DONADIEU'S WILL

Georges Simenon

DONADIEU'S
WILL

Translated by Stuart Gilbert

A Helen and Kurt Wolff Book

Harcourt Brace Jovanovich, Publishers

San Diego   New York   London

HBJ

Requests for permission to make copies of any part of
the work should be mailed to: Permissions Department,
Harcourt Brace Jovanovich, Publishers,
8th Floor, Orlando, Florida 32887.

The Shadow Falls copyright 1945 by
Harcourt Brace Jovanovich, Inc.
Copyright renewed 1972 by
Harcourt Brace Jovanovich, Inc. This is a
translation of Le Testament Donadieu.

Library of Congress Cataloging-in-Publication Data
Simenon, Georges, 1903-1989
[Testament Donadieu. English]
Donadieu's will / Georges Simenon : translated by Stuart Gilbert.
2nd ed.
p. cm.
Translation of: Le Testament Donadieu.
ISBN 0-15-126310-8
I. Title.
PQ2637.I53T3713   1991
843'.912—dc20   90-46267

Designed by Camilla Filancia
Printed in the United States of America
Second edition   A B C D E

I

LA ROCHELLE

1

An usher crossed the lobby and, after opening the big glass doors of the Alhambra, held her hand out cautiously, to see if the rain had stopped. Then, wrapping her black cape more closely around herself, she moved back into the lobby. As if this were a signal, the woman who owned the candy stand on the sidewalk beside the entrance crossed over from the doorway in which she'd been sheltering, and stood by her display of nougats, caramels, and roasted peanuts. At the same time, the policeman at the corner of Rue du Palais began walking up the street toward the cinema.

This was a daily routine, and there was something comforting about it, as there always is in a familiar sequence of events. A person could know he was in La Rochelle, and that it was Wednesday. A yellow band across the poster outside the theater announced: COMPLETELY NEW PROGRAM. In most provincial French movie theaters the program changed on the weekend.

It had rained all evening, but a large umbrella sheltered the candy stand. Most of the people coming out made the same gesture the usher had as they glanced up at the sky. And perhaps a hundred of them, after a few steps, made the same observation, husband to wife or wife to husband:

"Good! It's cleared up at last."

But the air was still damp and raw. There had been no summer to speak of. The Casino had closed two weeks earlier than usual, and now, at the end of September, it felt like midwinter. There was a frosty glitter to the sky. Ragged clouds scudded low under a few pale stars.

Ten or twelve cars were waiting outside. There was a purr of starters, headlights blazed out, and they set off in the same direction, slowly, because of the policeman. They put on speed, once away from the crowd.

It was a Wednesday night like any Wednesday night in autumn. Two other details showed that this was La Rochelle and no other town. At the corner, everybody looked up at the Clock Tower to see the time: five minutes before midnight. Other theaters usually closed by eleven. The Alhambra closed later because the program included a vaudeville act.

The second detail was a sound, which those used to it seldom noticed: a low, persistent throbbing interspersed with the creaks of pulley blocks and tackle. Everyone could tell from it that the tide was rising in the harbor. The water would soon be level with the quays, and, from a distance, the fishing boats would seem grounded, high and dry, on the road.

Meanwhile, as in provincial theaters the world over in the thirties, the owner was visiting the box office to collect the day's take. An elderly woman, her hat already on, handed him a long buff envelope, on which were penciled columns of figures. They exchanged a few words, unheard outside the small glass cage. The bartender, always one of the last to leave, saluted them as he went by.

Now the owner had only to lock the entrance doors before retiring to the little attic he slept in, at the top of the building, next to the projection room. The auditorium was empty, its cavernous gloom emphasized by the single ceiling light that stayed on day and night.

"Good night, Madame Michat."

"Good night, Monsieur Dargens."

Old Mme Michat, who was a fearful woman, hurried as fast as she could down the deserted street, shooting a timid glance behind her at every corner, as she always did on her way home at midnight. Turning to the right at the end of Rue du Palais, she almost collided with a young man standing there smoking a cigarette.

"I'm sorry . . . Oh, it's you, Monsieur Philippe. I didn't recognize you."

"Many people tonight?" the young man asked.

"Six hundred and fifty francs came in."

Philippe Dargens, son of the Alhambra's owner, tossed his cigarette in the gutter. He lit another, gave an irritable look at the clock, then started up a narrow street that led, in a roundabout way, to the park.

Everywhere people were entering their houses; footsteps ceased abruptly, then came the slam of a closing door. Remarks exchanged by couples, unaware that sounds carry far at night, could be heard in the empty streets.

4

A breeze was blowing from the sea, and the air was saturated with moisture, which clung to the skin, leaving a salty taste on the lips. Philippe turned up his coat collar and read the time on his watch in the glow of his cigarette.

Headlights flashed in the distance from a car leaving the park. The young man swerved to his right and started walking alongside the high brick wall that bounded the gardens of the houses fronting Rue Réaumur. These were mostly private residences of considerable size, standing in their own grounds and owned by well-to-do citizens of La Rochelle.

After he had walked some fifty yards, a small door opened in the wall, and a dim figure showed in the doorway. Dropping his cigarette on the grass and heeling it in, Philippe stepped into the darkness of a garden.

A voice whispered: "Why didn't you come yesterday?"

His only response was a shrug, unseen by the woman beside him. As if to make her understand that it wasn't his fault, he patted her arm.

It was pitch-dark under the plane and chestnut trees, and the paths were carpeted with dead leaves. At the far end of the garden, a house loomed, a square black patch in the surrounding gloom. Only the wet slates on the roof glimmered faintly in the starlight.

"Do stay a while," she begged.

"Ssh! Don't talk now. I'll be back soon."

"Philippe!"

"Not so loud!"

"Promise me, then . . ."

This was the worst part. Only some thirty yards separated him from another low doorway in a wall, which led to the grounds of the next house. And it would take no more than a minute to reach it; hardly that. But it was a minute during which he felt Charlotte's small body straining toward his, her thin arms clasping him like tentacles that would never let go; an endless minute, tense with foreboding . . .

"I promise you, dear, I'll stay on my way back."

"That's what you said Saturday, but you slipped away without . . ."

He gripped her shoulders, feeling the small, sharp bones under the coarse fabric of her coat, and with an effort dabbed a vague kiss on her forehead.

"Don't worry. This time I swear I'll come."

5

She made a little sniffling noise. And he knew that for the next hour or so, all the time he was gone, she would stay there, sobbing in the darkness, waiting for him to come back.

But it couldn't be helped. Once he was in the next garden, this unwelcome prelude passed clean out of his mind, and he walked with brisk, free steps. A necessary evil—that was the way to look at it. Since he had no choice, the best thing to do was not to think of the return trip, of Charlotte's crude embraces, her fond, futile questions.

Brushing past iron chairs and a big round garden table, he walked quickly along the edge of the lawn, skirting the gravel path, on which his footsteps might be heard. When he was about ten feet from a French window, he saw a faint movement behind it.

The house was in darkness. Slowly the window swung open, as if of its own accord—just as, a few minutes before, the door in the wall had opened—and a white form could be dimly seen. Without giving any sign of recognition, Philippe thrust aside the branch of a rambler rose that hung across the window; he found it as readily as he did the light switch in his bedroom. Placing a foot on the stone plinth and a knee on the windowsill, he swung himself in.

White curtains fluttered in the night breeze. A bed that had been lain in was growing cold. Philippe wondered anxiously why the lips to which he pressed his mouth seemed less responsive than usual.

He was more puzzled to find that Martine had kept her underclothes on beneath her nightdress, and that she'd stiffened instead of yielding to his embrace.

"What's wrong?" he asked, so softly that the words would have been unintelligible to anyone unfamiliar with his voice.

In the dark, he could just make out a tense white face and fever-bright eyes intent on him. He knew, he could have sworn, that something had changed.

When he made a tentative move in the direction of the bed, Martine stopped him with a touch so peremptory that he felt certain she had planned it in advance. Deliberately, she forced him back toward the window, where she could see something of the expression on his face.

"Look at me!" she commanded, holding his wrists to keep him from putting his arms around her.

"What's come over you, Martine?" he asked, and, precisely because she'd told him to, he couldn't meet her eyes, and hung his head.

"Let me see your face, Philippe."

There was something dramatic, almost tragic, in Martine's attitude.

He was conscious of tension in the air of this silent, sleepbound house, in which the least creak of a floorboard or word spoken too loud could bring catastrophe.

Martine's brother, a sullen, suspicious fifteen-year-old, slept in the room opposite. And her mother was only two rooms away.

The whole house, from the top floor to the ground floor, was peopled by Donadieus, old and young: sons, brothers, a daughter-in-law. Philippe was standing at the window with the youngest girl of the family: Martine, who was eighteen.

Suddenly, and not for the first time, he felt a qualm—why, he didn't know. Perhaps it was because of those eyes staring at him, eyes in which no affection shone, no gentleness.

"Look at me!"

Again he was conscious of a slight recoil, so unlike her usual readiness to sink into his arms.

"I want the truth, Philippe. . . ." Tonight she was raising her voice, courting disaster. But there seemed no way to stop her.

"Where is Papa? What's happened to my father?"

"To your father?" he repeated.

He had no idea what she meant. The situation was maddening. Had he dared to speak above a whisper, it would have been easy to calm her down. Martine, he knew, was high-strung, and inclined to let her imagination run away with her. Most likely she had misunderstood some remark she'd overheard, and built up some fantastic theory about her father, in which he, Philippe, heaven knew why, was involved.

"Answer me."

"I don't know what you're talking about."

But how could he make a remark like that sound convincing when he had to whisper it? How could he hope to prove convincing when his face was all but invisible, lighted only by vagrant gleams from a few faint stars?

"I insist on knowing, Philippe. Don't look away. You . . . you've done something, haven't you?"

"I assure you, darling, I don't understand a word you're saying."

"That's a lie! Oh, I know you're quite capable of lying. But . . . Philippe!"

It was like a cry of despair. He could see the white patch of the bed glimmering in the darkness and near him, too near, those pale, insistent eyes.

"I've just come back from Bordeaux," he said. "I went there last

Saturday, as I told you. How can I know what's happened? What do you mean?"

She didn't seem to hear. He realized that she, too, was exasperated, on the brink, it seemed, of an outburst of anger, or of tears.

"Haven't you seen your father yet, Philippe?"

"I saw him for five minutes, at the theater."

"Didn't he tell you anything?"

"No. He didn't!" Unthinking, he had raised his voice.

She stared at the floor, unconvinced.

"Well, I simply don't understand," she murmured. "Maybe you really don't know what's happened. But I had a feeling it must be you who'd . . ."

Suddenly her self-control broke, and she started wringing her hands.

"Martine, for heaven's sake!"

"Don't touch me. I don't want . . ."

"What is it? Tell me what's the matter."

Steadying herself with an effort, she peered again through the shadows at the half-seen face in front of her. Then she made a gesture of hopelessness.

"I don't know. I thought . . . You could quite well have done it. Yes. I'd say you wouldn't stop at anything!"

"Martine!"

It was nerve-racking to have to bear in mind the presence of the other people in the silent house.

At last the girl said, in a slow, toneless voice:

"Something's happened to my father. He hasn't been seen since *last Saturday.*"

She emphasized the last two words as if that day was important. Philippe, too, exclaimed: "Last Saturday!"

That was the day he had last come to see Martine; the following morning he'd left for Bordeaux. And she . . . had she believed he wouldn't come tonight; would never come again?

In almost the same tone as Martine's, he repeated: "Last Saturday!"

It was Charlotte who, almost by chance, had been the first to smell something unusual in the wind, though not wholly by chance. She had an uncanny gift of detecting signs, however trivial, of anything wrong or unusual.

At quarter of ten on Sunday morning, Mme Brun was dressing for Mass in her huge house, once a manor house, whose grounds adjoined the Donadieus'. Charlotte was with her, and around the two there brooded, as always, the dead peace of a museum. Checkered by diamond panes, the morning sunlight played on innumerable small objects on shelves and tables, bric-a-brac in porcelain and silver, mother-of-pearl and coral; and on walls from which family portraits, sedate or simpering, looked down from their dark frames, and old prints were foxed with reddish glints.

Charlotte had, as usual, already been to church, and had done the morning's marketing on her way home. Now, in her everyday clothes, she was helping Mme Brun into her black silk dress. When that was done, she hooked the broad black band of watered silk that the old lady always wore around her neck, which gave it a quaintly elongated air, like the necks of the swans in the park.

Suddenly, though she had half a dozen pins between her teeth, ready for an emergency, she exclaimed:

"Well, I never! The Donadieus are starting for church, and the Shipowner's not with them."

Mme Brun looked quite startled. That Oscar Donadieu, locally known as the Shipowner, should fail to head the family procession to Mass was almost unbelievable.

"Are you quite sure?"

"Positive, madame . . . There they are." She pointed toward the road.

Though Charlotte was more of a companion to the old lady than a maid, she nearly always, out of inverted snobbery perhaps, addressed her formally, rarely omitting the "madame."

It was a fine morning, but the light was bleak, and there was a frosty edge to the air.

The big double door, with its ponderous brass knocker, had closed, and the Donadieu family was now walking up tranquil Rue Réaumur in a sort of ritual progress—but a progress lacking its chief participant.

Prayer book in hand, Martine Donadieu headed the procession. She was in a white dress, the dress she had worn almost every Sunday throughout the summer. Beside her walked her younger brother, Oscar, who had only recently started wearing long trousers.

Often, when the two women were sewing or doing embroidery, Mme Brun would talk about Martine, whose young grace appealed to her.

"I'm sure she's far the cleverest of the next generation," she would say. "She has her father's eyes."

She never noticed the wry smile that came to Charlotte's plain, prematurely old face when she talked this way.

"The boy," she would add, "looks like a poor specimen. I wouldn't be surprised to learn he's a bit feebleminded."

As usual, the two grandchildren, Jean and Maurice, in sailor suits, walked behind Martine and her brother. Then came the grown-ups: Michel Donadieu and his wife, Eva, whose dresses were always daring, by local standards, and, behind them, Jean Olsen, the son-in-law, and his wife, Marthe, née Donadieu.

The Queen Mother, as Charlotte called her, brought up the rear. Mme Donadieu was a big, stately woman, but she had to lean heavily on a cane.

"That's so," said Mme Brun, after a glance at the family. "The Shipowner's not with them. I wonder now . . ."

Still, his absence might have some quite simple, innocuous explanation.

As soon as Mass was over that Sunday, the big blue car was brought out of the garage. With its brass headlights, seating room for ten, and cut-glass flower vases, it wore its age, ten years, with dignity. Only the elder son, Michel, got into it. He drove off with the chauffeur while Mme Brun and Charlotte, watching at their window, commented excitedly on this new development.

"I'm certain something's happened!"

The unusual or unforeseen played no part in the life of the Donadieus. Their days went according to schedule, their movements so nicely regulated that any citizen could set his watch by them as surely as by the clock in the tower.

Though there were other shipping magnates in La Rochelle, Oscar Donadieu was *the* shipowner, and, as if by virtue of his status as chief of the leading clan—for the Donadieus were more a clan than a mere family—the definite article sounded like an honorific prefix. Fifteen years before, there had been a striking proof of his prestige. When he renounced Protestantism for the Catholic faith, five other Protestant families, five other shipowners, followed his lead.

A tall, broad-shouldered man, he looked like he could be one of those statuary columns in ancient temples, shoring up the roof. Unbowed, in spite of his seventy-four years, he was as firm in his opinions as he was upright in his dealings. He was held in such esteem that he was regularly called on to arbitrate in cases where large sums of money were involved.

The Donadieu stronghold was not on the same street as the family mansion, but down by the harbor, on Quai Vallin. Dim light prevailed in the thirty offices in the four-story building—the staff could hardly see to do their work, even on a summer day—and its façade was equally austere.

Across from it were coal dumps, and there were usually several colliers, flying the Donadieu flag, unloading Donadieu coal. Nearby was a railway siding, with waiting trucks, some refrigerated, and trawlers made fast alongside: Donadieu trucks and trawlers.

At exactly ten minutes before eight each morning, three men set forth from the house on Rue Réaumur: the Shipowner; his son Michel, who, though thirty-seven years old, hung behind him like a timid schoolboy; and Olsen, his son-in-law, five years younger than Michel, who had developed into a true Donadieu, punctual and precise of speech.

On arriving at the office building, each took charge of a floor, a department, and settled down in his sanctum behind a massive, baize-lined door. Each also had a floor to himself in their large house. The head of the family occupied the first floor with his wife and the two children, Martine and Oscar; the elder son, Michel, his wife, and their children had the second floor to themselves; the floor above was occupied by Olsen and his wife, Marthe, and their seven-year-old son.

Mme Brun and Charlotte knew the routine of the Donadieu household by heart, minute by minute. And their curiosity rose to fever pitch when the Shipowner failed to return, and on Monday morning his son and son-in-law, instead of going to the office at the usual time, lingered in earnest conversation near the gate.

"Perhaps he's gone on a trip somewhere," Mme Brun suggested.

"No, madame. It can hardly be that." There was an undertone of ghoulish excitement in Charlotte's voice. "They wouldn't be upset like they are if that was all."

"What's your idea, then?"

"You never can tell. . . ."

That was one of her favorite expressions. A peculiar little creature, Charlotte was, with a stunted body and a small, witchlike face. She had been servant at a convent until the age of thirty. Then something had happened to her, a tragic incident of which she never breathed a word to anyone. She had undergone an operation, and when Mme Brun took her under her roof, Charlotte was like a limp rag, sexless, without any interest in life, it seemed, except to please her employer. She would spend long hours daily bent over her embroidery, in the half-empty house, over which a gardener and his wife, who occupied a cottage on the grounds, kept watch as caretakers.

At noon on Tuesday, Charlotte cried:

"Come and look!"

So thrilled was she that she forgot her usual "madame." She had reason. With Michel, who had just returned, was none other than Monsieur Jeannet, the public prosecutor, and something in his demeanor indicated that this was no ordinary visit. There was surely to be a marshaling of the clan, a council of war, in the huge living room on the ground floor.

"I wouldn't be surprised if something terrible has happened."

Sometimes it really seemed that Charlotte had second sight. Though there was no certainty of any tragic explanation, what had happened was startling enough. Oscar Donadieu, shipping magnate and pillar of society, had inexplicably vanished.

On Saturday evening, he had gone, as usual, to his club, on Place d'Armes. Only on Saturdays—because the office was closed the next day—did he permit himself to remain there as late as midnight, to play bridge, for very low stakes.

But he had not come home at all last Saturday night. The other members of the household did not dare stay away from church, but no sooner was the service over than Michel hurried by car to the Donadieus' country house, in Esnandes. There had earlier been vain attempts to telephone, on the remote chance that his father had gone there.

"Nothing!" he'd announced on his return.

Sunday was the one day in the week when the three households gathered in the first-floor dining room—under orders. That Sunday there was an atmosphere of tension and worry. They had discussed the situation until they were tired of their own voices. Eva was for notifying the police. This merely showed how little she knew the Shipowner; otherwise she would never have dreamed of making such a suggestion.

Oscar Donadieu was the lord and master, and he alone could have indicated the correct procedure. But—he wasn't there! All they could agree on was that no steps should be taken that might cause gossip.

On Monday morning, Charlotte, from one of her numerous observation posts, had noticed something that never happened on weekdays: people moving back and forth from floor to floor.

Now the public prosecutor, the leading representative of law and order in La Rochelle, had called.

"I'll make discreet inquiries," Mme Brun said. "Needless to say, there will be no public statement, not a word in the papers."

And in the small hours of Wednesday night, Martine Donadieu, giving no thought to love, or to the bed and its now stone-cold sheets, stood shivering in her nightdress near the open window, questioning Philippe.

"Are you quite sure your father didn't tell you anything?"

"Absolutely sure."

"He was the last person seen with my father. They left the club together."

So clearly did that remark convey the suspicions of the family that Philippe began to lose his self-assurance. There was a slight tremor in his voice when he asked:

"Have inquiries been made?"

"Yes, but unofficially—so far . . . They were seen leaving the club. After that . . ."

Forgetting the other people in the house, they were raising their voices.

"But, Martine, surely you know my father would never—"

"Philippe! Look at me again."

Too many things had to be crowded into these uneasy minutes. Had they been able to talk at leisure, had there been light, so they could see each other, instead of furtive gloom, conversation would have been easier. As it was, they confronted each other almost like enemies.

"Martine!" Philippe cried impulsively, and there was something in his voice that made her waver. He realized that she was near the breaking point, that she couldn't go on standing bare-foot and shivering in the night breeze very much longer. Perhaps soon she would slip into his arms.

"I swear to you by all I hold most sacred," he began—then stopped abruptly.

She, too, grew rigid. A ribbon of light had appeared under the

13

door. Another line of light flashed at a right angle to it and slowly widened.

Instinctively, Martine gripped Philippe's arm. He hadn't had the presence of mind to hide behind the curtain.

A young voice, unperturbed, but oddly remote and dreamlike, came through the silence:

"Martine! Are you there? What's happening?"

They saw the tall, slim form of a boy in pajamas silhouetted against the light flooding in from his bedroom door as he peered through the shadows.

"Martine!" he called again.

"Hush, Kiki. Yes, I'm here."

Neither she nor Philippe dared to move. Kiki groped his way forward, still half-asleep. When he saw Philippe, he came to a sudden stop and glared at him.

"Kiki!" Martine whispered.

Everyone in the house called him by this pet name; it was as if they felt his father's Christian name was too grand for a boy.

"It's all right, Kiki. Don't . . ."

Suddenly he started sobbing violently, putting his hand over his mouth to stifle the sound. His sister slipped her arm around him and tried to draw him to her.

"Hush, Kiki. If Maman hears . . ."

But he went on sobbing. At last, in a paroxysm of childish despair, he sank to the floor. His sister crouched beside him, stroking his hair.

"There, there, Kiki. There's nothing to worry about." Glancing up, she said to Philippe:

"You'd better go. I can manage him."

"But—"

"No. He'll be all right once you've gone."

Every time the boy looked at the intruder, he was seized by a sort of convulsion.

"You see. Please go, Philippe."

Swinging his legs over the window sill, Philippe dropped lightly on the wet leaf-strewn grass. The experience had been unnerving, but once outside, he took a calmer view: "Well, Martine can fix things up with her brother. He's only a child; she'll manage it."

Glancing back on his way through the garden, he saw the glimmering rectangle of Martine's window. He quickened his pace and pushed open the little door in the wall, which closed behind him by itself.

At the same moment, he heard a voice calling his name.

"Yes?"

"Come, Philippe." Urgent fingers tightened on his arm.

His thoughts were in chaos. He felt as if he'd left behind him, in that silent house, a bomb that might explode at any time. Suddenly all the lights would go on, and there would be a burst of excited voices, hurried footsteps—a gathering of the clan.

But nothing happened. Nothing broke the stillness but the slow, deep rhythm of the tide and, now and then, the shrill creak of a pulley block, sounding like a sea gull's mew.

He hardly knew what he was doing, where he was being led. Fear possessed him, and immense disgust. What a bad business it had been, all these months, having to humor Charlotte in order to keep in touch with Martine; having to buy her connivance, not with money, but with lies, a pretense of devotion, but hardly even that! All he had done was deliberately, cold-bloodedly, stir the woman's senses, play on her passion. Yes, a bad business!

As usual, she took him to the arbor covered with rambler roses in the center of the garden. All the flowers and leaves had fallen, and the arbor looked like a derelict umbrella, only the ribs left. It was swept by the wet sea breeze, and the wicker settee was dripping.

"Philippe . . ."

That was how Martine, too, had begun. What was it both of them wanted so much to say to him?

"I can't stand it any longer. I'm so miserable. Oh, Philippe, if you would only understand . . . !"

She said this every time. Luckily, he couldn't see her face. On previous nights, he had summoned up the courage to give his lips to her mouth's kiss, to put his arm around her skimpy shoulders, to murmur foolish, conventional endearments. But tonight . . .

"Don't you understand that I . . ."

No! Tonight he was in no mood for explanations. He was waiting for the explosion, expecting every moment to see the windows of the house beyond the wall blaze with light, one after the other. . . . But nothing happened.

He pictured Martine kneeling beside her young brother on the carpet, her arm around him, and he wondered what she was whispering in his ear. Undoubtedly, both were crying, mingling words with sobs. She was probably pleading with him, saying things that made her blush for shame, while Kiki grappled with a nightmare, like those strange dreams he had when walking in his sleep. Martine had

15

told Philippe that her brother was a sleepwalker, and for that reason the windows of his bedroom had been fitted with bars.

"And all the time I know that you love that girl, that you're only using me as a tool. . . ."

"Of course not," he murmured weakly. "You've got it all wrong, Charlotte."

"But it's true—and sometimes I feel quite desperate. . . . Tell me what she said. What did you do together just now?"

"Don't!"

"I've been thinking. Monsieur Donadieu hasn't come back. I can't help wondering . . ."

In her voice he seemed to hear the same suspicion he'd heard in Martine's. He gazed up at the leafless boughs, the draggled clouds racing across the cold translucent sky. Then, almost angrily, he turned on her.

"That's enough, Charlotte."

"Yes, I've been thinking quite a lot. And I'd like to know . . ."

He made an abrupt movement. At all costs, he must stop Charlotte from voicing her thoughts, and, to silence her, he lived through one of the most odious half hours of his life, while his eyes kept straying to the next house, which remained in darkness.

2

Oscar Donadieu's body was discovered by a cart driver at nine on Thursday morning. Rain was still falling, but there was a silvery light above the sea that hurt one's eyes and showed up intervening objects in sharp relief. Driven by a northwester, the long gray-green Atlantic waves were casting showers of dazzlingly white spray on the jetties, and nearby buildings gleamed whitely in the level light.

It was a morning when La Rochelle resembled, in almost every detail, the old prints on the walls of Mme Brun's living room. The tide was out, and there was hardly any water in the harbor. The fishing boats had gradually settled into the brown expanse of mud, which was seamed by tiny channels.

A girl in black was setting out shoes in a shop window. From eight that morning, Michel Donadieu had been working in his office on the second floor of the Donadieu building. He had glanced at the clock several times, wondering when he could decently call the public prosecutor, no early riser, and ask if he had any news.

For the last few minutes, however, his thoughts had been elsewhere, because Benoit, the cashier, had come in with vouchers to be signed. Benoit, who had been with the firm for thirty years, and was one of its most trusted employees, had one defect: his breath smelled. And when, as now, Michel was sitting at his desk, with the cashier bending over him as he laid the vouchers one after the other on the blotter, this was painfully noticeable. But no one had ever dared tell Benoit about his problem. Michel was thinking of this as he scrawled his signature, with its ornate terminal flourish, on the slips in front him.

His brother-in-law, Jean Olsen, who managed the warehouses and shipping, had been called to the railway station, where there was some complication about a refrigerator car.

The cart driver, whose name was Bigois, had had his first drink of the day in a small bistro in the fish market. Whip on his shoulder, he walked by his horse along the quay. Wanting to spit, he moved to the seawall and leaned over.

A yellowish object in the mud, a little way out, caught his eye. It was a light overcoat, and, looking at it more closely, Bigois was almost sure he saw a hand sticking out of a sleeve.

"My God!" he exclaimed, but without real interest. "Looks like a body!"

It was with the same words and with his mustache still wet from the second white wine he'd drunk, that he reported his find to the policeman at the corner.

The corpse lay in an awkward place, where there was several feet of viscous mud. The policeman gazed at it dubiously, then turned and looked at a couple of fishermen who had come over.

"You'll need a pushboard," said one of them.

"What's that?"

By now ten people had collected, all gazing at the yellow lump in the mud, not realizing what it was. Nobody seemed willing to do anything, and the policeman was uncertain. Another fisherman broke the silence:

"There ain't no time to lose. Tide's rising, and once it gets him . . ."

At last the policeman made up his mind. Walking briskly to the nearest café, he called headquarters. By the time he got back, a pushboard had been produced—a boat-shaped contraption, like a very wide ski, that glided over the mud without sinking. An ancient mariner in a sou'wester navigated this strange craft. When he got it beside the body, he found it impossible to lift the body out of the mud, which held like birdlime.

A crowd gathered, and for a good quarter of an hour lingered in the pouring rain, gaping at the mud. The driver of the Rochefort bus, to his annoyance, had to leave before seeing the end of the attempt. There was time enough, however, for the superintendent of police to arrive; he, too, did no more than stand and watch the fishermen make a rope fast around the body and haul it up onto the quay.

He was horrified when he saw that the dead man was Oscar Donadieu, and furious with himself for having failed to supervise operations, especially because, in the process of being dragged up the seawall, the corpse had been rather badly damaged.

Reluctant to leave the body lying on the quay, they placed it on

Bigois's cart, and someone found a tarpaulin, reeking of fish, to cover
it. After that, the superintendent dashed off to the Donadieu building,
slowing to a more seemly gait as he approached it. He was shown at
once into the second-floor office, where the walls were papered with
imitation leather and adorned with colored sketches of boats flying
the Donadieu flag.

Michel, still signing vouchers, failed at first to grasp his meaning.

"I have the painful duty to inform you . . ."

Michel rose slowly and gazed blankly at the superintendent. He
hadn't the faintest idea what he was supposed to do. Bleak light fell
on his temples, from which the hair was receding, and glinted on the
massive gold signet ring on his left little finger.

He turned to his cashier.

"Call the railway station and ask Monsieur Olsen to come back at
once."

It seemed to him desirable that his brother-in-law be present. He
thought of calling his mother as well—but wouldn't it be rather brutal
to break the news over the telephone?

"Where do you wish the body to be taken?" the superintendent
asked.

"Where is it now?"

Rather shamefaced, the superintendent confessed:

"Oh . . . er . . . on a cart."

"Where is the cart?"

"Over there." He pointed to the far end of the quay.

But when they went to the window and looked out, they saw
Bigois and the cart directly below; he had evidently thought it would
save time to come here at once. Michel dabbed his eyes vaguely with
his handkerchief, though there were no tears in them. Yet he felt like
weeping, and under other circumstances would certainly have done
so. But the setting was wrong; there was a lack of dignity about it all
that ruled out any show of emotion.

"If it had been anyone but your esteemed father, I'd have had the
body taken to the morgue, as is usual in such cases."

Obviously that was out of the question. On the other hand, perhaps it would be irregular to suggest taking the body to the house.
Michel was still wondering what to do when the cashier returned.

"Monsieur Jean will be here in a minute, sir."

"Call the public prosecutor, please."

Throughout the building, everyone had stopped work. A woman

who had come to order coal couldn't get anyone to serve her. Down in the street, a crowd was keeping at a respectful distance from the tarpaulin-shrouded cart; some had gone so far as to take off their hats, under their umbrellas.

Michel gave a hasty explanation to the public prosecutor over the telephone, then turned to the superintendent.

"He says we'd better bring the body in here. The police doctor will be here in a few minutes. . . . Will you sit down?"

And so, borne by two members of his staff and Bigois, who, expert in handling heavy weights, took command, Oscar Donadieu entered his office for the last time. Instinctively, Bigois had started to lay the body on the big mahogany desk, but recalling that it was plastered with mud, he placed it on the floor. Olsen came rushing in, whipped off his hat, and asked:

"Does Mother know?"

"Not yet."

It was all so chaotic and unprecedented that no one knew what to do, what attitude to adopt. So far no tears had been shed. Members of the staff wanted to show their sympathy in some way, but had no idea what to do. It was the receptionist who suggested that the offices be closed and a notice put on the door.

Michel approved at once.

"Quite right. Yes, we'll have the blinds down. . . . You agree, Jean?"

The next question was whether to keep the employees at work, behind the drawn blinds, or send them home.

"I have the monthly accounts to write up," Benoit put in.

"In that case, you'd better stay. The others can go . . . except anyone who is absolutely necessary. . . . Oh, good morning, Monsieur Jeannet."

At last the representative of the law had come. He was accompanied by the police doctor, a florid, thickset man in his forties.

"I need hardly say how deeply . . ." the official began stiffly.

What everyone present felt most was acute embarrassment. The situation had found them all unprepared.

"Could he be placed on a table?" asked the doctor as he took off his coat.

Bigois was still standing by, probably hoping for a tip. But did one give a tip in such cases, Michel wondered. Having no idea, he did nothing.

"I suggest, gentlemen, that you leave the room while I'm making my examination."

Michel, Olsen, and the public prosecutor adjourned to the second-floor office, where Michel offered cigarettes. Now that the corpse was no longer under their eyes, they found it easier to talk.

"Do you think the body was in the water since last Saturday night?"

"What puzzles me," Olsen replied, "is why it wasn't carried out to sea."

There was nothing surprising about that, however. The entrance to La Rochelle's harbor is narrow, between the ends of two jetties. The tides had merely shifted Oscar Donadieu's body from one side of the harbor to the other, a foot or two beneath the surface of the water. Finally, it had stranded on a mud flat at the ebb.

Michel Donadieu was a stout, loosely built man, who, to conceal his ungainliness perhaps, always dressed with extreme neatness. He was subject to dizzy spells—there was said to be something wrong with his heart—and was always wiping perspiration from his forehead.

"I suppose I'd better go and tell Maman," he muttered.

Though no one dared put it in words, or even admit it to himself, all of them felt relieved that the mystery of the old man's disappearance had been cleared up.

Once the doctor had finished with the body in the office below, there would be nothing more to worry about. They heard him calling up the stairs, but he wanted only the public prosecutor, who hurried down. As Olsen paced restlessly up and down the room, Michel's face grew oddly twisted; he wanted to shed some tears at last, if only for appearance's sake.

When Jeannet returned, followed by the burly doctor, he was wearing his most professional manner.

"I much regret, gentlemen, that it is necessary to prolong your suspense, but we have found it impossible, so far, to form any definite opinion. The doctor wished me to inspect the body myself. In its present state of advanced decomposition—you must excuse my bluntness—"

"Don't mention it. We quite understand."

"—it is difficult to determine precisely the cause of death. In a word, I would be failing in my duty were I not to insist on a post-mortem. However, I may say this much: So far as we can judge from

21

our cursory inspection, there's no reason to believe that a crime has been committed."

In a way, of course, this made things easier. Now that the law had intervened, there was a cut-and-dried procedure to be followed. A police ambulance came for the body. Michel and Olsen were back at the house on Rue Réaumur at exactly quarter of eleven.

"Is your mistress in?" Michel asked the maid.

"She's in her bedroom, sir."

"Please ask her if she can come. We have something to tell her."

But it was Martine who came first, a music album in her hand, and to her Michel blurted out the news:

"Papa's body has been found."

She had no opportunity to ask for details before Mme Donadieu entered the living room, wearing a sky-blue dressing gown and a lace cap. She glanced at the two men and the girl, took a deep breath, and pressed her hands to her heart.

"Tell me what it is. Quick! Your father . . . I dreamed about him last night."

Now at last it was like a real bereavement. Michel made no effort to keep back his tears. Mme Donadieu turned very pale, closed her eyes, and sank into a chair, half fainting. Martine rushed to the kitchen for vinegar and a wet towel. Eva, Michel's wife, hurried into the room to see what was happening, and she, too, burst into tears, and exclaimed:

"We mustn't let the children come down. Martine dear, please run up and lock the door."

The cook had entered, sobbing noisily. Because the big carpet had been rolled up that morning for the parquet to be beeswaxed, they were penned together in a corner of the room. It felt like a crowd, with everyone getting in everyone else's way.

"Where's Kiki?" Mme Donadieu asked suddenly. "The poor child must be informed."

She was told that he had gone out early, without a word to anyone—which was unlike him.

When, a few minutes later, he returned, his face drawn and pale, his shoes caked with mud, his hair sopping wet, he found an atmosphere of gloom.

"You'd better have something to eat," the cook kept repeating. "You must keep your strength up."

No one except Michel, who always had an appetite, took her

advice. Standing, he ate some slices of cold beef, without bread or vegetables.

"When will he be brought here?"

"When they've finished the . . . the . . ."

Somehow, no one liked to voice the ugly term postmortem. From time to time, Eva went upstairs to attend to her two-year-old daughter. Her small boy, Jean, and Olsen's son, Maurice, who had somehow found their way downstairs, were adding to the confusion.

It was Martine and Kiki who looked most upset; their faces were almost deathlike. After a while, Martine slipped out. Some time elapsed before she was discovered lying on her bed, her body rigid, her teeth clenched on a corner of the pillowcase.

The *Courrier Rochellois* gave some details:

On leaving his club on Place d'Armes, M. Oscar Donadieu invariably followed the same route. Instead of going straight home, he had a habit of making a detour and walking past his office building and warehouses. It was a dark, rainy night, and he may well have lost his footing. . . .

It was so. Old Donadieu had settled habits—with advancing years he had become more and more the creature of routine—and this was one of them. Probably it pleased him, on his way home to bed, to have a final glimpse of the large office building looming up through the darkness, the sheds and warehouses, the funnels of his steamers. They were so many symbols of his wealth and the eminence of his business.

Little was said about it at the club. All the members were elderly, around the same age as Oscar Donadieu, and they went there, not so much for company, as to spend a few hours ensconced in a favorite armchair in front of an open fire, in an atmosphere different from that at home. That they were men of substance and assured position could be read in their serious demeanor and the measured terms in which they discussed even the most trivial subjects. Not that they wasted much time on trivialities; they knew each other too well for that. They had grown up together, gone to the same schools and universities; indeed, most of them, as a result of intermarriage between clans, were more or less nearly related to each other.

Because Oscar Donadieu had been president of the club, it was resolved at a special meeting of the committee on Thursday afternoon that the club would remain closed for a week in token of respect.

Then, with the same decorum, they sanctioned an outlay of five hundred francs for a wreath.

Frédéric Dargens was present and voted with the others. It all went so smoothly that an outsider would never have guessed that there was anything beneath the surface; that, only an hour before, Dargens had been in the public prosecutor's office, undergoing questioning.

An acute observer might have detected a certain eagerness, on the part of some of the members, to leave the room without having to shake hands with Dargens. And perhaps he might also have noticed some curious glances directed at the cinema owner's handsome, finely molded face, the slightly graying hair at his temples, and his humorous mouth.

"You must excuse me, Monsieur Dargens, for having sent for you, but I am informed that you left the club in the company of Oscar Donadieu on Saturday night."

The public prosecutor, too, had been politeness itself. True, the more conservative members of the club deplored the fact that Dargens owned and personally managed a theater, and one where there was vaudeville, with acrobats, dancers, and the like, between the film screenings. In addition, they did not like the fact that, instead of a proper residence, he camped out somewhere in his theater, and made no attempt to control his son, Philippe, who was rumored to be getting into bad habits.

There were other things against Dargens. He let himself be seen in cafés with professional dancers and cabaret artistes. Sometimes he even took them out for the day in his car, to some neighboring seaside resort. Moreover, his style of dress was regrettable; too exotic and Parisian, it clashed with local standards of good taste.

Nevertheless, he was a member of the club, which his father had founded and presided over until Donadieu succeeded him. Until the previous year, the Dargens Bank had been regarded as the soundest of the local private banks, and many of the leading families had accounts with it. When the crash came, and the bank had to close its doors, the liquidators had to admit that Dargens had acted in good faith, that the failure was due to sheer bad luck. He had sold everything he possessed—cars, horses, the big country house at Marsilly and the modern residence he had built in the new quarter of La Rochelle—to meet his liabilities, and he had gone far in covering them.

What his fellow club members held most against him was his idea of starting a cinema.

24

"That is quite correct, Monsieur Jeannet. I left the club with Donadieu. We walked together as far as Rue Gargoulleau. He turned down it after wishing me good night."

"Did you go straight home?"

"To the cinema, you mean? Yes." Why should he go out of his way to stress this rather embarrassing detail?

"But," the public prosecutor pointed out, "wasn't Rue Gargoulleau the shortest way home for you also?"

"Certainly. But you know what Donadieu was like. I could tell from his manner that he'd rather be alone; so I took the longer way, Rue du Palais."

"Did Donadieu lose much money when your bank failed?"

"He was paid eighty francs per hundred, like all the other creditors."

It was distasteful to have to question Dargens this way. However much he might try to harden his heart against him, he couldn't help but like the man. For one thing, he had such perfect poise, was so obviously well bred. Perhaps, too, the faint aura of bohemianism that hovered around him contributed to his charm; it was so foreign to the drab, humdrum environment of La Rochelle.

Twenty years earlier, his wife, who came from a good local family, had run away with a dentist. This was difficult to account for, considering how popular Dargens was with women, from every walk of life.

"I must ask you, once more, to excuse me for questioning you in this manner. But I wanted to make quite sure that—how shall I put it?—that no scope is given for malicious rumors, once the inquest is over. You understand what I mean?"

On leaving the public prosecutor's office, Dargens walked straight to Rue Réaumur and rang the Donadieus' bell. He showed no sign of discomposure.

It was, perhaps, the busiest and most trying moment of the day for the bereaved household. Jeannet had just telephoned to say that the police doctor's report had come in. No injury inflicted before death had been found on the body, and the authorities were satisfied that death was due to misadventure. It was, therefore, up to the family to make immediate arrangements for the funeral. When Dargens stepped into the hall, he heard Michel speaking on the telephone in his rather squeaky voice:

"Yes, bring the patterns at once, please. Black worsted—that's right, isn't it? We shall require . . . wait! . . . two . . . no, three men's suits, and two for the children. Yes. Tomorrow evening at the latest."

A black dress was spread on the sofa, and Mme Donadieu was inspecting it with her daughter-in-law.

"I assure you, Maman," Eva was saying, "I can't possibly wear it again."

It was Martine who noticed Dargens' entry. She promptly looked away and hurried off to her bedroom.

"I've come to see you . . ." Dargens began.

There was a brief hesitation, a slight tension in the air, before Mme Donadieu cried impulsively, hardly knowing what she was saying:

"My poor Frédéric! It's . . . it's very nice of you. . . ."

Michel was dialing another number, while Olsen studied the directory.

"I've come," said Dargens, "to see if I can be of any help. If you want any messages delivered or arrangements made, please don't hesitate to use me."

But they were no longer paying any attention to him—perhaps deliberately. He stayed a quarter of an hour; then, without betraying the least embarrassment, took his leave as the undertaker was being shown in.

In the next house, Mme Brun was being helped by Charlotte into a black dress before she sallied forth on a visit of condolence.

It was still raining heavily. At the hospital, a surgeon was patching up Oscar Donadieu's battered body as best he could before sending it to the family.

The windows had alternate panes of greenish glass, and in the glaucous light faces were in oddly sharp relief. All those in the lawyer's office seemed like graven images, incapable of change. Martine, for instance, sitting very straight, her slim white neck and her pale, tense face contrasting with the blackness of her coat; she could never be pictured other than as a young, high-strung girl. Kiki, his thin nose always looking slightly crooked, seemed more decrepit than usual; it was hard to believe he would ever grow up into a normal man.

These two looked the most stricken, as if they bore on their young shoulders the whole weight of the tragedy; as if they were its only victims, the only orphans.

Behind them sat their uncle, Batillat, from Cognac, wearing a look of studied gloom. He had been appointed deputy guardian of the children.

Mme Donadieu seemed almost unconcerned. She gazed calmly at the lawyer, who was opening the will with deliberate slowness, while Michel and Olsen, looking slimmer in their mourning clothes, affected, without great success, an air of bland indifference.

"This will was deposited with me by the deceased two years ago, and we may presume, I take it, that he made no subsequent will."

He paused and glanced at Mme Donadieu, who shook her head.

He started reading in the slow, unemphatic tones appropriate to such occasions. A moment came when Mme Donadieu gave an involuntary exclamation and said:

"I beg your pardon?"

"Shall I read the passage again? 'I devise my entire estate to my children, Michel, Marthe Olsen (née Donadieu), Martine, and Oscar. . . .' "

It cost Michel an effort not to turn and stare at his mother, whose breath he could hear coming in quick gasps.

" 'No part or parcel of the real or personal estate shall be alienated before all the children are of age.' " Michel frowned, as if trying to work out the implications of this clause. His mother leaned more heavily on her cane. " 'Provided that, should there arise at any time an urgent need for the conversion of some part of the estate into ready money, before the youngest of the heirs has attained his majority, a sale may take place; but it shall cover the whole estate, including the goodwill of the various businesses as well as the various premises thereto appurtenant.' "

All of a sudden, Martine realized that something had happened, looked at her mother, and for the first time tried to catch the sense of what the lawyer was reading.

" 'My wife shall enjoy a life interest of one-fourth of the total income accruing. . . .' "

Slowly, Mme Donadieu raised her hand to her forehead, hid her eyes, and remained that way. The lawyer was slightly flustered and stumbled over the long concluding phrases, trying to get to the end.

Michel was the first to rise.

"Maman," he murmured awkwardly.

She did not look up and kept her eyes hidden.

"Shall I open the window for a while?" the lawyer suggested. "It's rather close in here."

Martine, who had also stood, asked impulsively:

"What exactly does it mean? I didn't understand." Olsen signed to her to hold her tongue, but she went on: "Does it mean that Maman is . . . is disinherited?"

Then at last Mme Donadieu let them see her face.

"Yes," she said quietly.

"No, Maman!" Michel hurriedly said. "It's hardly that. A quarter of the income goes to you for life, and none of us can touch the capital."

The lawyer, who was on his feet, too, looked uncomfortable. Olsen, only an in-law, thought it best to say nothing.

"Come along, Maman." Michel began putting on his gloves. "We'll talk it over at home. I have no doubt—"

"Talk *what* over?"

"You know what I mean. We'll arrange things among ourselves."

The uncle from Cognac looked thoroughly puzzled. Kiki cast mistrustful glances at all the grown-ups.

Somehow Mme Donadieu conjured up a smile. Leaning on her cane, she drew herself up, murmuring:

"A quarter of the income."

Paying no heed to the others, she walked slowly to the door, and never had she looked so stately, so tall and majestic.

"Oh, Maman!" cried Martine, bursting into tears.

"Maman!" echoed Kiki shrilly. The tension in the air had affected him; he was losing control.

At first their mother took no notice of either. When at last she turned, it was to give them a severe look.

"What's come over you, children?"

"Oh, Maman!" Martine sobbed, unable, it seemed, to get another word out. While her uncle tried to calm her, Michel scowled.

"Now then, Martine! Don't behave like a silly child. . . . We'll talk about all this presently."

The click of typewriters could be heard from an adjoining room, where four clerks and a typist were at work. They had to cross this room to leave. Mme Donadieu turned again to her daughter, and said sharply:

"Don't make an exhibition of yourself, Martine! Stop crying." She rarely adopted such a tone with her children; only when seriously displeased.

Augustin, the chauffeur-valet, was waiting with the car. It was five

28

in the afternoon. A miniature carousel for children had been set up outside the lawyer's office, but there were no children on the wooden horses.

Martine ran through the outer office, pressing her hands to her face to hide her tears. No sooner was she home than she had a complete breakdown, almost going into hysterics. She had always been prone to attacks of this kind. Her body was shaken from head to foot; her jaws were clenched so fiercely it was surprising her teeth didn't break. She began making convulsive movements and digging her nails into her palms until blood came.

Mme Donadieu brought her cane down with a bang.

"Stop that nonsense! Do you hear?"

This only made things worse. Martine was now writhing on the floor, clutching at her mother's skirt. Michel said to Olsen:

"Ask your wife to come, please."

Marthe was the only one who could manage her sister at such times. Kiki had retired to a corner and was sitting there, gazing at the others with big frightened eyes.

Olsen ran out and shouted up the staircase:

"Marthe! Come down! You're wanted."

The smell of wax candles and chrysanthemums still lingered in the air. But the house had been returned to normal, everything back in its usual place. Mme Donadieu took off her black hat and gloves, gazed calmly around, and said in a voice they hardly recognized as hers:

"Now, if you don't mind, I'd like to be alone."

A large picture on the living-room wall showed her standing beside her husband, a bunch of roses in her hand. It had been given to her by her children on her silver wedding anniversary. Twelve years had passed since then, but Oscar Donadieu, in his black frock coat, with the Legion of Honor rosette on the lapel, looked exactly the same as he had on the day of his death: tall, austere, impressive, with a look in his eyes that no one, not even his wife perhaps, had ever understood.

Lying on the floor, Martine was crying passionately:

"I won't! I won't leave Maman!"

Her sister, who had their father's serious calm, tried to draw her to her feet.

"What's come over her?"

"Oh, nothing really . . . We'll tell you later."

Seated beneath the portrait, holding her cane, Mme Donadieu was beginning to lose patience.

"Am I to have any peace, or am I not?"

Martine sprang to her feet abruptly, stared at her mother, at the portrait, and then swept her eyes around the familiar room.

"Maman!" she began excitedly. "I can't bear it! I want . . ."

"Go away at once, please. I wish to be alone."

Events had moved too fast. Everyone's face was flushed. No one knew what to do next, and for a few minutes they gazed at each other helplessly. Then Olsen said to his wife, "Come!" and, taking her arm, led her out into the hall and upstairs.

"Why is Martine in such a state?" Marthe asked.

"I'll explain when we're upstairs."

Michel had already slipped away, and the old uncle had retreated to the dining room, for want of anywhere else to go.

After a final glance at her mother, a glance in which flickered a vague hope, which died out at once, Martine ran to her bedroom and shut herself in. Mme Donadieu remained seated beneath the portrait, and, huddled in an armchair at the other end of the room, the young boy stared at her, his eyes big with alarm.

"You, too, Kiki," his mother said irritably. And when he didn't seem to understand what she meant, she lost her temper. "For heaven's sake, go away. I don't want you here."

No one had any dinner that night, except the Olsens, who had put their son to bed earlier than usual, so they could speak more freely.

On the second floor Michel had a severe attack of palpitations. He was subject to such attacks, and they always terrified him, even made him whimper like a child.

3

Before the small door wedged between the Alhambra and the shop next to it had given its usual premonitory creak, Dargens heard the sound of approaching footsteps. He knew at once it was his son.

He knew many sounds, because he suffered from insomnia and rarely got any sleep until the night was nearly over. But no one knew this. He always went to bed at a normal hour. Lying on the sofa that served him as a bed, he would read for hours, and few sounds in the nightbound city escaped him.

Later, after putting his light out to make his first attempt to sleep, his senses became preternaturally acute. He took no sleeping pills, and he was not one of those who always bemoan their inability to sleep, and start the day with haggard, bloodshot eyes, inviting pity.

He had no knack for sleeping, that was all. Stretched on the sofa, he waited patiently, sometimes with his eyes wide open, for the night to pass. He heard the fishing fleet put out to sea with the flood tide, and could identify the horn of each trawler.

Only with the first stir of life in the streets of La Rochelle did he doze off, like a sentry whose relief has come at last. Since he never rose before ten, everyone thought he took life easy; even his son, not knowing about his insomnia, believed this.

Tonight was the fifth consecutive one when Philippe didn't come home until one. He had started this habit—for a habit it had become—two days after old Donadieu's funeral. Lying on the sofa in his dark room, Frédéric was wondering what the explanation was.

On this particular night he noticed a slight difference from the previous nights. After closing the street door, Philippe forgot to fasten the safety chain, and he spent some time fumbling for the light switch, like a man under the influence of drink or some violent emotion. His father followed his movements step by step.

The Alhambra was still under construction, and parts of the old houses that had occupied its site remained, among them the narrow passage Philippe had entered. It was cluttered with crates, stage sets, and other trash, and as a rule Philippe went through it warily. Tonight, he didn't bother. He nearly fell over some scenery, kicked it aside, tramped heavily up the stairs, and flung open the first door, which led to the balcony.

"He's forgotten to turn off the light," Frédéric murmured to himself.

Philippe had to cross the balcony, climb over a row of seats, and go down a narrow passage beside the projectionist's room. Finally, on the other side of the attic in which his father slept, he reached the recess, hardly larger than a ship's cabin, that had been made into his bedroom.

He had no idea that Frédéric's eyes were open. After walking past the sofa on which his father lay, he entered his tiny room, closing the door behind him. There, too, he didn't act as usual, but flung himself, fully dressed, on the bed. After a while, he changed his mind, sat up, and took off his shoes, letting them drop noisily to the floor.

Frédéric listened intently, because he could hear his son talking to himself, muttering phrases that sounded like cursing. Then, suddenly, his mood changed, and he started sobbing violently and thumping his pillow with his fist.

Frédéric swung himself to the edge of the sofa and pricked up his ears like an animal that has heard, in the distance, the cries of another of its kind. Never before had he known his son to weep. Even as a small boy Philippe had seemed quite impervious to grief. Now, the sound of his son's sobbing had a curious effect on Frédéric: in a way, it gratified him; it showed that the young man was human after all.

There were broken phrases between sobs, but it was impossible to make out the words. Philippe switched on his lamp, and a ribbon of light showed under the door. Half reluctantly, Frédéric began to move toward it; he felt he ought to do something.

On the threshold he hesitated. Just as he never mentioned his insomnia to anyone, so he always refrained from talking about his private affairs, and discouraged it in others. If there was one thing he loathed, it was a "scene," especially the kind involving a parade of unbridled emotion. It outraged his sense of decency.

He waited for a while, his hand on the doorknob, and when at last he stepped into the room, he was embarrassed.

Philippe sat up abruptly and glared at his father. His cheeks had telltale patches of moisture; his eyes were dark with anger. He had torn off his tie, and it lay on the floor.

"What do *you* want?" There was a vicious edge to his voice.

Trying to keep calm, his father lit a cigarette. Though he had not turned on the light in his own room, he had slipped a dressing gown over his silk pajamas; carelessness in dress was another of his antipathies. The contrast between his elegant attire, which might have graced the bedroom scene of a modern comedy, and his surroundings—the two dingy little bedrooms, littered with film canisters, tattered directories, and papers of all kinds—was striking.

"What do you want?"

As if to make it clear that he intended to stay for a while, Frédéric swept the papers off a chair and sat down. Watching his son's set lips, he cast about for an opening.

"Didn't she let you in?" he asked. It cost him an effort to get the words out.

For the last twenty years, ever since his wife had left him, he had cold-shouldered sentiment, staying away from subjects like this. Not that he was bitter. On the contrary, though his vaguely ironic smile superficially resembled that of a cynical man-about-town, it held much more charity, indeed real kindness, which embraced not only the young chorus girls in cheap dresses who asked him for engagements, but also his usherettes and beggars in the street.

But because this was his son, he made no attempt to hide his anxiety.

"So you knew!" The young man bristled. "Who told you? What have you heard?"

"That's not important."

"Excuse me! It has great importance. Who told you about . . . all that?"

"No one, my boy."

"Ah! Then you've been spying on me."

An ugly word. The fact that Frédéric had almost never had a heart-to-heart conversation with his son made it harder. He had watched him growing up, going his own way, without ever interfering. It would have been, to his thinking, an indiscretion to approve or disapprove. That was another of his inhibitions: an invincible reluctance to meddle in another person's life, even his son's.

Irritated by his silence, Philippe repeated angrily:

33

"So you've been spying on me. What a dirty trick!"

"I have not been spying. It was pure chance that . . ."

"What, precisely, do you know?"

This was so typical of his son. A minute or two earlier, he had been weeping his heart out. Now, in a flash, because his pride had been hurt, he had swung to an aggressive mood. He was shrewdly trying to find out what cards lay in his opponent's hand before committing himself. The older man gave a sad, rather disillusioned smile.

"What do I know?" he repeated. "Everything, my dear boy. But you needn't be alarmed. . . . For five nights, she's kept her window shut. That's so, isn't it?"

"Were you watching?"

"Of course not . . . But I know."

What his father had said was correct. For five consecutive nights, Philippe had been making his usual incursion into Mme Brun's garden and running the gauntlet of Charlotte's embraces—only to find Martine's window shut. Tonight, he had dared to tap on the pane, half thinking he'd provoke a scandal if there was no other way to gain his end.

The worst part was the return journey: the certainty that Charlotte was lying in wait beside that little door in the wall, knowing that she *knew*, and that her meager breast was swelling with preposterous hope. . . .

All his efforts to see Martine in the daytime had failed, too, though he'd waited hours at the corner of Rue Réaumur. One morning he had even thought of going boldly to the front door and ringing the bell like an ordinary caller. But the door would probably be slammed in his face by Augustin. Old Donadieu, he knew, had announced in the presence of the whole family:

"If that young no-good has the nerve to set foot in this house again, I'll throw him headfirst out the window!"

The reason was that, in the days when he used to see a good deal of the Donadieus, Philippe had tried to sponge off the old man in a particularly repugnant way. He had explained that he needed money to send to his mother; she had written to him from abroad, he declared, saying that she was completely destitute. Then, going up to the second floor, he had said the same to Michel Donadieu.

Fortunately, his father knew nothing about this. All old Donadieu had said to Frédéric was:

"You'd do well to keep an eye on your youngster. He's growing up badly."

Now, sitting on the edge of the bed, his face flushed with anger and despair, his hair tousled, Philippe was glaring at his father, who, the more embarrassed of the two, was fumbling for words.

"Have you had an argument?" Deliberately he chose a nonromantic term.

"No."

"Then what's gone wrong?"

Philippe felt he'd better change the tone of the interview and show himself in better colors.

"Everything's wrong," he said bitterly, "and it's because of you, if you must know." Seeing the look of amazement on his father's face, he went on: "Don't you realize that the whole family thinks it's odd that you were the last person to be seen with Oscar Donadieu before his death? It's common knowledge that you're hard up for money, and you haven't been any more welcome at their house than I. Except, of course, by the old lady and the pretty daughter-in-law, but you probably make up to them."

"Really, Philippe!" his father exclaimed, but gently, without a hint of reproach.

"And I have to suffer for it! It's unfair! Martine's changed completely; she suspects . . . all sorts of things. She asked me point-blank if I was the one who . . ." His voice broke on a sob.

Suddenly another fit of rage came over him, and he started gesticulating, shouting imprecations at his father, the Donadieus, the world at large. . . .

But he never stopped watching his father. And Frédéric, who at first had looked more disturbed than Philippe had ever seen him, was growing calmer. Indeed, there was now less concern than curiosity in his eyes as he watched his son's extraordinary behavior.

Casually, he remarked, lighting another cigarette:

"I thought you loved her."

For a moment, Philippe was quite startled.

"Who said I didn't?"

Obviously, there was nothing to be done, and, with a sigh, Frédéric rose. In his dressing gown, which had no like in La Rochelle, and silk pajamas that would have both shocked and delighted the worthy bourgeois, he cut a graceful, almost dandyish figure against this background of squalor and disorder.

"You're furious, you feel sick to death," he said slowly, "but you don't love her."

He regretted having let himself be lured here, believing that his son's tears were due to real grief, that he needed consolation. Now that he'd found out his mistake, he wanted to get away. It had been a cruel disappointment, too, because, in the darkness, he had been fool enough to have illusions that . . .

"Listen!" The young man jumped to his feet and was barring the way to the door.

Frédéric stood still and waited.

"I'm of age. I can do what I like. Promise me, on your honor, that you won't breathe a word to anyone, that you won't try . . ."

"Don't be a damned fool, Philippe," his father broke in, smiling in spite of himself, though he could feel that his eyes were moist.

Philippe was not satisfied.

"I want you to give me your word of honor. I know you're close to the old lady. If you say a word to her about it—"

That was enough—too much. With a quick thrust of his arm, which showed the muscular force beneath his frail appearance, Frédéric pushed his son aside, went back to his room, closed his door—and, for the first time, locked it.

So this was how things were between them, and he knew it was his fault, in a way. That strange aversion he had to meddling in his son's life—a sort of deference to others' foibles, or, perhaps, a sense of human dignity—had kept them at arm's length. And there was another, less obvious, reason for their estrangement. Watching the boy grow up, he had sensed a stronger, harder personality than his own, and he'd been afraid that any injudicious tampering might blunt its edge. It might also, irrevocably, turn against him a boy who had always been intractable, mistrustful of his elders.

His son had asked him, on his honor, not to betray his secret! Well, it only proved, once again, how little Philippe understood him.

He turned on the light and sat at his desk, a cheap, mass-produced one, littered with bills and writs.

Not yet rid of his debts, he was walking a financial tightrope, doling out small sums on account, resorting to every expedient to get films and equipment for his theater.

People who didn't know him said: "Better be careful. Dargens isn't to be trusted." Others remarked: "He's as proud as he used to be when he owned a country house, horses, cars, and all the rest of it."

Actually, there had been no great change in the man himself. He had been the arbiter of elegance in La Rochelle, the most sought-after guest, and he had a reputation for innumerable successes with women. He had known to perfection the art of living, and he knew it still. He wasn't in the least depressed by having to make do with a little attic room, and receiving periodical visits from bailiff's men. Usually, indeed, at these encounters it was the bailiff's men who ended up by eating humble pie, apologizing for their intrusion.

But Philippe was a tougher problem. He could hear him stamping up and down in his little room, muttering to himself, seething with rage. He was a young man up in arms against the world.

At four in the afternoon the following day, Frédéric Dargens was ringing the bell beside the heavy outer gate of the Donadieus' house on Rue Réaumur. Augustin, the chauffeur-valet, who was in the kitchen, touched the mechanism that released the latch. After crossing the paved courtyard, where the car had just been washed, Dargens went up the front steps and entered the hall.

"Madame is not at home," Augustin informed him.

"I know. I'm going upstairs."

The servant seemed put out at first, but gave a slight shrug, as if to show he washed his hands of it. What a dolt the man is, Frédéric thought, the sort of well-meaning fool who paves the way for tragedies!

In old Donadieu's lifetime, Frédéric had been a frequent visitor, coming several afternoons a week. Mme Donadieu, with whom he had been friendly since his early youth, was always begging him to come. The life imposed on her by her husband was almost that of a recluse, and it was a welcome change to talk to someone who could recount the latest gossip. Moreover, Frédéric was the only person she knew with whom she could speak frankly, in whom she could confide.

Not that she had much in the way of secrets, but she was a woman of great vitality, who probably wished she could lead an active social life, go to Paris once or twice a year, travel. It was a relief to have someone who could appreciate her point of view and understand the dreariness of her cloistered days and petty duties.

"My children don't understand me a bit," she would tell him. "They take after their father; Michel especially. When he was fifteen, he had quite a business, dealing in stamps at school. Then he developed a craze for model ships in bottles. . . ."

Michel's present craze was his fourth. He was never happy unless he had a hobby, but it had to be sedentary. When the ships-in-bottles phase was past, he had thrown himself with fervor into genealogical research. The walls of his living room upstairs were plastered with coats of arms, which he could explain learnedly, and he knew the family trees of all the leading families in that part of France.

For the last three months, he had been a fervent addict of the Yo-yo. After reading in a gossip column that the Prince of Wales was a Yo-yo enthusiast, he had promptly sent to Paris for a selection of various types, and he played with them for hours in the evening, after the children were in bed.

When it was almost five, Mme Donadieu would say, with a sigh:

"Now I mustn't keep you any longer, or Eva will be furious. . . ."

That was why Augustin's tone was so disapproving. Dargens was friendly with both women, mother and daughter-in-law, and his visits usually took place when their husbands were at the office. He alone was free at five o'clock. After having tea on the ground floor, he went up to the second, where whisky was waiting for him.

If Marthe, the elder daughter, wanted to see her mother for any reason, she would ask Augustin:

"Is *he* here?"

If he was, she preferred to wait, rather than risk encountering him.

On this particular afternoon, however, knowing that Mme Donadieu had taken her husband's place at the office, Dargens went straight upstairs and knocked on Eva's door.

"Come in, Frédéric. Sit here . . . I'm feeling rotten. Don't expect me to get up and be polite. Yes, help yourself . . . Well, what's the latest news, my friend?"

Her room was one that, not without much opposition from the family, Eva had turned into a boudoir, for herself alone. Of very different stock from the Donadieus'—her maiden name was Grazielli— she was as slim and languorous as they were burly and austere. She gave an impression of extreme fragility, but also of an intense capacity for passion. Hers was a dusky beauty, and on Frédéric's advice she had furnished her little boudoir exotically; it would have suited a Venetian beauty of the Late Renaissance.

After kissing her hand, and helping himself to whisky, he settled down on a cushion at her feet.

"Is Kiki better?" he asked.

"Yes. He may be getting up tomorrow or the next day."

On his return from the funeral, which had taken place in a downpour, the boy had had a shivering fit and been promptly sent to bed.

He, too, was delicate. Born when his mother was past forty and his father close to sixty, he had always been a difficult child, and lately his moodiness had become more pronounced. His mother attributed this to growing pains, Michel to lack of intelligence, whereas Olsen, more severe, said Kiki had an innately disagreeable character.

"You haven't seen my mother-in-law, I suppose," Eva said.

"No. I hear she's working at the office."

"Yes. She started going there three days ago, and I wonder what will come of it. Michel is terribly fed up; he tells me she insists on being consulted on the most petty details, and she answers the telephone herself. She wants to boss everything! Her explanation is that, as Martine's and Kiki's guardian, she regards it as her duty to watch over their interests. That's all very well, but . . . Frédéric, my life in this house is getting more impossible than ever. It's positively awful at times. I wonder if I can stand it!"

Downstairs, Augustin, the faithful chauffeur-valet, was wagging his head in reprobation of this tête-à-tête—though nothing could have been more innocent than the relationship between Eva and Dargens. Pretty though she was, she wasn't his type; he preferred women of sturdier build, more animated, less romantic. But, because Michel's interests were so narrow—genealogies and Yo-yos—this brief hour with Dargens was the one bright spot of her day. She would smoke cigarettes in a rather affected manner—though they made her cough—and watch Dargens, that ladies' man par excellence, seated respectfully at her feet, sipping her whisky, which was an exotic drink by local standards.

"I haven't any idea what's really happening in the office. Needless to say, I'm not allowed to set foot in it. That's just like Michel; he's a sort of cheap edition of his father. Yesterday, when I told him I wanted a car of my own—after all, why shouldn't I have one?—what do you think he said? That it wasn't the time for extravagance; in fact, we'll have to go slow for quite a while!"

The one window was curtained with heavy black material, which also covered the sofa and the floor cushions. No sounds from outside reached the small, dimly lighted room.

"Give me another cigarette, please. Thank you . . . The family's dreadfully worried, you know. It seems that no one really believes it was an accident. My father-in-law knew every stone of that quay, and it was most unlikely he'd trip over a hawser or a bollard or anything like that. He wasn't subject to dizziness, and he was always so alert, wasn't he? My mother-in-law hasn't said outright that it can't have been an accident, but she's hinted as much to me. . . ."

"Has she?"

"And for the last four days there's been another thing to worry us."

Dargens kept quiet, as quiet as when, at night, he waited for sleep to come.

"It's Kiki. He's started walking in his sleep again. I hear he gets out of bed and goes to his sister's room. One night, his mother heard him asking, 'Where is he?' "

The cigarette between Frédéric's lips remained quite steady as he gazed up at her inquiringly.

"They tried to get him to explain. But he wouldn't say a word more. Twice, his mother went to see him in his bedroom, when only Martine was with him. He started crying, but she couldn't get any explanation out of him. . . . What do you think about it, Frédéric?"

"Me?" His voice sounded so odd that she couldn't help laughing.

"Yes, you silly old thing! I want to know what you think about what I was telling you just now. I don't believe you heard a word. What was it I said?"

"That Kiki started crying. . . ."

"Yes—and what else?"

"That he wouldn't say why. . . . Probably he was feverish."

"But that's not all." Eva lowered her voice. "Sure I'm not boring you with all this family gossip? . . . You know there's nobody else I can talk to freely. . . . I heard it from Nurse—what I'm going to tell you now."

The nurse who looked after Jean, who was five, and two-year-old Evette. The hiring of this peasant woman from Luçon when Jean was born had been another subject of dispute between Eva and her mother-in-law. Mme Donadieu strongly disapproved of wet nurses, and refused to believe that Eva wasn't strong enough to suckle her own children.

"It was the day before yesterday, washday. All the washing, you know, for the three families, is done together, in a building behind the garage. Two girls come to do it, and we share the cost. . . . Sorry to inflict these details on you, Frédéric. You must be thinking, What a bore the woman is!"

He made a dismissive gesture. A ray of sunlight slanting down between the black curtains fell on one of Eva's satin slippers and bare ankle.

"I've never seen these two girls except at a distance. My mother-in-law tells me it's getting harder every year to find reliable ones. Nurse goes there to do my little girl's washing, because I don't want her things to be washed with the others'."

She hesitated, watching Frédéric's face to make sure he wasn't smiling at these explanations.

"All this sounds pretty trivial, I know; but you'll see; it has its importance. . . . Well, Nurse was out in the washhouse in the afternoon, and suddenly my mother-in-law blew in and started scolding the girls about the soap. I don't really know the truth of it, but it seems they weren't using the soap we give them, but a cheaper kind. Finally, my mother-in-law lost her temper and told the girls they were no better than thieves. Then one of them muttered, under her breath, but loud enough to be heard:

" 'At least in *my* family there ain't no murderers!'

"You know what my mother-in-law's like. That made her see red. She dropped her cane, went up to the girl, and shook her soundly. Then she asked her what she meant by that remark."

Frédéric lit another cigarette and took a sip of whisky, perhaps to maintain his attention.

"Sure I'm not boring you?"

"No. Go on, please."

"Oh, there's nothing much more to tell. The girl—she's our greengrocer's daughter, it appears—dried up when my mother-in-law started in on her. All she had to say was:

" 'If some of the neighbors hereabouts told all they knew, you wouldn't be so sure that Monsieur Donadieu fell into the water by accident.'

"Then she stamped off with her clogs on, and wouldn't even take her wages. The other girl came to fetch her shoes that night.

"What do you make of it, Frédéric? Can you guess what was in her mind?"

He took a quick puff at his cigarette and shook his head.

"I could see that Nurse was rather scared of telling me. I thought my mother-in-law would say something about it to us, anyhow to Michel. If she did, he hasn't breathed a word of it to me. Tell me, Frédéric, do you think someone killed him?"

"Well, really . . ."

"Oh, I know you're in a difficult position, since you're my mother-in-law's friend as well. And I know, too, that I don't count in this house. I'm nothing . . . less than nothing. They'd never dream of letting me into their secrets. But I keep my eyes open, and during these last few days I've noticed a change. Marthe, for instance, hardly says a word to me, and we used to be fairly friendly—in a formal sort of way. In fact, I never see anyone to talk to now. My father-in-law used to drop in sometimes to see the children; he didn't have much to say for himself, but it was better than nothing. Now it's like living in a big apartment house, where the tenants don't know each other."

She gave a sigh, adding dolefully:

"Oh, I'm so bored in this house, bored to death! When I think of my mother's luck! She's in Colombo now, with her husband."

Mme Grazielli, who had recently married again, was on her honeymoon, and she sent her daughter postcards from time to time.

"If he comes again, I'll tell everything. I'll tell them he killed Papa!"

"But he didn't, Kiki. Really, he didn't."

Kiki made no reply. He was feverish, so it was hard to be sure he understood what he was saying. Was he trying some childish form of blackmail on his sister? Martine couldn't make up her mind about it. She was acting as Kiki's nurse, spending all day in the overheated bedroom, concocting evil-smelling poultices and measuring out medicine drop by drop. Kiki would doze for hours, and when he opened his eyes, he'd stare vacantly at the ceiling. He'd started doing this when he was quite small—to be precise, when he'd been in a cast for a year owing to trouble with his spine.

The family had often said, "He's backward. But he'll catch up eventually."

Actually, he was backward only in certain respects. He was tall for his age and already had a light growth of down on his upper lip. At school, he was handled gently, because of his spinal trouble. If he got promoted at the normal age, it was mainly because he was the son of Oscar Donadieu.

He was, however, a voracious reader, tiring his eyes so much that in the evening he had to wear glasses.

"Listen, Kiki. You've got it all wrong. I assure you that Philippe didn't . . . didn't do anything to Papa."

He remained silent, and his eyes went blank. At such moments, he really gave the impression that, as people sometimes said, he "wasn't quite all there."

"You love me, Kiki, don't you? Well, if you breathe a word of this to anyone, I'll kill myself, right away."

He found a typically childish retort:

"You can't. You don't have a revolver."

Martine, who had a quick imagination, promptly rejoined:

"I don't need one. I'll climb out on the roof by the attic and throw myself down into the yard. . . . Why are you so nasty to me, Kiki?"

"I don't want him to come here."

"I've told you he won't come again."

"He came here—and then Papa died."

That found her at a loss. The boy's mental processes had something baffling about them, a sort of perverted logic, and she had no idea how to rid him of his obsession.

"He came here every night," Kiki continued. "I heard him."

"That's not true. . . . Only once or twice a week."

"That's it."

"What do you mean?"

"He came here on that Saturday."

"No," she lied desperately. "I assure you, Kiki, he didn't come that Saturday."

They had to speak in undertones, and when there were footsteps in the hallway and the doorknob turned, they stopped speaking entirely. On such occasions Martine put a finger to her lips and looked at Kiki beseechingly, but the boy disdained to make the least sign of agreement.

Sometimes it was his mother who bustled in, casting suspicious glances at the two of them and seeming to fill the room with her commanding presence. Or it was Michel, who paid visits only out of a sense of duty, discoursed learnedly on pneumococci, and studied the temperature chart with a knowing air. Or it might be Olsen, the most placid member of the family, with all the Nordic gravity of his grandfather, who had come to France from Bergen at the age of twenty.

"Feeling better, sonny?" he would murmur vaguely, and leave almost at once. He was always thinking about work: tons of coal and frozen fish, contracts and quotas.

"Kiki, do be nice. I'm your sister, aren't I? There's only we two. . . ."

She knew what she meant; in the big house, with families on every floor, the two of them were natural allies, a pair apart. Kiki, however, didn't understand, or understood differently.

"We *three*," he corrected. "Anyhow, if he comes again, I'll tell. . . ." He was getting excited; his temperature was rising. He sank

43

back on the pillow, his forehead moist with perspiration. "I'll tell them that Papa . . ."

"Hush! Someone's coming."

Hastily, Martine picked up a compress from the bedside table and laid it on her brother's forehead, hiding his eyes.

4

Lamps were lighted a little earlier every day as the city was settling down to the rhythm of winter on the Atlantic coast. A sharper, saltier tang came from the harbor, where the boats rocked higher on the flood, blocks and tackle creaking, and the little bistros on the quays reeked of hot grog and wet serge.

In La Rochelle, the dark forms of women, countryfolk and residents, clustered like moths around the brightly lighted shopwindows. From the street clerks could be seen bent over their desks under green-shaded lamps. In contrast with the animation of the main avenues, the side streets had a furtive air, and the rare gaslights served as meeting places for loving couples, who presently retreated into the darkness of convenient doorways.

Light shone in the windows of the Donadieu building on Quai Vallin, including those on the ground floor, whose iron bars gave the place the look of a prison. Had anyone climbed the mast of one of the schooners alongside the quay, he could have seen the faces of the people gathered in the big office that had been Oscar Donadieu's and now was his wife's.

An elbow resting on the desk, a fat blue pencil in her right hand, she was presiding, with Michel sitting beside her, Olsen standing, and three other men, each with papers in front of him, facing her across the desk.

When anyone called to see one of the Donadieus, the receptionist informed him in his most official tone:

"I'm afraid you'll have to wait, sir. The gentlemen are at a board meeting."

"Ah! Will it last long, do you think?"

A vague gesture indicated that the duration of such a gathering was unpredictable. The result was that in the waiting room, with its few lights, hard horsehair seats, and discreetly placed spittoons, quite a number of people kept crossing and uncrossing their legs and sometimes cast admiring glances at a man who had had the nerve to get up and pace the room, stopping now and then to gaze at the photographs of colliers and trawlers on the walls.

At last a baize-lined door opened; then another just behind it, of polished oak. Voices were heard, of people taking courteous leave, and a woman's crisp, clear tones:

"So that's settled. You'll all come to lunch tomorrow. We can thrash the matter out and, I hope, come to a decision."

The men other than the family were soon heard exchanging pleasantries in the big entrance hall, then on the steps.

"Can I give you a lift home?"

"No, thanks. I must stop at my office."

"I hope Madame Mortier's better."

"Much better, thanks . . . And how's your son-in-law?"

Collars were turned up, because a drizzle had started. The three men went on chatting for a minute or two, but their thoughts were elsewhere, and their eyes kept straying to the ground-floor windows.

"Good night," said Camboulives, adding in a whisper: "Well, we'll see what comes of it."

The office door had been closed by Michel, to the chagrin of the people in the waiting room, who had hoped to be admitted once the meeting was over, and now had to sit down again. Michel walked to the fireplace and leaned against the mantelpiece, on which stood a large black marble clock. Olsen, who, after all, was only an in-law, sat in a corner and folded his arms. Both men were looking glum, and Mme Donadieu pretended to be surprised as she resumed her seat at the desk.

"What's come over you?" she asked, looking at each in turn.

For a moment neither spoke; then Michel said:

"I can't help wondering how they feel about it . . . this idea of yours—of a business lunch, I mean. I could see they were startled already, having a woman act as chairman of our meeting. . . ."

Each month, there was a meeting of the leading coal importers: the Camboulives group, the Varins, and the Mortiers—the principal rivals of the Donadieus. Among themselves, they settled various business problems, especially their relationships with local authorities and the railway companies, and also the apportioning of quotas.

"I wonder if you realize," he added, "that business lunches are something quite unheard of in this town?"

"Well, they'll be heard of now."

"What's more, it won't serve any purpose. . . ."

"Wait and see!"

Michel shot his last bolt.

"Who's going to pay for the lunch?"

"I am."

It was on the tip of his tongue to remind her that on a quarter of the joint income she could hardly indulge in such costly whims. But he had already gone rather far, and he thought it best to leave the room, muttering something under his breath and beckoning to Olsen to follow him.

Mme Donadieu's idea of having a business lunch was more than an innovation; it ran counter to all local methods of conducting business. Still more flagrant, it ran counter to the Donadieu tradition: never had such people as the Camboulives and the Varins set foot in the big house on Rue Réaumur.

Nothing if not thorough, Mme Donadieu called for the car, and she left in it well before six o'clock. Five minutes later, the big automobile drew up outside the leading caterer's. Mme Donadieu, who had difficulty walking, stayed in the car, sending Augustin to summon the manager. A moment later he was obsequiously standing on the muddy sidewalk taking down the order.

"I want fillet of sole for—let's see—twelve people."

She proceeded to work out the menu with him in detail, and on the way home gave Augustin instructions through the speaking tube.

"Don't forget to go to the market early tomorrow morning, for flowers. And get out the service with our monogram, the one with the ship on it."

On her return home, she had a long conversation with the cook.

Michel found Frédéric Dargens in his wife's boudoir—or, more precisely, noticed Frédéric's hat in the hall, and waited for him to leave.

Not that he had anything against Frédéric, or felt any jealousy. He was naturally unsociable, and he preferred settling down to the evening paper when he got home, rarely bothering to go and see his small son. Ordinarily, he would have waited for an hour or more without the least impatience, and perhaps tried a new and improved Yo-yo that had come with the morning mail. But, for once, he had something to tell his wife, and he heaved a sigh of relief when he heard the front door open and close.

"Guess what Maman has done!"

Eva, who had drunk two glasses of port and was feeling a little hazy, merely stared at him.

"Would you believe it? At the meeting this afternoon she invited all the men there to come to lunch tomorrow."

"Here? In *our* dining room?"

"No. Downstairs. They must be wondering what's come over us. Anyhow, I made it clear to her that *we* won't pay the bill."

He could not understand why, on hearing this, Eva showed so little interest.

On the floor above, Olsen, too, was imparting the great news to his wife.

"We'll make ourselves a laughingstock," he grumbled. "A business-lunch conference! To discuss problems of the coal trade! Absurd, I call it."

"It was Maman's idea, wasn't it? Does she expect me to put in an appearance?"

"Er . . . I don't know, really. I suppose I should have asked."

Marthe did not go down to inquire, but fidgeted while waiting for her mother to deign to come up and tell her if she was or wasn't to figure in the impending lunch party. But the whole evening went by without any visit or intimation from the ground floor.

Tired and sulky, Kiki was reading in his room, his feet on the radiator. Martine was finishing a table runner she had started long before her father's death. Their mother was still conferring with Augustin and the cook.

"Now let's decide on the wines. . . ."

On the third floor, Marthe was now studying fashion magazines. Dress was one of her chief interests, and she specialized in the dignified and distingué.

On the floor below, Michel, in his shirtsleeves, was trying his new Yo-yo, while Nurse ironed underclothes in the linen room. The low clang of her iron could be heard at regular intervals, and Michel's voice counting:

"Seven . . . Eight . . . Nine . . . Drat!"

"Drat!" was his pet oath. Too well brought up to indulge in vulgar swearwords, he found this mild imprecation a relief in moments of annoyance.

"Fourteen . . . Fifteen . . . Oh, drat it!"

Eva was playing tangos on the phonograph.

Olsen, the best bridge player in La Rochelle, was at one of his card parties, to which he never took his wife.

The hours went by in sleepy monotone, broken only at long intervals by a sudden stridence from the direction of the harbor: the horn of a trawler putting out through the rain-swept darkness.

An adventure film was showing on the Alhambra's screen for a half-full house.

Next door to the Donadieus', Mme Brun was writing a letter to her daughter. She looked up to say:

"Charlotte! How about a warm drink? A rum punch, maybe."

Mme Brun was a greedy old woman, who made a cult of petty self-indulgence. One of her pleasures was writing letters to her daughter, her only child, who had married a member of the nobility and whom she saw, at most, once a year. For the letter-writing ritual, a really elegant escritoire was required, as well as paper of the best quality and taste, discreetly subdued light, which kindled vagrant gleams on her beringed fingers, and the knowledge that somewhere in the background Charlotte was busy with her needlework.

My dear daughter [she had written], I know that you will find nothing of great interest in this letter, but your old mother, living in her backwater, sometimes feels a need to . . . [And she would ramble on for five or six pages, which she might as well not mail, since her daughter certainly wouldn't read them.] I hear from Charlotte that our neighbor, the Queen Mother, is to have a business luncheon at her house tomorrow. It will create quite a stir in our little city. . . .

She put down her pen, smiling. They were going to have a bowl of punch all to themselves, she and Charlotte—like two schoolgirls sharing a forbidden feast in their dormitory. Some evenings, Mme Brun would call across the room:

"Charlotte! Let's have some crêpes tonight."

She adored crêpes, especially the kind that, after being soused in brandy like a Christmas pudding, are set ablaze. And she insisted on cooking them herself in a chafing dish.

"I'm glad about that lunch," she said to Charlotte. "It's an Event."

It was to be an Event that, because of an incident occurring at it, marked a turning point in several lives.

———

49

Was it by oversight or deliberate? Certainly Mme Donadieu had no liking for her daughter-in-law, Eva; and perhaps she felt some jealousy of Marthe, who went out more and had more friends than she had. She did not tell either young woman that she wasn't wanted at the lunch, but she held her peace—which came to the same thing.

After some hesitation, however, she decided that her two youngest children should be present.

Somewhat to the surprise of the family, she went to the office as usual at eight o'clock. But, while there, she called the house twice, to make sure that everything was going as planned, that Martine's new dress was ready, that the caviar had been delivered.

Camboulives, a southerner with a coarse, swarthy face and a booming voice, was something of an interloper among the magnates of La Rochelle, whose families had been in the shipping business for at least two generations. He was the only one who demeaned himself by going to cafés, playing cards with his skippers or anyone he could find, and sometimes coming home half drunk.

Mortier was a smaller, less impressive version of the late Oscar Donadieu, but with this difference: he had remained a Protestant, and indeed had become more bigoted with advancing age.

This business lunch was so remote from their experience that, feeling slightly nervous, they arranged to go to the house together.

"I'm afraid you'll find this place somewhat depressing, but, so soon after a bereavement . . ." Actually, Mme Donadieu looked anything but gloomy. Hadn't it been her life's dream to play the hostess? "This is my youngest daughter. . . . Martine, would you pass the port around?"

Kiki was in the black suit he had worn at the funeral, though it was now too large for him. The guests greeted him politely, as if he were a grown-up, but after some vain attempts to draw him out lost heart.

Michel, feeling very ill at ease, tried to behave as if he, too, were a guest. Olsen embarked on a long conversation with Varin, one of whose boats he had been wanting to buy for some time.

"I suggest, gentlemen, that we don't talk business until the coffee is served. . . . Monsieur Mortier, this is your place, on my right."

It was Camboulives who started the trouble. Any silence in the least prolonged got on his nerves. A moment came when the only sound in the room was the clinking of knives and forks. Since Kiki was sitting next to him, he turned to the boy and said the first thing that entered his head.

"You're at school, aren't you?"

"No," Kiki answered with a scowl.

"That's not quite correct," his mother put in. "He was to go back at the beginning of the term, but he was ill. In fact, he's not quite well yet."

Camboulives didn't have the sense to let the subject drop.

"What class are you in?"

An unfortunate question! Though Kiki was fifteen, he was not with others that age.

"He's three years behind," Mme Donadieu explained. "I'm afraid there's nothing to be done about it, though it's disagreeable for him to have boys of twelve as classmates."

Disagreeable for the teachers, too, having this gawky youth among the juniors, and unable to keep up in his work. And having to handle him with a certain deference because of the important position of his family. Their secret hope was that he would be removed from school and given a private tutor.

Warming to her subject, his mother went on impulsively:

"It's not my son's fault that he's backward. He had a serious illness at the most critical age. But I have little doubt he'll catch up with the others before long. He's going back to school next week, and—"

It came as a shock when the boy, so shy and taciturn, cut in with an emphatic:

"No!"

"What did you say, Oscar?"

"I said no. I won't go back to school."

It was an absurd situation. Under any other circumstances, Mme Donadieu could have coped with it easily, reprimanding the boy severely, and perhaps boxing his ears. But Kiki was out of reach, and Camboulives, a blunderer born, made things worse by asking:

"If you don't like being at school, what do you want to do?"

It almost seemed as if the boy had been waiting for this chance. His sister gave him an imploring look. But Kiki, made bold by the presence of strangers and the fact that for once he had an audience outside the family circle, declared emphatically:

"I want to go to sea."

"Don't pay any attention to him," said his mother, conjuring up an indulgent smile. "He's been feverish and doesn't realize what he's saying."

"I want to go to sea," the boy repeated.

"And what do you want to be, sonny?" Camboulives asked, with a broad smile. "Captain of a liner?"

"I don't care what. I'll ship out as a deckhand if I can't get anything else."

"Mother!" called Michel across the table, signaling to her to order Kiki out of the room.

She nodded. But unfortunately she was at the wrong end of the table. Pheasant had just been served, and all heads were bent over the plates. Mortier turned to the boy and looked at him thoughtfully.

"It's a hard life, a deckhand's. Do you think your health would stand it?"

"Please don't encourage him, Monsieur Mortier," said Mme Donadieu. "He's being foolish—and he knows it."

She gave the boy a severe look. He turned paler, and his lips quivered. But he said doggedly:

"I shall go to sea."

"Oscar!" she said sharply. "That's enough!" No longer caring about the company or keeping up appearances, she tried to get control of her son. Even Camboulives realized that he'd better keep his mouth shut. Raising his voice, Olsen said to the man beside him:

"By the way, as regards that cargo of cods' roe we were talking about yesterday . . ."

Mme Donadieu noticed that Kiki was getting up.

"Sit down, Kiki."

"I won't."

His one desire was to escape from the dining room and sob his heart out in solitude. He heard his mother's voice again.

"Sit down, I tell you, and eat your lunch."

Convinced that such an opportunity to assert himself would never come again, Kiki yelled:

"I'll run away to sea! I'll run away to sea!"

He was getting on everybody's nerves; on Martine's most of all, since she could see her brother had lost all self-control, and there was no knowing what he might say.

"Go to bed at once," said Mme Donadieu.

"All right, I'll go to bed. But I tell you, I'll run away—and no one's going to stop me."

He walked to the door, stopped on the threshold and, looking at the people around the table, said to his mother, in a quavering voice, but so distinctly that everyone could hear:

"Anyhow, the boats belong to me more than to you."

The clatter of knives and forks was replaced by dead silence.

Augustin saved the situation—by spilling half the contents of the sauceboat he was carrying on Monsieur Mortier's shoulder.

"Really, Augustin!" Mme Donadieu exclaimed. "What's come over you? Have you forgotten how to serve?"

No more words had passed between Philippe and his father on the subject of Martine. But the young man continued coming home at one in the morning, which showed that he still went every night to see if the window was open.

He had grown thinner, and sometimes smelled of drink on his return. The men at the garage just outside La Rochelle where he was assistant to the manager were puzzled by the change in him.

"He's like a bear with a sore head," the owner said. And he was relieved by Philippe's frequent absences. The young man's sour looks, caustic remarks, and especially his shrill, cackling laugh, bothered everybody.

Hour after hour, in the deluges of October, in the keen November winds, under the gray autumnal skies of the Atlantic seaboard, he kept hopeless watch in the vicinity of Rue Réaumur. He even gave Charlotte a note for Martine, imploring her to transmit it. Charlotte consented, but nothing came of it.

"It's not my fault," Charlotte explained. "She hardly ever goes out, and when she does, her brother's always with her."

Philippe had met them twice. Martine looked away quickly; Kiki gave him a long, defiant stare. Nevertheless, he persisted in his nocturnal visits to the Donadieus' garden, even though he had to endure, on the return journey, that unescapable half hour of hateful dalliance with Charlotte in the leafless arbor.

"I know you love her," Charlotte would whimper in his arms. "If you got what you wanted, you'd drop me like a hot brick!"

"Don't be silly," he protested feebly. "You know I'm awfully fond of you, too, Charlotte."

"Oh, stop lying! I know you don't mean it."

Each time he came back from the other garden, he was unable to conceal his rage and despair. And once, when Charlotte gave way to a fit of weeping, he turned on her furiously.

"Can't you understand anything, you fool? Don't you realize my whole career's at stake?"

"That's not true."

"Those high-and-mighty Donadieus have humiliated us long enough—my father and me—and it's high time we paid them back. Do you know the terms of the old brute's will? No, of course you don't; you never know anything!"

"Madame told me something about it."

"Well, one fine day I'll own that house—just you wait and see! And one fine day I'll bundle certain people out of it—by the window!"

That night he had been drinking heavily, and was indeed so drunk that Charlotte was scared. He had raised his voice, and Mme Brun, who, like most old women, was a light sleeper, might easily have heard.

One evening she had news for him.

"They're going away."

"All of them?"

"I don't know. But they've been packing all day."

It was a consequence of Kiki's outrageous conduct at the memorable business lunch. Surprisingly, Mme Donadieu did not severely scold him or even reprove him. Nor did she mention the subject to any of the others. But for two days she behaved as if Kiki had ceased to exist.

They had their meals together—or, rather, the boy sat at the same table, but usually he pushed his plate away after the first mouthful—and no one said a word. On the third evening, however, Mme Donadieu, after gazing for some moments at Martine, remarked:

"You're not looking at all well."

That was so. At no time was Martine's health really good, but lately she'd been looking ill; her face was white and pinched.

Mme Donadieu alone ate heartily all that was put in front of her. She rose early and left the house in a whirlwind of orders and injunctions to the servants, and, except for her legs, which made a cane necessary, appeared almost to have regained her youthful vigor.

"I think a spell of country air would do you good," she added.

This was all she said that evening. Next day, at lunch, she informed Martine that she had called Baptiste and told him to turn on the central heating in their country house.

"It should be ready by tomorrow."

Neither Martine nor her brother knew what she had in mind. Nearly every Sunday, Michel went to their house in Esnandes—the Château d'Esnandes, as it was called locally—for a day's rough hunting. Now, though he had heard his mother's telephone call, he was as much in the dark as they were.

Toward the end of the meal Mme Donadieu explained:

"Augustin will drive you there tomorrow. Both of you need a change."

After drinking her coffee, she went back to her office, where she had an appointment with a representative of the Merchant Service Board, for whose benefit she had ordered in a bottle of whisky. This, too, was unprecedented in the annals of the office on Quai Vallin, indeed of all the shipping offices in La Rochelle.

The car made an early start next day, at quarter of eight, so that Mme Donadieu could see them off. The sky was overcast, but the rain held off. In the distance, the boom of Atlantic breakers could be heard.

No addict of early rising, Eva stayed in bed, and Marthe merely glanced out her window, without opening it, because she was supervising her son's bath.

"We'll see you tomorrow. Michel will come, too, I hope. . . . You must be especially careful not to catch cold, both of you."

Kiki was wearing black knickerbockers, but, not having found any black stockings, he was wearing gray ones.

"Look after your brother, Martine."

Philippe was at the corner, at the wheel of a new car, which he was breaking in for his employer.

From her dressing room, in which she spent two hours each morning, Mme Brun watched the proceedings.

"They don't look too cheerful, any of them," she remarked.

"Why should they be cheerful?" Charlotte sneered. "They don't deserve to be."

Charlotte professed advanced, almost anarchistic ideas—much to Mme Brun's amusement. For, in spite of them, she submitted to being at the old lady's beck and call from morning till night. Her revolt was purely verbal.

After Mme Brun's husband had been relegated to an asylum—though she'd kept him out as long as possible—she had tried to establish a social circle among women her own age. She had failed.

"They're so stupid," she had confided to Charlotte. "Empty-headed old gossipmongers without an idea among them."

The truth was that Mme Brun, who was a de Marsan, one of the oldest and most respected families in the region—an ancestor had been high constable of France—couldn't bear being contradicted. Or, actually, only by Charlotte, who was the spirit of contradiction incarnate, and took full advantage of her privilege.

55

"If there was another French Revolution," Charlotte would begin, staring angrily at the next house.

"Yes?"

"I'd lead the way into that house. Those Donadieus are simply asking for it."

Inwardly, Mme Brun may have approved of these sentiments. She, too, had married a local magnate, of the Donadieu stamp, one of the leading distillers in the district, and he had compelled her for twenty years to lead a life resembling Mme Donadieu's, seemly and sedate.

Then he had gone mad—mad in the most ridiculous way; he thought he was a sheepdog!—and left her a handsome fortune.

"Look!" Charlotte exclaimed. "Really, one can't help feeling sorry for that poor boy. Your pious friends are always collecting money to send slum children to the seaside. Well, that boy lives at the seaside all year round, but I bet he's never allowed even to paddle in the sea. Their cook told me he was always begging for a bicycle. Can you guess what they told him? That children of his class didn't ride bicycles. They leave that to the lower orders! And I'm pretty sure they hardly ever let the boy have a piece of candy. They probably think eating candy is vulgar."

As for the two women, they were always eating, not candy, perhaps, but innumerable cakes and puddings steeped in rum, kirsch, or liqueur, which made them slightly tipsy, and put even Charlotte in a good humor.

"Suppose we make some crêpes, Charlotte, with Grand Marnier, for a change."

The two cars sped, one behind the other, across the wide plain north of La Rochelle, passing through a series of villages whose low white-walled houses mirrored the pale translucence of the sky.

"That was very silly, what you did, Kiki."

The windows of the car didn't close properly, so Martine had wrapped a blanket around her knees and her brother's. Usually they had to sit on the tip-up seats, the places in back being reserved for the grown-ups. This time they were traveling in state.

"What do you mean?"

"I mean you went the wrong way about it."

"But I really do want to go to sea. . . ."

"Yes, but you shouldn't have said so. Not like that, anyhow."

He was too young to appreciate feminine diplomacy. He turned angrily on his sister:

"Listen! I've had enough of being ordered around by you. I don't want any more of your advice."

"But . . ."

"Oh, shut up!"

Marshland stretched for miles on either side of the road. The sea was out of sight, but there was a strong salty tang in the west wind driving across the low area.

After a long silence, Kiki asked his sister a question that took her breath away:

"Martine, what did he do when he was in your bedroom?"

"Who?" she asked nervously, to gain time.

"You know who, all right. What did he *do*?"

She gazed at him, perplexed. Were his teachers right when they declared that he had the mind of a child of eleven or twelve in the body of an overgrown boy of fifteen?

"Why don't you answer?"

At last, looking out the window, she said slowly:

"He's my fiancé. . . . But of course you can't understand."

"Why did he kill Papa?"

"He *didn't* kill Papa. I swear to you he didn't. . . . I can't imagine who put such a ridiculous idea in your head."

Esnandes was in sight, and the square tower of the château, surrounded by a belt of trees, showed dark against the gray horizon.

Immediately in front of Martine was Augustin's broad back. And in her ear was a shrill young voice, persistent as a mosquito:

"How can you swear it, when you don't really *know*?"

"And you, Kiki"—in her exasperation she almost shouted at him—"do *you* really know?"

5

Martine ran out a side door while her brother was unpacking in his room. She was wearing her raincoat, boots, and an old felt hat. She had noticed that the car that had followed them all the way from La Rochelle was a new one, the kind Philippe's garage was agent for. Though she hadn't dared to look back long enough to make sure, she suspected he was driving it.

Her hands thrust deep in her pockets, some strands of wet hair straggling on her forehead, she tramped across the carpet of rotting leaves, trying not to break into a run and glancing nervously around, ready to hide if she saw anyone.

The Donadieus' country house was called a château because of its age and size. But it was really no more than what a former, less pretentious generation would have called a manor house. The surrounding country, as far as the eye could see, was flat, studded with clumps of trees and church spires. Around the gray stone building and the squat, slate-roofed tower ran a double row of chestnut trees. In front of the main entrance was a small park, and beyond this, enclosed by crumbling walls, a wood covering five acres, with oaks and lime trees, masses of ivy, a tangle of weeds and creepers, and infested with snakes and huge black spiders.

There was a walled yard behind the château, and beyond it lay the farm: a real farm, with cows, hens, ducks, and guinea fowl, a pig or two, manure heaps, and carts, now lying idle, shafts tilted skyward.

Martine had a glimpse of the farmhand employed by the Maclous, the caretakers. She hurried past him, looking away, to avoid being delayed.

When at last she stepped into a lane leading to the main road, she gave a timid glance over her shoulder, like a child playing truant. Passing a cottage, she vaguely heard someone shout a greeting but ignored it. She reached the junction with the main road and gave a little cry. She had expected to find the car waiting there; none was to be seen.

After a moment's hesitation, she started off in the direction of the village. Women gossiping on their doorsteps greeted her respectfully. Some remarked on how pale she looked; others noted that she was "quite a grown-up young lady now." Martine struggled on against the sea wind, her face set and tense.

There was a car parked on the right side of the road, but she saw that it was full of small cases—obviously a salesman's.

She walked past a house with a pine branch fixed above the door; the first bistro. Her nerve was beginning to go, and she was thinking of turning back, when at last it came in sight. Outside the only real café in the village, a car was standing, the new car that had followed them from La Rochelle.

Without a moment's hesitation, she entered the dark café, in which some farmhands were playing pool, and went to the bar, trying to appear at ease.

"A hot grog, please."

"Fernand!" called the woman behind the bar. "Hurry and get some boiling water. Mademoiselle Martine wants a grog."

Philippe was standing by the window, and he looked as pale and tense as Martine. But she had to listen to the chatter of the owner's wife.

"Will you be staying long, mademoiselle? It was such a shock for all of us, hearing about your poor father. . . ."

After hunting for a tumbler less thick than the usual ones, she polished it carefully with a clean dishcloth.

Martine, not noticing these attentions, deliberately let her hand-kerchief and a folded slip of paper fall to the floor.

For some reason, Philippe failed to see this, perhaps because he was too deep in thought. Nor did he come toward her, as she'd expected. Finally, she had to pick up the handkerchief and the slip of paper herself. After drinking the grog, she fumbled in her pockets.

"Oh, I'm sorry. I haven't brought any money. I'll pay you another day."

"That's quite all right, mademoiselle. Any time you're passing . . ."

There were tears of vexation in her eyes as she began to walk toward the door. On her way, she flicked the note toward Philippe—whether it fell on the table or on the banquette she had no idea—and hurried back through the village, paying no heed to anybody. A housewife standing on a cottage doorstep remarked to her neighbor:

"Why, she's even more stuck-up than her mother!"

On the slip of paper she'd written: "Tonight at eight, by the old iron gate." It was at the far end of the wood, and had refused to close for as long as Martine could remember.

There were no maids at the château. Old Mme Maclou and her sixteen-year-old daughter, who was lame, did the cooking and housework; Baptiste, her husband, looked after the furnace.

The rooms were huge and, because of the belt of trees surrounding the house, depressingly dark. The bedrooms had been divided by wooden partitions, in order to provide accommodation for the whole family in the summer. At this time of year, the house was empty, and it had a desolate, abandoned air. In some of the upper rooms the chests of drawers and wardrobes had been moved slightly, revealing patches of mildew and cobwebs on the walls.

Kiki spent the afternoon reading in his bedroom. They had dinner at six, as they always did in the country. At quarter of eight Martine began to fidget, and tackled old Mme Maclou, who had just started washing the dishes.

"You can leave it till tomorrow."

"But, mademoiselle . . ."

Martine was conscious of handling the situation clumsily, but she was too nervous, and angrily insisted.

"Didn't you hear what I said, Sophie? Leave the washing till tomorrow."

"Very well . . . Good night, mademoiselle. What time shall I call you in the morning?"

"Don't bother to call me. Good night."

Martine knew her brother hadn't gone to bed; he obviously suspected something. While she was putting on her raincoat in the hall, he suddenly appeared. She braced herself.

"You're going to see him, aren't you?" he asked.

"Listen, Kiki . . ."

"Answer my question. I know he's hanging around the house."

"Kiki, do please be sensible. I simply must have a talk with him— and nothing's going to stop me. . . . Look! Suppose you come with me. I won't mind a bit. And you can ask him any questions you like."

"I don't want to see him."

"Well, promise you won't tell."

"I won't promise anything. So there!"

He ran up to his bedroom, without saying good night. Still, she felt relieved. He seemed a shade less hostile.

She walked quickly down the drive, and as the distance between her and the house increased, a cloud of dark worries seemed to lift from her mind. All she knew was that she was going to Philippe; he was somewhere out there, in the shadows. Then, somehow, she was conscious of his presence, close by. A dark form moved from behind a tree, and she tried to whisper "Philippe!"

But she couldn't get a word out. She flung herself into his arms, overcome by dizziness. She shut her eyes, and in a sort of dream felt his lips straying over her hair, lingering on her eyelids, then at last, hot and feverish, pressed to her unresponsive mouth.

So still was the young body in his arms that Philippe was afraid for a moment that she'd fainted. Because of the raincoat, the kiss had had a faint smell of rubber, and she seemed cold as ice.

"Martine!" he murmured apprehensively.

He couldn't see her. Her face was a mere white blur in the darkness. Somewhere a dog started barking, but he paid no attention. A branch creaked. Was it only the wind?

How long she stayed motionless, inert, he had no idea. When at last she stirred, she seemed to be waking from heavy sleep. Gently, she freed herself, to be able to speak.

"Come . . ."

She made a movement toward the house. One of the upper windows was lighted.

"What about your brother?" he asked doubtfully.

"It's all right. Come!"

She tried to smile encouragingly, but her smile was like that of someone utterly worn out after a night of traveling or a long illness. Yet her voice was surprisingly steady when, on the way to the house, she suddenly asked him:

"Did you leave the car in the village?"

She led him up the steps, opened the door with her key, and switched on the lights in the living room.

"Come in here, Philippe."

It was he who now felt nervous; the matter-of-fact way in which she was handling things surprised him. He had never thought her capable of so much self-possession. She seemed to have forgotten all about her young brother, who was still awake upstairs, and the Maclous, who must have seen, through their curtains, the downstairs lights go on.

"Now, let's have a look at you," she said in a low tone. "Yes. You, too, are thinner. . . . Do sit down."

They were so used to meeting clandestinely, in a sleepbound house, that instinctively they moved on tiptoe, talked in whispers.

"I couldn't have stood another day of it!" Martine confessed, sinking wearily into an armchair.

Now and then, Kiki's footsteps could be heard immediately overhead, and each time he heard them Philippe couldn't help giving a start, though Martine remained quite calm. He had drawn a chair close to hers, and was trying to put his arm around her. But when he unbuttoned her raincoat, to feel the soft warmth of her body, she gently pushed him away.

"No, not yet. Sit quite still, please. I want to see your face."

Her steady gaze was disconcerting; that deeply pondering look in her eyes was new to Philippe. She seemed to be thinking hard, trying to make up her mind about something, perhaps about him, and she repeated absently:

"Yes, you've grown thinner."

"That's not surprising," he said. "For the last month, and more, I've been eating my heart out, looking for you everywhere. I came to your window every night, and—"

"I knew that."

He felt a qualm. She seemed so remote, so indifferent. Those calm, appraising eyes, her silences, the brief remarks she let fall—what was he to make of them?

"Why didn't you open your window?"

"I'd made up my mind never to see you again. There were moments when I almost hated you. . . . I've been thinking a lot. Tonight we must settle things between us. I want you, first of all, to tell me, quite frankly, what you had in mind when you . . . became my lover."

It had begun quite recently, but he felt as if ages had elapsed since that first hour of intimacy. Until then, he had known her vaguely, as he knew dozens of other girls, daughters of his father's friends, and he had never taken any special notice of Martine. What had prompted him suddenly to embark on a passionate love affair with her?

As a matter of fact, he'd never had much use for girls in that particular set; their manners, their way of talking, their amusements—everything about them jarred. In their company he always felt like a wild animal penned in with a tame, domesticated herd, and he made no effort to conceal his sense of superiority. Then, in the spring, a group of young people in La Rochelle had formed a committee to organize a Red Cross fete, and Philippe had deigned to take part.

Martine was far from being the prettiest of the group; pale, shy, with little to say for herself, she seemed younger than her years, and he had hardly given her a glance.

It was she who started it. One incident stood out in his memory. On the night of the final committee meeting, which took place in City Hall, he'd been fondling Mademoiselle Varin, a plump, flirtatious young woman, on a dimly lighted stairway. Martine happened to pass, and saw the girl nestling in his arms. Philippe attached no importance to this, but next day, when he took Martine's arm in a friendly way to give her some instructions before she set out with others to sell flowers in the streets, she turned on him angrily.

"Don't touch me! You're disgusting!"

Her behavior was so unexpected that it stuck in his mind all day. He arranged to meet her frequently during the fete, and that night, at the fancy-dress ball, he discovered the truth: Martine was in love.

The ball, too, took place in City Hall, where Philippe knew every nook and corner. Between two dances, he went up to Martine.

"Come with me for a minute. I have something important to tell you."

She was looking very schoolgirlish in a pale-blue dress of some flimsy, gossamer material. She hesitated, but he looked her in the eyes and laid his hand masterfully on her shoulder.

"Where are we going?"

They crossed a brightly lighted landing. Philippe opened a door, then closed it behind them. The room was in darkness and smelled of ink and blotting paper. Before Martine had time to realize where she was, he'd flung his arms around her; his lips found her mouth and stayed there so long that she was breathless when he at last released her.

"So that's that!" he said coolly. "Now you can call for help, or do anything you like. . . . I love you, Martine."

She ran out of the room without a word, and left the ball before it ended. A week went by before he saw her again, though he looked for her everywhere.

One night, Martine woke with a start and saw the shutter of her bedroom window opening. She was on the point of screaming when a voice whispered her name, and she saw a dark form astride the windowsill, then moving toward her bed.

He laid his hand on hers, wanting to touch her, to feel her nearness. Martine, however, was waiting calmly for him to speak.

Philippe found himself tongue-tied. They were so used to talking in undertones in a dark little room that this spacious, well-lighted living room gave him a feeling of constraint. When at last he spoke, the words came awkwardly.

"I was so tired of living around people I loathe and despise . . . and I felt I'd found somebody finally who was different. . . ."

She shook her head. She knew he wasn't being sincere. Even his tone lacked conviction.

The principal reason he had become her lover was that it flattered his vanity to find a young girl of Martine's social standing giving herself to him so readily—especially a girl belonging to the arrogant Donadieu family, who on the rare occasions when they invited him to their stronghold on Rue Réaumur always made him feel they were doing him a favor.

But what of the future? He had no idea what he wanted, or how to handle the present situation.

"You can't understand, Martine—and it's difficult to explain." He was conscious that his voice was strained, unnatural. To cover his confusion, he bent over and tried to kiss her.

"No. Not now. I want to understand. Because we've got to make a decision. I can't bear it any longer. I feel as if I'm suffocating. . . ."

"You see!"

"What do you mean?"

He jumped at the opening; on this subject, he could let himself go.

"I mean that you've summed it up in a word; you're suffocating. Suffocating because you're cooped up among people who don't know the first thing about life, real life; who creep around within four walls without even noticing there are windows. And if a ray of light happens to come in, they promptly draw the curtains, afraid they might be tempted to break free. . . . Please listen to what I'm saying, Martine.

Words are always futile—but I know you attach importance to them. . . .

"If there's one thing I abominate in the world today, it's a certain way of living; certain houses, and the people who entrench themselves in them, and imagine they're superior, and secure. Don't think I'm jealous of their wealth. It has nothing to do with that, I assure you.

"I detest the Donadieus and all they stand for, just as I detest the Mortiers and the Varins, and that ridiculous club, where a dozen pretentious old fogies doze in big armchairs, thinking they're the lords of creation—until the day they're moved into the family vault, which will be no great change in their condition.

"I hate your sister and her husband. I hate that precious brother of yours, Michel. I hate them because they're missing splendid possibilities. Watching them is enough to make one despair of mankind. . . .

"You were the exception. You were determined to make something of yourself. I could see it in your eyes—rebellious eyes!"

For the second time, she shook her head. Again, in this tirade, she'd been conscious of a jarring note. But Philippe took no notice.

"If you fell in love with me, it was because you guessed that I was an animal of a different breed. You knew that with me there'd be no more walls, no more shuttered windows. I never spoke of marrying you, because nothing would induce me to enter that prison of a house you live in, where I'd run the risk of becoming just like the other inmates.

"I don't have any money now. But I can make any amount I like, if I set my mind to it. Yes, I'm certain—I've always felt it in my bones—that I can shape my life whatever way I want. Nothing will stop me. . . .

"So, if you have confidence in me, all I have to say is let's go away together. Wherever you like. Whenever you like."

She wished he'd said it more simply, without all the rhetoric. From the way she looked at him, he guessed she was wondering again: Is he sincere? Or is he playacting?

When they had been together in her bedroom, there had been no time for such speculation. Only in the mornings would a dark cloud of doubt settle on her mind. Mornings of bitterness, almost of aversion to him. Yet, when night came, forgetting all her resolutions, she would leave her bedroom window open, once more.

Physical desire had nothing to do with it—her senses were as yet unawakened. What she wanted was something very different, but she couldn't have put it into words.

She was looking at him almost as she might have the morning after one of his nocturnal visits.

"Why don't you want to marry me?" she said slowly. "What's the real reason?"

"Because everyone would say I'd married you for your money. Because you're a Donadieu; and you have a share in the estate. If I became a member of the family, well, everybody would be sure I'd squander it all."

He was handsome, almost as handsome as his father, she thought, with his burning eyes, finely molded nostrils, dark hollows in his temples under his thick brown hair.

"Do you remember the question you asked last time we met?" he said.

She looked away. She'd rather not be reminded of that. Was she to blame if the atmosphere in the house after her father's disappearance had affected her, too? And perhaps a sense of guilt had put strange ideas into her head. . . .

"I should have left at once," he went on, "and never seen you again. There are moments when you have the Donadieu outlook on things—however much you try not to. Do you understand, Martine? When I got home, I broke down completely. My father was quite worried. So I decided to go away."

"Why did you stay?"

Amazing girl! She asked it quite coolly, in an almost casual tone. Once more he was puzzled by the curious faculty she had of combining extreme matter-of-factness with a capacity for rapturous emotion.

Kiki was still pacing in the room overhead. There was an embarrassing propriety about this interview in the main room of the château, so different from Martine's bedroom.

"I didn't go away, because . . ." He paused. A new idea had waylaid him, and this, too, involved playacting, but he had no doubt he could carry it off.

"Because?" Martine prompted.

"No. I'd rather not say."

She fell into the trap, as he'd foreseen. She even sat up in the armchair and said imperiously:

"I insist on your telling me."

"I'm afraid you'll be angry. But . . . since you insist . . . Well, it

66

was when I heard about your father's will. The whole town was talking about it, of course."

"What on earth are you getting at?"

"Do you remember the question you asked me that night? Not very kind. Was I a murderer? Well, I have a perfect right to put forward a theory of my own about your father's death—if only to clear myself. I remembered a certain detail. . . ."

"What detail?"

She bent toward him eagerly, but he seemed reluctant to continue.

"Tell me," she insisted.

"You remember the last time we met before it happened, on a Saturday?"

"Of course I do . . . Well?"

"In that case, can't you remember something curious we noticed?"

"Something curious? No. I don't remember."

"At a certain moment—surely you haven't forgotten—we heard a noise. . . ."

She kept quite still, looking at him with troubled eyes. Yes, she remembered now. While they were in bed, they'd heard the sound of a key turning in the front door, which faced Rue Réaumur, then footsteps in the hall. She'd whispered: "That's strange. I didn't know anyone was out."

While the footsteps receded up the stairs, they'd held their breath to listen, trying to tell if they stopped on the second or third floor. But the noise of a passing train made this impossible.

"Now do you understand?" Philippe said, lowering his eyes.

"But it . . . it's unbelievable!" Her brother? Her brother-in-law? "Why must you put such horrible ideas in my mind?"

"You insisted, didn't you? I'm sorry, dear, but I've got to defend myself as best I can. For your sake, as much as for mine."

Again she exclaimed: "Oh, I can't stand it any longer!" She glanced irritably up at the ceiling.

"Does he know I'm here?" Philippe asked.

She nodded. She was worn out, her thoughts in chaos. There was a short silence before Martine touched him lightly on the arm.

"Tell me what your father said."

"About what?"

"I mean when he saw the . . . the state you were in?"

"Oh, I didn't let him know the reason."

The look that crossed Martine's face told him that he had made a mistake. She wasn't in the least ashamed of her conduct. Right now, she was so bewildered, so uncertain, that she would have welcomed advice or assistance from anyone whatever. In a faraway voice she asked:

"Well? What are we going to do?" Then, seeming to wake from a dream, she added impulsively: "I'm *not* going back to that house. I couldn't stand another hour in it. . . . Philippe, we simply *must* do something."

She had kept her head enough to watch his expression, and could see he was uncertain what to say. For the first time, she noticed that his mouth had a curious twist that made his face look almost sinister sometimes. It was such a moment now. Why, she wondered. Who, or what, had provoked his anger?

He seemed to be studying the floral pattern of the carpet, the molding of a table leg. During the silence, they could hear a cow lowing in an outbuilding.

Suddenly he jumped to his feet, and at last looked her in the eyes.

"All right! Let's go away together. Right now." The fierceness of his voice startled her, and she hesitated before getting up from her chair. "I take it you're prepared to stick it out?"

"To stick *what* out?"

"Your name will be mud in La Rochelle, for one thing. And, for a while anyway, you may be desperately poor."

He blushed when he heard her say, in a low voice:

"Are you afraid of going away with me?"

It was almost true. At this crucial moment, his courage was faltering.

"Afraid? . . . Yes, for you—not for myself."

He was conscious that he was not rising to the occasion, but the banality of his surroundings had a deadening effect: the too-bright room, Mme Donadieu's big tapestry-upholstered armchair, one of her canes standing in a corner where she had left it, the old-fashioned marble clock on the mantelpiece, above which hung an oval mirror scarred with damp spots.

"Did you leave the car in the village?" She forgot that she had asked that question before. Suddenly a new thought came to her. "Philippe!"

"Yes, darling?" Another slip! He'd said that "darling" too casually.

"I'm going to tell Kiki."

"Tell Kiki? Why on earth do that? He'll only make a scene—and go get the farmer and his wife, probably."

"No, he won't. I'm sure Kiki won't let us down. He's . . . like us."

What did she mean by that? He had no time to think. She had run to the door and was calling up the stairs.

There was movement again in the room above. After a long pause, they heard a door opening, and the boy's voice.

"What?"

"Come down."

"Is . . . is anyone with you?"

"Never mind about that. Come downstairs."

They could tell how reluctant he was by his slow footsteps on the stairs. Martine's eyes were roving restlessly from place to place. When her brother appeared in the doorway, she took him by the hand.

"Now, Kiki, I want you to be very nice and try to understand. I cannot face the thought of living any longer in that dreadful house, and I'm going away with Philippe. One day, it will all be all right; you'll see—and you and Philippe will be great friends."

She was not looking at her brother as she spoke, but at his reflection in the mirror, which emphasized the crookedness of his nose. Quickly, she turned away.

"Philippe, please explain to him."

"There's no need," the boy said in a stifled voice. His Adam's apple was heaving convulsively. He added, in a whisper: "What about me?"

"You'll stay here. Tell Sophie tomorrow morning that I've gone. But there's no need for them to know you saw us. . . ."

Standing on the threshold, he motioned for his sister to come nearer. When she did, he murmured:

"Are you really sure?" Meaning "Are you really sure he didn't kill Papa?"

Instead of answering, she kissed him, and dried the tears in her eyes.

She knew there was no time to lose, or she'd break down completely.

"Shall I take anything with me, Philippe?"

"No," he said, hoping to end this more quickly. But Kiki reminded her:

"Your medal."

"Where is it?"

The medal was a small gold disk with the Virgin's effigy, a gift from Sophie, who had presented one to each of her employers' children for their first communion. These medals were regarded by the family as mascots.

Kiki was running up the stairs, glad, perhaps, to escape from the atmosphere in the living room. Martine turned to Philippe.

"Are you sure you won't regret this?" There was a faint tremor in her voice.

Instead of answering, he kissed her. Martine still didn't know how to kiss. She merely parted her lips a little and waited submissively. Now, she felt like bursting into tears, but she kept hold of herself.

"Here." Kiki had come back with the medal. She hugged him, and he whispered in her ear:

"You'll come back for me, won't you?"

A branch creaked outside the window. Philippe took a quick step toward the door.

"We'd better go."

"Yes. I'm ready."

Perhaps she would secretly have been pleased if, at this moment, something had cropped up to prevent her from going. She didn't dare look at Kiki, especially in the mirror, which brought out the queerness of his face.

"Here's your hat," the boy said.

A rush of cold, moist air enveloped them when they stepped outside. The wind was rising; clouds were scudding across a moon that was near full.

Hand in hand, they hurried to the old iron gate, the farm dog, who knew Martine, trotting behind them. No light now showed in the château.

"The car?" Martine panted.

"Over there. At the corner."

"Let's hope . . ."

They did not hear a forlorn cry across the darkness:

"Martine! Martine!"

But Mme Maclou heard it. She sat up, tossed aside the big eiderdown, and said to her husband:

"That poor child's walking in his sleep again. I wonder if I ought to go and see. . . ."

He went on snoring, and after a few minutes she, too, was asleep.

The damp had affected the engine, and Philippe had to press the starter several times. At last the two headlights sprang to life, flooding the lane with greenish light from the hedgerows. At the first bump, Martine gave a slight start, but her voice was even when she asked the young man beside her:

"Where are we going?"

6

Before opening her eyes, she had been dimly conscious that someone nearby was vainly trying to start a car. Also that the sun was shining and—though she had no idea how she knew this—that she was in the country.

Abruptly, she opened her eyes, and looked at the bed beside hers. It was empty; Philippe had evidently gone out without waking her. Raising her arms to her breast, she realized that she was naked, and quickly, with the sheet wrapped around her, reached out for her underclothes, which were lying on a tattered rug beside the bed.

She could still hear someone cranking a car outside, and it was easy to picture it: one of those antiquated tall vehicles that quiver like a startled horse the first time the engine fires.

A gentle ticking on the marble-topped bedside table caught her ear. It was Philippe's watch; it showed ten minutes to ten. Why, as she bent forward to see the time, did she suddenly feel sure it was Sunday, and catch herself thinking of the service just beginning at the Donadieus' parish church?

She was still exhausted, in mind and body. It was as if she had been given a severe beating, which had left her aching. Mentally, her fatigue took the form of vast indifference, a total lack of emotion, or interest in the future. Strangely, however, she felt exceptionally lucid. She examined the room, sitting up in bed in her chemise—for, even alone, she could never bear to feel her body naked.

What a funny room! she thought. Unlike any she'd seen before. The furniture was shoddy and mass-produced; though most of it seemed relatively new, it was beginning to show signs of wear. The wardrobe, for instance, had lost a leg and was propped against the edge of the mantelpiece. In its mirror-paneled door, she caught a glimpse of her reflected self, and hastily looked away. What surprised her most was the incongruity between the furniture and the room containing it: large, finely proportioned, with two tall windows and an elaborately molded ceiling. Obviously in its better days this place had been a real château, much more imposing than the Donadieus' so-called château at Esnandes. Glancing out the window, she saw sunlight playing on a spacious park. Someone was still trying to start that reluctant engine, and there was a dog somewhere; she could hear it scratching in gravel.

Her eyes lingered, for some reason, on an enormous sofa upholstered in green velvet, with a tall Empire cheval glass beside it; then on a plump white statuette, a cheap Venus, standing on the mantelpiece. The walls, she now noticed, were hung with studies of the nude and suggestive prints. Then something else caught her attention. Sniffing, she detected a curious, rather unpleasant smell, which somehow seemed to be linked with the pictures. It came, as far as she could judge, from the next room, in which she could hear people talking. There was, she noticed, a communicating door.

"Where are we going?"

When she'd asked that question in the car last night, she'd already stopped worrying about the future; come what might, she was prepared to face it. If she felt some vague unrest, it was because of the darkness, the racing clouds, the sudden gusts driving across the marshes, which rattled the windows of the car and made it sway.

Philippe had gone first to La Rochelle, where he'd parked outside his father's theater.

"You may have to wait a while," he'd warned her.

She had waited placidly, as if what was happening was not charged with momentous consequences for her whole future. The truth was, she was too tired to think; she'd reached a stage where nothing seemed to matter. And when Philippe came back, she didn't ask him what he'd been doing, or why he looked so annoyed.

He had run up to his father's office. But Frédéric was out, and Philippe had ransacked his drawers for money without success.

For the last few days, Frédéric Dargens had been cultivating a new mistress, a slim young dancer who had been performing between films the previous week. He'd kept her on as much out of charity as because she had a quaintly attractive little face. Had Philippe gone down to the waterfront, he would have seen the lights still on in the Café de Paris, the chairs piled on the tables for the nightly mopping, and he might have noticed his father, sitting at a table near the bar, waiting for the girl to finish her sandwich.

When he started the car again, Philippe was looking truly gloomy. He had less than a hundred francs with him. The station was closed, and there was no train until 5:07 in the morning. But it would be rash to go by train; Martine might well be recognized, and they would be traced immediately. As for the car, it belonged to the garage, and his boss would set the police on his trail if he made off with it. So his position seemed quite hopeless. . . .

To his surprise, Martine promptly went to sleep, her head resting on his shoulder. Unsure what to do, he drove slowly through the city. When he reached the outskirts and a road leading east, beside a canal bordered by tall trees, he remembered that, about a mile and a half farther on, there was a small inn kept by an old, white-haired black man, where bedrooms were provided for lovers.

He stopped the car outside the inn and rang the bell. But either the man didn't hear or he was afraid to open his door in the middle of the night. After ringing several times in vain, Philippe turned the car around and drove back to La Rochelle.

On the return trip, he took the road along the waterfront; this time, the Café de Paris was in darkness. Feeling that he could think better if he was not driving, he stopped the car again. The city was plunged in silence, except for a faint sound of receding footsteps: some belated nightbird going in the direction of City Hall.

Martine gave a little moan; she was in an uncomfortable position. As a last resort, he decided to try the Château de Rivedoux, some six miles outside the city. Whether Martine was really sleeping, and whether she was conscious of these strange peregrinations, he had no idea.

The château gates stood open. The park was in darkness, and there were a number of drives and roads crossing it, but Philippe found his way easily enough, since he had been here several times before. He drove to the back entrance and blew his horn. As he stepped out of the car, a big dog ran up; it did not actually snap at him, but the way it sniffed his legs was far from reassuring.

Knocking on the door had no effect, so he threw a pebble at one of the windows on the second floor. It opened, and a dim form could be seen leaning out.

"Who's there?"

"Philippe. Philippe Dargens. Let me in, please."

No light was switched on; when the door opened, the conversation between him and the woman standing there took place in darkness.

Martine had only a blurred memory of what followed: being helped out of the car by Philippe and led through a pitch-dark hall that seemed never-ending. Her last memory was of a woman saying in a wheezy asthmatic voice: "You'll find a towel in the wardrobe, dearie."

A moment later she relapsed into dreamless sleep.

It wasn't one detail only that seemed wrong. Almost everything she set eyes on was so strange that Martine gave up trying to make sense of her surroundings.

This place was obviously a château, one in the grand style. Stepping out of the room, she found herself in a long, gray-flagged hallway with pointed windows overlooking a spacious quadrangle. But the quadrangle wasn't merely ill-kept—that wouldn't have surprised her—it, too, had a look of incongruity. In a patch of sunlight beside the unmown lawn, which had in the center a group of marble nymphs, an aged crone sat huddled in an armchair. Both the old woman and the chair were out of place in the courtyard of a château. The chair was the Voltaire type, with a very high back, and it exuded horsehair from every pore. The old woman, whose lank gray hair hung to her sagging shoulders, was wearing the most hideous garment Martine had ever seen: a flannelette dressing gown mottled with enormous pink and yellow flowers.

The hallway led to a lofty room with a remarkably handsome timbered ceiling. When she entered it, Martine was confronted by, of all things, a player piano—the kind that works when a coin is put in a slot. At the far end was a doorway—the one, Martine supposed, she'd come in through last night. Beside it was a small bar, with an array of bottles. Café tables were dotted here and there. On the floor, a two-year-old child was playing with some dirty rags.

"Shall I serve your early breakfast here?"

Turning around, Martine saw a woman, younger than the one in the courtyard but even dirtier, staring curiously at her. She, too, was in a dressing gown, and her shoes were down-at-heel.

"Would you like some café au lait?" the woman continued.

"No, thank you. Not now."

As Martine stepped out of the doorway, she came on the man trying to start a car. It was impossible to tell his age; it might have been anything between thirty and fifty. He had shifty eyes, towlike hair, and was wearing carpet slippers. Holding the crank in his right hand, he was mopping his brow with the other. With a sigh, he pointed to the car, the hood of which was up.

"Can't think what's wrong with her. But Philippe will be along soon."

"Has he been gone long?"

"He left just after eight. Asked me to tell you not to worry."

Though the park had been allowed to run wild, its size gave it a certain dignity, and the open gates were flanked by huge stone lions. Beyond them stretched a green expanse of meadow, and a mile or two away the spire of a village church showed above a clump of trees.

"Had breakfast?" the man asked.

"Not yet."

"A proper mess, ain't it? But give me a month or two, and I'll get it all cleaned up."

Martine wondered idly what he meant. Did he include the two slatternly women in the "proper mess"? Her strongest impression of the oddness of this place had come from them. Even if she'd known the man's name—Papelet—it would have meant nothing to her. She had only the vaguest notion that in the neighborhood of the La Rochelle barracks there was a street shunned by decent people, where windows were always shuttered, doors left ajar.

Papelet ran two of the largest establishments on that street, though it was his mother, the old creature in the flannelette dressing gown, who owned them.

The previous summer, the Château de Rivedoux had been put on the market, but there had been no buyers, nobody prepared to face the heavy expense of making it habitable. Papelet had bought it, for the same reason he'd bought a broken-down car: nothing pleased him more than buying things that no one wanted and tinkering with them at his leisure.

He had repainted the hall himself, pale green with a stenciled fresco of gaudy red tulips. The player piano was another bargain, picked up at a tavern, where it had been replaced by a radio.

One evening, a group of young men and girls had turned up at the château, asked for drinks, and after that for rooms. This had given Papelet the idea of furnishing one or two bedrooms for the weekend use of couples from La Rochelle. There wasn't much money in it, but, as he pointed out to Mme Papelet, "every little bit helps."

"Hasn't my wife shown you around?" he asked Martine. His wife was the woman who had proposed café au lait, and the small child crawling on the floor was his son.

Because it was a Sunday, the streets were empty, except for church-goers, when Philippe drove into La Rochelle. He stopped at the Alhambra and let himself in with his key. His clumsy movements betrayed the state of his nerves, and he made more noise than usual crossing the gallery and opening his father's door.

He cared nothing for the fact that Frédéric wasn't alone, that a woman's head could be seen on the pillow, her face half hidden by the sheet.

"I want to talk to you," Philippe announced, without looking at his father, who sat up abruptly.

"Oh, it's you. . . ."

Frédéric glanced at his watch and scrambled out of bed, after a quick look at the girl, who opened a sleepy eye, then closed it, reassured.

"Let's go to your room."

At a glance, Frédéric saw that his son's bed had not been slept in.

"Hurry up! I want another hour's sleep—if I can get it. I may as well tell you at once, if it's money you're after . . ."

"It's more serious than that."

Frédéric, who had put on his dressing gown, seated himself on the corner of the table and lit a cigarette.

"I've run away with Martine."

Philippe had anticipated an outburst of indignation, followed by a violent scene. But his father merely murmured, "The devil you have!" and looked at his son with mild surprise, almost as if he didn't think him capable of such an action.

"No need to go into details," Philippe continued. "That's how things are. Martine has left home, and I'm responsible for her now."

"I suppose you realize the risks you're running?"

"I do. I know she's a minor."

"Well?"

"All I want is money for our fare to Paris. After that, it's my problem. I'll manage somehow."

Frédéric left the room abruptly, and Philippe wondered what that meant. A moment later, his father came back and tossed his wallet to him.

"Here you are!"

The wallet contained no more than a hundred and fifty francs.

"That's all you have? What about yesterday's receipts?"

"You know they're collected every evening."

"What in hell am I to do?"

Half-asleep at first, Frédéric was gradually becoming his normal self. Now and then, he cast a shrewd glance at his son, who was staring glumly at the floor.

"Couldn't you get some money for me before noon? What about your friends at the club?"

The only answer Philippe got was a shrug. He began to feel quite desperate.

"Damn it all!" he cried. "What on earth am I to do?"

"How can I know? . . . But tell me this: are you really in love with her?"

"That's my business. . . . Look, the main thing is to get away at once. She's at—"

"Stop! I'd rather not know where she is. And I may as well warn you that, the moment you've left, I'll go straight to Rue Réaumur and tell my old friend Mme Donadieu what's happened."

The girl in the bed, who was wide awake now, got up and opened the door an inch or two, asking in a husky voice:

"What's the matter?"

"Nothing, my dear."

"What's Philippe been doing this time?"

"Something silly, as usual. No. More than silly. Something really nasty."

"Father!" cried Philippe, as Frédéric started toward his room.

"Well?" There was a tremor of anxiety in Frédéric's voice. He realized that, in his present state, his son was capable of anything. "Would you like me to give you my advice?"

"No."

"Then what were you going to say?"

"Oh . . . nothing."

Philippe grabbed his hat from the bed, hurried through his father's room, and ran down the stairs into the auditorium. He left by the stage door, and a quarter of an hour later was driving the car into the garage where he worked.

"Is Denis here?" he asked the man at the pump.

"I think he's in the office."

Philippe found the owner of the garage, who was only a little older than he was, in breeches and gaiters, about to leave for a day's hunting in the marshes.

"I've must have a word with you. It's extremely important. A matter of life and death . . ."

Denis looked at him with surprise, but said nothing.

"I've run away with a girl," Philippe went on. "Martine Donadieu. I need some money immediately. I'll pay it back all right; I promise you."

"What's this yarn you're telling me?"

"It's the truth."

"Well, I haven't any money here. Or very little." He had opened the till, and now took from it three hundred and fifty francs. "Sorry, but that's all I can lay my hands on."

"I'm taking the car with me. You'll have it back within a week."

Philippe was out the door before the garage owner knew it. He ran to the entrance, shouting:

"Philippe! Stop!"

But Philippe was already in gear and was soon well away.

Michel Donadieu got up at six, warmed the coffee left in the pot the night before, and waked his brother-in-law. Laden with guns and cartridge pouches, the two men left in the big blue car. All the others were still asleep, as they were at that time almost every Sunday in winter.

At Esnandes, they found old Baptiste waiting at the iron gate, smoking his first pipe of the day, a shotgun slung across his shoulder, and the dogs capering around him.

"Starting right away sir?"

"Yes."

Early though it was, shots could be heard in the distance. The sun was rising, and smoke was curling from the Maclous' chimney.

"Has my sister settled in all right?"

"Yes, sir. She came yesterday, with Master Oscar. They're still in bed, I imagine. . . . Let's try that stubble, to begin with. We're sure to put up a hare or two."

They fanned out, while the dogs ran ahead, noses to the ground. It was Michel who fired first, bowling over a hare. Baptiste trudged forward through the stubble and, after finishing the animal off and emptying the bladder, put it in his bag.

Other guns and dogs were seen, and greetings were exchanged.

It had struck nine before Olsen bagged his first hare. The plain stretched out for miles on all sides, dotted with church spires, and everywhere now, in marshes and fields, men with guns on their shoulders were outlined against the growing light.

On several occasions Michel and his companions approached the château. No one was visible, and all the blinds were down.

Meanwhile, in the old house on Rue Réaumur, Mme Brun was dressing for Mass. Charlotte's eyes were red-rimmed, as if she hadn't slept.

Frédéric Dargens was ringing at the door of the next house. When it opened, he said to Augustin:

"Tell Madame Donadieu I'd like to see her."

Without waiting to be shown in, he entered the living room, and he heard a voice say:

"Ask him to wait, Augustin. I'll be there in a minute."

A good quarter of an hour went by, during which he heard footsteps and children's voices overhead, where they were dressing for church. Mme Donadieu failed to see him at first when she came in, and seemed puzzled. Then she discovered him standing in a corner, staring gloomily at the carpet.

"I'm sorry to have made you wait. I hadn't finished dressing."

He found he'd quite forgotten how he'd planned to break it to her. On a chance, he said:

"Any news from Esnandes?"

"News from Esnandes? What do you mean?"

"I have something to tell you. Please sit down. . . . And do keep calm. If you start making a scene, I'll leave at once. . . . My son is a young blackguard. Last night he ran away with your daughter."

"With Martine?"

"Yes. They've been having an affair for some time, I believe. . . . Well, that was what I had to tell you—and it wasn't a pleasant task, you may well believe."

Mme Donadieu stared at him, incredulous.

"Really, you must be mistaken. Martine would never do a thing like that." Her smile showed absolute confidence in her daughter. Then, as if some memory had crossed her mind, her mood changed abruptly. "Who told you?" she asked nervously. "For heaven's sake, say something. Can't you speak?"

But without waiting, she hurried to the telephone.

"Esnandes one, please. Yes, one. Put me through quickly, please."

She started pacing up and down the room, making distracted gestures. Suddenly she rounded on Frédéric.

"Where are they?"

"I don't know. Philippe came to see me this morning, to ask for money."

"Did you give him any?"

"All I had: a hundred and fifty francs."

"What on earth do they think they're going to do? They must be— Hello? . . . What's that? . . . No answer? Nonsense. Ring again, please. I know there's someone in the house." After a moment she said nervously: "Don't cut me off. Ring again. . . . Is that you, Sophie? . . . Don't shout into the telephone. Hold it farther from your mouth." Old Mme Maclou had never learned how to speak on the telephone. "Yes, that's better. It's Madame Donadieu speaking. Has Martine gotten up yet? . . . What? . . . You haven't seen Master Oscar either? Sophie, you've got to find them. At once. Look for them outside. Master Oscar must be somewhere around. Hurry!"

She could picture the old woman running down the back hall, where the telephone was, and out to the drive, wondering, no doubt, what it was all about.

"Do you have your car with you?" she asked Frédéric.

"I haven't a car now."

She glanced out the window toward the garage.

"They've taken ours. And the absurd thing is, it's the château they've gone to—for some hunting. . . . Will you try to get a car somehow?"

Frédéric noticed that her eyes were dry; she had kept her head remarkably well. Without leaving the house, he called the nearest garage, while Mme Donadieu, glancing toward the ceiling, murmured: "I wonder if I ought to let them know."

No, she decided, there was no need to tell "them." Martine was still under her control, and so, of course, was Kiki. This was her business, and nobody else's.

Some minutes later, a car drew up outside, and Mme Donadieu and Frédéric got into it.

"To Esnandes, please. . . . Yes, the château. As quickly as you can . . . No, don't drive too fast," she added hastily. She was always nervous in a car.

"It's incredible! How did it ever happen?"

"Oh, the way such things usually do happen, I suppose."

"But . . . what are we going to do about it?"

"Don't ask me."

"Surely they can't have taken Kiki with them."

People were coming into the city for Mass as they drove out. They saw others, with guns on their shoulders, trudging across the stubble fields. Near the château, Mme Donadieu noticed three men about to cross the road. Tapping the driver's shoulder, she told him to stop.

"Michel! Jean!" she shouted. "What are you doing? Don't you know what's happened? Martine's run away . . . with Philippe. Kiki, too."

They could see old Mme Maclou making frantic gestures near the entrance gates. For a quarter of an hour she had been shouting to the three men, who couldn't hear her.

Michel clenched his fists and gave Frédéric an ugly look.

"Just let me lay my hands on that young swine. I'll wring his neck!"

"Don't talk nonsense," said his mother, sighing. "You know quite well you won't do anything of the sort."

Of them all, it was Mme Donadieu who had remained in control, especially as far as Martine was concerned. As regards Kiki, she showed more alarm. She had herself telephoned to all the police stations in the vicinity.

"We must give them Martine's description, too, and Philippe's," Michel insisted.

"Don't be so absurd!" Then she turned to Frédéric, whom the others were eying mistrustfully. "The poor child must have been dreadfully upset. He's so high-strung. I imagine he's hiding in some corner of the grounds, crying his heart out. . . . He hasn't even put on his good suit."

Mme Maclou had provided coffee for everyone, and Michel, who could never resist the sight of food, wolfed down half a dozen sandwiches, but with a tragic look on his face.

"Shall I telephone the house?" he asked when he had finished eating.

"Certainly not. Aren't there enough of us here already?" Mme Donadieu shuddered at the prospect of a general irruption of the family, with her daughter, daughter-in-law, and grandchildren shedding tears or uttering cries of indignation.

"How do you think he managed to see her?" she asked Frédéric in an undertone.

"I daresay he went to her bedroom at night."

"And—just think!—none of us heard a sound." There was a note in her voice that could have been admiration for Philippe's audacity. "Well, I suppose the only thing now is for them to get married."

"What!" barked Michel, who had caught her last remark. "Do you mean to say you'd let my sister marry a cad like Philippe?"

She cast her gaze ceilingward as if to convey to Frédéric that he wasn't to pay attention to Michel's cantankerousness.

Only toward eleven o'clock did she begin to show signs of real alarm. The various police stations had called, one after the other, to report their failure to find a trace of Kiki, and it was now certain that he was not hiding in the house or on the grounds.

Michel had started eating again. Exasperated, Mme Donadieu spoke harshly to him:

"I never saw such a useless lot of men! Take the car and look for him yourselves, instead of hanging around here. Ask in the villages and railway stations. Do anything you want, but for heaven's sake do *something*."

When she saw Frédéric getting up, she added: "No, Frédéric. I'd rather you stayed."

When the others had left, she remarked with a faint smile:

"Had anyone told me, when I was a girl of sixteen, that this sort of thing was going to happen to me in my old age . . ."

She left the phrase unfinished. Frédéric said nothing; his thoughts had harked back to his youth and hers, when she was a plump, sprightly girl of sixteen, regarded as slightly wild by the matrons of La Rochelle.

The telephone rang. It was Eva.

"Are you there, Mother? Do you know if Michel will be back for lunch? Someone called just now to find out if Frédéric was here, and hung up immediately."

"Thank you, Eva, for letting me know. . . . I don't think Michel will be going back yet."

It was probably Philippe who'd called.

Events had moved too fast. Mme Donadieu was too tired to be capable of any great emotion.

"Really, it's all so difficult." She sighed. "I hardly dare think what would have happened if poor Oscar had still been alive."

Sophie, having roasted three partridges, shot that morning, had laid the table as if nothing unusual had happened. But no one entered the dining room.

"What do you think of Kiki, Frédéric? You can look at him with an outsider's eye, if you know what I mean. The family thinks he's . . . well, not quite all there."

"He's a very sensitive boy, I would say. He takes things too hard. It's no worse than that."

They couldn't keep their eyes from straying to the telephone. Shots could still be heard in the fields, but fewer and fewer, since it was now the dinner hour.

"He was born so much later than the others, you know." Mme Donadieu's tone was almost apologetic. "Why, Michel is old enough to be his father!"

Toward three, she gave up the struggle to keep awake. She lay back in the big armchair and closed her eyes; now and then her lips moved in her sleep. . . .

Night was falling when at last the telephone rang. Frédéric frowned when he heard a voice say: "Luçon police station."

It was there that Kiki had been discovered, lying by the road just outside town, completely worn out. On seeing the policeman, he had made a feeble attempt to escape. Finally, he had confessed that he was heading for the nearest port—intending to run away to sea.

Mme Donadieu listened in amazement to Frédéric's report of what he had been told over the telephone.

"But Luçon's twenty-five miles from here! How on earth did the poor child manage to go all that distance?" The thought of it made her burst into tears. "We'll start at once. Let's hope we can get a car."

The big car wasn't back yet; Michel and Olsen were still scouring the countryside. Fortunately, however, the La Rochelle car had stayed; the driver was reading the paper in the Maclous' kitchen.

"Kiki's been found!" Mme Donadieu announced triumphantly. "Sophie, if Monsieur Michel comes back, tell him to return to La Rochelle at once. We're going to Luçon."

As she was stepping into the car, it suddenly occurred to her that she hadn't used her cane once throughout the day.

7

It was like a scene from a fairy tale; simple, yet somehow touched with magic. Philippe was driving back to the Château de Rivedoux, whose turrents could be seen above a belt of trees. A light veil of morning mist hung on the countryside, but the sun was shining through, and drops of dew were sparkling on grass and hedges.

There was a sharp bend to the left, and a clump of brambles hid the continuation of the road. The moment he had rounded it, the avenue leading to the château came in view; the iron gates, flanked by the stone lions, were standing open. And there, bathed in silvery radiance, was Martine, walking toward him, quite relaxed, as if this were her home. She was dressed in black, and her hair was rippling in the morning breeze. The big dog, which hadn't known her the previous day, was nuzzling up to her with clumsy demonstrations of affection.

She put her hand up to shield her eyes, and when she recognized the driver of the approaching car, gaily waved to Philippe. There was nothing dramatic about it, but the moment was tense with possibilities; the slightest gesture, each fugitive expression, could have incalculable consequences.

The window beside the driver was open. When Philippe came up to her, Martine leaned inside the car.

"Have you managed it?" When he nodded, she asked: "Are we going away?"

She wasn't afraid in the least. On the contrary, she was taking the adventure lightheartedly. Even on waking in this queer château, so unlike anything she had seen before, her first reaction had been a cheerful giggle. She had already made friends with the big dog and was calling him by his name, which was Castor. On her way past, she had given the old witch in the flowered dressing gown a bold smile.

Another detail caught her eye, and made her feel more vividly that she had been transported into a world of romance. It was a suitcase in the back of the car, which hadn't been there the previous day—Philippe's suitcase.

"Are we leaving now?"

She was sure they were when, after stopping the car, he left the engine running. He went up to Papelet, who said something to him that sounded like "Any luck?"

The two had a whispered conversation; Philippe was apparently trying to talk the older man into doing something. They moved into the hall where the player piano was and talked for several more minutes.

"Well, we'll be off," Philippe announced, coming out again.

"Really, mademoiselle, you should have something before you start," said Papelet politely. "May I bring you a glass of port?"

"No, thank you."

The idea of drinking anything in this goblin's castle amused her. She was struck by Papelet's familiar tone as, waving his hand, he shouted after Philippe:

"Au revoir, my boy!"

After leaving the park, they had the sun directly in front, and Martine closed her eyes.

"Who are all those funny people in the château?" she asked, leaning toward Philippe.

All Philippe found to reply was:

"Oh, Papelet's quite nice really. . . . And he's rolling in money, I think."

She was vaguely annoyed by this answer. Though she knew too little of the world to guess Papelet's occupation, or the use to which the château was being put, she felt instinctively that there was something shady about both.

The mood passed quickly. After all, why should she resent Philippe's having taken her to that place? It was just the sort of thing you would expect of him. Perhaps, indeed, she loved him all the more for this streak of rebellion, for his deliberate flouting of convention. He always went all out. Right now he was driving straight ahead at the highest speed he could get out of the small touring car.

"Won't you tell me where we're going?"

He glanced at her with the same smile she'd seen on his face when he caught sight of her coming to meet him outside the château. Then, too, he had been struck by her fearlessness. Far from looking scared, she had more color than usual. And her tone had been quite cheerful when she asked where they were going, the tone she might have used if they were starting out for a ride on a Sunday afternoon!

She seemed to understand his smile, for she smiled back.

"We're going to Paris," he said.

"I'm thirsty."

"We'll stop when we're farther from La Rochelle."

For the first time, she was able to observe him at her leisure, and, half-unconsciously, she fell to studying his face, seen in profile. Aware of this, he held the pose docilely. She began by trying to distinguish the resemblances and differences between Philippe and his father. Sometimes Philippe's face looked more clean-cut than Frédéric's, perhaps because it was a trifle longer and his nose more aquiline.

On the other hand, his eyebrows were rather bushy, and his forehead somewhat receded, whereas Frédéric's was particularly straight.

"What are you thinking about?" When she didn't answer, he added: "No regrets?"

"What about *you*?"

No. Philippe was reconciled to the change in his life, and getting used to it already.

"My first idea," he explained, "was to keep off the main road, in case we were followed. But I've thought it over, and I'm pretty sure your family won't want to have a scandal; they'd rather hush it up."

Again her thoughts went back to her family, and their vast gloomy house on Rue Réaumur; but only for a moment. She'd caught sight of a small café with whitewashed walls, a rough wooden bench in front, and hens pecking around the doorstep.

"Stop, Philippe."

Despite what he'd just said, he glanced uneasily behind; this did not escape Martine.

There was a homely smell of onions and pine cones in the little parlor. A red-cheeked woman stepped out of the kitchen, drying her hands on her apron.

"What'll you have?" Philippe asked.

"A glass of white wine, please."

It was an unforgettable moment, a landmark in her life. The café was a grocery as well, and, pointing to a box of crackers, Martine said:

"Buy me some."

There were other moments, other details of their journey to Paris, that were destined, like this one, to stamp themselves on her memory—for all their triviality. That steep hill, for instance, soon after Niort, where, in the marketplace, a shooting gallery had been set up. Halfway up the hill, Philippe sounded his horn to warn a very small car panting up the gradient in the middle of the road to draw over to the right. Apparently its driver didn't hear. Philippe kept his horn going full blast for a good half-minute. Through the back window of the car in front, Martine had a glimpse of a young man at the wheel, a girl nestling against him.

The more impatient Philippe grew, the more determined seemed the driver of the other car to bar the road. Suddenly the girl looked around, said something to the man beside her, and the car swirved hastily to the side.

As they passed, Martine glanced at the couple in the car. The driver, a young farmer with a toothbrush mustache, gave her a sheepish grin, while the girl laughed frankly as she smoothed her ruffled hair.

There was another incident that stuck in her mind; it took place much farther on—after they'd left Poitiers, as far as she could recall. They were driving by a high stone wall that seemed endless. Behind it lay, no doubt, some vast domain. Martine kept looking for the entrance gates, in order to have a glimpse of the house in which the owner of this huge estate lived.

Suddenly Philippe, guessing what was in her mind, remarked:

"One day we'll be rich—richer than the fellow who owns that estate. Anyhow, I bet the house is just as dingy and depressing as your parents' place."

Nevertheless, she kept her eyes fixed on the wall, waiting for the gap. When it came, they failed to see the house. It evidently stood far back, hidden by trees.

She didn't want to stop for lunch; she was not hungry in the least, she said. Instead, she was eager to get to Paris. The air grew chilly with nightfall, and for an hour or more there was the usual exchange of "amenities" with motorists who wouldn't dim their headlights.

"The tank's nearly empty," Philippe remarked when they were nearing Paris.

He stopped outside a showy modern place to fill up, and persuaded Martine to have a drink in the lounge attached. It was utterly unlike the little café where she'd had the glass of white wine. It looked like a stage set, with its enormous crescent-shaped bar, luxurious chairs, tall stools, white-coated bartenders, and the silvery flash of cocktail shakers.

"Do we have far to go?" Martine was feeling drowsy after her cocktail, and had half a mind to ask for a second.

"We'll be in Paris in an hour."

"Where will we sleep?"

Philippe's only answer was a laugh as he helped her into the car.

There was a look on Philippe's face that stamped itself on her mind so strongly that ever after it was hard to picture him with any other. What day was it he'd had that look, she wondered. Yes, the third day, the morning after she'd slept naked for the last time for want of a nightdress. She'd been quite prepared to put up with such small inconveniences, because the room made up for everything. It was the most attractive room she'd ever known.

It was in a big new apartment building in Montparnasse, at the end of Boulevard Raspail. Hundreds of young couples like them lived in it, she had discovered. She had seen and talked to some of them in the elevator, on the way to or from her marketing.

The apartment was thoroughly modern. Once the bed was made and folded away, it had the appearance of a small, well-appointed living room. It also had a private balcony, a bathroom, and a tiny, labor-saving kitchen with an electric stove. The walls were distempered in bright colors, the furniture was modern, and the lighting was indirect.

The balcony was the great attraction. On the first day, Philippe had bought a robe for Martine in a neighborhood shop, and she used it as a dressing gown. For the beginning of winter, the weather was remarkably mild. There was bright sunshine every morning, tinged with a faint blue haze, and Martine would step out on the balcony, wrapping her robe tightly around her because of the slight chill in the air. From her seventh-floor eyrie, she gazed down at the ceaseless tide of traffic in the street below. When she turned, she could see Philippe shaving in the bathroom, the door of which stood ajar.

In the early morning, most of the people living in apartments facing south went out on their balconies to sun themselves. A young man next door daily put in a quarter of an hour of physical exercise, with an air of grim determination that always made Martine laugh.

That look on Philippe's face—she could recall every incident leading up to it. He had left as usual in his car, which he kept in a garage nearby. Martine had tidied the apartment, taking her time over it, and dressed. As she was about to start out to do the marketing, she saw a car draw up below; Philippe stepped out of it. She waited for him by the elevator.

"Come." He took her arm and led her back to their room. She noticed that he was breathing rapidly. After drawing her toward the window, into a patch of sunlight, he took his wallet from his pocket. "This afternoon you'd better buy a nightdress, or pajamas, and whatever else you need. . . . Oh, and you'd better get a light dress, too; there's no point in your wearing mourning here."

He took some thousand-franc notes from his wallet—she couldn't see how many—and handed her one, adding in a casual tone:

"Will this be enough?"

She gazed at him wide-eyed, puzzled, perturbed. It was then she saw that look, that unforgettable look, on his face—a look of arrogance, with, behind it, some less acceptable emotion: a desire to wreak vengeance on something, perhaps the world at large.

"Philippe! What have you done?"

He led her to the balcony and pointed down.

"Don't you see? It's not the same car. I've exchanged mine for an older one. It runs quite well—and I made eight thousand francs on the deal."

"But . . ." After a moment she got it out, and, to her surprise, found that she was smiling. "But the other car didn't belong to you!"

"That's all right." He laughed. "I'll pay Denis ten times its value someday, if I feel like it."

She could see he was vexed, and she tried to make amends.

"Oh, of course. If you do that . . ."

With a slight shrug he cut in:

"Just you wait and see. I'll make all the money we can want, once I get started."

"I'm sure you will, Philippe."

"Anyhow, we have enough now to keep us going for several weeks, haven't we?"

"Yes indeed."

Nothing would be gained by protesting. He was made that way, and people had to take him as he was. Most likely he didn't even realize . . . When he'd made her stay at that grotesque château, for instance, she hadn't said anything. It would have served no purpose, anyhow. And perhaps, she thought, it's precisely this—this blind spot, as some would call it—that gave him his driving force.

The Donadieu family doctor, a cautious man, had declined to take the responsibility; he gave them the address of a colleague, a specialist in Bordeaux.

The first plan had been for Mme Donadieu to go alone with Kiki, but, the night before, Olsen had come down to announce that his wife intended to accompany her.

"She has some shopping to do in Bordeaux," he explained.

That was only a pretext. After a long conversation with her husband, Marthe had gone to the floor below.

"Can I have five minutes' talk with you, Michel?"

"Certainly. What is it?"

Without replying, Marthe glanced meaningly at Eva and the nurse. Michel took the hint and walked into his study, followed by his sister.

"Do you propose to let Maman take Kiki to Bordeaux by herself?"

Without thinking, Michel picked up a Yo-yo and started playing with it.

"What can I do about it?"

Marthe made a gesture of annoyance.

"Do put down that wretched toy and listen to what I'm saying. It's important. . . . Do you think we can depend on her to tell us the truth if it's something serious and . . . and steps have to be taken?"

At first he looked merely puzzled; then an expression of alarm settled on his face.

"I was reading yesterday," his sister continued, "the article in the medical encyclopedia about cases like this."

"Do you really think . . . ?"

"I came to no conclusion. But I do think one of us should be present when the specialist gives his opinion."

"Who do you think should go? Maman's sure to guess. . . ."

"I'll go." She heaved a sigh, as if deploring that she had to shoulder, unaided, all the family responsibilities.

They decided that it was wiser to travel by train than by car. Ever since his abortive escapade, Kiki had been so listless and taciturn as to seem really ill, and they had been watching over him with almost excessive solicitude.

"Are you sure you're not cold, Kiki?" "Aren't you too hot, so near the fire?" "Take a second helping, dear. If you don't eat, you'll never get back your strength."

And, though the train was overheated, they wrapped him in a heavy afghan. Marthe, who had brought a book, read the whole trip.

"We'll be just in time for the doctor," she said as the train slowed down.

"Oh, are you coming with us?" Mme Donadieu sounded surprised. "I thought you had shopping to do."

"I'll do it afterward."

Her mother made no comment, but she had understood. Since Martine's disappearance, she had been conscious of a change in the attitude of the other members of the family toward her. It was as if they held her responsible for what had happened. Marthe had been the most hostile of all.

When her mother had suggested that Marthe, whose son was seven, should send him down now and then to keep Kiki company, Marthe had considered it, then shaken her head.

"No. I hardly think that would be wise."

"Why not?"

"I'd rather he didn't see too much of Kiki. Please don't make me explain."

The specialist asked the two women whether they wished to be present while he was making his examination, obviously hoping they would answer "No."

But they remained, and for a quarter of an hour watched him tapping and auscultating the boy's chest. Kiki bore it with surprising patience.

"Am I hurting you?"

"No."

"Do you ever feel a pain here?"

"No."

"Take a deep breath, please."

Obediently Kiki took a deep breath.

"Do you have a good appetite?"

"Yes."

"Why did you run away?"

No answer. Looking around, the doctor saw the eyes of Mme Donadieu and her daughter intent on the boy. With a grunt of annoyance, he got up.

"If I'm to get any result, I must ask you to leave him alone with me. I can see he's nervous with you here."

The two women retired to an adjoining room. No sooner had they left than the doctor changed his manner completely, smiled, and said in a jovial tone:

"Put your shirt on again, young man." Then he added quickly: "Your sister's a bit of a tartar, isn't she?"

Kiki eyed him suspiciously, and remained silent.

"What games do you play when you're not at your lessons?"

"I don't play games."

"Well, whom do you talk to?"

"I don't talk to anyone."

"You *must* have a dull time! What *do* you do?"

"I read books."

"Know how to swim?"

"No."

"What? You live at the seaside, your father was a shipowner, and you can't swim? . . . Perhaps you ride?"

"No."

"Don't you have horses?"

"My brother and brother-in-law had some, but they were sold last year. We had to set an example, Papa said, when he cut the staff ten percent."

"What put the idea of Sables d'Olonne into your head? Had you been there before?"

"No. I looked on the map and saw it was the nearest seaport—except Rochefort, and people know us there."

"Ever been to Paris?"

"No."

"Where *have* you been?"

"Only to Berck. I was in a sanatorium there for six months."

"Which of your sisters do you like best?"

"Martine."

"How old is she?"

"Seventeen."

"Why didn't she come with you today?"

"Because she's gone away." Abruptly he added: "Please don't tell Maman I told you. She went away with Philippe. I'm quite sure now he didn't kill Papa."

"What on earth are you talking about?"

"Never mind. Don't ask me anything else, please. . . . Tell me, am I really sick? Too sick to go to sea?"

"Well, you're not up to it right now, I'm afraid. It will depend . . ."

"On what?"

"On the sort of life you lead the next year or so. You must develop your muscles, fill your chest out. And you must learn to breathe properly; that's essential. . . . No, you're not strong enough to be a sailor yet."

The boy was staring at him, thinking hard.

"Is that all?" he asked, after a short silence.

"Once you've put on another twelve pounds, you'll be fit for anything—but not before."

"Twelve pounds," Kiki repeated thoughtfully.

The specialist had much the same advice to give in the talk that followed with Mme Donadieu and Marthe.

"I do not altogether agree with my colleague in La Rochelle—that the boy has a predisposition for what we call '*fuga*.' That's to say, flight, or running away from home. I wouldn't be surprised if he never tries to run away again. But I strongly advise you to make his life as cheerful and healthy as possible, to encourage him to play games, and to discourage him from reading."

"Don't you think, doctor," Marthe began, her tone vaguely ominous, "the fact that he was born when his mother was over forty and his father almost sixty may have some bearing . . . ?"

"Not necessarily," said the doctor, after a quick glance at Mme Donadieu.

"I mention that because my sister, who is only two years older than Kiki, resembles him in some respects. I'm afraid I mustn't speak more clearly. But I'd be glad to know one thing: do you consider Kiki a normal child?"

She was taken aback when he asked blandly:

"May I ask exactly what you mean by 'normal'?"

"Well, for instance, do you think he's fully responsible for his acts?"

The doctor, who had been eying her shrewdly, retorted:

"Do you know many people who are fully responsible, as you put it, for their acts?"

Marthe sprang to her feet, looking daggers at him.

"You are deliberately misunderstanding me, doctor. Really, I'm amazed. . . ."

"My dear lady, you're much mistaken; I understood you perfectly well. . . . Now, if you'll excuse me, I'll write out, not so much a prescription, as a few suggestions, which I hope you will follow. In my opinion, there's no reason the boy shouldn't go back home, provided . . ."

That evening, when her husband returned from his office, Marthe vented her indignation to him.

"That specialist was most disappointing. He didn't even try to find out if Kiki has some congenital taint." And, in a lower voice: "It's quite possible that Papa got infected with . . . with some disease after we were born. In the article I read, it says that most cases of this kind are due to heredity."

"Cases of what kind?"

"Of running away from home. *'Fuga,'* they call it. The doctor wouldn't even listen when I told him Kiki had had trouble with his spine."

"Do you know who he is, this guardian of hers they're talking about?" Charlotte's voice was so shrill, and she looked so fierce, that Mme Brun burst out laughing.

"You may laugh," said Charlotte sulkily, "but nothing will convince me she hasn't run away with Philippe."

"Nonsense!"

"I tell you, I'm sure of it. Of course, the family pretend she's staying with her guardian, but that's just eyewash. What the servants told the milkman was the truth: she's eloped with that young man."

"You mean Philippe Dargens, I suppose?"

"Who else?" When really angry, Charlotte could look almost murderous. "Where do you think they've gone?"

"What does it matter? Wherever that poor girl is, she's better off than she was at home."

"Do you really think that?"

"Certainly I do."

Charlotte was set on having the last word, and she had it.

"Well, if that's how you feel, you'd do better not to say it. Because, in that case, there's no reason for poor girls like me to keep straight."

As Charlotte usually did on her "bad days," as Mme Brun called them, when her digestion was out of order, she flung out of the room, slamming the door, and shut herself in the linen room, where she could be heard grumbling.

Didn't Marthe have something of the same feeling toward her mother? She had been a model of propriety in her girlhood; indeed, her father had seen to it that she wouldn't be otherwise. She would never have dreamed of going to a dance without a chaperone, as Martine had been known to do, and the cook had always escorted her to and from school.

Now, she was profoundly shocked by what appeared to be the crumbling of the old regime. Martine had eloped with a young man, and the whole family was dishonored. Yet Maman deliberately, it seemed, refrained from talking about it; and not because the subject was painful, but because the rest of them took it so tragically. One evening, when they had been getting on her nerves, she had even defended Philippe:

"After all, he may be quite a decent young man for all we know. His father says he has brains."

Had such a remark been made two months earlier, in Oscar Donadieu's lifetime, or had any member of the family dared to find excuses for a shameless girl like Martine, the house would surely have rocked on its foundations! Marthe was appalled by the change that had come over her mother, by her moral laxity.

This business with Kiki was another case in point. From what she knew of her father—and, as his favorite daughter, almost his only confidante, she had known him through and through—she felt convinced that he would have taken a most serious view of his son's escapade. Instead of taking the boy to a doctor, he would have packed him off to a reformatory, or some such institution, probably in some foreign country.

Hardly was the old man in his grave when everything changed. It seemed taken for granted that a boy should be allowed to make a scene at a formal lunch and to run away from home. His sister . . . !

"I hate to say such a thing," Marthe told her husband, "but I put it all down to Maman's influence. A demoralizing influence, I'm afraid. It's as if she's suddenly gone crazy. Do you know, she's actually been talking of spending a month this winter on the Riviera, and taking Kiki with her."

"She can't have meant it!"

"I assure you she spoke quite seriously."

"But where's the money to come from? We'll have at least five more boats laid up before the month is out, and I'm afraid we'll all have to cut down on expenses."

"Have you told her that?" By "you" she meant both Michel and Olsen.

"Not yet. But we will."

"Has the staff any suspicion of what's happened? I mean, about Martine."

"I really couldn't say."

"Yesterday, when I was at the hairdresser's, I saw old Mme Brun, and she gave me such a funny smile."

"Mme Brun! *She*, at least, has no right to criticize us. Why, when her husband went off his head and had to be locked up, she didn't even shed a tear. On the contrary, it was quite a scandal, the way she started carrying on. The 'Merry Widow,' everyone was calling her, and . . ."

"Listen!"

"What?"

"Someone's coming up. Have a look."

He tiptoed out of the room and, leaning over the banister, saw Frédéric on the landing below. He was on his way to visit Eva. They were going to sip liqueur and smoke cigarettes in the boudoir with the black velvet curtains.

"He should be more careful."

"Who?"

"My brother. One day there will be trouble, mark my words. Do you know, Eva refuses to wear a crepe veil; she says it makes her eyes smart!"

Marthe was tall, statuesque, and her black dress made her look even more so. Olsen, several years younger than his wife, and secretly rather in awe of her, had now made three attempts to go on reading his book, but she had frustrated him each time. She switched to a new topic.

"Are the crews still talking of a strike?"

"Yes, I'm afraid so. I've been told that it's part of a deliberate plot to make things difficult for us this winter."

"A plot? Who's behind it?"

"Camboulives. He's going to stand as a candidate at the next election, I hear, and he goes around proclaiming that his father was a fisherman and he started life as mate on a trawler. Currying favor with the masses, of course."

"Why shouldn't Michel contest the election? He'd have quite a good chance, I'd say."

The lampshades made a soft, warm glow in the room. Olsen tried again to read, but his wife returned to the attack.

"What does Maman say about it?"

"All I know is that she's asked Camboulives to lunch again."

"And of course you two take it lying down!" Marthe exclaimed indignantly. "If things go on like this, I'll start going to the office myself, like Maman. Something must be done. . . ."

Here, too, as in the rooms below, a portrait of Oscar Donadieu hung on the wall, but it was only an enlarged photograph.

That night Martine and Philippe went to a movie. They gave hardly a thought to La Rochelle, or the talk that must be going on about them, in the Olsens' living room, in the Donadieu offices, at Mme Brun's. They had no idea that Michel was threatening to go to Paris to track them down—among the city's four million inhabitants! Or that Olsen was talking of laying a complaint before a magistrate, and Marthe was bemoaning her mother's apathy. Or that all were united on one point: the necessity of avoiding any public scandal—which was why the days went by without any move being made.

Watching the cartoon, Martine felt a little thrill of pleasure, like that she had experienced in the café where she'd drunk that glass of cellar-cool white wine. It had come to her again one morning on the sunlit balcony outside their room—a fleeting rapture for which she was unable to account, but of which she could never have too much.

Without thinking, she laid her hand on Philippe's arm and nestled against him. Then a man immediately in front blew his nose loudly—and the spell was broken.

8

. . . that I am very happy, and I send you my love and best wishes for
the coming year.

December had been a month of gales and deluges of rain, marked
by catastrophe: the *Marie-Françoise*, a three-master that had weathered
many a storm off the Newfoundland coast, went down with all hands
off Ile d'Oléron.

New Year's Day was no better. Though the rain held off, an icy
wind swept the streets, forcing its way into the house, under doors
and through the chinks around window frames.

"I don't know how the rest of you are feeling," Mme Donadieu
grumbled, "but, personally, I'm frozen."

She was wearing a fur coat in the living room. Something was
wrong, evidently, with the central heating. Kiki was sitting on his
bedroom floor with his back against the tepid radiator, and the others
were no better off for warmth. Olsen was particularly unfortunate,
since he was suffering from a severe cold; his nose was as red as a
tomato, and his face swollen almost out of recognition.

"I've always said it's impossible to warm this house with the furnace we have. It's much too small for a place like this." Mme Donadieu
had been making this lament every winter for twenty years or more,
to no avail.

Something had to be done to celebrate New Year's Day, but now
that Oscar Donadieu was dead, the ritual was changed. Indeed, slowly
but surely, the old order was dying. It was a wonder the portrait in
the living room could keep that look of stolid satisfaction!

On the excuse that it was too cold to venture out, and, anyhow,
one isn't obliged to attend church on New Year's Day, Mme Donadieu
stayed at home, contrary to precedent.

The servants had gone to Low Mass at seven. Mme Donadieu did not emerge till eight, and she was wearing a weekday dress. As she was walking past the dining room, she heard a slight noise. Looking around, she saw Kiki standing in the doorway, with Edmond beside him.

Kiki was in his Sunday suit; so was Edmond. So ceremonious was their attitude, they might as well be wearing gloves.

Mme Donadieu's first impulse was to walk away without saying anything. She always felt like this when confronted by the young tutor or by any of his "doings," as she described them to herself.

It was Michel's idea, this introduction into the household of a private tutor for Kiki. He had advertised in a professional paper, and one day a young man had presented himself. He was so timid that he could hardly get a word out at first, and so overawed by his surroundings that he was seen to bow to one of the portraits in the hall. He was studying for a classical degree. A room had been fixed up for him on the top floor, where the servants slept.

Obviously, this was one of Edmond's doings. He had told Kiki to put on his Sunday best, and now he was nudging him with his elbow.

"Maman dear, as a new year begins today, I take this opportunity"—Kiki hesitated, and she almost expected the young man to prompt him—"of assuring you that I will do my very best to please you throughout the . . . the coming year, and . . ."

"Splendid!" she cut in hastily, giving him a kiss. "That's very sweet of you, Kiki. And I wish you a very happy New Year, darling, and, above all, better health. Happy New Year, Edmond."

"Permit me, madame, to offer you my best wishes and my hopes . . ."

Thus the day started. Next it was Augustin's turn; he said his little piece while serving the morning coffee. Then the cook's; she held the door ajar and poked her tousled head in.

"Thank you very much," said Mme Donadieu. "And the same to you."

Meanwhile, she could hear people moving in the rooms above, and on the stroke of nine the Olsen family trooped down. They were in their best clothes and had a formal manner. Marthe pushed her seven-year-old son to the front and, a paper in his hand, Maurice began reciting his New Year's wishes, sometimes pausing to look up at his mother for approval. The recitation ended with ". . . my dearest grandma, whom I love with all my heart."

"I won't kiss you," Olsen mumbled. "I'm afraid of passing on my cold."

The Olsens left to present their New Year's wishes to Olsen's uncle, who was Norwegian consul in La Rochelle.

There remained the second-floor household, Michel and his wife, whose footsteps could be heard above. As for the staff—clerks, crews, and workmen—they had been dealt with the previous evening, when there had been bestowed on each a glass of port—or, rather, a red wine masquerading as port—and a couple of cigars.

The bell rang. Augustin opened the door. Frédéric entered the room without waiting to be shown in, went up to Mme Donadieu, and lightly kissed her cheeks.

"All the best, my dear," he said with an affectionate smile.

He noticed a tray standing on the table, with port, crackers, and cigars ready for the morning's callers. It was a custom of the house, going back as far as he could remember.

"All going well?"

"I'm through with one group." She smiled. "I'm awaiting the second visitation. Kiki gave me a regular speech."

"I have something for you, too."

He took out of his pocket an envelope from which the stamp had been peeled, as if it had been through the hands of a collector—a detail Mme Donadieu noticed at once. From the envelope Frédéric extracted two letters, one of which he handed to her.

Dearest Maman, I can't let the old year end without writing to tell you that I am very happy, and I send you my love and best wishes for the coming year. Martine.

That was all. Surprised, and more affected than she cared to show, Mme Donadieu gazed at Frédéric, as if asking what this meant. Then her eyes fell on the second letter, which was covered with writing in a small, neat hand.

"This is from Philippe," he said. "There's no reason why you shouldn't read it too."

Dear Father, First let me say that Martine and I send you our greetings and the usual wishes for the New Year. In my last letter—

Mme Donadieu looked up quickly. Frédéric, who understood the look, hastened to explain.

"He's written to me twice. He didn't have much to say. Only that he was well and getting on all right."

He rose, poured himself a glass of port, and lit a cigar.

I asked for news from La Rochelle, and especially I asked you to tell me quite frankly what people are saying about us.

She stopped reading. There were footsteps on the stairs. Michel came in, holding his five-year-old son by the hand. Eva had the baby in her arms—an unusual sight.

Three kisses for each. On the left cheek, then the right, then the left again. It was a family tradition. The little boy, younger than Marthe's, had no prepared speech to deliver.

"It's dreadfully cold in here," Michel observed.

His eyes fell on the decanter at once, and he poured himself a glass of port. He gave a vague nod to Frédéric, with whom his wife was exchanging greetings, and raised his glass.

"Here's best wishes!"

He was looking worried and out of sorts. His eyes had a curious shiftiness, and there were dark rings under them.

"The committee meetings are most exhausting," he had thought fit to explain to his wife, who hadn't asked him anything.

He was presiding over a committee for the erection of a statue of Gérard Dampierre, near the Clock Tower.

With his port, he ate several crackers. The sight of food, as always, rousing his appetite.

"Why don't you light the fire?" asked Eva. "We've had one going all morning."

"You know quite well that this fireplace never draws. I'd be smoked out."

"Has Marthe been down?"

"Yes. She's gone out with her husband and Maurice."

Mme Donadieu was anxious for them to leave. She had the two letters in her hand, and, as ill luck would have it, Eva, who had a knack for indiscretion, noticed them.

"Isn't that Martine's writing?"

"It's an old letter I discovered in my desk."

"Oh, is that all? I thought perhaps she'd written. . . ."

"That would be the last straw," mumbled Michel, his mouth full.

"Well, I'm afraid I must be going up again," said Eva. "The baby, you know . . ."

"Yes, yes. I quite understand."

"You'll drop in before you go, won't you, Frédéric?"

Michel followed her out, announcing that he had an appointment.

A mingled smell of port, sweet crackers, and cigar smoke hung in the air; the characteristic smell of New Year's Day in the Donadieus' living room.

"Don't you think Michel has aged a good deal lately?" asked Mme Donadieu when the others had left.

Frédéric looked away, to hide a smile. He knew very well the cause of Michel's "aging." In fact, he had it in his pocket.

It was a small weekly newspaper, printed in big type on very heavy paper, and oddly named *The Laundry*. The first issue had appeared two days before. Under the name was a line in italics: *For the Weekly Cleansing of Our Civic Life.*

A general election was due to take place the following spring, and the business of the Dampierre monument was a pretext for a preliminary skirmish. Chosen ostensibly to do honor to an eminent citizen of La Rochelle, the committee was composed of the most reactionary elements. Michel Donadieu had consented to be its president.

A week after the first committee meeting, hostilities had opened: *The Laundry*, an extremely scurrilous publication, had been deposited in a thousand mailboxes and posted on the walls of public lavatories.

AN OPEN LETTER TO M. DONADIEU, JR.

We do not propose, in this our first issue, to liquidate for good and all the honorable gentleman above named, who has recently announced his wish to represent the citizens of La Rochelle in the Municipal Council. The Augean stable was not cleansed in a day, and M. Donadieu, Jr., need feel no immediate alarm; we shall proceed by gradual degrees. Week by week we shall throw fresh light on a certain rather sordid mystery, a blemish on our town's good name, of which many of our citizens have an inkling, but few dare to speak openly.

By way of hors d'oeuvres to a repast we promise our readers will be gargantuan, we will lead off with a brief questionnaire.

Is it a fact that, on December 23, Mlle Odette B., age 23, a typist employed in the palatial Donadieu building on Quai Vallin, took the train to Bordeaux in the company of a woman in black, who lives some miles out of town and whose house is resorted to, clandestinely, by young ladies who have (as the saying goes) got into trouble?

Is it a fact that, shortly before these two ladies took the train, Mlle Odette B. had a heart-to-heart talk with her employer, M. Donadieu, in his sanctum, and that at this interview she burst into tears repeatedly, and ended up by fainting?

Is it a fact that one of our least estimable citizens, who recently bought an ancient château near La Rochelle—with a view to using it, we presume, as the country branch of his chain of "houses" in town—might have much to tell about certain meetings previous to the one described above, and of a much more cheerful order, between our Grand Panjandrum Junior and his typist?

And that, alas, these meetings had consequences, which involved an appeal to the services of the obliging dame in black?

And that, her efforts having failed, there was a hurried journey to Bordeaux to consult a specialist, and Donadieu in an incredible burst of generosity handed to the said specialist the, to him, enormous sum of two thousand francs?

And that since then he has been quaking in his shoes, awaiting a message from the clinic, to which he dare not telephone?

We feel sure the answers to these questions would be highly interesting, but we foresee that none will be forthcoming; in which case we will publish a further list, on another topic.

After all, Oscar Donadieu has not been buried so long that an exhumation, followed by another post-mortem, is ruled out.

The article was signed "Fiat Lux."

One morning, Olsen, a copy of *The Laundry* in his pocket, entered Michel's office.

"Is it true, what's said here?"

There was no need for an answer. Olsen had only to look at his partner's woebegone face to realize that it was true, though Michel tried to prevaricate.

"Well—er—it's a fact that she's been ill. But I had nothing to do with it, I assure you. I wasn't her first, or only one, by any means. She's . . . that sort of girl."

"What do you propose to do about it?"

He had no idea, and merely murmured sulkily:

"I wish I knew who the swine is who writes that filthy rag!"

Frédéric could have told him. Little went on in La Rochelle that escaped him, and he knew, better than anybody, the personalities of its inhabitants.

And the personality of Dr. Lambe, the writer of the article signed Fiat Lux, was remarkable in its way. During the five years he had been practicing in La Rochelle, he had been an inconspicuous figure. A lean, bilious-looking, middle-aged man, he lived in a small house near the barracks, not far from the street of ill fame from which Papelet derived his wealth. His practice brought him little; he didn't even have full-time help, and opened his door himself after six o'clock. Most of his patients were farmhands from the surrounding countryside.

As recently as a fortnight before, he had passed for a nonentity. He belonged to no club, had no dealings with local bigwigs, and was never seen in cafés.

Then, out of the blue, he had launched this rag, *The Laundry*. Did he have political ambitions, and want to place himself in the limelight? Or was he merely a blackmailer? Nothing was known of his intentions, and everybody was waiting eagerly for his next move. Some said that Donadieu would prosecute, and was sure to win his case. Others said that *The Laundry* would stop appearing; the Donadieus were rich enough to see to that.

Frédéric naturally refrained from showing this paper in his pocket to Mme Donadieu.

"What's he doing?" she asked. Her thoughts were still with Martine and Philippe.

"I haven't any idea. But he says he's getting on all right."

"If you'll excuse me, I'll go on reading."

In my last letter I asked you to write me poste restante, Neuilly. I especially asked you to let me know how things were at your end, but all you thought fit to reply was: "Everything's the same as usual."

Mme Donadieu looked up, and Frédéric smiled rather sadly.

I must say that was rather mean of you, considering I've always treated you as a pal, and I hoped you'd do the same. Also, if I wanted this information, it was more for Martine's sake than my own.

Do you still see the Donadieus? If so, I wish you would explain to them exactly how I feel about it. I can't forget that I was always treated by them as if I were a pariah; that Oscar Donadieu threatened to throw me out the window if I came again!

Well, I didn't go out the window but out the door, and if Martine went with me, I can assure you it was entirely of her own accord.

We have been in love for a long time. If her father hadn't taken such an absurd position, I'd have gone about it in the normal way, and asked for his consent to our engagement. After his death, I would certainly have approached Mme Donadieu, but Martine begged me to take her away at once; she couldn't stand the atmosphere of that house a day longer—and I don't blame her.

I tell you all this because I could see, when we met the last time, that you disapproved of my conduct.

Frédéric kept his eyes on the back of the letter as she read it, and, though he knew it by heart, he was reading it again. From time to time, Mme Donadieu shot him a questioning glance. He merely shrugged.

"Is it true?" she asked.

"Yes, I'm pretty sure it's true."

Try to put yourself in my place. I'm twenty-five. I'm what they call a ne'er-do-well, because I didn't have the luck to step into a fortune or a soft berth in an office on Quai Vallin. That is not your fault, I know; but it's a fact we have to face.

In spite of these handicaps, I have managed to pay my way, and I'll go on doing so; more successfully, perhaps, than some others, who had an easier start.

If I had proposed marriage to Martine, they'd only have said I was a fortune hunter and, of course, turned me down. As it is, I can hold my head up, and tell them boldly: "We love each other, Martine and I. Nothing will part us. We can stand on our own feet, and we ask no help from anyone." That would be the truth. I am earning enough to provide for us both, in a simple but quite decent way.

Perhaps you might convey this to Mme Donadieu, who may possibly understand. But it's no use saying anything to Michel or to Olsen; they would simply foam at the mouth!

Martine is quite happy. At first I was rather anxious about her health. But she assured me she had always been like that and, at home, no one worried about it. However, I took her to a specialist. He asked questions about her family and gave her an X-ray examination. He was particularly interested to hear about Kiki's spinal trouble, and he prescribed a change of diet.

She has to eat twice as much as she used to, and take long walks, for three hours a day. She sleeps with her window open, and, on the doctor's advice, we'll go to the seaside in the spring.

But it will be a very different seaside from the one patronized by the rich folk of La Rochelle, who are satisfied with glimpses of the back end of a port. You understand, I hope. . . .

For the rest, do as you think fit. This letter isn't in any sense a "feeler." I know that, if I proposed going back to La Rochelle, Martine would be up in arms at once.

If I write like this, quite straightforwardly (you will learn nothing by trying to read between the lines), it's because I have in mind a possible contingency. You know what I mean? Martine's being a minor, her guardian's consent is necessary for our marriage. And it is possible that something may happen before we get it.

Once again I assure you that we are perfectly happy; Martine has no idea that I am writing to you at such length. As a matter of fact, it was all I could do to get her to send a few lines to her mother for the New Year; without me, she'd never have thought of it!

As for money, I'm not doing too badly. I have gone into partnership with a friend, and we have launched a business that may develop into something really big. I will only mention that we have just gotten an option on the construction of a new breakwater for a big seaport in North Africa. I may have to go there within the next few weeks, so we may be absent for some time.

Please yourself about answering this letter. And form your own opinion. I know only too well that there's always a gulf of incomprehension between two generations. With all your broad-mindedness you have never really understood me.

                                          Affectionately yours,
                                          Philippe

"What's he getting at?" Mme Donadieu asked.

That, indeed, was the problem: how was this letter to be understood? For all its inconsequence, there seemed to be a definite idea behind it. There was even a postscript, which was not its least revealing element.

If you show this letter to anyone, please destroy the envelope, because of the postmark. Not that this matters; we are not living anywhere near Neuilly. And I hardly think they will get the police to look for us. Still, with a man like Michel, one never knows, and it's best to be on the safe side.

"What's your opinion of your son, Frédéric?"

He rose, smiled, and took a sip of port before answering.

"When I was his age, my father predicted that I'd end my days in jail, because I'd bought a horse, only half the cash down. Soon after that, I signed an I.O.U.—it was quite aboveboard, and I paid when it fell due. My father, who had never borrowed money in his life, not even for his biggest ventures, told me I was bringing discredit on his name."

She saw his drift, but would have preferred something more explicit.

"It was Philippe I asked you about."

"You should put that question to someone of his generation."

He refused to sit in judgment on his son. There was much that displeased him about the young man; some things that Philippe did seemed to him outrageous. Yet who could say which of the two generations was in the right?

True, the letter was cold. But there had never been much display of sentiment between him and his son. And that might well be his fault, because of his almost morbid horror of showing his feelings.

He knew Philippe to be capable of sharp practice on occasion; he had learned of his failure either to send back or to pay for the car he had taken from the garage for his journey to Paris. But one had to allow for the atmosphere in which he had been living recently: in a tiny, shabby room, with a bankrupt father harassed by creditors. In addition, it was true that Philippe had no compunctions in his dealings with women, even with an innocent young girl like Martine. There again, was he wholly to blame? At his last meeting with his father, hadn't he found a young dancer in his father's bed?

Frédéric was inclined to hope that this lack of scruples was merely a passing phase, that the young man was sowing his wild oats.

Still, this letter . . . If Frédéric had spoken his mind, he'd have said it was "a nasty piece of work." For one thing, it didn't ring true. It had a studied vagueness and evasiveness, and, moreover, not to mince words, more than a hint of blackmail. The way he talked about Martine, for instance, about her health and the visit to the specialist. That allusion to a possible contingency was an obvious suggestion that a baby might be on the way. Even his insistence on Martine's contentment with her lot and her refusal to hear of returning to her family . . . There was something dubious about it.

In fact, though he didn't dare say so, Frédéric was quite disgusted, and he couldn't help wondering if the letter hadn't produced the same impression on his old friend Mme Donadieu, who was still holding it, frowning and deep in thought.

"After all . . ." she murmured, then fell silent and glanced again at the letter in her hand. "After all, Frédéric, perhaps he's right."

He looked at her, wondering what she meant.

"In truth, I know very little about Martine," she continued. "Now that I've been watching her brother so closely, I wouldn't be surprised if Philippe's telling the truth. She may well have determined to leave home at all costs."

"Yes, that may be so."

"In that case, it was rather a fine thing he did, your youngster. It needed some courage to saddle himself with a young girl under such conditions."

He was half inclined to warn her: "Hold on! Don't exaggerate his heroism." But, instead, he nodded and temporized.

"Yes, poor boy, he hasn't had an easy start in life."

Abruptly, he looked away. An odious thought had just crossed his mind. Watching Mme Donadieu's face, he had noticed a sentimental, almost sensual look in her eyes. At the same time, a picture had risen before him of Philippe, in the full flush of his twenty-fifth year, with his handsome, clean-cut features, his easy grace. It would not be surprising if this woman at the turn of life should feel indulgence for the young man; for Martine, too, from whose adventure she derived, perhaps, a vicarious thrill.

For over thirty years she had been starved of every pleasure except the mild amenities of family life. And now this letter, which seemed to exercise a curious fascination on her, had probably awakened feelings outside Frédéric's ken.

"Michel, needless to say, will be difficult to deal with. He seems to think that, as the senior male member of the family, he has stepped into his father's shoes, and carries on accordingly. . . . Really, he overdoes it. And my son-in-law backs him up. One would think that those two had the honor of the Donadieus in their keeping. Marthe is nearly as bad. Can you imagine what she said to me the other day?"

"What?"

"It was about Edmond—Kiki's tutor, you know. I didn't even choose him. Michel placed the advertisement and dealt with the answers. Well, sometimes after dinner Edmond stays on in the living room for an hour or so. Once or twice I've had a game of checkers with him, when Kiki was in bed. And, do you know, my daughter told me I shouldn't do this—it might cause gossip! . . . What makes it so ridiculous is that the poor boy's young enough to be my son, and so shy that he apologizes when he wins a game. Her latest idea is that he shouldn't have his meals with us, but in a room by himself. Needless to say, I put my foot down about that. . . . Go and see what they're doing."

"Who?" Frédéric sounded puzzled.

"Kiki and Edmond."

He did as she asked, and knocked at Kiki's door.

"Come in."

He noticed that Kiki put his hand behind his back, to hide the cigarette he was smoking. Sitting with his back to the radiator, his legs across another chair, the boy was reading. Seated at the table, his cheek propped on his arm, Edmond was playing chess by himself. Seeing Frédéric, he sprang to his feet.

"Don't bother to get up. Go on with your game."

"I'm sorry. I didn't see you come in. I was trying to work out a problem—the Fool's Mate, they call it in my book—but I'm stuck."

It was a sunless day, and the room was darker because of the trees outside. Smoke hung in the air, though Edmond was not smoking. The room had the cheerful disorder of a student's, and the two youths seemed quite at ease.

"Happy New Year, Kiki, dear boy."

"Happy New Year," the boy responded, sounding surly. He regarded Frédéric as being in league with "the old gang"—his mother and the rest of the family, Martine excepted.

"Have a smoke." Frédéric held out his cigarette case.

"No, thanks."

"Oh, come now! One should start smoking at your age. I did. . . . What's that you're reading? Ah, *The Viscount of Bragelonne*. Which reminds me: I have a complete set of Dumas that isn't doing anything. That'll be my New Year's present to you, Kiki. Monsieur Edmond, would you mind coming to my place for it this afternoon?"

"Certainly, Monsieur Dargens. With pleasure."

No detail of the scene escaped Frédéric's notice. He realized that Kiki was devoted to his young tutor, heart and soul. For the first time in his life, perhaps, the boy had found a friend, someone in whom he could confide. And the room, too, seemed to have come alive; its dreariness had given way to an atmosphere of warmth and well-being.

"Did you say you were trying the Fool's Mate?"

"Yes."

"Well, you've moved the wrong pawn. See! If you don't get the queen clear . . . May I show you?"

In five moves, Frédéric announced checkmate with a smile. As he walked to the door, he reminded Edmond:

"Don't forget to come for the books. . . . Au 'voir, Kiki."

On his return to the living room, he found Mme Brun there, clad in rustling silk, as usual. He bent to kiss her hand and give the season's greetings.

"What news, friend courtier?" she asked playfully.

He looked at her questioningly.

"Yes, that's how I always think of you. You're the last of our courtiers; you have all the graces of the old regime. And aren't you attached to the court of our charming hostess? Also, I hear, you often have a cup of tea with the fascinating Eva."

"If it's as you say," he said, smiling, "that's because I've never dared to knock at your door, greatly as I'd like to."

Mme Brun beamed on him, then resumed her conversation with Mme Donadieu.

"You were saying, dear, that Martine . . . ?"

"She's in Paris, staying with one of our cousins. It was so dull for her at home, you know. That's how it always is for the youngest in a family, isn't it? Their brothers and sisters are married and have children when they're just starting life. I quite understand how boring it must seem, being shut up with a lot of older people who have quite different tastes. As Frédéric was saying just now . . ."

He shrugged evasively, conscious that Mme Donadieu was trying to shift the onus of the conversation to him. He got up and poured himself some wine.

"I think I'll have a glass of port, too, Monsieur Dargens," said Mme Brun. "And one of those honey puffs, please. I simply dote on honey."

She was a woman who doted on everything—never merely liked it—and would go into raptures as profuse over a bakery bun as over a culinary chef d'oeuvre.

"Thank you, Don Juan."

Frédéric knew what the old lady wanted in response.

"A Don Juan out of luck. You aren't on his list of conquests."

The familiar New Year's atmosphere had changed with Mme Brun's coming; her slightly malicious archness irritated him. When he heard her saying, with a pretense of innocence: "How's your son, Michel? Isn't he in?" he thought: Yes, you old cat. I wouldn't mind betting you have a copy of *The Laundry*.

"It must be a fearful strain for him," Mme Brun continued, "having to shoulder the responsibility for such a large business at his age."

What drivel the woman talked! Michel was thirty-seven, and what did the "responsibility" amount to?

But Mme Brun had come with the intention of saying certain things, and she said them.

"How lucky he is to have a wife who helps and understands him so well. As your next-door neighbor, I feel, if you don't mind my saying so, a special interest in your family, and . . ."

"Have another honey puff," Frédéric cut in.

"No, thank you. By the way, what's the latest news of your young scapegrace?" She had promised Charlotte to mention Philippe, and was keeping her word. She had even promised to say: "If he doesn't turn over a new leaf, there won't be breathing space left in La Rochelle. How many young toddlers do we owe to him already?"

And she said it. Then, for all her natural effrontery, somewhat abashed, she beat a quick retreat, murmuring something about a call to pay on the mayor's wife.

9

Above each desk, a small, green-shaded lamp hung low, with the effect that each man bent over a little pool of brightness that intensified the darkness around him. Some of the older members of the staff, used to oil lamps or gaslight, even added a ring of cardboard to their lampshades, to restrict the light even more. Caught in the beams from a street lamp on the quay, flurries of raindrops glittered on the windowpanes.

MANAGER. FISHERIES. This was Mme Donadieu's department, and she, too, seemed penned within the circle of light cast by a green-shaded lamp standing on her desk. Pencil in hand, she was listening to a long explanation from a man seated facing her, hardly distinguishable in the surrounding gloom. He was her legal adviser, and the subject under discussion was the new quota system and its bearing on the import of sole and cod from Holland.

MANAGER. WAREHOUSES. SHIPPING. Here, as it happened, Olsen was taking things easy for the moment. On his desk, an illustrated magazine lay open at an article on golf, and while he read he was idly penciling grotesque little figures along the margin. His busy time was in the morning, at flood tide. Moreover, the weather had been so stormy for the last few days that the fishing fleet had been unable to put out.

MANAGER. ANTHRACITE, BRIQUETS. This department, on the second floor, was always the busiest, and often Michel Donadieu, in the course of a discussion with his brother-in-law, would say haughtily:

"Where would we be if it wasn't for my briquets?"

There was some truth in this. The briquets, made of amalgamated slack, and, owing to their shape, known as ovoids, brought in twice as much as the fisheries did. You could hardly enter a cottage or farmhouse in that part of France without seeing, on the wall, a calendar depicting an object like a big black egg embellished with a colored filigree that was quite a work of art, and blazoned in gold letters: "Donadieu Ovoids. The Perfect Fuel."

Michel was talking to one of his rural agents, a burly man in hobnailed boots that had played havoc with the red carpet. Twice during their conversation, Joseph, Michel's "office boy," had come in and whispered something in his employer's ear.

"Didn't you tell him I was out?" Michel asked petulantly.

"Yes, sir. I told him."

"Well?"

"He said he'd heard your voice."

"How did he seem? Excited?"

"I couldn't say, sir."

Michel glared at Joseph, whose obtuseness had been proverbial in the office for nearly forty years.

"Damn it all, can't you give me an idea of how he's behaving?"

"He's sitting on a chair."

"Yes, yes. What I mean is, does he look—er—calm?"

"Well, he seems anxious about the time. I keep my watch on my desk, and he's got up once or twice to look at it and then his own."

"Tell him . . . yes, tell him I'm in the middle of an important business meeting and won't be free for an hour or two." Turning to the agent, he said, louder: "Sorry for this interruption. I agree to your proposals and hope to look in on you someday next week. Good day . . . No, you'd better leave by that door."

He pointed to a door leading to another office; that way the man wouldn't cross the anteroom on his way out. For some moments Michel remained standing, his head outside the zone of light. Abruptly, he came to a decision, pressed a bell, and turned toward a heavy door, which opened at once.

"Is he still there?"

"Yes, but he told me he could wait only twenty minutes more. He's driving the 9:12."

"What's that?"

"It must be a train, sir. He's wearing a railway engineer's cap."

"Do you mean he has it on?" Michel couldn't repress his vexation at the idea of someone sitting in the anteroom with his cap on.

"No, sir. I meant he had it on when he came. He's taken it off."

"Ask Monsieur Olsen to come and see me for a moment."

Michel walked to the window and gazed thoughtfully at the rain-swept quay, a passing umbrella, the vagrant gleams on the dark surface of the harbor. He was in a brown study when the door opened, and he jumped when he heard footsteps.

"Oh, it's you."

Olsen was in gray; his manner was calm and cheerful—as if nothing was the matter.

"Shut the door, please," Michel said. "Did you notice anything?"

"Where?"

"In the anteroom."

"There are five or six people waiting."

"And one of them is . . . Listen, Jean! Baillet's out there."

"The devil he is! Are you going to see him?"

"What would you advise?"

"Why didn't you have him told you were out?"

"I did."

"Or you were engaged?"

"Nothing will make him budge."

"Any idea of the mood he's in?"

"I asked Joseph. It seems he keeps looking at the time. That might mean anything."

While speaking, Michel unlocked the left-hand drawer of his desk and took out a revolver, gingerly.

"Jean, *you* see him. He has nothing against you, and you could explain much better . . ."

"Why on earth should *I* see him? What a ridiculous idea!"

"I don't see anything ridiculous about it," Michel retorted sulkily.

The trouble was that Olsen refused to take this business seriously, and wasn't in the least impressed by his brother-in-law's panic or the revolver on the table.

"Is Maman still here?"

"Yes."

In her office, directly below, every footstep in the one above could be heard, even what was being said, if the voices were at all loud. Indeed, during Oscar Donadieu's lifetime, Michel had always entered his office on tiptoe whenever he arrived late.

"Don't you understand? I'm afraid he's going to make trouble."

"That's possible. But it's no reason for not seeing him."

"Would you mind being present, anyhow, while I see him?"

"Oh, I don't mind, if you want me to. But it'll look rather silly."

"I wonder if he's armed?"

Joseph knocked at the door and announced that the gentleman was in a hurry, because of the 9:12.

"Show him in."

Michel's heart sank; nevertheless, he put the revolver back, taking care to leave the drawer slightly open. Olsen retreated to a dark corner and sat down. A moment later, the door opened and a gnomelike little man came in—his head hardly reached Michel's shoulder. He had a narrow, ferrety face and knobby hands.

"Monsieur Baillet, I believe?" said Michel.

"That's my name." The man remained standing, cap in hand.

"Sit down, please. I'm sorry to have kept you waiting, but I was exceedingly busy. I can give you only a few minutes, I'm afraid; I have an appointment with a representative of the Chamber of Commerce for—"

"I won't keep you long. I've got to be back soon, to drive the 9:12."

"Ah, yes. You're a railway engineer, I understand."

"Yes, and I've been one these thirty years. Ain't Odette never told you?"

Fumbling in his pocket, he cast his eyes around the room. On catching sight of Olsen puffing a cigarette in his corner, he frowned as if he sensed a trap. Then, very cautiously, he seated himself on the edge of the chair to which Michel had pointed.

The deeply furrowed forehead gave the impression of a man who has seen much trouble or had a hard life. When Michel made a slight movement, he gave a violent start. Abruptly, he whipped a paper out of his pocket and held it up.

"You've seen this, eh?" *The Laundry*, of course. After a few moments' silence, he went on: "This is man to man, ain't it? Your dad, he was a proper man, I've heard tell, and I reckon you maybe take after him. So I says to myself, 'We'll have a straight talk, Monsieur Donadieu and me. And if he's a man like his old dad, he'll tell me the truth.' "

In his little zone of light, Michel nodded gravely; it was going better than he'd expected. So far the engineer had kept his eyes fixed on the floor; now he looked up.

"So that's it. I've come to see you."

Michel gave a slight cough before speaking.

"That paper is a scurrilous rag, of course. . . ."

"I found it in my mailbox. I couldn't believe my eyes when I saw that about 'Odette B.'—meaning my daughter."

The two men were equally embarrassed. To hide this, Baillet took a big silver watch from his pocket and looked at the time.

"Is it true that Odette's gone to a specialist?"

Michel would have been happier if he could see his brother-in-law, but Baillet was between them.

"It's an absolute lie."

"And is all the rest a pack of lies? What they say about her being in trouble, meaning in the family way? I must say, I never noticed nothing, though we live in the same house. . . . But we don't see much of each other, 'cause I'm on night trains mostly. . . . Odette takes after her poor mother: she's tight as a clam about her own affairs."

"She's an excellent stenographer and typist."

"That don't surprise me. At the school where she was, they thought a lot of her; the head man told me she was the best student of her year."

Was the interview going to continue along these lines, merely an exchange of commonplace amenities? No. Quite suddenly, when he least expected it, Michel saw a look of suspicion come into Baillet's eyes and heard him say, though without any show of feeling:

"So that's all you got to say about it? What's written in this paper's a lot of dirty lies? My daughter ain't in trouble, or anything like that? . . . All right. Then tell me straight: where is she now?"

"Hasn't she let you know?"

"All she told me was that you gave her a thousand francs besides her pay to do a job for you, in Bordeaux."

"Yes. That's right."

"At the time, I didn't pay no attention. I'd been driving the 4:34, and she's a bitch. What's more, it was freezing pretty near all the way to Paris. . . . Why did you pick her for that Bordeaux job?"

"Because she's also my confidential secretary."

"Is it here she works?" He cast another glance around the office.

"No." Michel pointed to a door. "In that room."

"By herself?"

"Yes."

Baillet seemed to be trying to figure out the conditions under which his daughter worked, and the relationship between her and her employer.

"Well, if that's how it is," he suddenly remarked, "I'll go there myself."

"Where?"

"To Bordeaux. But I can't go right away. I've got to drive the 9:12 to Paris. Then I have forty-eight hours off. Yes, I'll go to Bordeaux, and see for myself. . . . But wait! You ain't told me where she's staying. She didn't give me her address."

"At . . . at the Hôtel de la Poste, I believe," Michel answered quickly. He vaguely remembered staying at a hotel of that name during his military service.

"Good. Then I'll know if you've been bluffing, or if you're straight. After that, I'll have a word with that there Dr. Lambe."

He picked up the paper, which had been lying on the desk, folded it in four, and put it in his pocket.

"I don't want you to make no mistake, sir. I ain't one of the goody-goody sort, and I know what girls are like nowadays. . . . Accidents will happen, as they say. Still, there's some things . . ."

His cap in one hand, he held out the other rather diffidently. Michel was almost more uncomfortable than the engineer to shake hands.

"I'll be in again one of these days and tell you how she is."

The door opened and closed. Michel remained quite still for some minutes before summoning Joseph.

"Has he gone?"

"Yes, sir."

"Are you quite sure he's left the building?"

"Well, I saw him going down the stairs."

"How did he look?"

"Like someone going away."

Michel scowled. "All right. You can go. If anyone wants to see me, say I'm out."

"There's the inspector from the gasworks. He says he has an appointment."

"Tell him I'm very sorry, but I'm not feeling well. Ask him to come again tomorrow."

At last Michel was free to turn to Olsen.

"Well, what did you make of it? Either the man's a half-wit, or . . ."

"I agree."

"What do you mean?"

"I think as you do: either he's a born fool or he's playing some deep game."

"Do you think he believed what I said?"

"It doesn't seem so, considering that he's going to Bordeaux."

"Ah, yes, Bordeaux . . . Jean, will you do me a favor? It might look odd if I went there myself. Would you mind going to Bordeaux tonight? Odette's well enough to be moved, I would say. Please take her to the Hôtel de la Poste and . . . do the necessary. You understand? She'd better say I sent her to collect statistics at the shipping office."

Looking anything but pleased, Olsen asked:

"Suppose the doctor says she can't be moved?"

"Oh, it would only be a matter of putting in an appearance at the hotel for a few hours. Once her father's seen her . . ."

He started pacing up and down, ignoring his mother's presence below. Once, without thinking, he switched on the light in Odette's little room. He gave a slight shiver; the air there seemed cold and dank.

Strictly speaking, it wasn't a separate room, but an annex to Michel's office, and this peculiarity, indeed, had been his undoing. The window was high in the wall, and the panes were of frosted glass, like all those on this side of the building. Thirty years before, Oscar Donadieu had noticed that employees were apt to waste their time gazing at the houses opposite; so he had had frosted glass put in, little dreaming . . .

A small desk with a typewriter, a file cabinet, some curtained shelves—no more than that. The notebook Odette had been using on her last day there still lay beside the typewriter.

She was no beauty; not even pretty. Unlike her father, whose smallness had been a surprise to Michel, she was exceptionally tall, one of those gawky, austere-looking young women who give an impression of relentless virtue. Though only twenty-two, she had already lost her youthful freshness, and looked ten years older; perhaps as a result of working in his cell-like little room, she had a gray, washed-out complexion.

But even so, it had happened, though so slowly as to be almost imperceptible. It was at this hour, five o'clock, when the lights had been turned on, and over each desk in the Donadieu building a head was bent, aureoled by the yellow glow of a green-shaded lamp, that it had begun.

"Mademoiselle Odette," Michel had called.

He dictated some letters, which she took down in shorthand, standing beside his desk. She had always refused to sit down in her employer's office. Another incidental cause, perhaps!

". . . and we propose in the near future to undertake the manufacture and sale of . . . of . . . Let me hear what went before, please."

He had been walking up and down, but stopped behind her, as if to see what she'd written, though he could not read shorthand. As he bent forward, his shoulder brushed hers.

That was the first of several successive phases, each of which lasted for weeks. During the second phase, he remained seated, but moved his chair close to Odette and gently stroked her hip. She went on working, as if unaware of this. Then one evening, when his caresses became slightly bolder, she looked around and said, rather weakly:

"No . . . Please don't . . ."

He hardly gave a thought to her in the daytime. Only when night was falling and the lights went on did a craving he could not resist come over him suddenly.

"Mademoiselle Odette! I have some letters to dictate."

On one occasion they were all but caught by Joseph. Michel had pushed his chair back only just in time.

At last an evening came when, greatly daring, he walked into the little room off his office, where she was typing letters.

"Show me that last letter, please. There are some changes."

She was seated at her typewriter, and he was standing behind her. He had only to bend forward to have her in his arms.

"Careful!"

"Why?"

She pointed to the frosted window, on which their outlines could be seen from outside, like figures in a shadow play. . . . So she consented! So . . .

The next evening, he placed the lamp between them and the window, so their shadows wouldn't show. She tried to free herself.

"Please, Monsieur Michel . . . You mustn't do that."

"Why not?"

"Suppose your wife . . ."

But really she was easy game. Presently he returned to his office, and stood for some minutes by the window, calming down and running a comb through his hair. From that moment until the same hour the next evening, he almost hated her, and saw as little of her as possible, addressing her with involuntary curtness.

On one evening only had there been a departure from this ritual. A big stock of jute was being sold in Niort, where a firm of importers was being liquidated. The Donadieus used large quantities of jute for their coal sacks. So Michel had the idea of taking Odette with him in his car, on the pretext that her services were needed.

On the return journey, he had driven with one hand and fondled her with the other. Yielding to an uncontrollable uprush of desire, he had turned off the main road, driven to Papelet's château, and asked for a room. Odette had been nervous and on the brink of tears. But after he had persuaded her to drink two glasses of port, her scruples were dust before the wind. . . . "Accidents will happen," as old Baillet had observed. Was it then that the accident had happened?

"What am I to tell my wife?" Olsen asked peevishly.

"Oh, you can think up some story, can't you?"

"What if Odette refuses to come with me?"

"She won't. She'll realize it's in her interest as much as ours."

"I'd better give her some money, hadn't I?"

"Yes . . . Not too much, though. It might look suspicious if it came out."

"How much?"

"Let's see. . . . Two thousand francs."

"Shall I take it from petty cash? What shall I make the voucher out for? . . . Ssh! Your mother's coming."

The tapping of her cane on the stairs was a blessing; it always gave warning of her approach.

"What have you two been up to?" she asked Michel. "I could hear you walking back and forth."

"Oh, nothing important. We've been discussing a . . . a contract."

Perhaps some instinct told her he was lying. She looked around the room suspiciously, and even seemed to sniff the air.

"I have something to tell you, Michel."

"At the moment, I'm . . ."

"Of course! Whenever I want to talk to you, you're up to your eyes in work. But this time you won't put me off. . . . Frédéric's just been to see me."

"Here?"

"Why shouldn't he come here? He's had another letter from Philippe, who's doing very well in Paris. He even sent a thousand francs for his father to give to the man who owns the garage where he worked—an installment on the car he took. In my opinion, that's a very good sign."

"It would have been a better sign if he hadn't taken the car at all."

"Don't be tiresome!"

Michel turned to Olsen.

"That's settled, then. I can count on you?"

"All right . . . As you say, it's necessary."

Michel sat down again, facing his mother with his usual sulky look.

"We'll have to come to a decision sooner or later," she said, "and the longer we put it off, the worse it will be for us. People are beginning to suspect something. It's all very well our saying that Martine's gone to Paris to study art. But—a Donadieu studying art? You must admit it doesn't sound convincing."

She said "a Donadieu" almost as if she were not one of the family. Indeed, half unconsciously, she drew distinctions. For her, Michel, especially, typified the essential Donadieu, and so, of course, did Marthe; Olsen, too, though an outsider, almost qualified to rank with them, so precisely had he fallen into line.

Eva was definitely no Donadieu. But, though Mme Donadieu had no great liking for her, she had to recognize her independence and originality. Eva was, in fact, a foreign body in the household, her exoticism symbolized by her pseudo-Oriental boudoir, with its black curtains and aggressively nonbourgeois atmosphere.

One couldn't be sure about Kiki yet. He had Donadieu phases, but others, too; sometimes he had the Donadieu look in his eyes, and sometimes a very different one, which worried his mother.

"We must," she concluded, "put our heads together and settle it one way or the other. If necessary, I'll ask her guardian to come and give us his views."

"I don't see the need for all this haste."

"That's because you don't know . . . I happen to be better posted on the facts than you are. Philippe writes regularly to his father, and Frédéric—I must say it's very good of him—lets me see the letters."

"Written, no doubt," sneered Michel, "with the idea that you should see them."

"I don't agree. But, even if you're right, it makes no difference. None of you knows the first thing about Philippe. He went to Paris without a penny in his pocket, and with a girl on his hands, and he's made good without help from anyone. In fact, he can get on quite well without us."

"So can we, without him."

Michel had almost forgotten about Odette, and Olsen's errand. Hearing the car start, he moved nervously in his chair; he would have preferred Olsen to take the train.

"What's the matter?" his mother asked.

"Nothing."

"That was Jean, wasn't it? Where is he going?"

"To Bordeaux. He's meeting an Italian importer there tonight."

His mother looked at him for a moment before returning to her subject.

"As I was saying, we can't go on ignoring Martine's existence. And the longer we wait, the worse . . . I mean, the greater the risk of a scandal. In his last letter, Philippe said quite clearly that he thought there was a baby on the way."

Michel's shoulders sagged. That last remark had made him crumple completely. He felt incapable of standing up to his mother. If only Olsen were already back, with news from Bordeaux!

"Well, Maman," he began, then fell silent.

"So that's settled," she said briskly, getting up. "I'll write tomorrow to her guardian. We'll see what he has to say."

"Very well."

He closed the door behind her, but it opened again at once.

"There's still three people waiting," Joseph announced.

"What do they want?"

"Two want jobs as agents for the briquets. The other one . . ." He paused.

"Well, get it out, man!"

"I think he's an insurance agent. He says . . ."

"Tell him I've left."

"But they must have seen you when I came in."

"Say I've left by another door."

His mind was in chaos. He felt like weeping, but the tears wouldn't come. And he was tired, dog-tired.

After lingering in his office till the anteroom was empty, Michel went straight home. Through a ground-floor window, he glimpsed Kiki and his tutor playing Ping-Pong on the dining-room table.

The staircase was in darkness. He could hear a child whimpering: his daughter, Evette. As he entered his own apartment, he noticed the smell of Turkish cigarettes, and had noticed Frédéric's coat and hat in the hall. He was about to walk past the open door of his wife's boudoir, when he heard her calling him.

"Yes, I'm back. What do you want?"

"Come here a moment, please."

He found them, as usual, sitting on cushions on the floor.

"Good evening, Frédéric," he mumbled.

"Do sit down," said his wife. "I called Frédéric and asked him to come and tell us what he'd do if he were in your position."

He had his mother's gift of intuition, and had known before entering the room that something disagreeable was in store.

"Why *my* position?"

"You know quite well why." She pushed toward him with her foot a folded copy of *The Laundry*.

Her sandaled feet were bare, the toenails painted scarlet. As usual, she, too, was puffing a cigarette, and a blue smoke cloud coiled above their heads. The light was even dimmer than in the office on Quai Vallin. In one corner squatted Eva's latest exotica, a fat bronze Buddha, around which, to amuse herself, she had installed a little shrine, complete with offerings and joss sticks.

"There's no need to look so glum," she continued. "I'm not going to scold you. But I suppose you realize this business might land you in a lot of trouble. What do you propose to do about it? . . . Nothing, evidently!"

He scowled at Frédéric. Why must they drag this fellow into all the family affairs?

"Does my sister know?" he asked.

"Marthe? Yes, she knows. In fact, it was she who brought me the paper. She doesn't want your mother to see it. She told me to let her know the moment you came back."

"What does *she* want?"

"We must agree on how much to offer. . . . I suppose it's a question of money. Don't you agree, Frédéric?"

"In my opinion, the first step to take is to make sure the girl isn't made to undergo a risky operation."

Michel winced. That was the one thing he didn't want to be reminded of. He pulled himself together.

"Oh, it's not so bad as all that."

"Shall I call Marthe?" his wife asked. "She must have heard you come in."

Eva's method of summoning her sister-in-law was peculiar. All she did was rap the radiator with her knuckles; the pipes communicated her message to the room upstairs.

When Marthe joined them, she sniffed disgustedly.

"What a smell! Let's go up to my room."

Upstairs, the atmosphere was always crystal-clear, and decorum reigned.

"No, I'd rather stay here," said Eva. Though it was six in the evening, she had little on under her kimono, and the mere thought of going up the drafty staircase made her shudder.

Marthe, consenting with bad grace, went to the dining room to get a chair, a real chair.

"Well, Michel, what are you going to do about it?"

Deliberately, she ignored Frédéric, of whom she disapproved on principle. Now particularly all the Donadieu instincts in her were in revolt against the presence of an outsider.

"Where's Jean?"

"He's gone to Bordeaux. It would take too long to explain. Odette's father came to the office this afternoon."

"Did you see him?"

"Yes. He's going to look her up tomorrow, he said. I told him she was at the Hôtel de la Poste, and that I'd sent her there to do a job for the firm."

"He's a Breton," Frédéric put in.

"Well, what if he is?"

"Oh, nothing . . . But I happen to know the man, and, as I said, he's a Breton."

Marthe shrugged impatiently, while Michel, who had no experience of Bretons and their proverbial tenacity, tried in vain to guess the point of Frédéric's interjection.

"He's an engineer on night trains," Michel explained. "I gather it's really that swine Lambe he's got his knife into."

Frédéric put in another remark.

"For the moment, yes. But once he's had a talk with Lambe, he'll have it into someone else."

"Can't you keep your mouth shut?" Marthe exclaimed irritably.

"I'll keep it shut after I've said one thing more: there's someone here who's within an ace of being hauled up before the public prosecutor."

Marthe could contain herself no longer.

"And there's someone else here who's been within an ace of getting jailed for the last five years."

"Thanks for the kind reminder." Frédéric bowed ironically and got up.

"No, don't go!" begged Eva. Looking at the others, she added:

"Don't you realize he's the only one who can advise us what to do? If only Marthe would get off her high horse . . ."

"Perhaps you'd rather I leave?" suggested Marthe with a sour look at her sister-in-law.

Michel hardly heard what was being said; he felt like an inexpert swimmer who has ventured out of his depth and is groping for a foothold on the beach. Once more he pulled himself together.

"Now let *me* speak, for a change. I've done everything possible, to the best of my belief. This afternoon I announced my resignation from the monument committee. That's what Lambe was after, isn't it? And I will not be a candidate at the next election, however good my chances. As for the girl . . ."

Eva didn't show a trace of jealousy; indeed, she was looking at her husband with new interest, surprised that he had it in him to embark on such an adventure.

"It's a matter of money," he continued. "I'll be able to deal with her easily enough."

"Unless she dies," Frédéric put in.

"What then?"

"There'll be an inquest."

"That can't be helped. . . . Anyhow, it was her idea, not mine."

"What idea?" asked Marthe.

"The idea of . . . of getting rid of it. She told me she knew where to go, and everything would be all right."

While he was speaking, they had heard the sound of the front door opening. Mme Donadieu's cane was now tapping on the stairs. Presently her voice, whose piercing tone had always vexed her husband, said:

"Good! I see you're coming to your senses. Well, what have you decided? Fetch me a chair, Frédéric."

There was a short silence. Mme Donadieu, who was out of breath, sank heavily into the armchair.

"My view is this. The sooner we get them married, the less trouble all around. And I'd have you know that Frédéric hasn't tried to talk me into this. Quite the contrary . . . Isn't that so, Eva?"

"That's so," murmured Eva, whose thoughts were elsewhere.

"Well then?" Mme Donadieu was struck by the gloomy looks of the others, and wondered what the reason could be. "All right, if you are going to take it like that, I have a little surprise for some of you. Go and get my marriage certificate, someone, and Michel's birth certificate. I'll ask you to compare the dates. You'll notice . . ."

"Maman! Stop!" cried Michel, jumping to his feet.

"I will, if you'll explain. . . ."

"Don't say any more, Maman. Or at least wait until we're alone."

"Don't be absurd! Do you imagine Frédéric doesn't know?"

"Stop, I tell you!" Michel's voice rose to a scream, and he stamped his foot. He seemed to be on the brink of hysterics.

10

No single person could claim to know the whole story, from start to finish, and of those who knew fragments of the truth, many thought fit to keep these to themselves. Moreover, as in most cases of the kind, these people were not acquainted with each other, so there was no question of pooling their information.

There was no agreement, even on the weather. If questioned, some would have told you, "It was raining, a real deluge," and others, "It was a moonlight night, and freezing hard."

Both would have been referring to the same night: the night that followed Baillet's visit to Michel. Soon after the engineer left La Rochelle, the light drizzle changed abruptly to a downpour; people in the street took to their heels, and got home drenched to the skin.

But at the same hour, for Baillet, it was a clear night. On leaving Niort, he saw a full moon riding low in a pale wintry sky, and frost flowers began to form on the windows of the train.

He was at his post, one arm resting on the steel rim of the engine's cab, peering ahead through the small circular lookout window, watching for the signals, while his fireman swung his shovel behind him.

Miles and miles of rails in glimmering recession, flanked by silvery seas of meadows and black scarps of woodlands; a clangor of dark iron as the train crossed the Loire; at each stop a self-important stationmaster fussing up and down the train . . .

Olsen did not reach the clinic, which was on the outskirts of Bordeaux, until ten o'clock and, had he not seen some lights still on in the building, would probably have postponed his visit to the next morning. He had thought it wiser not to take the chauffeur, and his left arm and shoulder were soaked through, from the rain driven around the windshield.

Here, as in La Rochelle, it was raining heavily. The outer gate was locked, and Olsen was kept waiting in the downpour for five minutes.

To add to his distress, a large dog just inside the railings growled savagely at him.

There was nothing of a hospital about the place, no rows of beds in white-walled wards, no uniformed nurses, no stretchers on rubber-tired wheels to convey patients to the operating room. It was more like a rest home—for the kind of rest Odette needed.

A man with a small pointed beard opened the door and led Olsen into a vestibule, from which he had a glimpse of three people at a bridge table in a dingy-looking dining room. Two of the three were young women, and for a moment he wondered if one might be Odette.

"This way, please."

The bearded man was the doctor. He showed Olsen into his consulting room. Raindrops sparkled on his beard, since he had had to cross a strip of garden to open the front gate. Olsen explained his errand in as few words as he could, adding:

"You understand the position, I hope? It's most desirable that tomorrow, when her father comes to Bordeaux, he should find her at a hotel."

At first the doctor hemmed and hawed—to make his visitor appreciate his importance. After tugging at his pepper-and-salt beard, he rose heavily to his feet and said:

"Under these circumstances, I have no objection. Perhaps you would prefer that *I* talk to her?"

"That would make things easier. You're used to handling such situations, of course."

After leaving the room, the doctor returned almost immediately, to Olsen's surprise. Looking at him hard, he said:

"There's one point we overlooked. Suppose that, for some reason, she doesn't return here? . . ." Seeing that Olsen had not grasped his meaning, he added: "It would be best to settle the account at once, I think. I'll make out the bill."

This he proceeded to do, with painstaking deliberation, carefully figuring out how much to write for each item. Meanwhile, Olsen supposed, the three women at the bridge table were still waiting for him, to resume the game; Odette must be already in bed, perhaps asleep.

"You will not require a stamped receipt, I take it?"

A good thing, Olsen thought, that I brought a large sum of money with me. I wouldn't want to give this fellow a check.

The doctor went out to get Odette, and was gone for a quarter of an hour. As Olsen had noticed, he did everything with exasperating slowness. And he was quite capable of having stopped on his way, to finish the bridge hand. At last the door opened, and Olsen saw the doctor standing in the dimly lighted corridor.

"Here's Mademoiselle Odette. She is quite agreeable to going with you."

In the dim light, Olsen had a glimpse of a tall, gaunt young woman in a black coat, with a very pale face and expressionless gray eyes. She greeted him rather shyly.

"I must apologize, mademoiselle," Olsen began, "but—"

"I've explained," the doctor interrupted, and shepherded them to the door, obviously wanting to get back to his bridge game.

When they were at the gate, Olsen asked:

"Would you rather sit in back, or beside me?"

She chose to sit beside him and, to make conversation, said:

"Has it been raining like this for long?"

"All the way from La Rochelle . . . Were you in bed?"

"Yes, but I hadn't gone to sleep."

"Don't you play bridge?"

"No."

Bordeaux at last! He knew the city well, but invariably lost his way when entering it, and found his bearings only near the center. The Hôtel de la Poste, he discovered, was nowhere near the Central Post Office, but in a side street behind the Opera House, flanked by small cabarets with photographs of half-naked girls outside.

"Michel"—yes, surely, with her, there was no need to call him Monsieur Donadieu—"suggested that you'd better tell your father you were sent here to collect statistics at the shipping office."

"Yes, that would sound all right. Anyhow, I won't have any trouble with Father."

"Sure you're not feeling too tired?" He was haunted by the fear that she might faint or be taken ill.

"No. I'm much stronger now. Will I have to stay here long?"

"He'll let you know when to come back."

"Suppose Father asks the hotel people how long I've been there?"

Olsen shrugged. There were bound to be some risks, but he'd done all he could. At the hotel, he was about to get out and ring the bell, when Odette discovered the night porter and went to talk to him. Evidently she explained things satisfactorily, for soon the door closed behind them.

He didn't feel like facing the hundred-and-sixteen-mile journey back to La Rochelle, and he was extremely hungry. So, after a belated dinner at a brasserie, he drove to a hotel he knew in the center of the city and slept the night there.

Baillet reached Paris at midnight. He prowled around the dimly lighted station for half an hour before discovering a freight train leaving for Bordeaux. On seeing his uniform, the guard cleared a place for him among a stack of fish boxes, and even offered him a cigarette.

This took place at the Montparnasse terminus. In the Montparnasse district at the same hour, Martine was sitting opposite a fair young man, while Philippe, beside her, chatted with a small, anemic-looking young woman. They were in a cabaret and were drinking champagne.

The two couples had become friends, and Martine had already danced twice with Albert Grindorge, the fair young man. Mme Grindorge, who seldom went out at night, was wearing an ill-fitting dress of gold lamé. Philippe had danced with her.

For them, too, this evening was a kind of climax, the outcome of a sequence of trivial events, which none of them could have recapitulated in full. Martine could have said something about the early stages, her gradual discovery of the shops in this part of Paris—of one, especially, that provided ready-cooked dishes that she found delicious. But oftener than not, no sooner had she prepared a little dinner in their room than the telephone rang.

"That you, dear? Take a taxi and meet me at Etoile. We're eating out." Sometimes it wasn't Philippe who called her. "Monsieur Dargens wants you to meet him at La Chope, on Rue Montmartre," a voice would say.

She would go there and find Philippe with a group of people she had never seen before, to whom he introduced her as his wife. While they ate, the men talked business, a different kind of business every time.

In the afternoon, sometimes, Philippe sent her to a cinema, where he joined her later, after telling her to leave a message at the box office to say where she was sitting.

Arm in arm they walked home down the brilliantly lighted streets, and Philippe, who hadn't the slightest domestic instinct, always found a pretext for lingering on the way. Either he wanted a drink or he was famished; or he would insist on stopping at some American bar, where he hoped to meet a fellow who might be useful. In fact, he seemed to have a horror of returning to their apartment.

Martine enjoyed this life. It was never dull, for one thing. In fact, it was more like a game they were playing. Nothing they did seemed to matter in the least, and she had no idea that the last month's rent had not been paid. . . .

Then came that memorable evening when Philippe said to her:

"I want you to buy a new dress, something really chic. I have a friend in one of the big stores who'll lend you a fur coat. We have a very important lunch tomorrow."

It was their first lunch with the Grindorges. Martine felt ill at ease the whole time because of the fur coat that didn't belong to her, and about which Mme Grindorge had commented admiringly.

The Grindorges were an amiable, rather naïve couple. The man showed his admiration for Philippe; indeed, there was something of a schoolboy's hero worship in his attitude. And Mme Grindorge was equally impressed by Martine. "Oh, my dear, how clever you are!" she kept exclaiming at everything Martine said or did.

Yet Grindorge was no provincial; he was the son of a successful Paris businessman who had recently retired, after making a fortune of many millions of francs.

Philippe had had the luck of appearing on the scene just after young Grindorge had stepped into his mother's estate. Twenty-four hours after that meeting, they had agreed to join forces in a business venture, Grindorge putting up the first hundred thousand francs of capital required. By the beginning of January, they had their own workshop and a staff consisting of a typist and half a dozen white-aproned girls, who spent most of their time wrapping bulky packages. Their firm was named P.E.M.

"What does it stand for?" Martine had asked.

"Absolutely nothing!" Philippe chuckled. "That's the whole point—to keep 'em guessing!"

P.E.M. imported phonograph motors from Czechoslovakia, and had fake-mahogany cases made at a joinery on Rue Saint-Antoine. The management included a clever young Russian, known as Monsieur Ivan—or, for the benefit of outsiders, as "our engineering expert"—under whose supervision the girls rapidly assembled the phonographs and packed them in cartons for delivery.

The company's advertisement read: "A Super Phonograph for the absurdly low price of two hundred and twenty-five francs! This unique offer, which is made to launch our new phonograph, is for a strictly limited period, after which the price will be considerably higher."

The phonographs cost the firm about eighty francs apiece, and young Grindorge, who previously had lost money on everything he set his hand to, was staggered by the orders pouring in with every mail. One day he had a twinge of conscience about the articles they were selling.

"Are you sure they work all right?" he asked Philippe.

"Oh, they run quite well for a month or two. Then they break down, of course. But that doesn't matter. When we've sold ten thousand, we'll switch to something else."

The two couples spent their evenings together. Grindorge was greatly smitten with Martine, but too shy to make advances. One evening, when they were dancing together, he asked, with a blush:

"I hope this doesn't tire you too much?"

"Not at all. Why should it?"

"Oh! I thought . . . dancing might not be good for you right now."

Philippe had spread the news that his wife was going to have a baby—though nothing was less certain.

Blushing still more deeply, Grindorge went on:

"My wife, you know, had such an awful time with our first."

There were now two children in their pleasant little apartment in Neuilly.

As soon as Philippe had some cash, he sent a thousand francs to his former employer, through his father, as a payment on account for the car he had taken. But he left even Frédéric in ignorance of his address in Paris.

If you have any urgent reason to communicate with me [he wrote], put a "Personal" in the *Petit Parisien*. "Frédéric wants to get in touch with Philippe," or something like that. For the moment, I'm up to my ears in work—fifteen hours a day!—because I have to do everything myself.

Baillet, the engineer, was sleeping in a freight car reeking of fish. A draft played on the nape of his neck, and sometimes, in his sleep, he ran his hand across it, as if to flick away a fly. He recognized each station by its sound, and half woke at each stop, only to relapse again into heavy sleep.

On Saturday, they got up at different times. Philippe, though he had gone to bed in the small hours, left for the workshop at eight. Martine opened a sleepy eye, and promptly dozed off again. There was bright sunshine, but the air was cold, and Philippe had trouble getting his car to start. As he did every morning at work, he ran his eyes down the "Personal" column of the *Petit Parisien*. There was nothing for him. . . .

In La Rochelle it was still raining, and the sky was so overcast that Michel could hardly see his face in the mirror hung on the window latch. Once again he thought that he really must get a shaving mirror with an electric light, like the ones he'd seen in a large store, but always put off buying.

He was knotting his tie when the telephone rang. The call was from Olsen, still in Bordeaux, to announce that all was well and he was just starting back.

Eva came in while her husband was on the telephone, and asked, without much interest:

"Who is it?"

"Jean. He's fixed it up, thank goodness."

She was still half-asleep, her cheeks moist, her limbs languid. With a low sigh, she raised her hands to settle her dark-brown hair.

"I must say you're a disgusting lot," she murmured.

Michel dropped his eyes, conscious that this was only too true. But that didn't prevent him from eating two poached eggs, toast, and marmalade. He had spent some years in England, and affected English ways. He could hear his little daughter whimpering in the nursery. His small son was splashing in his bath.

He put on his raincoat, chose one of his oldest hats, and walked, his hands thrust deep in his pockets, to Quai Vallin. As usual, he first entered the first room on the left, where the mail was sorted.

Mme Donadieu arrived rather late, because she had spent some time scolding Edmond, Kiki's tutor. Once again she had caught them attempting absurd gymnastic feats in the morning room.

"I won't have you doing circus tricks like that in the house. Do you understand? We engaged you as a tutor, not an acrobat."

It was hard on Edmond, who was boyishly proud of showing off his muscular development. After all, he looked far from robust, and in early youth had been thought to be consumptive.

"Watch!" he would say to Kiki, and proceed to do some prodigy of equilibrium. "Now suppose you're being attacked. It doesn't matter how much stronger the other fellow is—this is the position to take. It's a jujitsu stance, really."

Now Kiki could think of nothing but jujitsu, chest measurements, circles on the horizontal bars. Clenching his teeth and perspiring freely, he worked to emulate his instructor's feats.

"Why not have an iron bar clamped to this wall?"

In fact, they had plans to convert the morning room into a fully equipped gymnasium—until Mme Donadieu put her foot down. But the only effect of her embargo was a transfer of the scene of their activities to a damp, secluded corner of the garden.

A bumper haul—four thousand hake—and, unfortunately, Olsen, who should have been in charge at this point, was not there. On the quay, men in sea boots were floundering in pools of brine as they packed the fish into crates streaming greenish water from melting ice. The sea was neither rough nor smooth; gray, edged with white, it merged into the lowering sky.

The freight car was held up for nearly an hour at Poitiers. But Baillet, who was awake, managed to slip across to the Bordeaux express and settle down in an empty first-class compartment. He was soaked through and reeked of fish.

In Bordeaux, Odette was doing her daily regimen as best she could, unaided; this was difficult in a hotel, because she didn't want to attract attention. At nine, she went downstairs and strolled around the lobby until she saw the manager alone in her office.

"I have something to ask you, madame. If my father comes to see me, would you be kind enough to say I've been staying here for some days?"

She looked so pathetic that the grim-faced woman in black finally consented.

"Will you be staying long?"

"Quite likely. I find your hotel so clean and comfortable."

After that, she went to a stationery shop, bought pencils, shorthand notebooks, and files, which on her return she spread out on her bedroom table, to give the impression she used the room to work in. But she moved slowly, as if she didn't care. . . .

Her father arrived just as she was sitting down for lunch. They were like strangers, with little in common except that they lived in the same house—a cottage on L'Homeau Road, with a green fence and a small front garden planted with marguerites and marigolds. Odette's mother had met her death fifteen years before, in an ironic way—by catching pneumonia at a neighbor's funeral.

As a rule, Baillet was on duty when others slept, and went to bed when others started their day, with the result that he and his daughter rarely met. He had glimpses of her leaving for the office, or coming back and settling down to do typing for a local lawyer who was writing a history of La Rochelle.

Though not overawed by her in any sense, he couldn't help being conscious of the gulf between himself and this well-educated, neatly dressed girl. She lived in a different world, was almost a young "lady." And one day she'd told him she had seven thousand francs in the savings bank.

What perhaps impressed Baillet most was that a cleaning woman was never needed; their house was the best kept on their street. His daughter's efficiency amazed him; he had no idea when she got up, but he could enter any room at any hour of the day and always find it spotlessly clean. The windows were washed every week, the floors were always glossy with beeswax, the kitchen stove as clean as if unused. Yet she never seemed to hurry; he had never caught her with her hair untidy, or perspiration on her face.

As for talking to her—well, for that they'd have needed to be more used to each other. On entering the hotel in his shabby blue suit, with the little bag containing his work clothes in his hand, he found he'd forgotten all he'd meant to say.

He saw her sitting by herself at a small table in a corner of the dining room.

"I'm in Bordeaux by chance. So I thought I'd look you up."

"Stay and have lunch with me," she suggested.

Baillet looked so ill at ease when the waiter came and stood beside him, pencil in hand, that Odette gave the order, selecting things she knew her father liked.

"Nice here?" he asked vaguely.

"Well, I'm here to work, you know." She lowered her eyes.

"Yes, you're collecting . . ." He floundered for the word, and was grateful when his daughter helped him out.

"I'm collecting statistics at the shipping office."

"Is it . . . far from here?"

"On Quai des Chartres."

It had been on the tip of his tongue to ask the meaning of that word "statistics," but he changed his mind. With one of his fellow railwaymen, he wouldn't have hesitated. But somehow he did not like admitting his ignorance to his daughter.

"You ain't looking too fit. Feeling seedy?"

"No. I'm quite all right. I've never had much color, you know. I take after Maman."

It lasted an hour. He tried to throw out hints, and once, watching her from the corner of an eye, remarked:

"There's one trouble when you're away; it's about the . . . the laundry . . . the washing, I mean."

Would she understand his meaning?

But Odette replied, quite naturally:

"Doesn't Madame Bourrat come to do it for you?"

Without realizing it, he overate and drank too much.

"Eh, well, I'd best be off." He rose ponderously and gazed at his daughter, frowning slightly.

It was difficult to guess his state of mind. Clearly he didn't *know*, but something, a germ of mistrust, had taken root in his slow-moving brain.

Michel had invited Olsen to lunch so they could have a talk. Eva pretended not to be listening to what they said, and left the room when dessert was served.

"Well? What exactly did she say?" Michel asked eagerly.

"Nothing. She seems to have no ideas of her own. She just does as she's told."

"She didn't—er—say anything against me?"

"No. She struck me as being very much run down, almost too weak to talk. . . . How's your wife taking it?"

Michel shrugged. What had happened hadn't changed things much between them. The breach had taken place two years before, exactly a fortnight after Evette's birth. They had engaged a young girl as nursemaid, and one day Eva had caught Michel with her in a dark corner of the hall. All she had said was:

"You should be more careful. Jean might have seen you."

That night she'd slept in another bedroom, and after that they'd always slept apart. This was one of the reasons Michel sometimes frowned when he found Frédéric in his wife's boudoir. What could he do about it? An altercation would have served no purpose—and anyhow, he wasn't really sure if he felt jealous.

"I hear there was a great commotion, almost a fight, at the fish market this morning, over the large amount of hake that came in.

137

Something about a change in the way the auction was conducted. Camboulives says he'd fixed it up with you, but . . ."

As usual, they were back in the office by two: Mme Donadieu, Olsen, Michel. It was the hour of Kiki's geography lesson, and while he laboriously sketched a map of France, Edmond made notes for the thesis he had to submit in a few months' time. In the next house, Mme Brun was writing a long letter to her daughter, who had gone to the Tyrol for the winter sports.

> I am beginning to suspect that Charlotte has a secret. It's too absurd for words! As our esteemed ancestor Mme de Sévigné might have written, it's something that outsoars one's wildest fancy. I really think, in fact I'm positive, that Charlotte is—in love!!
>
> But with whom? That's what I'm trying to discover. The trouble is, she's diabolically cunning. I've found her in tears a dozen times, and each time she's had the presence of mind to think up an explanation. . . .

"Now listen, Joseph," Michel was saying. "If that fellow Baillet comes again, tell him it's absolutely impossible for me to see him."

Though he did not voice his thought, it struck him that, in view of the dangers of the situation, perhaps Joseph should be given a weapon of some kind. "We'll see about that later," he murmured to himself. Then he rang for the bookkeeper, with whom he remained closeted for an hour, engrossed in work.

Baillet had to make two changes on his return journey, and it was quite dark when he reached La Rochelle. He had six hours before he went on duty again. He crossed the city on foot, and on reaching his cottage fished the door key out of the flowerpot in which he always hid it when he went out. When he opened the door, he saw at least a dozen copies of *The Laundry*, which had been pushed through his mailbox, lying on the floor. These were only the overflow; the mailbox was filled to the brim with copies of the paper.

No one actually saw him return, since all the neighbors were at supper. And a man on a bicycle who'd ridden past the cottage noticed nothing unusual.

At the Café de la Paix on Place d'Armes, a game of *belote* had been dragging on for half an hour, and one of the players, a man who owned a wallpaper shop, remarked irritably as he drank his third Pernod:

138

"Won't this damned game ever finish? My wife will give me hell when I get back!"

Standing nearby, a napkin under his arm, a waiter was watching the game, only with great difficulty restraining himself from pointing out the players' mistakes.

Two trawlers, one flying the Donadieu flag, the other Varin's, were exchanging blasts of their horns, as each tried to reach the fairway first.

In Paris, Martine was alone, trying out records she'd bought with a thirty percent discount, because of P.E.M., on the phonograph. She was waiting for Philippe, who was due back any minute. . . .

Subsequently, medical experts were to fix the time it happened as approximately 7:30. So far, the only definite clue was that the victim's stomach was empty. But when did he usually eat? No one seemed to know. After his cleaning woman left, he had his house to himself, and none of the neighbors knew much about his habits.

In fact, the police found them singularly unhelpful. Asked if they hadn't heard the doctor's bell ring, they looked blank. True, one old woman said, yes, she'd heard a ring; but, because she fixed the time at 5:00 or thereabouts, that didn't help.

The one established fact was that, during the time when most of the inhabitants of La Rochelle were eating dinner, and the rain was lessening, a scene of the utmost savagery had taken place in Dr. Lambe's hallway.

In the hallway, not in his consulting room. His visitor hadn't waited to be shown into it. The moment the front door closed behind him, he had struck the doctor, from behind, most probably, with a heavy hammer. Thirty-one distinct hammer blows could be counted, but there might have been more.

When the cleaning woman came at 7:00 the next morning, the hall was a shambles. Fragments of brain were spattered on the walls. Because it was Sunday morning, the discovery attracted less attention locally; most people were at early Mass, or enjoying a late morning in bed. And, in spite of the bad weather, a fair number of people had gone to the country for a day's hunting, among them the adult male members of the Donadieu family.

Dr. Lambe had always been unpopular; there was something sinister about him. Yet, though he died unregretted, no one could help being shocked by the brutality of his end.

Michel and Olsen heard the news at noon, when they got back to the château at Esnandes. Baptiste, who had been with them, kept casting surly glances at Michel, who had been shooting abominably, missing pheasants that had risen almost under his nose.

"Three rabbits—that's the morning's bag!" he announced scornfully to his wife, who was busy in the kitchen.

She had a message from the house for Michel.

"Madame Donadieu wants you to return immediately."

At first, Michel supposed she meant his mother, and he had a qualm of fear. However, on questioning Mme Maclou, he learned that the call was from his wife.

They had the big blue car, as usual; Olsen drove. Unknowing, they passed the cottage where Baillet lived.

He had not appeared for duty at the railway yards, and a substitute had to be found. The train he should have driven left on time. Still, the railway officials thought it best to notify the police.

It was almost certainly on purpose that Frédéric had persuaded Mme Donadieu to have a game of chess with him in the ground-floor living room. When she saw the men returning, she merely remarked:

"I suppose there wasn't anything to shoot. The poachers have been very busy lately."

At three o'clock, Eva appeared in the doorway.

"Could you come up for a moment, Frédéric?"

"What is it?" There was a shade of anxiety in Mme Donadieu's voice.

"Oh, nothing really . . . Michel wants to have a word with Frédéric; that's all."

Upstairs, Frédéric found the two men and Marthe waiting for him.

"What do you make of it? . . . You've heard what's happened?"

"About Dr. Lambe? Yes. The police are looking for that engineer, Baillet. He's not been seen since last evening."

"It was he who did it, of course," Marthe put in emphatically.

"I suppose so. That, anyway, is what the superintendent at the Central Police Station thinks. I had a talk with him this morning."

"Did he say anything about us? I mean, about my brother?"

"No. So far, your brother's not involved."

"What would you do, in our position?" This time it was Marthe who asked the question.

"I? Nothing."

Eva had taken on herself the task of keeping Mme Donadieu company downstairs and diverting her attention.

"People are beginning to talk about Martine," she was saying. "They're wondering what the truth is about her absence."

Soon after, there was a series of conversations, on one floor or another; sometimes by twos, sometimes by threes, and at least one almost-complete gathering of the senior members of the family.

Meanwhile, Kiki and his tutor were at a soccer final, because of which there were only about a hundred people in the Alhambra that afternoon.

Nerves were so frayed that Marthe actually shed tears, and Michel shut himself in his room, threatening to "go off the deep end" if he wasn't left in peace.

"My view is"—Marthe had dried her tears and was speaking in her usual rather peremptory voice—"that it's high time for Martine to come back. We can't afford to leave any loophole for suspicion, considering how things stand with us."

Oddly enough, it was Frédéric who demurred.

"Really, I don't see what you can have against it." Marthe seemed quite annoyed. "Do you think Martine isn't a good enough match for Philippe?"

Frédéric gave way finally, when, at about 8:00, they were having a makeshift meal of sandwiches.

"Do you know his address? . . . Oh, of course you must, since he writes to you."

"I don't know his address. But I'll communicate with him." And from the Donadieus' he called the *Petit Parisien* office.

"Frédéric wishes to get in touch with Philippe."

The "young couple," as their friends called them, were dining with the Grindorges at a restaurant.

Police in the whole area around La Rochelle were on the alert that night.

II

SAINT-RAPHAËL

11

What always happened at 10:00 was as stereotyped as the behavior shown in a type of insanity well known to psychiatrists. The sufferer, having experienced once an erotic thrill he'd never known before, returns at stated periods—as for an anniversary—to the same place of bought illusions, hoping to regain that first rapture. He insists on the reproduction of all the circumstances, down to the least word or gesture, of that unique experience.

At 10:00 in the evening, the third and last rubber of bridge at the Brasserie de l'Univers was well under way. Play had begun, as usual, immediately after dinner. Michel Donadieu always sat two chairs' distance from the players, and, though he didn't know any of the four men, a curious relationship, subtler than that which follows on an introduction, had grown up between him and them.

One thing, for instance, that certainly interested the bridge players, and, quite aware of this, he enjoyed their puzzled glances, was his performance with the powder box.

Three of the players were elderly men, well-known figures in Saint-Raphaël, one of them being the leading real-estate agent. They wasted no time on preliminaries, hardly pausing to greet each other before settling down around the table.

"Hurry up with the cards, Ernest," one of them shouted to the waiter.

After the first game had started, Michel came up, sat down in his usual place, and watched the fall of the cards with an expert eye. When a hand had been played with special skill, he would make a little gesture of appreciation, which the others had come to look for.

Yet he never exchanged a word with any of them. He always wore plus fours of English cut and material and brown brogues, which he cleaned himself, so they were always immaculate, whatever the weather or the time of day.

He waited until the clock struck 9:00 before producing the powder box. Then he gazed at his reflection in the mirror facing him. It was a traditional French restaurant, with marble-topped tables, imitation-leather banquettes, and mirrors paneling the walls.

Delving with thumb and forefinger into the yellowish powder that filled the box, Michel took out a pill little larger than a pin's head, laid it on his tongue, and washed it down with a sip of Vichy water. A simple ritual, on the face of it. However, the pill contained no ordinary drug, but one that doctors prescribed rarely, and for no trivial complaint. It was digitalis. Then there was the box. Most people would have used the pillbox supplied by the pharmacy; but not Michel. For a while he had toyed with the idea of buying an antique silver comfit box he had seen in the window of a curio shop. Finally he had decided on the gold powder box, which was more delicate and more original.

Michel was a sick man. Within the last few months, he had grown inordinately fat, and his features, never particularly clean-cut, had become coarse and bloated.

When the big white wall clock struck 10:00, he beckoned to the waiter and paid for his drinks, taking the money from a small pigskin purse. By then, he had a good idea which players were going to win the final rubber.

The seafront was empty at that hour, and the only sound was a murmur of small waves and leaves rustling in the warm Mediterranean breeze. Though the month was April, nights were so mild that a coat was not needed.

Saint-Raphaël seemed deserted; shutters were closed in all the houses. As Michel walked away, he knew the men in the brasserie were wondering where he could be going at this hour. And this knowledge did not displease him.

He took the second turn to the right; then, turning right again, entered a street parallel with the seafront. On it a small café was still open, the Provençal Bar. It was a sordid little place, badly lighted and dingy, with a zinc bar and two tables. The staff consisted of an aged couple, the owner and his wife.

It was a wonder anyone would want to drink in such depressing surroundings. Yet there were always two or three people lounging against the bar: railwaymen, hotel employees, and other workmen.

Michel, in his plus fours, looked grotesquely out of place.

"A small Vichy, please."

He had informed them that the Vichy they supplied was not authentic Vichy water, but came from a neighboring spring.

"Very sorry, sir," the owner had replied. "But this is a small place, and we don't have much choice."

When Michel appeared, the other customers stopped talking and eyed him curiously. Sometimes he produced his powder box, carefully selected a pill, then put it back again, murmuring to himself:

"No. No more tonight."

He guessed that when he left, somebody would ask:

"Who's he?"

Who, indeed, was he for these people? A rich, well-dressed man— a "nob," as the old owner would say—who came here every evening, and afterward waited for someone at the service door of the Hôtel Continental.

This, too, was a daily rite. He took his stand a hundred yards from the café. Some nights he wasn't the only one waiting there; among others, the girlfriend of one of the kitchen staff was often seen pacing up and down, her high heels clicking on the sidewalk.

Eventually, Nina came running out, almost colliding with him in the darkness. He flung a protective arm around her and pressed her to him for a moment.

"Not too tired, dear?"

"Not at all. The hotel's almost empty."

Arm in arm, they walked the empty streets until a neon sign appeared: BOULE ROUGE. A muffled sound of music throbbed in the warm air as they went down a short flight of steps. When Michel drew back the red plush curtain, the proprietor or the headwaiter— or both together—hurried forward to greet him with an obsequious "Good evening, Monsieur Emile."

He smiled affably as they escorted him to his table. Then Nina said, "Excuse me," and disappeared into the ladies' room.

This daily arrival was quite an event for the little cabaret, which made little money. Usually, the only ones there were a few penniless youngsters, a so-called Spanish dancer, and two girls, always the same pair, whose task it was to stay until two in the morning, dispensing glamour.

In fact, this nightly round, beginning with the hour or so of bridge-watching at the brasserie, and ending when Michel got back to the villa in the small hours, had replaced for him the genealogies and Yo-yos of his nights in La Rochelle.

Wearing a thin black dress he had bought for her, which showed to advantage the lines of her young body, Nina returned and sat beside him, smelling of face powder and the liquid soap provided in the ladies' room.

Their table was at the back of the room, in a sort of alcove bathed in the rosy glow of a small lamp. Everyone knew what was expected: the band prepared to strike up a rumba; the proprietor signaled to the two girls to get ready; the young men, knowing they were expected to help to create an atmosphere of gaiety, asked the girls to dance. Then Michel, too, rose and did some steps with Nina, who was teaching him the rumba.

"Am I improving?"

"Yes, you're coming along fine. You're very supple. That's the great thing, isn't it?"

He wasn't supple; merely flabby. He stole a glance at his reflection in the mirror over the bar.

After a few turns, he sat down again, his arm around the girl's waist, and they whispered.

"Needless to say," he had told her, "Emile isn't my real name. You mustn't mind if I don't tell you what it is."

"You mean you don't trust me?"

"No, it's not that at all. It's just . . . I'm too well known."

"What do your do?"

She made a game of trying to guess his occupation.

"I know! You're a famous writer. Or a newspaperman."

He smiled, made a vague gesture.

"Ah, if I could only tell you the story of my life, my poor little Nina."

Poor she was, little Nina Pacelli. Her father, a quarryman, was out of work oftener than not. Never, before Michel came on the scene, had she set foot in such a place as this, and at first she had hesitated.

"Oh, I couldn't go there dressed like this. It's much too fancy!"

"With me, you can go anywhere."

She hadn't quite sized him up yet, but she had an inkling of the part he wanted her to play. She had already told him that she had five brothers and sisters, and they had only two rooms.

"How many sleep in your room?"

"The two kids sleep with Dad and me; the rest in the other room. It's a squeeze, I can tell you!"

This seemed to please him; it was what he'd hoped to hear, apparently.

Pointing to his tiepin, she'd asked:

"Is that a real pearl?"

"Yes, of course."

"It must have cost an awful lot."

"Oh, no. Only four or five thousand."

The cabaret, upholstered in red plush, was overheated. It was as if it stayed open solely for the benefit of Michel and Nina, and, indeed, Michel always scowled if the red curtain was drawn aside and some chance customer dropped in. Everyone knew that "the rich gent" was the protector of the little chambermaid, and out to give her a good time.

"I want you to tell me frankly, Nina . . ." he began.

"What?"

"What I asked you yesterday, and the day before." His fingers were twitching; his cheeks were slightly flushed.

The question he had asked her twice was:

"Have you ever . . . been with a man?"

She only smiled demurely.

"Why won't you tell me?" he insisted.

"What difference can it make to you?"

She was seventeen, slim and lithe, but with an almost matronly bust out of keeping with her otherwise childish figure.

"Your fiancé has never . . . ?"

She had confessed to him that she was engaged, that her young man was doing his military service at the Brest arsenal.

"Ssh! That girl is listening."

His senses were tingling, and he began fumbling with her dress. When he grew too bold, Nina pushed his hand away, with a little laugh.

"Stop that! Behave yourself!"

"You might be nicer to me, dear. You would be, if you understood; if you knew the dreadful time I was having before I met you. I got into trouble over a woman. . . ." Something pushed him to play the risky game of half-confessions. "It was a close call. I almost got arrested."

"Whatever did you do?"

"I suspect they're still talking about me in . . . in a certain city. Yes, Nina, you really should be nicer. . . . And my health is terrible. I have tachycardia. Do you know what that is? All of a sudden my heart starts racing, like a car's engine. Once, I nearly passed out. They managed to slow it down just in time. . . . Right now it's slow; under fifty, I'd say. Feel my pulse. No, that's not the place. . . . Here."

She held his wrist docilely.

"Notice anything?"

"No." Should she have said "Yes," she wondered.

"My pulse is as weak as Napoleon's. He had the same disease, you know. . . . Nina darling!"

"Yes?"

"Why won't you answer my question?"

"What question?"

"You know quite well."

"You *are* a silly!" She gave a nervous laugh. "Anyhow, if you're that ill, you shouldn't excite yourself like this."

There were times when he scared her, especially in the red glow of the alcove, which made him look fatter, more like an ogre. Like a great fat slug! she thought. And when his fingers started twitching, creeping over her thin black dress, she wanted to jump up and run away.

"Tell me you love me, Nina, just a little."

"You know I do."

"Then kiss me."

After a quick glance around the room, she dabbed her lips on his cheek.

"I can see you're thinking of something else," he grumbled.

"Don't be so silly. . . . But it must be getting late."

Usually their departure was the signal for closing. The bartender, jingling glasses on his counter, was showing signs of impatience.

"Good night, Monsieur Emile." The owner hurried forward obsequiously when he saw Michel stand up.

"Good night, Monsieur Emile," echoed the headwaiter.

And the checkroom girl said, with a smile:

"Good night, monsieur. Pleasant dreams!"

In the empty street, they felt a slight nip in the air.

"I wouldn't mind betting"—Michel chuckled—"that they think we're going to . . . hm . . ."

"Oh, do keep quiet!"

He accompanied her as far as the railway bridge. She lived about a hundred yards beyond, judging by the time he heard her running and the sound of a door opening and closing. She always refused to let him come past the bridge. She was ashamed, he supposed, of letting him see the hovel she lived in.

"Good night, dear. You'll answer my question tomorrow, won't you?"

"That depends. . . ."

"No. I want you to promise."

"Well . . . maybe."

He had to cross Saint-Raphaël from one end to the other to reach Villa des Tamaris, and he always dreaded the long, lonely walk across the sleeping town. He looked nervously around when he heard footsteps behind him and avoided dark patches or crossed them almost at a run. It seemed hours before he came to the gate, walked through the garden, and unlocked the door.

On this particular night, he saw from the street a light in the conservatory, which now served as a morning room. It differed from the other rooms only in having glass on three sides.

Villa des Tamaris had been rented by the Donadieus for three consecutive years in his father's lifetime, when Michel was ten or twelve. It was exactly as he remembered it, even its antique furniture and dingy brocade curtains. The only change was that the plants had been removed from the conservatory, making the long, narrow room look like an aquarium.

The idea had come from Marthe. When Michel had his heart attack, and the doctor advised a prolonged rest, she had thought at once of Villa des Tamaris. The attack had taken place three months earlier, just after Dr. Lambe's murder. Michel had collapsed one afternoon at work in his office. He was carried to the house at the point of death, it seemed, and for hours the doctor had doubted if he would pull through.

Martine had come home the day before. Philippe was staying at the house, and, to account for his presence, their engagement was to be publicly announced. Oddly, Marthe, who might have been expected to resent his intrusion into the family, had come to regard him as an ally.

"He should be kept out of the way as long as possible," Philippe had remarked, referring to Michel.

A clinic was suggested, but Michel wouldn't hear of it. Not that he minded being an invalid; indeed, it was rather a relief. But the mere word "clinic" terrified him. He was convinced he would never leave it alive.

"How about the pine woods around Arcachon?" Mme Donadieu suggested. "I'm sure we could find a nice house there for him."

The doctor vetoed this. The Arcachon climate was too enervating.

"The Mediterranean coast would be much more suitable."

Then Marthe remembered the villa in Saint-Raphaël.

The days that followed had been nerve-racking for the Donadieus. Old Baillet had let himself be arrested tamely enough: more precisely, he had been found on the morning of the second day sleeping like a log in his cottage.

Eva had flatly refused to stay in the house.

"It's on account of Jean," she explained. "He keeps asking awkward questions about his father. You know what boys of five are like. I'm going away for a while with Nurse and the children." She left without even saying good-by to her husband.

Marthe was afraid to venture out; she felt that she'd be stared at in the street.

Those five days were a nightmare. Even Olsen began to lose his calm; he was afraid his visit to the clinic in Bordeaux would be discovered. One morning Philippe tackled him.

"Where is she now?"

"At the Hôtel de la Poste, I suppose."

"Is she seriously ill?"

"I couldn't say."

"Ill or not, it's absolutely necessary for her to come back to her job at the office."

"But—"

"I'll go and see her."

The circumstances attending Philippe's arrival had been such that his presence now seemed almost to be taken for granted. So much so, that one night when they had sat up late, talking, he had slept on a sofa in the living room.

As if the family didn't have anxieties enough, Kiki chose this moment to have one of his "attacks."

"Michel had better take Kiki with him to Saint-Raphaël," Marthe suggested.

It seemed a good idea. The lists, so to speak, had best be cleared: invalids and wounded removed to a safe distance. Michel, who had dreaded the idea of being left to his own resources, welcomed the prospect of having the company of Kiki and his tutor.

"I had a long swim in the sea this morning," wrote Kiki, proudly, to his mother in mid-January.

One evening, Philippe brought Odette back, and she resumed her work at the office.

The local paper announced "the engagement of Mlle Martine Donadieu and M. Philippe Dargens. Owing to the recent family bereavement, the wedding will be a very quiet one."

After an expert glance at her sister's figure, Marthe had decided to ignore Martine completely. Mme Donadieu wept copiously, but her tears were no more than a suitable display of motherly feeling.

Frédéric was seldom to be seen; there were rumors that the Alhambra might have to close down shortly.

Eva went to Switzerland with her children, and a week before the wedding, which was to be in mid-February, sent a telegram, which served as pretext for a general review of family affairs. Eva asked for money to be telegraphed at once, because, in her haste to get away, she had left with only two or three thousand francs.

It was Olsen who took the lead: he asked Mme Donadieu, Marthe, as her brother's representative, and Philippe to meet in his office.

"This is how things stand," he began, watching the faces of the others to see how they would react. "Each of the Donadieu heirs is manager of a department of the business, and, as such, draws a salary of fifty thousand francs a year."

In Saint-Raphaël, Kiki was bathing in a warm sunlit sea, but rain was falling steadily outside the windows of the offices on Quai Vallin.

"As a consequence of his marriage, Philippe will be entitled to a post of the same order, and I propose that, for the present, he take over Michel's department and draw the salary attached to it."

Philippe's face was quite expressionless. Marthe, who was watching him, was favorably impressed by the young man's calm.

"Now, as regards our financial situation . . . At the end of each fiscal year, the profits are, of course, distributed among the shareholders; in other words, the members of the family. I think I should let you know that for the last three years there have been *no profits*; our balance sheet has shown a loss."

"I see," said Philippe quietly.

He had understood. He would have to make do with a relatively small income: fifty thousand francs a year. Moreover, this accounted, in some measure, for the curious atmosphere in the house on Rue Réaumur, which had puzzled him for some time.

Two days later, Marthe started another hare.

"It's out of the question that my sister should stay here, or even in La Rochelle, after the wedding. We don't want the whole town to know that she was two months along when she got married."

Again Philippe agreed. Not once had he been heard to protest against what might be called a Donadieu mandate. Bearing in mind that they would have to live on fifty thousand francs a year, he suggested that Martine join Michel and Kiki in Saint-Raphaël. "They could share expenses," he pointed out.

Meanwhile, Martine possessed her soul in patience. She saw little of Philippe, and when he talked to her, it was almost always about practical matters. The arrangements for the wedding gave rise to heated family debates. Frédéric had declined to act as principal witness at the ceremony. So, deliberately, to defy public opinion, Varin and Camboulives were enlisted for this function.

Michel stayed in Saint-Raphaël. It seemed wiser to give the impression that he was seriously ill.

The ceremony held little interest for Martine; only one thing caught her imagination: the astounding fact that it was her bedroom she shared with Philippe on their wedding night.

But something was weighing on her mind.

"Philippe dear, why shouldn't we go away together, you and I? We'd be much happier almost anywhere else."

"We'll do that later."

"When?"

"When the Donadieu finances have been straightened out. You understand, don't you?"

No, she couldn't understand why he should fall into Donadieu ways so readily, be more of a Donadieu than she was: going to the office at eight sharp every morning, and hurrying through lunch when he had a busy afternoon ahead of him. Nor could she understand why he and Marthe got on so well together, or his affability toward Olsen.

"I'll come to see you every other weekend while you're in Saint-Raphaël," he promised her. "Once the trial's over, we'll see what can be done."

And he went on sleeping at the house and having his meals with Mme Donadieu.

"Come in." Philippe opened the door of the aquarium.

He had heard Michel's steps on the gravel path, then in the hall. Martine was sitting in an armchair, looking pale and tired.

"I've been waiting for you," Philippe continued, "for the last several hours. My train got in at nine-thirty."

"Really?"

Michel, who was perspiring slightly, sank heavily into a chair. Some of the sandwiches Martine had made for Philippe remained on a plate beside him, and Michel promptly reached out for one. His inability to set eyes on food without wanting to eat had grown even more pronounced since his illness, and every afternoon he spent a good deal of time in local English tearooms.

"We're leaving at six tomorrow morning."

"Eh? What's that? Who do you mean?"

"You and I, of course . . . Martine, you'd better go to bed. Michel and I are going to have a little talk."

"You won't stay up too late?"

"Oh, no. It'll only take ten minutes."

The ten minutes proved to be an hour. Philippe was in no mood for trifling, and several times rapped out a peremptory "Now listen, Michel!"

Since his marriage, and indeed ever since he'd been invited to return to La Rochelle—after all, it was they who had summoned him—he'd called the Donadieus, his mother-in-law excepted, by their Christian names.

"I won't ask you how or where you've been spending the evening, but I must ask you to hear what I have to say. The case is coming up for trial in three days."

Michel made a feeble bid for the young man's pity by putting on a woebegone air and fumbling in his powder box for a pill.

"What do you think will happen?" he asked miserably.

"That depends on how we handle it. Do you know Limaille?"

"The lawyer?"

"Yes. He's a nasty fellow. I've had dealings with him. . . . Well, it's Limaille who's defending Baillet."

"He'll do all he can to make things awkward for us, I'm afraid."

Limaille was thirty and had started from nothing. Though he worked like a galley slave, he had failed to reap the success he thought himself entitled to. The truth was that nobody trusted him, and important cases never came his way. His practice was confined to poorer clients and shadier cases.

"I've been talking with Limaille," Philippe said, lighting a cigarette.

He was dressed as he had been in the past, and had neither put on weight nor lost it. Yet he had changed considerably—above all, in his bearing and expression. He was a young man very sure of himself—"cocksure," detractors might have said—strong-willed and somewhat arrogant.

"Limaille has withdrawn his plea for a medical examination."

"Medical examination?"

"Anyhow," Philippe went on, ignoring the question, "it is no concern of the examining magistrate. All he has to find out is when, how, and why Baillet killed Lambe. No complaint has been laid in regard to the illegal operation."

"I don't quite follow. . . ."

"Surely it's simple enough. The Baillet-Lambe business is just an ordinary murder case. But suppose the trial were to be adjourned for further inquiry into the allegations regarding Odette's illness? And suppose Limaille persuaded the court to examine both cases together? I could see that that was what Limaille was angling for; he wanted the case to become big, thus shoving him into the limelight. That was what he was after when he asked the magistrate to have inquiries made into the allegations published in *The Laundry*. He even talked of starting proceedings on behalf of his client."

Michel nearly had another heart attack. He was picturing the excitement in La Rochelle, the police questioning the woman to whom he had sent Odette, and the doctor in charge of the clinic, and the manager of the Hôtel de la Poste. . . .

Philippe had been watching his face with amusement. "Limaille, you'll be glad to learn, has backed down. . . . Starting in September, he's to be legal adviser to the Donadieu companies, with a handsome salary."

"I see. In that case, there's no reason for my going to La Rochelle."

It wasn't merely Nina he was thinking of, or of the sunlit ease of the Riviera. He had a feeling that only here was he safe; in La Rochelle, heaven knew what trouble was waiting for him.

"There *is* a reason," Philippe said. "Odette is being called as a witness for the defense. I have no idea what sort of questions Limaille will put to her once she's on the witness stand. I don't trust the man altogether; he has the reputation of being unreliable. And Odette is still feeling far from well. I'm in a position to know, since she is now my confidential secretary. It's absolutely essential for you to have a talk with her, and no later than tomorrow. That's your job; I can't do it for you."

Unthinkingly, Michel took another sandwich.

"I've done my best to prime her," Philippe went on, "and I've been fairly successful. But there's always the risk she may lose her head when she's confronted with her father. She thinks you've forgotten all about her, and, for all I know, she may be feeling angry. I've done my best; I've told her that you're at death's door, and . . ."

"Suppose she won't listen to me?" Michel put in dolefully. He was clinging to his drab but carefree life in Saint-Raphaël—to Nina, the little café, the cabaret, the bridge players at the brasserie—to the safe routine of the new life he'd organized for himself.

"An hour's talk with her should be enough. Then you can come back here. We'll go into the details tomorrow, in the train. . . . Good night now. We have to make a very early start."

They did not shake hands. Philippe tiptoed into his room and crept into bed as quietly as he could, thinking that Martine was asleep.

But he heard a small voice beside him.

"Well? What plots have you two been hatching?"

"Never mind now, darling. Try to sleep."

"No. I want you to tell me. . . ."

"I'm trying to save your family from getting into a dreadful mess."

A sleepy voice murmured:

"Very nice of you, dear." Suddenly she woke up completely and clasped him in her arms. "Why should you bother about all that? We could be so happy . . . anywhere together . . . away from all of them!"

He kissed her, and gently freed himself.

"Don't talk, please."

"But I want to know. What can it matter to you if my brother . . . ?"

"Please, Martine dear, do let me sleep. I'll need to have all my wits about me tomorrow. It's no easy job I've taken on, I assure you. Once I'm through with it, we'll have a quiet life together. All I ask is for you to let me have a free hand for the next few days."

She felt like weeping—why, she hardly knew—but only sighed.

"Why?"

"Don't ask. You'll understand someday. . . . I've got to get up at five tomorrow." He settled into the position in which he always slept. There was a whisper in his ear:

"Philippe!"

"What is it?"

"Sure you're not getting tired of me?"

"I love you more than ever."

"Then why, why . . . ?" For days and days, in her exile at Saint-Raphaël, she had been dreaming of those golden months in Paris. "Oh, Philippe dear," she sobbed, "let's go away together. Anywhere. I can't see why you . . ."

"Please don't talk, darling. I really must sleep."

He had a strenuous day, several such days, ahead of him, and a restless body pressing against him irritated him. He changed his position again, saying sleepily:

". . . night, Martine."

"Good night, dear."

He was conscious that she stayed awake, lying on her back, gazing up into the darkness. Evidently sleep did not come to her for a long time, because when, at five, he got up and dressed, she did not stir.

He went at once to Michel's room. Michel gave him an imploring glance and moaned:

"I'm feeling rotten."

"Hurry up and dress. I'll get coffee ready." He went down to the kitchen.

The rent for the villa was high, so they made do with only a cleaning woman, an Italian, who came at seven.

To her surprise, on entering the kitchen she found the gas stove still warm, some tepid coffee in the pot, and bread crumbs on the table.

For a moment, she wondered what had happened. Then, hearing movements in Kiki's room, she merely shrugged—it was no concern of hers—and set about her work. As usual, she laid the table for four in the former conservatory.

12

At the station, the taxi driver promptly asked Michel:

"Where to, sir? Quai Vallin or Rue Réaumur?"

It was Philippe who answered.

"To Quai Vallin. As fast as you can."

It was five o'clock, and the office closed at six. An hour was a short time for what had to be done. On the way from Saint-Raphaël, few words had passed between them, because, unfortunately, they never had the compartment to themselves. Michel had read a detective story; Philippe gazed out the window.

When the taxi stopped at the Donadieu building, Michel dragged himself out sullenly, produced money with studied slowness, and left Philippe to pay the fare.

Inside, he was quite startled to see the young man run up the steps four at a time, greet Joseph with a friendly wave, and push open a heavily padded door. Michel had vaguely heard that things had changed, but only by hearsay; seeing was another matter. It was even more disquieting to see Philippe pick up the letters on the desk— letters addressed to Messrs. Donadieu—and hear him call:

"Mademoiselle Odette! Please come!"

When she stepped out of her little room, he saw that she was dressed exactly as in the past.

"Would you please give Monsieur Michel a hand," said Philippe, moving to the door, the letters under his arm. "If anyone wants to see me, I'll be in Monsieur Olsen's office."

So that was that! The rest lay with Michel. . . .

Forgetting that the girl had been through a long course of priming by Philippe, Michel was prepared for the worst, now that they were alone together. He expected hard words, reproaches, or a flood of tears.

Nothing happened. Odette remained standing in front of his desk like a model employee waiting for orders.

"Shall I get my notebook, Monsieur Michel?"

It suddenly struck him that she had changed; she looked more awake, and—what surprised him most—much more intelligent. He had never thought of her as a young woman with a mind of her own; she had seemed to him a stolid, painstaking employee, if somewhat obstinate, as is often the case with those who have won certificates at training schools.

As she stood waiting, Michel, more and more embarrassed, drew the little gold box from his pocket and heaved a sigh.

"I'm a very sick man, my dear."

He took out a tiny pill and swallowed it, grimacing.

Odette watched without any show of interest, then remarked:

"I'm ill, too."

"I know. We're a pair of sick people—sick in mind and body, I'm afraid." He was feeling his way, hoping to find some opening for saying what had to be said. "Has Philippe told you what the doctor says: that I should have complete rest for some time?"

"Yes, he mentioned it."

"And that any violent emotion might . . . be my death."

"I know."

He had been playing a part, watching himself from outside. Suddenly he realized how dangerous his position was. That simply dressed young woman standing in the middle of the office, once *his* office, held them all in the hollow of her hand. Tomorrow, or the day after, when she was on the witness stand, a few words from her could bring the house of Donadieu to ruin, could get him sent to jail for heaven knew how many years. He bit his lip, then murmured brokenly:

"Odette!"

"Yes?"

"You can't imagine what I've suffered, and how miserable I am now. I did a wicked thing. I admit it. I couldn't resist the temptation of . . . of your youth, of everything about you." Tears of almost sincere remorse gathered in his eyes, and he buried his face in his hands. After a moment, he looked up. "Believe me, I'd willingly give ten years of my life to atone, to make you well again. . . . Tell me the truth, Odette. Are you still very ill?"

"Yes." She said it quietly, without a trace of emotion.

"Do you . . . do you suffer much?"

"What does that matter to you?"

"Odette, if I go down on my knees and beg you to forgive . . . ?"

"What good would that do?"

Was there a veiled menace in that question? Hardly knowing what he was doing, he sank to his knees and stretched his arms out to her.

"Odette, I implore you to forgive me. Haven't we all suffered enough?"

"Please get up, Monsieur Donadieu."

"Not before you tell me—"

"Please get up. Somebody might come. . . ."

He rose, stumbled across the room, and sobbed with his face to the wall. He had a feeling of helplessness; nothing he could do or say would influence her. She was implacable. All was lost!

Typewriters were clicking in other offices; somewhere a telephone was shrilling. A voice could be heard dictating a letter. Philippe was sitting on the corner of Olsen's desk.

"How does he seem?" asked Olsen anxiously.

"Same as he's always been, and always will be."

Olsen looked away. It wasn't the first time Philippe had made remarks like this about the Donadieus.

"What was her attitude?"

"Indifference, as far as I could judge."

They could only wait.

"How's your wife?" Olsen asked, to fill the silence.

"Quite well, thanks."

It was between these two brothers-in-law that relations were coldest. Each seemed to be observing the other warily, trying to discover the chink in his armor. One day Marthe had asked her husband:

"Well, what do you think of him?"

"I think . . . he's better than I'd expected," Olsen replied, with a hint of reluctance, but, for truth's sake, giving the devil his due.

"What does Michel find to do all day in Saint-Raphaël?" Olsen asked.

Philippe made a vague gesture. He neither knew nor cared. He was listening for sounds from the room below. After a few more minutes, when he could hear nothing, he ran downstairs and into an adjoining room, where he put his ear to the keyhole.

". . . ask anything you like," he heard. "Needless to say, I make myself responsible for your future. You can stay on here, of course, as long as you choose."

"No," she said. "I'll leave the city once the trial is over."

"Where will you go?"

"I haven't decided. Monsieur Philippe's promised me an allowance equal to what I'm earning now." Philippe grinned; he could picture the look on Michel's face when he heard this. "And he's promised, too," the girl went on, "that if my father is sentenced to transportation, he'll see that he escapes within two years at most."

"Quite so; you can count on us," said Michel firmly. "What I'd like to have is your assurance that you'll hold out in court, whatever pressure they bring to bear on you, and whatever questions you're asked."

"Yes. I won't say anything."

"I can depend on you—absolutely?"

"I promised Monsieur Philippe, and I shall keep my word."

Philippe smiled again. He had neither wept nor cajoled, but almost every day he had put aside his work at some point and called the girl to his side.

"Odette, my dear, how are you feeling today? Let's have a look. You've been crying again, I can see. And all on account of that damned fool of a brother-in-law of mine! He isn't worth it."

He chaffed her, refused to see the bad side of things.

"I suppose you're going to tell me the usual sob stuff about 'a young girl's honor,' and a ruined life, and all the rest of it?"

The first time, she looked at him reproachfully.

"It's no laughing matter for me, Monsieur Philippe. My life *is* ruined."

" 'Ruined'? Not at all! For one thing, you're much prettier than you used to be. Yes, you are. Only look at yourself in the mirror over the fireplace. . . . There now; can't you see? And in two or three months you'll be quite well again. So what's the point of crying over spilled milk, making yourself miserable for nothing?"

"I . . . I don't know."

"No point whatever. In fact . . . Look! Suppose you and Michel hadn't . . . done what you did, or there hadn't been any complications?" She was still dabbing her eyes with her handkerchief, sobbing—but less sincerely. "In that case, you'd have kept your job with us, for years most likely. And you'd have developed into a dried-up old maid. You're the kind who gets like that, my dear, quite easily. Of course you might have found a husband; but then again, you might not have. Isn't that so?"

"At least I wouldn't have been a . . . a bad girl."

"That's not true!"

"What do you mean?"

"I mean that you weren't such an innocent little thing when my brother-in-law started with you. Isn't that a fact?"

"Well, I once had a . . . a boyfriend."

"Exactly. And now, thanks to what's happened, you're an interesting person. You've gained experience, and had a romantic adventure, like a heroine in a film. In a day or two, everybody in town will be talking about you; they'll discover that you have 'glamour,' as they'll call it. Michel will see that you have a comfortable income, and you'll be able to lead a peaceful or an exciting life, as you choose. Really, you're a very lucky girl, my dear."

It was amazing how readily she let herself be convinced. He could see she was drinking in his words, picturing the future he painted in such rosy colors.

"You'll have a husband—or, if you prefer, you can have a host of lovers."

"Don't be horrid! All men disgust me."

"That's nonsense. Take me, for instance; I don't disgust you, do I?"

She remained silent. Philippe was quite aware that Odette admired him, and that her feelings toward him were growing daily more ardent.

"I suppose you're worrying about your father. Of course it's hard on him, but let me ask you this: Was he ever a happy man? No. Well, now he's in prison . . ."

"Do you think that's nice for him?"

"It may not be nice, but, given his temperament, I wouldn't say he feels it deeply. He'll be convicted; they'll send him to a penal colony. But we'll see he doesn't stay there long; with money, one can always fix it up. And he, too, will be in a position to insist on my brother-in-law's providing for his future. He can settle down somewhere, and do nothing for the rest of his days, if he feels like it."

Several times he had succeeded in making her smile.

But at the interview with Michel, she wasn't smiling. Persistently, he handled it the wrong way: protesting too much, indulging in self-pity, and trying to exonerate himself.

"Answer me frankly, Odette. Did I use force on you? Wasn't it of your own free will that . . . ?"

Somehow she couldn't help glancing toward the corner of the office where he had embraced her the first time.

"And then afterward, when a baby was on the way, was it I who . . . ?"

"Please stop!"

"I will if you'll stop looking at me like that, as if you loathed me. I know I did wrong, but I'm paying for it now. My wife has left me; I'm like a stranger in my own house; I've had to go into hiding; and I'm dangerously ill, into the bargain."

A bell clanged in the elevator shaft; the offices were closing. Philippe opened the door and professed surprise at seeing Michel and Odette.

"Still here, you two? . . . Mademoiselle Odette, has anyone called me?"

"No, Monsieur Philippe."

"Coming, Michel?"

Before leaving, Philippe stepped over to the alcove, where Odette was putting on her hat.

"Please say something to reassure him. For my sake."

She seemed to hesitate. But, on her way out, she paused when passing Michel on the landing and said in a low voice:

"You have nothing to fear from me."

Eva was still in Switzerland with the children, so Michel dined with Mme Donadieu and Philippe in the ground-floor dining room. It struck him that his mother had changed, though he couldn't have said exactly how. Watching Philippe's behavior, as if he were quite at home here, he could not keep his eyes from straying to the big portrait of his father on the wall.

"Can she be depended on, once she's on the witness stand, Philippe?" Mme Donadieu asked.

"Absolutely. I was pretty sure before. But I thought it best for her to have a talk with Michel."

Michel looked down. That talk had left a detestable impression; it lingered with a bitter taste. And the changed atmosphere of the house added to his discomfort.

It seemed extraordinary, almost uncanny, that only a few months should have brought such changes. He found himself picturing the dining room as it had been during his absence, with his mother and Philippe having their meals together.

There had been a sort of fatality about it, he decided, and no one had attempted to stem the downward slide. So now Philippe was eating, chatting, and quite at his ease in the family home; while in Saint-Raphaël, Martine was soon to have a baby. . . .

"I suppose you know," his mother said to him, "about the plans we're making for the coming winter."

"What plans?"

"There'll be another family in the house. So I will move out to the lodge, with Kiki. Marthe, as the eldest, wants to have the ground floor. Philippe and Martine will have the third floor. You, of course, will stay where you were before."

Sometimes, from the way she looked at the two men, it was as though she was comparing one with the other. After a long glance at Michel she said:

"You haven't changed. You eat just as much as ever—and just as fast."

Michel was an ugly eater. Not only did he take enormous helpings, but also he gobbled his food, no matter what it was.

"You've put on weight," his mother added.

"That's because of my heart. Having a slow pulse often has that effect, it seems; though it makes some people thin. Strange, isn't it?"

"How's Martine doing, Philippe?"

"Quite well, Mother."

That "Mother" was another shock for Michel. Yes, the old order had changed, with a vengeance! To his surprise, Marthe came down before dinner was over—which was contrary to all Donadieu etiquette.

"Finished your dinner already?" her mother asked.

"Yes. Jean's gone out."

She drew a chair up to the table and started chatting with Philippe as if he were a well-established member of the family!

"Seen the lawyer again?" she asked.

"Yes, it's all fixed. He showed me the jury list. With any luck, the case should be over in one session. And no awkward questions asked."

To her brother she said:

"You know the changes that are to be made—about the division of the house among us?"

"Yes."

"I wrote to Eva about it, but she hasn't answered. I suppose you know she keeps on asking us for money?"

He nodded vaguely. The curtains were drawn, and the city noises were a mere distant murmur.

Next door, Mme Brun was gossiping with Charlotte.

"Michel's come back," she said. "Do you think he'll have the nerve to put in an appearance at the trial?"

"Not likely!"

"I wonder if he really knew what was going on. . . ."

"What can that matter to you?" Charlotte had grown surly to the point of rudeness. And she no longer showed any pleasure when Mme Brun proposed one of their crêpe orgies. For Philippe's wedding, she had sent a large, grotesquely large, bunch of flowers with a card cryptically inscribed: "Best wishes, all the same. . . ."

Mme Brun took Charlotte's retort placidly, and went on:

"I still think that it was Michel, when he learned she was enceinte, who persuaded . . ."

Charlotte stood up abruptly.

"I'm sick and tired of talking about those horrible people." She walked toward the door. "Good night."

"But it's only nine."

"Maybe it is, but I want to go to bed. Don't I have the right to go to bed if I feel like it?"

Left to herself, Mme Brun fell back on writing a long letter to her daughter. "Michel has abruptly returned from the Riviera, where he was taking a rest cure. In my opinion, that means . . ."

Marthe was asking her brother:

"When are you going back?"

Philippe answered for him:

"Tomorrow morning."

Though none of the Donadieus attended the trial, it was as if they were all, in flesh and blood, in the courtroom. Somehow their presence was felt—behind each word spoken, each question put to a witness; even on the judge's bench. As chance would have it, there was a break that morning in the long spell of bad weather. The sun came out; the air was as bright and warm as on a spring day.

The most prominent figure at the trial was Limaille, the lawyer, and he was watched with eager interest as he bustled up and down

166

the corridors, the wide sleeves of his gown flapping like a huge crow's wings. What would he have to say? Was he about to make a frontal attack on the Quai Vallin stronghold?

There was surprise, not to say disappointment, when the prisoner was marched in by two guards. He was such an insignificant figure, not at all like the ferocious beast they had expected to see. He was in his Sunday best and, with his white collar and cuffs and ready-made tie, looked like a peasant dressed for a country wedding, or a funeral. He did not seem agitated; only on a close look was a hint of panic seen in his eyes.

When he was being examined by the judge, he seemed to wonder if the questions were addressed to him. He kept looking around at his guards, as if asking them to help him out, while his counsel whispered instructions in his ear. Now and then he braced himself to answer:

"Yes, your honor . . . No, your honor."

He felt the lack of his engineer's cap, which he could have twiddled, to calm himself. Without it, he didn't seem to know what to do with his hands.

"Did you strike Dr. Lambe with this implement?"

"Yes, your honor."

"Did you deal your victim at least thirty-one blows with it?"

There were the expected exclamations of horror from the public.

"Yes, your honor."

The judge looked up severely. "Silence!"

At certain moments, the prisoner's calm might have been taken as proof of callousness. But generally it was obvious this was not the case, and even the judge seemed to have little heart for questioning him. The man in the dock was a poor devil of limited intelligence; there was nothing to be got out of him. Indeed, the only remarkable feature of the case was that a man so meek and insignificant should have worked himself up to the point of murder.

"Next witness."

The courtroom was crowded, and everyone craned his neck toward the witness stand.

Slowly, Odette moved forward. So unself-conscious was her manner that she might have been entering her employer's office, notebook in hand, to take a letter.

"As daughter of the accused, you are not required to give your evidence on oath, but you are nonetheless obliged to state the truth and nothing but the truth. . . . My first question is this: **Were you** aware of your father's intention to commit murder?"

Odette answered in a low voice, her eyes fixed on the judge, and someone at the back of the court cried, "Louder!"

"Speak up," the judge said. "And please turn toward the jury when you answer. . . . When your father came to visit you in Bordeaux, did either of you mention the article in *The Laundry*?"

"No, sir."

"Were you not surprised at your father's coming to see you?"

"I really couldn't say. . . . I forget."

There were still cries of "Louder!" from the back. Odette swung toward the interruptors and gave them a scathing look.

"Had you read the article in question when your father came to see you?"

Her answer was inaudible, but everyone saw her shake her head.

"Now that you have read the article, will you kindly inform the court if the statements made in it are true?"

Baillet seemed plunged in a sort of stupor, cowed perhaps by the pomp and circumstance of the law, the robes and ritual, and the sight of all those people staring at him as if he were some strange, dangerous animal.

"No, sir," said Odette firmly.

"You understand my question? The court is not concerned with references to other parties, which are irrelevant to the present proceedings. What I ask is whether the allegations relating to you are true."

"They are not true."

"Am I to take it that none of them is true?"

"Yes, sir."

"You never ceased working for the firm employing you, even for a few days?"

"No, sir."

"You went to Bordeaux under instructions from your employers, in the ordinary course of your duties?"

"Yes, sir."

The judge turned to the public prosecutor, then to the jury; finally his eyes settled on Maître Limaille.

"Has anyone any further question to put to this witness?" he asked, following that quickly with "Thank you, mademoiselle. You can stand down."

That was all. There was a change in the atmosphere of the crowded courtroom—a general sigh of relief, or regret, from those who had been hoping for sensational disclosures. Still, it had been a near thing; one answer different and a leading family of La Rochelle would have been humbled to the dust.

"Next witness."

A railwayman took the stand, one of a series of witnesses who testified that Baillet had an excellent character and was the mildest of men.

In answer to questions by counsel for the defense, a medical witness said:

"After a careful study of Baillet's mental state, I am convinced that he was not wholly responsible for his acts that evening." This was perhaps the most distressing part of the evidence, because the doctor, after his patient had released him from his obligation to secrecy, went on to state that Baillet had suffered in early life from a specific disease that had permanently impaired his constitution.

There were yawns among the public, who had expected something spicier. Instead, they had to listen to a series of dull, mildly sordid depositions.

"The court will now hear counsel for the defense."

Limaille was as disappointing as the witnesses. He spoke briefly and to the point; in fact, his speech was a model of decorum.

"Try, gentlemen of the jury, to put yourselves in the place of my unfortunate client. Suppose a scurrilous rag were to publish a grossly offensive article defaming the wife or daughter of any one of you . . . For political reasons, the deceased sought to sully the good name of one of the most respected families of our city, and, as an indirect consequence, a decent workingman, with thirty years of loyal service to his credit, now stands before you in the prisoner's dock."

This colorless allusion was the only reference to the Donadieus. The rest of the speech was an appeal for sympathy for Baillet—which was superfluous; one had only to look at the wretched man to feel sorry for him.

When counsel for the prosecution addressed the jury, no one was much surprised to hear him add:

"While looking to you for a verdict of 'Guilty' of the charge of manslaughter, I see no reason why you should not give him the benefit of extenuating circumstances."

Philippe was in his office with Mme Donadieu and Olsen, and

none of them had much to say. For all Philippe's assurances that everything would go well, they couldn't help feeling uneasy. The telephone shrilled, but it was only Michel, calling from Saint-Raphaël.

"No, nothing yet," Philippe replied. "I'll call you when it's over."

Just then, by chance, apparently, Frédéric strolled in. He had been in the courthouse and had found its atmosphere so depressing that, seeing his face, they thought he was the bearer of bad news.

"Acquitted!" was all he said.

His eyes were fixed, not on Philippe, but on Mme Donadieu. He dabbed his forehead with his handkerchief before taking out his cigarette case.

"Acquitted!" Olsen echoed. "Well, I'll be damned!"

Then a curious thing happened. All four could not help glancing nervously toward the door, as if they expected to see a menacing form loom up on the threshold: Baillet on the warpath!

"What did he say?"

"Nothing. In fact, he didn't seem to understand the verdict. Limaille went and got his daughter. She burst into tears and flung herself into her father's arms." From Frédéric's tone, they could tell he had been deeply moved.

"How did the public react?" Philippe asked.

His father frowned slightly, as if thinking, That's the only thing that interests you, my boy! He turned to his son.

"The public? They were completely taken by surprise, as far as I could judge. It was quite a sensation, in fact. A lawyer standing next to me said to a man beside him, 'A neat piece of work, eh?' "

"And so it was!" Philippe smiled.

There wasn't open war between father and son, but they seemed to live in different worlds. Whose the fault was would have been hard to determine, though Frédéric's attitude of mistrust might well account for it, at least in part.

The Donadieus, however, had all reached a favorable opinion of Philippe; indeed, Mme Donadieu sometimes seemed to have more confidence in him than in her own children.

Marthe, if still a shade aloof, was grateful to Philippe for having kept his head and piloted the family so skillfully through its troubles.

Olsen, too, was forced to admit that in business matters Philippe was his equal, and vastly superior to Michel. But, like Frédéric, though for other reasons, he couldn't overcome his mistrust of the young man. Asked to sum up his feelings, he might have said: "I'm wondering—what's his game?"

There was something almost uncanny about the readiness with which Philippe had adapted himself to Donadieu ways and to the exigencies of the business. What was he aiming at? Was he the sort of man to be content with being merely one of the Donadieu heirs? He never even hinted at a desire to have his salary of fifty thousand francs increased, and he regularly paid his share of the rent for the Saint-Raphaël villa. Nor did he ever make a decision without first consulting Mme Donadieu and his brother-in-law.

Even in such details as the lighting of his office—which was quite inadequate—he made no attempt to break with precedent. He could easily have had a better lamp installed, but he refrained from doing so.

"Now that that's over," said Mme Donadieu, "what about the future? We'd better come to some arrangement—about our vacations, for instance—hadn't we?" Without thinking, she looked to Philippe for the answer.

"There's no need for any immediate change that I can see. Michel had better stay on the Riviera all summer. We can go there for our vacations in succession. When it's my turn, I'll take Odette with me as my secretary; everyone will find that quite natural. Then Michel can settle on her the lump sum he's promised, and she need never come back to La Rochelle."

"What about her father?"

An unpleasant reminder. They'd provided for every contingency except his being acquitted. What were they to say to Baillet, and how would he react?

Just then, footsteps were heard on the stairs. Without waiting to be shown in, someone knocked at the door and entered quickly. Philippe was the first to look around, and he could not repress a slight start when he saw Odette walk calmly past them to her office, taking off her hat.

Afraid that Mme Donadieu might make some remark, he said hastily:

"If you'll excuse me, I'll get on with my work." He pointed to the correspondence on his desk.

"Will you call Michel?" asked Olsen, but Philippe scowled him into silence, and shepherded them out, his father included.

When he had closed the door behind them, he saw the girl standing beside the desk, a faint smile on her lips. She was swaying slightly, as if from some emotion.

"Well, Odette, my dear . . ." he began.

She made an effort to appear composed, and said shyly:

"Were you satisfied with me, Monsieur Philippe?"

He realized that they were on the brink of an emotional scene—he was almost as moved as she was!—and that it must not be allowed to mature. He walked across the room to the window and flung it open.

"Was I mistaken when I said we'd fix things up all right?" he asked cheerfully.

She looked at him inquiringly, as if wanting him to be more explicit.

"Now," he hastened to add, "I'll ask you to carry on as usual for the next few months. When I go south in the summer, I want you to come with me."

"Will you be working any more today?" She picked up her notebook.

"No . . . I'll only ask you to get Saint-Raphaël for me."

She did so—reluctantly, he guessed; but he judged it necessary to ask this of her.

"Thanks, Odette. Now you'd better go to your father."

"Oh, some friends of his have taken him off with them," she said rather scornfully. "I don't know where they've gone. To some bar I suppose."

Philippe could picture the railwayman and his cronies drinking themselves to intoxication in some low bar.

"Hello? That you, Michel?" He gestured to Odette to leave the room, and made a speaking trumpet of his hand. "Can you hear me? . . . Good! All's well. He was acquitted. . . . Yes? . . . I tell you it's quite all right. . . . No, there's nothing to worry about. I'll write this evening."

Odette, who was on the landing, heard the click of the receiver as he hung up. She went back to her office to get her hat, moving with a slowness that showed her reluctance to go without hearing the words she was waiting for. Her hand on the doorknob, she looked wistfully at the young man.

"Good night, Monsieur Philippe."

"Good night, Odette." He would not meet her eyes.

When the door had closed behind her, he heaved a sigh of relief.

13

The door key was so heavy there was no question of carrying it. Yet, neither Baillet, though he prided himself on his carpentry—the elaborate henhouse in the back garden was his handiwork—nor his daughter, for all her resourcefulness, had ever thought of getting a new lock for the front door.

Before the engineer's arrest, there was only one key, and it was always kept in a cracked flowerpot standing on the windowsill to the left of the door. This hiding place was hardly a secret; once, when Baillet and his daughter were out and the chimney caught fire, the neighbors promptly showed the firemen where to find the key.

While her father was in custody, Odette had continued leaving the key in the flowerpot, for lack of anywhere else to put it, and when she saw him going off with his friends to celebrate, after the verdict, it never occurred to her to whisper to him:

"You'll find the key in the usual place."

Night was falling, and it was turning chilly, when she entered the quiet street where they lived. Most of the cottages were the same humble kind, with small gardens in front and behind. There were no streetlights, but arc lamps strung up at long intervals.

As Odette opened the gate, she noticed there was no light in the front room. With a movement that had become automatic—she had been making it since she was quite small and had to climb on an empty box, kept near the window for her use—she plunged her hand into the flowerpot. She had quite a shock when she found nothing in it, and took it down to make certain.

After that, she knocked on the door, though she was fairly sure that, if her father was home, there would be a light showing, because the shutters didn't close completely. She was dead tired. She went back to the street, where she had a clear view in both directions. No one was in sight.

Of course, it was an exceptional day; so no conclusions could be drawn from a detail like this. Possibly her father had been home and, without thinking, put the key in his pocket when he left again.

Her clothes were too thin for the cold night air, so she did what she had sometimes when she was little: she walked around the house, climbed on the kennel—its last occupant had been dead ten years—and scrambled in through a window that could be opened from outside, because the latch was missing. The room into which she stepped was a small scullery next to the kitchen.

Nervously, she fumbled for the light switch. It seemed to her there was something different about the atmosphere. Still, she could see nothing abnormal; the kitchen was not particularly untidy, though a cupboard door stood open and there were some crumbs on the oilcloth.

What struck her most was the unusual smell. Where could it come from? Opening a door, she entered what they called the parlor, though actually it was furnished as a dining room. It was a room that was never used except when visitors came, and it usually smelled of damp and beeswax.

Now, when Odette turned on the light, she discovered that the air was thick with smoke. Then she understood. The lace doilies and ornaments had been shifted from the table, and in their place was an array of glasses, the best ones. A box of cigars, reserved for visitors, lay open. The air reeked not only of cigar smoke but also of brandy and men's sweat.

Without stopping to think, she hung up her coat and hat, took an apron from a peg, and put the kettle on. Then she opened every window, because the smell in the house was making her feel sick.

Obviously, her father had been entertaining his cronies here. That was natural enough, but he shouldn't have used the best glasses, or left them standing on the polished table, making rings all over it. After washing the glasses and putting them back on their shelf, she wiped the table, and when some of the spots wouldn't come off, she went over them with furniture polish.

She wasn't hungry, but was dropping with fatigue. After finishing the table, she sank into an armchair. For some minutes she let her gaze roam the room, lingering on the framed photographs on the walls. Then, with a little sigh, she closed her eyes.

She remained conscious of time passing, and heard the last bus from Charron go by, and, soon after, the Paris train. About half an hour later, there was the sound of heavy footsteps outside, a key rattling in the lock. Before opening her eyes, she was aware that the person at the door was having trouble opening it, and had a moment of panic. Suppose it wasn't her father!

She rose, yawning, and made sure the room was neat, while footsteps sounded in the hall. No longer nervous, she opened the parlor door.

Then she felt frightened as she looked at the man who loomed in the shadows. It was her father, yes, but almost unrecognizable.

He was still in his best suit, the one he had worn for the trial. But his lips were tight, his jaw was thrust forward aggressively, and his eyes had a queer glitter she had never seen before. Suddenly he barked out:

"What the hell are you doing here?"

Odette almost burst into tears. She understood. Only twice in her life had she seen her father drunk, but she had a vivid memory of both occasions, especially the one following her mother's funeral.

"What is it, Father?" she asked timidly.

He grinned, a thing he rarely did. It made him look even more alarming.

"Clear out!" he bawled, steadying himself against the door frame.

For a moment she thought she'd misunderstood, and waited, keeping quite still.

In the tone of a man who is holding himself in, but cannot answer for what he will do next, he repeated:

"Will you clear out!"

She realized he wasn't drunk in the same way as before. There was a strange fixity in his eyes, and his features were rigid, as if he were controlling them by a tremendous effort.

"Please, Father, listen! I . . ."

"Ain't I told you to clear out, you bitch? I'm through with you. And you know damn well why."

Suddenly he seemed to lose control; he burst into tears and shook convulsively from head to foot. Odette was so scared she could hardly think.

"All right, Father. I'll go. Don't take on so. Please listen . . ."

"Shut your mouth!"

"But I want to . . . to explain."

"I don't want to hear no more of your lies, my girl. Get a move on! Can't you see it's all I can do to keep myself from giving you what I gave that blasted doctor?"

She started to go to her bedroom, thinking she could spend the night there after barricading herself in. Perhaps in the morning her father would be calmer.

But he took a step toward her, snarling: "Get on with it!" Tears were still rolling down his cheeks. "Take what you want, but get out of this house *at once!*"

To her surprise, he walked into her bedroom and switched on the light. She saw him hauling a suitcase, the only one they had, from the top of the wardrobe.

She seemed paralyzed; she couldn't get a word out, or even shed a tear. Her body was limp. Propped against the bedpost, she watched her father with bewildered eyes.

Clumsily, with the jerky movements of a drunkard, he opened the wardrobe door, wrenched clothes off their hooks, and bundled them into the suitcase.

"Why don't you lend a hand? . . . Guess you think I'm drunk. Well, I may've had a drop or two, but I know what I'm doing. And don't you get the idea I'll change my mind tomorrow morning."

There was something tragic in his grief, tragic and grotesque. Those who had seen him that morning in the dock, an insignificant little wisp of a man, dazed and pitiful, would not have dreamed he was capable of such intensity of emotion.

"For God's sake, hurry up!" There was almost a note of pleading in his voice. "Don't you understand? . . . No? Well, that dirty swine of a lawyer, that . . . Limaille, had the goddamn gall to offer me *their* money—same as they're giving you. Could hardly keep my hands off the bastard's throat!"

His voice broke on a sob, and a fit of dizziness came over him. Odette thought he was going to pass out. But another spasm of rage convulsed him and, losing control, he started screaming:

"Get out, you bitch! Get out!"

He fumbled in his pockets and finally produced a small red card, which he held to her eyes. It was a membership card in the Communist Party; a brand-new one, issued that afternoon.

"*Now* do you understand?"

To him, that piece of cardboard was the symbol of his revolt, of his break with all that his life had stood for until today.

He stumbled back against the wall, on the edge of collapse, and with vacant eyes watched his daughter as she slowly moved toward her hat and coat. With a last burst of energy, he picked up the suitcase and flung it down in front of her.

"Don't forget your things."

Odette made a final effort.

"Listen, Father! I assure you . . ."

She could see he wasn't listening; he was nursing his grief, working himself up for another outburst. As she opened the front door, she heard a strange blurred sound behind her—was it a snarl, a hiccup, or a sob?—and then she started running down the street, the suitcase slapping against her leg.

Though not particularly heavy, the suitcase was awkward to carry, but she slowed down only on reaching Porte Royale. Two young corporals on their way back to the barracks stared at her and made some remark. But there were other people around, coming from the center of the city; the show at the Alhambra had just ended.

For a while, Odette lost her bearings, but soon she saw the Clock Tower, and discovered that it was after midnight. Beyond the clock lay the harbor, where the tide was near full, making the masts of the fishing boats rise higher than the nearby houses. On the waterfront the Café de Paris, where she sometimes went on a Sunday afternoon to listen to the music, was still open.

In a sort of dream, she walked to a table and sat down on the banquette behind it. When a waiter came, she stared at him for a few moments as she tried to realize where she was.

"What can I get you, mademoiselle?"

"I don't know. . . . Oh, yes; a cup of coffee."

Some time passed before she noticed that the café was getting ready to close: most of the chairs were stacked on the tables, and half the room was in darkness. She could hear two half-drunk young men near the bar exchanging confidences at the top of their voices.

"So I says to her, 'If you think you can play that sort of game with me, my pet, I tell you straight, there's nothing doing.' "

Odette's eyes settled on a man she recognized. She had seen him only that afternoon, but for some reason she couldn't recall who he was. He had graying hair and was sitting beside a rather shabbily dressed woman who was probably a chorus girl. He looked at Odette, and there was a curious intentness in his gaze.

She saw him bend toward the woman, say something to her as if to excuse himself, and start walking across the sawdust-strewn floor in her direction. As he approached, Odette was racking her brain to remember who he was.

There was something so strange in this that she half wondered if she was dreaming. But she could still hear the two young men loudly discussing their love affairs.

The gray-haired man bowed to her formally and said, in a low voice:

"May I sit beside you for a moment, Mademoiselle Odette?" Then, seeing she didn't recognize him, he added: "I'm Frédéric Dargens, Philippe's father."

She nodded, guessing that he had noticed the suitcase and was wondering about it. When the waiter came with the coffee, he murmured:

"May I suggest you not drink coffee right now?" Turning to the waiter, he said: "Bring a hot toddy."

She made no protest. Indeed, she felt vaguely drawn to this man, who obviously understood life well and handled things tactfully.

"So you missed the train?" He smiled, glancing at the suitcase.

She felt like bursting into tears, but managed to fight them down. When he gently patted her arm, she found something consoling in his touch.

"There isn't another train until morning. . . . You can't stay here all night, you know."

He was choosing his words carefully, and they were intended to convey more than their surface meanings.

Abruptly, Odette came out with it, and she could hardly believe it was she who was speaking. She had never been one for confiding in friends, and at the office she had a reputation of being standoffish. Now she heard herself saying:

"My father turned me out of the house!"

"I guessed that when I saw the suitcase."

She didn't stop to wonder how he could have guessed what, for her, had been a complete surprise. Glancing at the woman sitting near them, she said fretfully:

"Why does she keep staring at me like that?"

Frédéric murmured an excuse and went to whisper something to the woman. Shrugging her shoulders, she picked up her bag and shabby fur coat, and walked out.

"I told her to go to bed," Frédéric explained with a smile.

"Why?"

"Because we must have a little talk. You can't roam the streets all night, obviously. For one thing, you might be seen, and that wouldn't help matters. . . ."

She made a gesture of indifference.

"Now then!" said Frédéric with mock severity. "Don't be childish! Try to see things in their proper light. . . . But I wish you'd drink that toddy."

"It's too hot."

"Drink it anyway."

The young men sitting near the bar were watching them. The cashier and the waiter, used to Frédéric's late hours, showed patient resignation.

"Remember that nothing in life is final—least of all its tragedies."

She found his voice soothing; it resembled Philippe's, but was warmer and gentler. Also his "Don't be childish!" had reminded her of Philippe, who had the same way of regarding others as children and taking them under his protection. What was it Philippe had said to her? That it was wrong to think her life was ended. Why, it was only beginning.

How easily she had let herself be convinced by Philippe—she, whose father had killed a man on her account; she, who was known to all as her employer's mistress, and a girl who had undergone a secret operation; she whose good name was lost forever!

Now Philippe's father was assuring her that "nothing in life is final," and she had to admit that the details of the tragic confrontation she had just had with her father were already growing dim. Later, perhaps, she would recall them vividly, but now they were like something she had read in a book, or dreamed.

The room seemed hot, and she unbuttoned the collar of her coat. After finishing her toddy, she could feel the blood coursing in her veins, her temples throbbing. The voice beside her asked:

"Do you love Michel Donadieu?"

She promptly shook her head; then blushed, remembering. . . . And somehow she couldn't help thinking of Philippe, of the times he called her to his side, not to dictate, but to talk to her about her personal problems.

He'd told her, half laughing, half in earnest, that she'd acquired "glamour," that she'd had "a romantic adventure, like a heroine in a film." He'd said more in this vein, but she couldn't remember the exact words. It was more his tone, his manner, that lingered in her memory.

It all came to this: he was urging her to become cynical ("It's best to be 'hard-boiled'!"), to keep her end up ruthlessly, to cease being a "victim."

What he'd said was more or less this:

In the world of nature there are animals that eat others and animals that seem born to be eaten: wolves and rabbits. Don't be a rabbit!

Frédéric, she guessed, was not so hard. Perhaps, indeed, what he meant was something different.

"As luck would have it, you've not been able to lead the sheltered, regular life you seem cut out for. So you'll have to make do with another. See what I mean, Odette?"

She nodded, and dabbed her forehead with her handkerchief; she was perspiring slightly after the hot toddy.

"Anyhow, you're in a better position now to face life, aren't you?"

"I'm not well yet," she said sadly.

"I know. . . . But suppose I tell you that fifty percent of the women I know have been through what you've been through?"

"Is that really so?"

"What did they say to you at the office?"

"They want me to go to the Riviera later on, with Monsieur Philippe. For appearance's sake. I'm to work there for a time. Then they'll settle money on me, or give me a monthly allowance, and I can go. . . ."

"Where?"

"I don't know."

"What have you decided to do?"

"I haven't decided anything . . . not yet."

At last the noisy young men left the café. The waiter promptly seized the chairs they had been using and stacked them on the table.

"What would you advise me to do?"

Frédéric hardly felt justified in advising her to reject the Donadieu offer. He had no idea how far Odette was capable of fending for herself. So he replied, vaguely:

"I advise you to . . . live your own life. . . . By the way, have you any money with you?"

"I really don't know."

Then she remembered seeing her father, after bundling her clothes into the suitcase, throwing in something else, something that looked like the old leather wallet in which they kept some savings.

"Shall I have a look?"

She dreaded being left alone. With nervous haste, she opened the imitation-leather suitcase, fumbled among the jumble of clothes, found the wallet, which had been one of Baillet's few wedding presents, and opened it.

"Yes, there's money here. What do you think I should do?" she asked again.

She had a feeling that it was Philippe who would answer her, through his father's lips.

"The first thing to do is to get out of this café. It's long past closing time, and they want us to go. After that, we'll see."

For a moment she thought he might have an ulterior motive. After paying for the drinks, he picked up the suitcase, and for the first time in her life she had a door held open for her by a smiling, elegantly dressed man.

It was a moonlit night, the air dry and crisp. As they walked along the waterfront, Frédéric was wondering what to do.

"Of course, you could spend the night at a hotel," he said at last, linking her arm in his with an easy, protective gesture. "But everyone would hear about it tomorrow, and gossip would start. A train doesn't leave until 5:07."

"What train?"

"Does that matter? The best thing, in my opinion, is for you to leave La Rochelle and have a good long rest. Then you'll be able to make plans and decide where to go: to Paris, for instance, or to some quiet country town, if you prefer it."

She decided quickly. "I'll go to Paris."

"Now listen, please. What I'm going to suggest may compromise you, though there isn't much risk, really. If you weren't so tired, I'd advise you to walk around until your train leaves. As it is . . . Look, I'll leave the door of the theater ajar, and you can make yourself snug in one of the dress-circle boxes. I'll see that you get away before five."

He didn't trouble to listen to her answer; he knew she would do anything he suggested. After lining up three well-padded chairs at the back of a box, near a radiator, he watched her settle down on this makeshift couch and close her eyes.

In his little room in the attic, he found the woman who had been with him at the café—an acrobat past her prime, who was now out of a job.

"Who was that girl?" she asked.

"Nobody you'd know."

"Well, I'd never have thought it of you—leading young girls astray at your time of life! She's young enough to be your daughter."

He responded with a laugh.

"That's a sign of age, my dear. Didn't you know that? Old fellows always want them young!"

In Saint-Raphaël at the same hour, Michel was leaving the Boule Rouge with Nina. He was tired after his journey, but he exaggerated, tottering like a man on the brink of collapse. Now and then he halted with a faint gasp, and pressed his hand to his chest dramatically.

"Another evening gone, and you haven't answered my question yet," he said reproachfully.

He was still harping on the same theme; he had let his curiosity develop into an obsession. Each day he resolved to have it out with the girl, even to use violence if she refused to answer. His eyes fell on a wooden bench.

"Mind if we sit?" he said. "I think my pulse is slowing down again."

Nina complied with bad grace. She didn't believe his stories of a pulse that slowed down, without rhyme or reason, so far as she could judge. Plump, pink-cheeked, he didn't look in the least like the victim of a dangerous disease.

But somehow tonight she felt uneasy. The silence of the sleep-bound town affected her; she wished there were people still walking around.

"Come closer, Ninette."

He had a string of pet names for her: Ninette, Ninouche, and even, garbling a name he had seen in a Russian novel, Ninouchka. Silly business, she thought, but she took care not to tell him so. He was a rich man, and rich people, as she knew, were apt to be odd. Some of the women staying at the Continental, where she worked, were like that; they had the craziest habits. One woman brought her own sheets with her, black silk. She said white sheets kept her awake.

Nina let herself be drawn toward him, and made no protest when his hand cupped her firm young breast. After all, there was no great harm in that. The trouble was, this didn't satisfy him. He was always trying to go farther; give him an inch and there was no knowing what he'd take! Cautiously, trying to divert her attention, he became more enterprising, and when, at last, she thrust his hand away, he complained and said he was sorry—only to start over again a moment later.

"Can't you realize it proves my love for you, my wanting to . . . to do that?"

"It proves you're a man; that's all."

Then he began talking about his past in a sad voice. "I've been through such a terrible time, Ninette."

She knew her cue.

"Ah. You're thinking about that fellow who's doing time on your account."

"He isn't. They acquitted him."

"Well, then, I can't see what you have to worry about."

"You can't see? Don't you understand that that man has got his knife into me? One of these days he'll track me down and . . ."

"What did you do to make him feel like that?"

"Oh, there was trouble about a girl . . . a woman."

"His wife, eh?"

His hands were roving again and, though she struggled hard, there was no detaching them. It was as if the tentacles of some large, hungry creature had fastened on her body. For the first time, she felt frightened of him.

"Ninouche . . . Ninouche darling . . ." His hot breath fanned her cheek.

"That's enough!" she cried. "Can't you leave a girl alone? Take your dirty paws off me. If you don't, I'll . . . I'll bite!"

Suddenly she did. Michel's nose was right in front of her mouth, and she gave a vicious snap.

He sprang to his feet with a strange, aggrieved expression, like that of a child who has been unjustly scolded. After fumbling for his handkerchief, he dabbed at his nose.

"You can't say I didn't warn you," she muttered, straightening her dress. "You're the limit! Always trying to find out what don't concern you. You should know better at your age."

In his plus fours and argyle stockings, he looked grotesque as he wiped the blood from his nose, which seemed fatter, more bulbous now.

"Fed up with me?" she asked. Then she rose and turned to walk away. "Because, you know, you only have to say the word . . ."

"Please don't go," he begged her. "Surely you can stay a few minutes more."

183

The only light came from the moon and a few pale stars. For a while, they were silent, and Michel pretended to be blowing his nose when a policeman walked by. Nina was the first to speak.

"It's all your own fault, really. Why must you start that business every time? You know I don't like it."

"Then . . . answer my question!" Despite his smarting nose, Michel was still gripped by his obsession.

"What question?"

"You know perfectly well."

"You mean, if I've . . . if I've been with a man?"

"Yes, that's it," he muttered uncomfortably.

"All right! I *have*. . . . Now, are you satisfied?" Sullenly, she turned her back on him.

"Who was he?"

"The man I'm engaged to, of course."

"The one who's at Brest, in the arsenal?"

"Who else?"

"Ninouchka dear, come nearer."

But it was he who went to her, and he pressed her to his breast tenderly, whispering in her ear:

"Then why won't you . . . with me?"

"It ain't the same."

"Why not?"

"Because it ain't. . . . Now, come along; I want to get some sleep tonight."

"You'll meet me tomorrow as usual, won't you, dear?"

"Depends on how I feel."

"What's the matter? I haven't offended you, have I? Look, Nina, if you like, I'll promise . . . not to start that again."

"That's what you always say."

"This time I really mean it."

She burst out laughing. They were under a streetlight, and she had just noticed two big drops of blood on Michel's nose, one of them hanging on the tip, about to fall.

"Why are you laughing?"

"Sorry. I can't help it. You're so funny."

But she said it almost affectionately. He *was* funny, so different from other men she'd met. He reminded her of a fat bumblebee in a kitchen, blundering up against the walls.

"No. Don't start that again. I want to get back."

"What about tomorrow?"

"Wait for me at the usual place. Maybe I'll come. . . . What will your sister think when she sees your nose?"

Though, for safety's sake, he called himself Monsieur Emile, he was always coming out with things, and Nina knew quite a lot about his family. She knew, for instance, that his sister was staying with him and was going to have a baby, that she telephoned her husband every day, and each call cost eighteen francs for three minutes.

She had also learned that his young brother, a delicate boy, had developed a passion for gymnastics, and spent hours attempting the wildest acrobatic feats, helped by his tutor.

Actually, Kiki's latest hobby was boat-building. He had sent for a pamphlet, *Build Your Own Boat*; he'd seen the advertisement for it in the boys' paper he subscribed to. He'd bought the necessary wood and tools and set to work. Edmond had given him a hand, and was now equally enthusiastic about it.

They were continuing their gymnastic exercises with equal ardor, however, and sometimes quarreled when Kiki maintained he could beat Edmond at certain feats on the horizontal bars. They had taken Martine's measuring tape, and were always checking their biceps, calves, and chests.

On reaching the railway bridge, Nina gave Michel the usual parting kiss. He was seized by panic at the thought that perhaps she wouldn't meet him again. And another thought was hovering in the back of his mind: perhaps some other man . . .

Suddenly an access of desire came over him; there was nobody in sight—why not here and now? She seemed to guess what was in his mind and, slipping from his embrace, ran quickly under the bridge, calling over her shoulder:

"Au 'voir, dear."

One more unpleasantness, the day's last, had to be faced: the journey home, haunted by fears of being waylaid by some nocturnal prowler. As he hurried along, he felt his strength failing, and decided to take his pulse the moment he got home.

An eerie sense of loneliness came over him as he entered the silent house. One would never have thought it occupied by four persons—not counting the child that was on the way. There was none of the vague animal warmth, the homely atmosphere, pervading a house that is lived in.

Michel had the largest bedroom, also the barest. Its emptiness was like something he often felt within himself, which led him to prolong the moments when he held the soft warmth of Nina's body against his, and to hunger for her kisses, with their faint savor of garlic, which he had come to love.

Slowly, with the preciseness he brought to everything he did, he undressed, folded his clothes, and felt his pulse. Then he gargled, and finally walked, barefoot, to the door to turn off the light, because the switch beside the bed didn't work.

14

Philippe's visit to the Hôtel de France, one morning in early February, would have drawn little attention had it been noticed at all. In the big hotel dining room, which looked like a refectory, he lunched merely with a young couple who had arrived earlier in the day and had registered as M. and Mme Grindorge.

In the afternoon, the Grindorges went sightseeing in La Rochelle—for once, it wasn't raining—and Philippe, it so happened, was standing at the door of one of the company warehouses when they passed. After greeting them, he showed them around the refrigeration plant, then over a trawler and a collier, and finally through the briquet factory.

There was nothing surreptitious about it. He could be seen from the windows of the offices on Quai Vallin; though, as a matter of fact, no one happened to be watching.

Nor did the arrival of a tall, thin, bearded Russian at a small hotel near the station attract any notice. The manager and staff treated him with deference, because when he registered, he wrote Civil Engineer after his name, which was so long and unpronounceable that, to simplify things, they addressed him as "Monsieur Ivan." On the third day after his arrival, he came back in a small six-horsepower car he had just bought.

After that, Monsieur Ivan was out all day, driving around the city and stopping at various garages to buy small quantities of gasoline.

Toward the end of March, there was talk in La Rochelle about the liquidation of the Rossignol garage, which, badly situated between one-way streets, and also not well equipped, had been losing money for some years.

Then one fine day Rossignol paid his creditors in full, gave his garage a new coat of paint, and announced that he had gone into partnership with a wealthy Russian engineer, a Monsieur Ivan. At the beginning of April, a new sign appeared above the garage entrance: ROSSIGNOL & CO., TRUCKING AND HAULING. A fortnight later, ten enormous late-model trucks were lined up in the street outside the garage, each of them blazoned, in big red letters, ROSSIGNOL & CO.

The conversation came around to this subject as Philippe and Mme Donadieu sat at the table one evening in early May. Summertime had begun, and they could now eat by daylight, though even on sunny days the dining room was dark and the air damp, because of the big trees. Mme Donadieu had formed the habit of dining tête-à-tête with Philippe, who usually had something interesting to tell.

"Know what I've been thinking about, Mother?" he asked that evening in a casual tone.

Naturally, she said "No," and looked at him inquiringly.

"Some enterprising fellow has just set himself up as a trucker here. I haven't any idea what sort of stuff he proposes to carry, but I saw his fleet of trucks the other day. There are ten of them, all big and brand-new."

Mme Donadieu, who knew that Philippe rarely spoke without some definite purpose, listened attentively.

"Today, I heard something that, if true, might make a good deal of difference to us. I was told that the man who's running the business—he's a Russian, by the way—has been to see Varin twice. . . ."

"Yes?" She still didn't know why he was telling her this.

"The explanation may be that he approached Varin with a proposal to deliver his fish. But there's another possibility: I wouldn't be surprised if he offered to distribute Varin's briquets, in competition with us. Ten fast trucks delivering, in rural districts, to customers' doors. We'd have difficulty against that."

Not for the first time, she was impressed by Philippe's business acumen. No other member of the family had had the faintest inkling of this danger—a serious danger, because the briquet part of the business was the only one showing a profit.

In the same casual tone, Philippe went on talking while he ate.

"I haven't had time to go into the matter at all thoroughly. But one thing's obvious: our delivery service is shockingly out of date. I'm afraid it wouldn't be any use asking the bank for another loan, to buy new trucks. . . . Cheese, Mother?"

After helping himself, he rang the bell.

"Some more butter, please, Augustin."

Philippe waited until the man had gone before continuing.

"As a matter of fact, I have an idea, but I don't know yet if there's anything in it. It's this: suppose that, instead of selling our coal ourselves . . ."

Had Olsen been present, he'd have made an angry protest. Mme Donadieu, however, merely leaned back in her chair and waited.

"Instead of *distributing* our coal ourselves, I should have said. Suppose we were to delegate that service to a subsidiary company? You'll tell me, of course, that this is ruled out by the will. Under its provisions, we're not allowed to dispose of any part of the business before Kiki comes of age. My answer is that this wouldn't be *disposing* of any branch of the concern. . . ."

She put her elbows on the table and gazed at him intently; she had a feeling that this moment might have serious consequences.

"Let me make myself clear, Mother, if you don't mind. We would, of course, go on buying coal in England and bringing it here in our colliers. We would go on manufacturing our briquets. But in the handling of these, there would be a slight modification. For our retail sales, we would set up a new company, a subsidiary, which would buy our stocks at an agreed price and provide the delivery service for the area we now supply."

"Who would run this subsidiary you're speaking of?"

"*We* would. In conjunction, of course, with the garage owning the trucks. It's quite simple, really. We supply the goods; they supply the transport."

So far, so good. What remained to be said needed more careful handling. Philippe stood up, lighted a cigarette, and took some long puffs on it before continuing.

"At first sight, I grant you, there doesn't seem much point in tying ourselves to another concern. But it would be to the advantage of us all—especially to your advantage, Mother. As things stand, the profits on our coal are eaten up by the fisheries and shipping departments. And you, of course, have no direct interest in the business. The result is that each of us has to struggle along on fifty thousand francs a year, and it looks as if next year we won't get even that. Also, when Kiki comes of age, you'll have only a pittance, perhaps nothing at all."

He was conscious of the portrait on the wall gazing down severely, but this didn't embarrass him in the least; quite the contrary. The thought that he was playing fast and loose with the provisions of the old man's will, defying the domestic tyrant on his own ground, tickled his fancy.

"Of course, the subsidiary company would be an independent

concern. Each of us would hold a certain number of shares in it, and yours would be in *your own name*. Thus the profits wouldn't pass through the Donadieu accounts. . . . Well, this is just a casual idea that crossed my mind."

It was nothing of the sort—a fact of which Mme Donadieu was perfectly aware. She had had ample time to take Philippe's measure, and, though indulgent toward the young man, she was not his dupe.

He knew what he was about, and, no doubt, had his ax to grind. Still, when all was said and done, wasn't he less dangerous to her than her son and daughter, who were all for strict compliance with the will?

His proposal, she saw clearly, was nothing but a scheme for bypassing the restrictions imposed by Oscar Donadieu, and regaining some freedom of action with the estate.

"What is it?" she asked impatiently when Augustin entered.

"Madame Marthe wishes to know if she can have a word with you, madame." . . .

"Good evening, Maman," said Marthe, bestowing a quick kiss on her mother's forehead. Her "Maman" had sounded as aloof as the most formal "madame."

Mother and daughter often let two or three days go by without seeing each other. Marthe alone still kept to the ritual instituted by Oscar Donadieu, and announced her visits.

"You can stay, Philippe," she remarked when her brother-in-law started to leave the room. "What I have to say concerns you, too."

In other words, like him, she had something up her sleeve, and it was probably delicate, because Olsen, who abhorred family discussions, hadn't come. Marthe was much better at that sort of thing, rarely yielded ground, and never lost her head under any circumstances. This was her greatest asset.

Philippe expected her to begin with one of her usual acid comments, because, since he and Mme Donadieu had started eating together, the latter smoked and had a liqueur with her herb tea after dinner.

But no. After Augustin had lighted the lamps and shuffled out of the room, Marthe began in what was, for her, quite an amiable tone.

"It's about vacations. Jean and I were discussing that at dinner, and it struck us that it might be a good thing if you took yours first—immediately, in fact."

The family had already agreed that, since they'd gone to the expense of renting the Saint-Raphaël villa for a long period, the most practical course this year would be for each household to vacation there in turn. At present, Michel, Martine, and Kiki and his tutor were in the villa, but there were other bedrooms.

"We mustn't forget," Marthe hastened to add, "that the weather on the south coast is quite different from ours. In fact, if you postponed your visit until July, you might find the heat rather trying. . . . Then there's Martine." She glanced at Philippe, as if to enlist his support for what she was about to say. "You've seen her last letter to Philippe, haven't you? It seems that she'll have her baby a little prematurely, some time in June. So you'd be there when it happens."

Mme Donadieu was amused. She had a shrewd idea of what was at the back of her daughter's mind. At this time of the year, there was no one on the Riviera, and Marthe wanted to be there at the height of the season. Her next remark clearly gave her away.

"I've just had a letter from Françoise." This was Mme Brun's daughter, the one who had married well. "She says she'll be in Cannes in July, and she hopes to see me. Saint-Raphaël's quite near Cannes, of course. . . ."

Mme Donadieu nodded. There was no point in holding out against her daughter, whose tenacity, once she set her mind to anything, was proverbial in the family. Meanwhile, she saw a way of turning the situation to her own account.

"Very well," she said. "I don't mind going now. But on one condition: that I take Augustin and the car with me."

Marthe grimaced.

"Well, I'm not sure if we can spare the car. I must ask Jean what he thinks."

She went upstairs. After quite a long absence, she came down, still looking glum.

"Jean agrees about the car, though not having it will be a nuisance for him. But he won't hear of your taking Augustin. There's got to be a man here in the daytime."

They discussed this for some time. Mme Donadieu had not learned to drive. Engaging another chauffeur would be too expensive.

Then Philippe had an inspiration. Why not take Baptiste, the caretaker of Château d'Esnandes?

Marthe jumped at the idea, but her mother was less enthusiastic.

"I can't see Baptiste driving a car on the Riviera. For one thing, he looks like such a . . . such a rustic."

Finally they reached a compromise. Baptiste was to be made presentable with chauffeur's livery.

On the day before the one fixed for her departure, Mme Donadieu was as excited as a young girl off for her first vacation on her own. She had ordered two half-mourning dresses, explaining that full mourning was uncalled for, and anyhow would look ridiculous on the Riviera. The car was crammed with luggage, Baptiste resplendent in brand-new livery.

Nothing further had been said about the subsidiary company, though Mme Donadieu had had two more meals alone with Philippe. Only when about to leave did she remark, with affected casualness:

"By the way, how do you propose to carry out that plan you were speaking of the other evening?"

"I'll have to talk it over with Jean and Marthe, to start with. If your signature is needed . . ." His gesture indicated that in that event he would hurry south to see her.

"Any message for Martine?"

"Tell her I'll be coming in a few days. And she's to take great care of herself and wrap up well in the evenings. I believe the night air can be treacherous in those parts."

Mme Brun and Charlotte were at their window, the former counting on her fingers.

"Let's see. How many of them are left, now that the Queen Mother's gone? Marthe and her husband, and Philippe. Only three. Why, the house is practically empty!"

She descended on the villa like a whirlwind, and created as much disturbance as all the others put together.

Martine, who was more or less an invalid, usually stayed in her room, which was on the second floor and had a balcony. Her only exercise was an hour's stroll each evening on the seafront—and that only because the doctor had insisted.

Mme Donadieu took little notice of Kiki, hardly bestowing a glance on the boat, which was nearly finished. Her first brush was with Michel, who was annoyed when he saw the car. On the day after her arrival, Mme Donadieu made an inspection of the villa, noting which faucets were dripping, which shutters failed to close, and she exclaimed indignantly at the forlorn aspect of the living room, the emptiness of the conservatory.

That evening, a contractor, summoned by her, made his appearance, and went away with a long list of repairs and alterations to be carried out at once.

"Won't it cost a lot?" Michel ventured to ask.

"That can't be helped. This place isn't fit for human habitation; it's falling to pieces. I can't imagine how you've lived with it all these months. Of course, you're out so much—and you never come home until three in the morning, do you?"

This thrust home had the intended effect. Michel made no further protest, merely sighing when his mother indulged in some new extravagance. One morning, a complete set of garden furniture was delivered to the villa.

"You don't expect me to stay cooped up indoors all day, I hope," she said, noticing her son's expression.

Another day, a crate arrived containing an assortment of liqueurs, mineral waters, cigars, and cigarettes.

"What on earth do we want with all this?" Michel couldn't help asking.

"Oh, I have some friends coming tomorrow afternoon. . . . You've not been here, I suppose, without making some acquaintances. Well, I've done that, too—and they're very nice people. They belong to one of the important families in Mulhouse."

She was brimming over with vitality, busy from morning till night, and devoted barely two hours a day to her daughter. She had the grounds, which had been running wild for two years, cleaned up, the glass roof of the conservatory washed, and got some exotic plants to garnish it.

Michel wondered how she'd made the acquaintance of these new friends of hers, the Krugers. The explanation was simple; they had started talking in a teashop, and three days later were bosom friends.

The Krugers were Alsatian, and owned big woolen mills in Mulhouse. They'd bought the Saint-Raphaël villa in which they now were staying, and they used the same system as the Donadieus: various parts of the family—there were no fewer than fifteen—occupied the villa in turn.

A hundred yards from Villa des Tamaris was another villa, with spacious, well-kept grounds and tall wrought-iron gates. In the afternoon, its occupants could be seen leaving for the Valescure golf course in a large tan car, and sometimes, on gala nights, for the Casino in Cannes.

Mme Donadieu was interested, and asked who they were. She learned that the villa was owned by an eccentric rich old English-woman, whose whim it was to have a little court of young men in attendance.

"I'll get to know her," she decided.

She continued spending. The dresses she had bought in La Rochelle looked dowdy and depressing in the brilliant sunshine of the South, so she had new ones made. She did not pay for them at once, but said:

"I want these things delivered to Villa des Tamaris. I'm Madame Donadieu. You know the name, of course; we're shipowners in La Rochelle."

The bills could wait. In Cannes, she was even "wilder." For the first time in her life, she gambled. True, she risked only a hundred francs, and she had beginner's luck, winning three hundred after the croupier had explained how to place her bets and so on.

It was at the table that she achieved her purpose: she struck up an acquaintance with the opulent Mrs. Gabell, whom everyone, despite her age, called Minnie. Her husband, Mme Donadieu learned, was a big whisky distiller.

Meanwhile, Michel fumed with suppressed irritation. If there was one thing he loathed, it was disorder. He liked his days adjusted hour by hour to a fixed schedule, to breathe familiar air wherever he might be. He also needed to be a leading figure, as he had been in La Rochelle, where Oscar Donadieu's elder son was definitely "somebody."

His mother had changed all that. The Krugers—the girls, to his disgust, were plain and had no charm—were at least the equals of the Donadieus, and they had brought two cars.

When, escorted by a couple of her courtiers, Mrs. Gabell came to tea, Michel was annoyed to see that the young men's clothes were cut quite differently from his, being, he assumed, the last word in masculine fashion in Paris or London. In addition, they asked him tiresome questions, such as:

"Don't you play golf?"

He did, but so badly that he would rather give up going to the course than play in their company. And:

"I suppose you spend the winter in Paris?"

Then they started discussing the attractions of various European capitals and New York, and the technicalities of polo, which one of the young men played.

There seemed no point in trying to keep up; no doubt they found him as boring as he found them. He had only one resource: his heart complaint. On this subject, anyhow, they couldn't compete.

Sometimes, when they came, he went upstairs to his sister, but Martine had developed a curious irritability and was often quite short with him. Once, he ventured to give Kiki some suggestions about the building of his boat, but the tutor quickly made him realize he didn't know what he was talking about.

O. has left town abruptly [Philippe told him in a letter], but I don't think you need to worry. It probably means that she's decided to start a new life somewhere else, which is all to the good.

Comparing Nina with Odette, he decided that in some ways she was more satisfactory; in others, not. She was less docile than Odette, but she stirred his senses more. Though he had spent quite a lot of money on her, she still refused to do what he wanted. And there was a cloud on the horizon: in two weeks, she told him, her young man would be coming on leave. If only he could persuade her to become his mistress before the fortnight was up!

Even the climate got on his nerves. In the sun, it was too hot; when he moved into the shade, he started shivering. The night air made him feverish.

At meals, his mother kept talking about a big dinner party she wanted to give, at which the Krugers were to meet Mrs. Gabell and her satellites, and also a Geneva doctor she had met at the Casino.

Philippe, when he came for a weekend, seemed to approve of this. After a brief conversation with his mother-in-law about his project of a subsidiary company, he asked Michel to go for a stroll along the seafront with him.

"I've discussed it with Olsen," he said, "and he seems to be coming around to my view. From the look of things, this year's balance sheet will be even less satisfactory than the last one. The banks are beginning to make difficulties. And, as you know, our family expenses aren't getting any less. Your wife's just written for another four thousand francs."

"Is she still in Switzerland?"

"No. She's moved to San Remo."

"With the children?"

"She didn't mention them in her letter."

"Really, I think she might have let me know . . ."

Philippe tapped him lightly on the arm.

"Listen, Michel. As I said, we're in a tight corner, and the question is how to get out of it."

Though he had little real interest in the family business, Michel had the Donadieu squeamishness on certain matters; he was genuinely shocked by the proposal to launch a subsidiary company.

"Surely it . . . it would be a breach of the provisions of the will, wouldn't it? We were expressly forbidden to alienate any part of the business."

"This wouldn't be alienation. We wouldn't be parting with anything; we'd merely be delegating certain activities to another group."

In the glance Michel gave Philippe, there was as much rancor as resignation. He knew the others regarded him as a fool, and that he was under Philippe's thumb; that his mother was trading on his weakness when she alluded to his coming home at three in the morning; that Philippe was doing likewise when, almost in the same breath, he referred to Eva and to Odette. It was hitting below the belt, but he wasn't in a position to retaliate, or even to protest.

"What does Marthe say?"

Marthe was his last hope. She was as much a Donadieu as he was and, as she had often shown, inflexible on points of family honor.

A picture rose before him: the portrait of his grandfather, the Founder of the House, a naval architect with a big fan-shaped beard like that of a Jules Verne hero. That stern, dour face said at once that this man—another Oscar—had never felt the least temptation to stray from the narrow path; that all his life had been hedged by rules and self-imposed restrictions.

So compelling had his personality been that his wife, Michel's grandmother, had never seemed to count in the family history. She had carried self-effacement to the point of fading out of existence a few months after she had provided her lord and master with a son. Michel felt convinced that, after her death, there had been no other woman in his life.

This first Oscar had been succeeded by Michel's father, who had carried on the Founder's work, and built up not only a fortune, but also a dynasty. Under his sway, the rigid principles Michel's grandfather had imposed on himself were extended to the household: his wife, his children, the servants.

Little by little, habits had crystallized into hard-and-fast rules, a family code the basic principles of which no one, during the lifetime of the second Oscar, had ever dared question.

Then came *his* death—and with the thought of it a frown settled on Michel's face. He had never fully accepted the theory of an accident: that his father had stumbled in the darkness and fallen into the harbor. What was the true explanation?

A new thought waylaid him. Why had he not been given the name Oscar, in accordance with family tradition? Because of his mother, he had been told. She had never liked the name, and they did not want to upset her after a hard confinement. Many years later, the name had been bestowed on the last-born Donadieu; but they had made haste to substitute a nickname, Kiki.

Now, the last chapter of the family history was epitomized, it seemed, in this ambitious young man walking at his side under the plane trees bordering the seafront; in Philippe, who was expounding the most efficient method of distributing their coal and the various ways in which the will could be construed.

If only, Michel thought, I didn't have a weak heart . . .

But no! For once, he was honest with himself, as he sauntered in the sunshine filtering through the leaves, and admitted that, even if he were perfectly fit, he would probably submit as he was doing now. Suppose, however, his father had died when he, Michel, was twenty? There was no way to know. He had always been a weakling, and his inferiority was constantly brought home to him, even when hunting on Sundays. How often, when he fired at a pheasant, had Baptiste fired at the same moment, from behind him, and when the bird plunged down, exclaimed in a tone that just failed to convince: "Good shot, sir!"

From early childhood, he had been under his sister's thumb. Marthe had always known her own mind, and she had very soon taken his measure. Though he was the boy and older, it was Marthe who laid their sparrow traps, wrung the birds' necks, and roasted them at the kitchen fire.

As for Martine and Kiki, they had never counted. Their father had made no secret of his aversion to his puny, dull-witted younger son.

Yes, Marthe was the only one who might have made a stand. But Philippe had assured him that Marthe consented. . . .

As if this weren't enough, he had to endure the spectacle of his mother, who should still be in full mourning, plunging into a whirl of pleasure and behaving like a woman half her age.

This morning, Michel felt exceptionally clearheaded. He could see that, since his father's death, he had gone to pieces, whereas his mother seemed to have taken a new lease on life. Yet why . . . worry? He was a sick man, he needed rest—and Nina gave him quite enough trouble. If there was anything to be done, others must do it.

He dropped wearily onto a bench—as it happened, the very bench on which he had been sitting when the little chambermaid bit his nose.

"When are we to sign?"

"Immediately. I have all the documents with me. Mother has agreed."

"And Kiki's guardian?"

"I'll see him on my way back."

The sea was calm as a lake; he felt that it would be a joy to plunge into those blue depths and find oblivion. Young men in white flannels were strolling in the sunlight; women in flimsy dresses or bathing suits were lounging on the sand below. Two Navy planes were circling over the bay.

Yes, why worry? What could he do? Already it was an effort for him to recall the look of the Donadieu stronghold in La Rochelle, overshadowed by its immemorial trees and steeped in the damp of Atlantic gales.

"They're to pay a million for the distribution rights."

"For how many years?"

"Ten."

He would have done better not to bring this up. Legally, no doubt, it could pass muster. But, in practice, it would defeat the intentions of Oscar Donadieu, whose will expressly safeguarded the minors' rights.

"I have the figures with me, if you'd like to see them," Philippe added.

But it was easy enough to juggle figures. One thing was certain: if some capitalist was prepared to pay a million francs for the rights, they must be worth more than that. And if Philippe . . .

"Also, each of us, Mother included, will receive twenty shares in the new company."

At that moment, had Michel seen a possible ally anywhere, Marthe, or Olsen, or Martine, or even one of the senior members of the staff, who with the years had acquired much of the Donadieu mentality, he might have made a stand, defied the young man beside him.

"Mother included," Philippe had said. In other words, his mother had been bribed, as indeed they had all been, by an offer of ready cash at a time when they were short of it. He thought of his mother, right now sitting with the crazy old Englishwoman, who was wearing a white jersey dress and a big white cape. For the first time, he glimpsed what had lain behind his father's will.

One evening, the old man, bringing to bear on this the perspicacity he brought to every problem, had drawn up the clauses of his will, which were so baffling at first sight. No doubt he had foreseen the course of events; had guessed that his wife, at the age of fifty-six, free at last from his restraint, would kick over the traces and play fast and loose with Donadieu tradition. Quite likely he had also foreseen that Michel would yield supinely, that Marthe would accept a new order. . . .

Never before had Michel asked himself if he loved his father; now, at last, he felt a touch of filial devotion, and with it a tightening of the heart. Almost without thinking, he took his gold box from his waistcoat pocket and put a digitalis pill on his tongue. Then he began coughing violently, because the pill wouldn't go down. For a moment it seemed as if he might be sick. Passersby were beginning to stare, and Philippe slapped him on the back two or three times.

"Come along to that café over there. You can sign the agreement after you've had something to drink."

Just then Kiki and Edmond walked by. They were carrying their cockleshell boat down to the beach for a trial trip. Both were in bathing suits, which revealed their lean young bodies. Their eyes were sparkling with excitement.

My dear Frédéric—You'll be surprised to see that I am writing from San Remo; no doubt you thought me still in Switzerland. I told you nothing in my last letters. I'd had a great shock and I preferred to wait till I could collect my thoughts.

You know the kind of hotel we were staying at, and the kind of people one met there, and, worst of all, the kind of conversation one had to put up with. From morning till night, I heard nothing but disquisitions on TB, but the subject bored me, and I never paid much attention.

Well, I'm getting to believe that there's a sort of fatality guiding one's actions. I chose that hotel to get away from the rotten life I'd been having, and into a new atmosphere. And, of course, I had the usual ideas about mountain air, and the virtues of a simple, healthy life in restful surroundings.

There was a nice young doctor staying at the hotel. (No, don't jump to the obvious conclusion, Frédéric dear!) We saw a good deal of each other. He told me his lungs were affected. What struck me most was his enormous zest for life. You could see it in his eyes, in his gestures, in everything he did. So much so that I sometimes felt almost embarrassed when I was with him, because there was something so *frantic* about it all.

Then one day my little boy, Jean, fell ill: a cold to start with, which developed into bronchitis. Anywhere else, I wouldn't have felt much anxiety. But here I'd heard so much about lung trouble that when my nice young doctor proposed taking him to a colleague for an X-ray examination, I consented.

I hope you'll never have to live through an experience like that, and hear somebody say gravely, "We have to have a blood test." Then he asked me such questions as "Did his father suffer from tuberculosis? Was there any trouble of the kind in your childhood?" All I knew was that, when I was only a few months old, I had a bad bout with pneumonia; in fact, the doctor had given me up.

Those were two horrible days. Séances in front of the X-ray screen, sputum tests, and the rest of it.

Then came that "Yes," which makes you feel like sinking into the earth, and one by one all your poor little illusions are blown away to nowhere! You know you're cut off from the world of normal, healthy people, and have become that pitiful, half-dead creature, "an invalid."

The strange thing is the quickness of the change—from health (one believes) to sick. And promptly—that's almost the worst thing about it— one gets the invalid mentality, starts walking like an invalid, fussing about one's health, taking precautions.

So that's how things stand, my friend. Jean is consumptive. And poor little Evette has some lesions, too. And they got it, not from their father, but from me.

I don't feel like writing to Michel, but when you next see him, perhaps you'll let him know. He will understand why I had to ask for money so often these last few weeks.

Since I am the most seriously ill, I have left the children in the best sanatorium in that part of Switzerland. Evette is in no great danger, they tell me; the lesions should heal in a few months. It may take longer for Jean, a year or so, they think, but there's little doubt he, too, will recover.

As for me, no, I'm not out for pity or the glamour of the dying heroine in a play—as you're probably thinking, you old cynic, you! But they're talking of a pneumothorax. A word I've heard pretty often here, and each time I hear it, I get gooseflesh all over.

They assure me that in two or three years, if I take care of myself and live an invalid's life, I have quite a good chance. My doctor friend begged me to stay in Switzerland, and nearly scared me into doing so.

But I realized that if I stayed, it would mean that for the rest of my days I'd have to live in that sanatorium atmosphere. You can't imagine what it's like. One has to see *them*, to know. And that's where I belong! The most awful thing, perhaps, is how the doctors encourage them to hope, even when there's no hope and the family has been warned to be ready for "bad news."

That, Frédéric, is why I've come to San Remo. I didn't really choose it; I picked it out at random from a list of resorts on the Italian Riviera. I pictured endless sunshine, mimosas—alas, they're over for this year—and a divinely blue sea.

I have come here to think things over, and make plans. In three years— if they aren't lying to me, as they usually lie to TB cases—I'll be fit to return to the old life in La Rochelle.

I know what my mother would advise. She's a true Italian, and would prefer six months of "crowded life," especially if she'd never known a better one than—well, you know what it was like—to the dull business of "lingering on."

My doctor friend—he's blond and comes from Lille—writes to say he wants to join me here, and burn up in two hectic months what little is left of his lungs. I'm telling him not to come.

An Englishman, an officer in the Indian Army, who always spends his leave in Italy, is making love to me, and I must say he does it nicely. Yesterday he took me to Monte Carlo in his speedboat; it does fifty miles an hour, and I wished it could go even faster! I treat myself in a sketchy sort of manner. But I smoke forty cigarettes a day, to the despair of my doctor.

Don't give me advice, please. I don't need it. The only thing is to let the sunlight and the marvelous air here do their work.

Write to me poste restante. And please don't say anything that will only make me feel worse. I suppose you'll think it's up to you to give me a fatherly lecture, but you wouldn't mean a word of it. If you were in my shoes, I know exactly what you'd do!

So I have the choice between . . . No. One can hardly talk of "choosing" when one is cornered.

Nurse has stayed with Evette. Everyone here calls me Señorita!

The real tragedy, believe it or not, is that I haven't any money left. They dole it out to me in ridiculously small sums. Of course, the family doesn't realize that a day may come when a telegraphed money order will decide things for me, one way or the other.

Don't think too badly of me. Remember how I struggled to "fit in," especially in the early days. If you believe in heredity, take into account what my mother's like; when I last heard from her, she was in Tahiti. I wonder if she, too, is consumptive, or if I got it from my father, whom I can't remember at all.

Who knows? Perhaps by the time you get this letter it will all be over. In fact, I'm so much inclined to think this, that at long last I may as well confess something to you, Frédéric, my friend. I felt like crying—isn't it absurd!—when I wrote "my friend." You were the man with whom the girl I was, greedy for life and love, should have thrown in her lot.

I can see you smile. Never once did you dream of making love to me. I had only the crumbs from your table, but how I treasured them! And no one in that dreary household ever guessed, not even Michel, who used to grumble, but had no idea. Can you imagine why he grumbled? It was because he thought it was you who'd taught me to smoke!

That's what they're like!

I hear the speedboat buzzing around almost under my window. If I am false to you tonight, it won't be with a man, an army officer from India, but with a speedboat that is doing fifty miles an hour, in a dream world of moonlight, where there are no such things as lungs!

Clasp my hand hard, as you used to do each evening when you left me—how I loved the pressure of your warm, dry fingers!—and say in that "special" voice of yours (I can hear it now across the noise of the speedboat):

"Good night, little girl!"

Yours forlornly,
Eva

15

Leaning against the bar at the Boule Rouge was a swarthy young man, whom Michel recognized as one of Mrs. Gabell's friends. Obviously of Middle Eastern origin, perhaps a Turk, he was known to everyone as Freddie. Michel nodded casually and gave no more thought to him. He had more serious things to think about: Nina's fiancé was due to arrive in two days, and he still had not achieved his goal.

Indeed, he had made no progress whatsoever. In the pink glow of the alcove, he was following the usual procedure, the girl submitting with more reluctance than usual to his clumsy pattings and pawings.

When she got up and went to the ladies' room, Freddie came and sat beside Michel.

"A juicy little piece, eh?" he said with a knowing leer. From his tone he might have been as intimate with her as Michel was. Paying no attention to the scowl that greeted this opening, he continued:

"She's at my hotel, on my floor, as a matter of fact. I've often noticed how washed-out she looks in the morning, and I guessed she'd been making a night of it." In a slightly lower tone he added: "Getting what you want?"

That was how it began. Nina reappeared, and Freddie went back to the bar.

"So you know that gigolo?" she remarked. "He's on my floor."

What prompted Michel, after seeing her home as far as the railway bridge, to return directly to the Boule Rouge and have a whisky-and-soda with Freddie at the bar? He may have drunk two glasses of whisky—though his doctor had warned him on no account to touch alcohol—because, less than a quarter of an hour later, he was talking to Mrs. Gabell's gigolo as to a boon companion.

"You see how it is, Freddie? The only problem is finding a place. She won't hear of going to a hotel. And at my place, of course, there's all my family around."

Freddie, too, had had a great many drinks, and both men were at the stage when one swears eternal friendship and develops fixed ideas. The idea now obsessing them was how to enable Michel to have his way with Nina.

Suddenly Freddie had an inspiration.

"I've got it, dear fellow! Why not drop in and ask to see me? When you're shown up to my room, I'll toddle off to the barber's for a shampoo or something. While I'm gone, you ring for the chambermaid. After that . . ."

He guffawed. Michel patted his pockets, and turned to the bartender.

"Chalk it up, please, with the rest."

He had run up a pretty big bill. . . . It was three-thirty before they left the cabaret, together, and for another half hour they roamed the streets, arm in arm, reluctant to go to bed. At last Freddie went into the Continental.

When Villa des Tamaris came in sight, Michel was surprised to see lights on in nearly all the rooms.

At six that evening, Dr. Bourgues had been sent for. Martine was complaining about feeling considerable pain.

"I know what I'm talking about," the doctor reassured her. "You have two or three days more to go, at least."

But at one in the morning, he'd had an urgent call from the villa. After a glance at Martine, he announced that it would be rash to move her, even though a bed had been reserved for her at a clinic. He telephoned for a nurse.

For some reason, Michel was annoyed by the sight of all the lights. There was no one in the conservatory when he entered. Noticing a cake on the table, he cut himself a slice. People were moving around upstairs, but he felt no inclination to see what was going on. His wife had had two children, and Marthe had had hers at home, so he knew all about confinements and associated them with a sickroom and a disagreeable smell. He scowled as he helped himself to a glass of the whisky put out for the doctor and munched a second slice of cake.

Someone opened the door, and he saw Kiki, in pajamas, looking scared.

"Isn't it over yet?" the boy asked. He had tried to persuade Edmond to sit up with him, but without success. He was now very upset.

Meanwhile, Baptiste was busy in the kitchen putting kettles on, and the nurse kept running up and down the stairs.

Michel wondered what to do. To go to bed as usual might seem callous. He was no longer wearing his plus fours, but a new summer suit, which he was afraid of creasing if he dropped off in an armchair. He crept upstairs, changed into an old outfit, and went down again.

The drinks took effect, and he fell at once into a heavy sleep. Even so, he was dimly conscious of what was happening. Finally, he woke with a start and became aware that his mother and the doctor were in the room and had been talking for some minutes.

It was an odd feeling, to wake up like this in the conservatory, which he had never before seen in early daylight. Light was flooding in from every side and from above as well. When he turned his head, he had a glimpse of the vividly blue sea and fishing boats that seemed to be floating in midair.

"Is it over?" he asked, rubbing his eyes.

"Yes. But you'd better not go up yet. She's sleeping."

"A girl?"

"No. A boy. He weighs six pounds, which isn't bad considering he was born nearly two weeks early."

Then Mme Donadieu persuaded Michel to leave, because she had more to ask the doctor. Kiki, who had fallen asleep at last, was wrestling with a particularly unpleasant nightmare. The cleaning woman was opening windows, letting the brisk morning air sweep through the house.

"That you, Philippe?" Martine's voice was a mere whisper. The nurse was holding the telephone receiver for her. Little spots of sunlight danced on the white bedspread.

"What? . . . Oh, you were asleep? . . . Philippe, I have something to . . ." She couldn't get the words out, and the nurse patted her shoulder encouragingly.

"That's all right, madame. Don't hurry!"

"Philippe, we . . . we have a son!"

Martine's bed faced the sea, and the window had been opened, since it was a fine, warm morning. But her tears blurred everything; she couldn't even see her son in the cradle beside the bed.

"What? Please speak louder, Philippe dear. Yes . . . a boy. No. I'm all right, really. But I'm glad it's over. He's bigger than they expected: six pounds. . . . You're coming today? . . . What? . . . Not at once? . . . What did you say?"

She couldn't hear clearly. She was too exhausted. Sinking back on the pillow, she signed to the nurse to take the receiver.

"Yes. I'm the nurse. . . . She's a little tired. . . . Oh, no, nothing serious. Just weak . . . By the night train? You'll be here at six-thirty tomorrow morning? . . . I'll tell her."

Martine made a quick gesture to show she wanted the telephone again. All she said was:

"Bye-bye, Philippe. Come as quick as you can."

The nurse explained:

"Your husband has an appointment this afternoon, to sign a very important contract. He told me you knew about it, and you'd understand."

She hardly heard what the nurse was saying. Everything was growing blurred, merging into a golden mist: Philippe, the contract, her baby, the blue sea, and a white speedboat churning up snowy streaks of foam. . . .

She woke with a start. She'd just dreamed that it wasn't true, that she hadn't had a baby.

"Where is he?" she cried.

"There's His Majesty." The nurse smiled, glancing at the cradle. "Had a nice sleep?"

It was nearly noon, and the curtains had been drawn to keep out the glare. There was a distant sound of music: a band was playing at one of the cafés on the seafront, where people were having cocktails before lunch.

"Your brothers have come, madame. They want to see their nephew."

The whole day went by like that: long spells of drowsiness, brief visits from the family. The doctor came twice. Mme Donadieu, after excusing herself, went out to tea; there was no point, she said, in letting the Krugers know. True, they had no contacts in La Rochelle, and need not learn the date of Martine's marriage. Yet they might as well be on the safe side. . . .

Michel stayed a quarter of an hour with his sister, remarked dutifully that it was a fine sturdy baby and that the noise it was making was a sign of "character." Kiki fidgeted, and wouldn't approach his sister's bed; in fact, he seemed rather annoyed with her.

Martine woke only twice during the night. A low light was on; the nurse was dozing in her chair; the child, in his cradle.

"What's the time?"

"Quarter past six, madame."

"Wasn't that a train whistling just now?"

"It couldn't be his train—unless it's ahead of time."

"Open the windows, please. Fix up the bed, and give me the mirror and a damp towel. Oh, and my powder box, too, please."

Everyone else in the house was asleep. The cleaning woman could be heard opening the front door.

"That was a train, wasn't it?"

"Yes, but it was going in the direction of Marseilles, I think."

"I suppose he'll take a taxi."

"If he can find one at this hour."

After a long wait, during which the minutes seemed to crawl, they suddenly speeded up, flashed by like seconds. A car purred in the distance, then coming toward the villa. It stopped outside the garden gate. There was a sound of footsteps on the gravel; a moment later, on the stairs.

"Please go," Martine said to the nurse.

And there Philippe was, in the doorway, looking, heaven knew why, much taller and asking breathlessly:

"Martine! Where is he?"

He had shaved on the train. His cheeks were cool, and he brought with him the smell of clean, fresh air.

While he bent over the cradle, Martine looked at him anxiously. Did he seem slightly put out? Didn't his son come up to his expectations? He seemed afraid to touch the baby, only putting his hand out cautiously, as if . . .

Suddenly he flung himself on the bed and hugged Martine so hard she gasped for breath.

"Oh, Philippe!" she panted. "What's come over you?"

He was crying. Never had he wept like that before, his whole body shaken by sobs.

"Martine darling! I'm so happy!" He straightened up and dried his eyes. Then he frowned when he saw how pale and tired she looked.

She could read every fugitive emotion on his face, and she understood, too, when his gaze settled on the sunlit sea. The expression he had now was characteristic: his eyes, mere slits, had an almost fierce intentness, and his lower lip jutted forward truculently. He was holding Martine's hand so tight that she winced. Abruptly, he dropped it and stepped back from the bed.

"You'll see!" he exclaimed.

He seemed unable to keep still, and paced the room, stopping as often at the window as at his son's cradle. The sun hung just above the horizon; gulls skirmished for small fish discarded by the fishermen; a municipal watering cart rumbled along the seafront.

"Has he come?" Mme Donadieu asked the cleaning woman.

"Yes. I heard a gentleman go upstairs."

She hesitated. No; better leave them to themselves for a while.

"You can't understand," he was saying. "But I wish you'd try to see things from my point of view . . . or, better, feel the way I do about them."

Never had Martine seen him so emotional, so little master of his feelings. As he stood at the window, gazing toward the sun, he seemed to be letting the level light seep into every pore. He had flung off his coat, and his shirt looked dazzlingly white; he was wearing a belt, and the sinewy yet graceful lines of his figure showed clearly.

"I nearly threw over everything to come here by the first train, when I got your message yesterday. I suspected you'd feel hurt if I didn't, that you wouldn't understand. . . . But . . . look at this!"

He picked up his coat, took out some papers, held them in a sunbeam, then placed them on the cradle.

"Was it as fine as this yesterday?" he asked.

"Yes."

"So it was in La Rochelle—for a wonder! The first decent day we've had for ages. At three, we all met in my office: Goussard, the lawyer, Grindorge . . ."

"Did you have lunch with them?"

"With Grindorge and his wife, you mean? Yes. Why?"

"Oh, no particular reason. Go on . . ."

It was at that lunch that Philippe had announced the great news to his friends.

"Martine's done it!"

"Yes? A boy or a girl?"

The Grindorges, who had two children, were not impressed. All that seemed to interest Mme Grindorge was whether Martine would suckle the child herself.

"Of course she will!"

"Don't be too sure. That's what I said, but the doctor put his foot down."

Philippe had laughed away any doubt. And now he was gazing

down at the cradle, on which lay the documents, among them a big blue contract form.

Martine, who was eagerly watching his face, saw him frown. He had heard footsteps on the stairs. He stepped quickly to the door and opened it. Mme Donadieu had at last decided to come up.

"Well, what do you think of your son?" she asked in her strident voice.

Philippe dabbed her forehead with his lips, and murmured:

"Later, Mother, if you don't mind. I'd like to be alone with Martine for a while."

He closed the door. Then, standing beside the cradle, he said in a low, pensive voice:

"Do you know, all sorts of thoughts chased through my head last night on the train. . . . Somewhere in Russia—in the Caucasus, I think—there's a fellow named Smirnoff, or some such name. For several years he's been getting remarkable results from crossing various kinds of fruit. For instance, he's crossed an apricot with a cherry, by a special technique of his own, and the result is a new sort of fruit, totally different from either a cherry or an apricot."

"Why on earth are you telling me this?"

He pointed to the baby in the cradle.

"Because I wondered if he'd be a little Donadieu or a little Dargens."

"Why not a mixture—fifty-fifty?" She smiled.

"No."

He started pacing the room again, and she realized that he was not talking on the spur of the moment. No; this problem had been haunting him for a long while.

"I want our son to be, like Smirnoff's fruit, something brand new, unique—the beginning of a new dynasty." His eyes shifted from the child to his wife's face. "And I've been wondering whether, when you come back to La Rochelle, we should go on living in your mother's house. Better not, I think. It's too damned 'Donadieu' for me. . . . Sorry! Maybe I shouldn't worry you with these details right now."

"On the contrary."

"What do you mean?"

"I mean, I've been hoping we wouldn't live any longer in that gloomy house, or even in La Rochelle."

Why did he smile, and why did his eyes take on that steely look she'd often seen in them when certain subjects were broached. He walked to the window and, gazing out, murmured, as if to himself:

"No. We won't stay there much longer."

She caught the words, and her face lighted up. But somehow, with all her pleasure, she couldn't repress a vague worry.

He came back to the cradle, and she watched him pick up the documents and flick them with his fingers to make sure they were all there before replacing them in his pocket. Again she was struck by the neat precision of his gestures.

"It's odd," he remarked, "but, to create a new species, one has to use an old, well-established parent stock."

He had never studied botany, or genetics, of course. Indeed, he'd never studied any subject deeply. But he had a flair for garnering scraps of knowledge that might come in handy, and a keen sense of reality. It was enough, for him, to skim the contents of a five-hundred-page book for a quarter of an hour or so to grasp what was essential in it—essential for him, that is.

These modern theories of genetic control, and the possibility of breeding new species, had caught his fancy. Once more, he planted himself beside the cradle and gazed intently at his son. Actually, the baby struck him as rather uglier than the general run.

Watching him, Martine felt her anxiety becoming more precise. She was almost certain he was keeping something back.

"What *is* on your mind, Philippe?"

He seemed to come out of a dream.

"Oh, nothing."

But something was on his mind, though it hadn't taken definite form yet, and he could not have found words for it. The things he had just been saying, his sudden emotion, the sea, dotted now with small white boats, the noises of the house—all seemed merged into a whole from which a new element, a new feeling was growing. A feeling that was in some way disquieting; Martine saw his brow pucker.

"Come here," she said.

It seemed an effort for him to leave the cradle, but he sat down on the edge of the bed, ran his hand through his hair, and smiled down at her.

"What were you thinking about, Philippe?"

"It's hard to explain, but I'll try. . . . For those fishermen down there, it's just a fine spring day like any other. And yet there's a new being, here beside us, who's just come into the world. No one has the faintest idea of what he'll become, but he has every possibility in him, every single one we can imagine. Do you understand what I mean?"

There was a note of exaltation in his voice that bothered Martine even more.

"Possibilities of great success or disaster. Possibilities of carrying on my work, the job I've set myself, or . . ."

"Philippe!"

"What?"

"Oh, nothing . . . Philippe darling, I love you so much and . . . Oh, how I wish we could be together always, just we three!"

He stood up, a sulky look on his face.

"There you are! That's just like a woman! When I was talking to you about . . . about . . ." He couldn't find the words. For all its vagueness, it was something of enormous importance—of that he was certain. And she hadn't even mentioned the contract he'd brought, though it counted for as much in their future as the birth of their child!

It had been in his mind when he talked to her about the Russian and his experiments. He, Philippe, was, so to speak, a graft on the Donadieu family tree. And very soon the rest of it would be so much useless timber. The new company had just been launched and, on the motion of Grindorge, the principal shareholder, Philippe was its chief executive.

And now a child was born. . . .

"Why are you looking like that? Have I said something wrong?"

"No, dear. Don't take any notice. . . . I haven't had any breakfast yet, not even a cup of coffee."

"Poor darling! Go downstairs at once and have something."

"All right. I won't be more than a few minutes. I'll only have a snack."

"You needn't hurry. Nurse has . . . has quite a lot to do to me, you know."

He didn't, but he preferred not to know all the unpleasant, not to say squalid, details involved with his son's birth.

"Ask the nurse to come, please." She got the words out in a rush, and he thought she was going to cry. In a surge of compassion, he put his arms around her, and her tears flowed freely.

"Martine," he murmured, "darling little Martine. You mustn't mind the way I talk. Of course I don't mean to hurt you. But I'm a man, you see, and a man's mind works differently from a woman's. It's our son I'm thinking of all the time, I assure you. But I think of him on different lines."

"You haven't even taken him in your arms!"

That was because he hadn't dared. Somehow that little lump of almost fluid flesh intimidated him.

"Shall I?"

"Give him to me."

He picked the child up gingerly, kissed the top of its head without any pleasure, and placed it on the bed beside Martine, who was now smiling through her tears.

"Ask anyone who knows about it, and you'll be told he's a very nice-looking baby."

"I'm sure he is."

"No. You think he's hideous! . . . Hurry off and have breakfast. And don't forget to send the nurse; it's high time she took care of me."

When he left, she gave way to a fit of weeping—why, she had no idea. All she knew was that she needed what her old nurse used to call "a nice, good cry." The current nurse remarked sagely, as she started her chores:

"Madame, that's how they are. They can't help it really."

"Who?"

"Men, I mean—husbands—for the first few days, anyhow. They don't feel the same about it as we do."

She was wrong. Martine wasn't unhappy, and she had no grievance against Philippe. She was crying because . . . she felt like crying.

Philippe breakfasted with Michel in the conservatory. There was not the least trace on his face of the emotional crisis he had undergone. That was something about him that often amazed Martine: his capacity for regaining self-control at a moment's notice. Still, there was a shade of anxiety in his voice when, as he helped himself to marmalade, he asked his brother-in-law:

"It went all right, didn't it? I mean, she didn't have much pain?"

"I don't think so. I was down here, in that armchair, all the time, and I hardly heard a sound from her room."

"How are *you* feeling now?"

Actually, Michel, in a light suit and suede shoes, looked exceptionally fit. But Philippe's question was enough to make him pull a long face and say lugubriously:

"My pulse is still terribly slow. I'm feeling rotten. . . . Oh, by the way . . ." He paused.

"Yes?"

"I've had a letter from my wife. Guess where she is."

"In San Remo." Philippe bit his lip at this slip.

"How did you know?"

"My father had a letter from her."

"Oh, did he? What did she tell him?"

"That she'd moved to San Remo."

"Was that all? . . . Really, I can't make head or tail of it. Her letter reads like a business letter—asking me to meet her. She suggests Cannes or Nice, to more or less even our travel expenses. I gather that she has something important to tell me, and we'll have to reach a decision. She didn't mention where the children are."

"They stayed in Switzerland."

"Oh! . . . Isn't it strange! Your father knows more about my family than I do. What on earth can she be up to, all by herself in San Remo?"

Philippe was watching the play of light and shadow in the garden. Sunlight came flooding through the glass roof, and he felt an agreeable drowsiness stealing over him. Probably it was the effect of the long night journey by train. He hardly heard what Michel was saying, until some words caught his attention.

". . . ask for a divorce."

He quickly became alert.

"What's that? Are you intending to divorce her?"

"Of course not. I said, 'provided she doesn't ask for a divorce.' That wouldn't do at all, would it? . . . Have you any news of . . . of that girl?"

"Personally, no. But I believe my father's heard from her."

"Well, I'll be!" Michel sounded quite indignant. "He seems to hear from everybody; whereas I . . ."

His expression was so comic that Philippe couldn't help smiling. Michel gave him a sour look.

"I'll ask Maman to let me have the car tomorrow afternoon, to go to Cannes. Then I'll learn what it's all about."

There was a knock at the door, and the nurse put her head in.

"Madame says you can come now."

"Is she by herself?"

"No. Madame Donadieu is there."

"Say I'll be up in a few minutes."

He had finished his breakfast, but he still had something to say to Michel, and he began by locking the door.

"The agreement was executed yesterday. We need only your signature and Marthe's now. Albert Grindorge has put the agreed sum, a million francs, in the bank. So each of us has a credit of two hundred thousand. I've brought you ten thousand in cash, in case you happen to be short of ready money."

He got a pen and ink. Michel rose heavily, scrawled his signature, then carefully chose a pill from his gold box and put it on his tongue.

Upstairs, Martine was becoming impatient.

"Why doesn't he come?" she asked her mother.

The nurse ventured to intervene.

"He's talking to Monsieur Michel," she explained. "I guess it's about business, because they locked the door."

"But the doctor will be here any moment," Martine grumbled. Then her face lighted up as she added, to her mother: "He's promised to let me know today the results of the test—of my milk, you know. I do hope it will be all right."

There were footsteps on the stairs. Philippe was putting his wallet in his pocket as he stepped into the room.

16

In the telegram, sent to answer Michel's letter, Eva had said: "Three sharp, Carlton, Cannes."

The masts of all the yachts in harbor were steeped in sunshine as the tires of the big blue car squelched on the asphalt. Baptiste, in the full flush of his promotion to chauffeur on the Riviera, drove down the long, resplendent avenue in a sort of ecstasy, and Michel had to rap on the glass between them to persuade him to stop outside the cream-white façade of the Carlton.

Some people hadn't finished lunch, and almost all the seats under the colorful umbrellas on the terrace were occupied. After threading his way among them, Michel went up to the hotel's desk.

"Is Madame Donadieu in?"

The man, looking dubious, examined the pink-and-white slips on a board and, just to make sure, ran his eyes over the visitors' book.

"Are you quite sure the lady's staying here?"

All the people on the terrace were speaking English. Girls in the sketchiest of bathing suits brushed against him with their bare shoulders. Gloomily, he waited on the top step, surveying the crowd with half-closed eyes.

"Michel!"

At first, he couldn't tell where the voice had come from.

"Michel! This way!"

He saw a hand waving to him above one of the deep wicker chairs. As he made his way to it hesitantly, a tall young man sprang from the chair beside Eva's.

"Let me introduce Captain Burns."

The young man held out his hand, and its grip made Michel flinch.

Obviously, he had been wrong to expect his wife to dress for the Carlton terrace as she had done in La Rochelle. Still, she'd really carried it too far. She was in a flamboyant yachting outfit, the kind seen in musical comedies; a sailor's cap with a huge gold badge on it was perched at a rakish angle on her thick brown hair. From her chair she extended a languid hand, saying in an exaggeratedly affectionate tone:

"Sit down, my dear. What will you have? . . . Bob, would you order a whisky-and-soda for my husband—and then go for half an hour's stroll somewhere?"

Eva seemed intoxicated—with sunshine or with love—and there was something almost indecent in this unabashed exposure of her joy. With her moist red lips, darkly glowing eyes, and attitude of absolute abandon, she might have been an incarnation of the languor of the South, at one with her environment, with the light and color, the palm trees, and a sea too blue to seem real.

While the waiter served the drink, she gave her husband a prolonged stare.

"You haven't changed a great deal. Fatter, that's all."

He had to struggle not to lose his bearings. He had to remind himself that this woman was his wife; that only an hour ago he had been lunching with his mother, Kiki, and Edmond at the villa, which was pervaded now, as he'd heard his brother remark, by "the smell of a baby."

An ear-splitting din drew his eyes seaward. It was Burns, at the wheel of a big speedboat, putting out from the hotel dock, followed by the admiring gaze of the crowd on the terrace.

"Well, Michel, I'll tell you how things stand."

A rather curious thing was happening. In La Rochelle, when they had something private to say to each other, they always spoke English. Now, too, though most of the people around them were English or American, they fell into the old habit and spoke that language—which, perhaps, was really more suitable for what they had to say to each other.

"I suggest you smoke a cigarette, or a cigar. Yes, a cigar. That may help. . . . I wonder if you've guessed that I chose this place deliberately. With all these people around us, we'll have to keep our heads and talk quietly—and that's just as well. . . . Tell me first, has Martine had her baby?"

"Yes."

"A boy?"

He nodded, and lit a cigar, as she had suggested, his eyes fixed on the speedboat weaving snow-white circles on the blue. After a moment's silence, he, too, asked a question.

"Where are the children?"

"I left them in Switzerland. . . . Well, since I don't really know where to begin, I may as well begin at the end. And please try to remain calm, and not make a scene in front of all these people. . . . Captain Burns is my fiancé; my fiancé or my lover—it comes to the same thing really." She gave a quick glance around to remind him once more that there were people within earshot. "You don't have anything to say? That's sensible of you. . . . Or perhaps you remember that I never once reproached you for . . . for the things you did?"

Fortunately, Michel had his cigar; it helped him to keep calm. There were people only a few feet away, and Eva was talking in a low voice, but with a studied air of casualness.

They could still hear the roar of the speedboat sweeping around the bay, and couldn't help following its gyrations with their eyes.

With an effort, Michel spoke, feeling it was up to him to say something.

"I don't understand."

He had lowered his eyes, and now he noticed that Eva was wearing gold sandals and her toenails were dark crimson.

"That's because I began at the end. Careful, Michel; the head-waiter's watching. A month ago, I learned quite suddenly that I had TB. . . . No, don't move. You needn't be anxious about the children. Evette will be cured in a few months, and your son within a year at most."

"What are you saying? . . . Listen, Eva! We absolutely must go somewhere else to talk."

"Don't get up! And please don't raise your voice. When you've heard everything, you'll see it's all quite simple, really. . . . When the doctor told me, I was quite stunned at first. And then a sudden craving came over me to enjoy life while I could. I left the children behind. People will say I'm a heartless mother, and all the rest of it, but I don't care."

"I see! You went off your head." Michel said it quite seriously; he suspected that the shock had really driven her crazy, and he was wondering if he ought to exercise his rights and force her to go back with him to Saint-Raphaël.

"Perhaps I did—or almost. But please listen to the rest of what I have to say."

It was as though she had given much thought to this meeting, weighed every word that must be said. Leaning back in the big chair, with her legs crossed, she was gazing at him curiously, with a new interest. She seemed perhaps to be wondering if she had really lived six years with this man.

"Remember, Michel, what my life's been like. Could you truthfully say that we fell in love with each other? . . . I suppose you found me a change from the other marriageable girls you'd met, members of the wealthy families of La Rochelle. By local standards, I was 'daring,' 'original,' somewhat 'fast.' Mind you, I'd left school at seventeen, and I was twenty when you married me. So I'd had three years of comparative freedom—quite cheerful years, as I remember them: lots of dances, drives to the small casinos on the coast in summer, balls at City Hall in winter—and, of course, a few flirtations. The least a girl can expect, isn't it, if she's not too prim or unattractive?"

"But, good God, Eva . . . !" Michel began, rising from his chair. The setting of their conversation, the animated crowd, and the buzz of voices seemed so grotesquely out of keeping with what Eva was saying—and with what he would have to say.

"Do, please, keep still. Have another whisky, if you feel like it. . . . You'll notice, Michel, that I haven't said a word of reproach to you."

"You'd need some nerve to do that!"

"Let's put it this way: we both made a mistake. The very first night, I think, you realized that . . . that I wasn't your type at all. Don't shake your head. There's no point, now, in fooling ourselves. As for me, I did my 'wifely duty,' as I believe they call it—and, to be frank, it always was a duty, not a pleasure. The wonder is that two children were born to us."

"That's enough!" It was as if a dentist's drill were jabbing at a nerve; and its sound was the buzz of the speedboat circling the bay, where that damned Englishman was showing off to the gaping fools on the terrace.

"Try to stick it out a few minutes more. I'm nearly finished. . . . You must admit I gave you an easy time; I never made scenes, as a good many wives would have done. We'd scarcely been married a year when you started running after servants, typists, any poor wretch of a girl you could get into your clutches, and it didn't seem to matter what you did with them. I wonder if poverty and helplessness haven't a sort of perverse attraction for you. . . ."

He blushed when he saw an elderly Englishman looking at him with an odd expression, and whispered to Eva:

"Not so loud!"

"Oh, no one's listening. Bring your chair closer, if you like. . . . Yes, that's better. . . . If I don't take precautions, I have two, or at most three, years of life before me; and even if I do, there's no certainty I'll recover. So I ask you just this—the only thing I'll ever ask you: Give me my freedom. I promise to accept whatever conditions you impose. You can keep the children if you wish to. . . . That shows you, doesn't it, the point I've reached? If you prefer, we'll divorce; or we can have a legal separation. I leave it to you. And there won't be the least publicity. Bob is going back to India next week; I'll go by the same boat, and will probably live in Simla." She was nervously fingering a large Indian bracelet Michel hadn't seen before, and her eyes were moist. "Well . . . I'm finished."

She called the waiter and ordered a cocktail.

"You'll have another whisky, won't you? Yes, do . . . Waiter, a rose and a whisky."

Her little laugh when she saw Michel hastily finishing what remained in his glass had a jarring note.

"You're the same as ever, I see," she said.

Michel would have given much to be through with the next half hour. The idea of making a decision then and there, on the crowded terrace of a hotel, seemed to him preposterous.

"Now let *me* say something, for a change," he began. "You must come back with me to Saint-Raphaël. We'll have a serious talk, and then . . ."

She shook her head.

"No, Michel. I won't go to Saint-Raphaël. Unless you have me arrested by the police, I'll be leaving with Bob in half an hour. We came from San Remo by sea. There's a cool breeze in the evenings, and I must be back before it starts. That's why I made our appointment for three sharp. . . . Perhaps you feel I shouldn't have brought Bob with me. As a matter of fact, I thought it was the decent thing to do, a proof of friendliness. . . . And we'd better part friends, hadn't we?"

"I really believe you're completely crazy."

"You've said that already. And you're wrong." She was showing more animation; feelings she had intended to repress were welling up. "But if I have gone crazy, what's the cause? That horrible, sinister—yes, sinister!—house of yours in La Rochelle. Do you remember how your father refused to let us go away, even for our honeymoon— because it was the cod season? Your cod seasons! Your precious ovoids! And there was I, in that mausoleum of yours, treated like an outsider, almost a pariah. . . . None of you ever regarded me as a member of the family. I defy you to say otherwise!"

"Well, if you hadn't persisted in seeing people like Frédéric . . . Ah, that reminds me. Don't you think it was rather . . . rather tactless of you to write to him before writing to me? It was only by chance, through Philippe, that I learned you'd moved to San Remo."

She shrugged disdainfully, and lit another cigarette, on which her lips left red smudges.

"Just now," Michel went on, "you were talking about servant girls and typists. Well, what about *you*? Can you assure me there was never anything between you and Frédéric?"

That should get her on the raw! He was paying her back in her own coin. Forgetting where they were, he had raised his voice.

"Frédéric never wanted it," she said regretfully.

"*What?*"

"I mean that, if he'd wanted me to, I'd gladly have been his mistress. In which case, I'd have told you about it, needless to say."

How long was it since Oscar Donadieu's death? Less than a year. And now a Donadieu—for she was one by marriage, and bore the name—was confessing brazenly that . . . To make things worse, he, Michel, couldn't work up any real indignation. True, the setting was against it, what with the heat, the glare from the sea, the persistent buzz of that infernal speedboat . . .

"Well, Michel?"

"Well what?"

"You agree, don't you?"

"The family will never hear of a divorce."

"Then let's content ourselves with a separation."

"What about your English friend?"

Her eyelashes fluttered.

"It won't make any difference. He can't marry me. . . . Even if he could, I'd never agree to it."

"But, good heavens . . . !" he exploded.

She guessed what was in his mind. That she'd be going to India as a . . .

"Yes, I'll be a woman on her own. There's no need to use an ugly term, is there? . . . You needn't worry about the family honor; I'll resume my maiden name."

She was watching her husband, and suddenly she felt a wave of disgust. It was as if he exhaled the fetid atmosphere of that hateful house in La Rochelle; it hovered around him, an almost visible miasma.

"Let's get it over with. I haven't said anything about the financial side of it. There's really nothing to say. I give up any claim I may have, and I ask nothing from you."

"These matters should be settled in writing, before a notary."

"All right, have a document drawn up."

"Your signature will be required."

She called the waiter.

"Ask one of the pages to come, please."

She told the boy to bring the Cannes directory. Michel looked quite startled.

"What's your idea?"

The speedboat had stopped at last, and the Englishman could be seen stepping onto the dock, a tall, clean-cut figure against the blue of sea and sky.

"Wait."

Eva fluttered the pages of the directory, nicked with a red fingernail one of the names in a column.

"Don't forget the name: Maître Berthier, notary. I'll see him at once and give him a power of attorney. Then you can arrange things with him, to your best advantage."

Burns was approaching. With a smile and a wave of her hand, she let him know he should leave them together for a few minutes more.

"So that's that, Michel. I'm sorry to have rushed you like this, but there was no help for it. Curious, isn't it, the way things have turned out? . . . If Jean hadn't had bronchitis, I suppose I'd have carried on for another two or three years, without knowing about my own health. We'd have gone on living together, you and I, almost like strangers under the same roof. . . . We're well out of it, both of us, when all's said and done. Don't you agree? You're a free man again."

"A very sick man, too," he mumbled.

"Nonsense! You fell ill because you were in a bad situation with that girl, and your being ill made things easier. When it's all forgotten, you'll be well again. People like you are never really ill."

"What on earth do you mean?" Michel sounded quite offended.

"Don't be vexed." She smiled. "Let's part on good terms. The truth is, though, that a man like you, the complete egoist, is trouble-proof. When anything seriously threatens your peace of mind, your body sets up what the doctors call—yes, I've learned quite a lot of their jargon lately—a defensive reflex: your heart begins to wobble at a convenient moment. . . . Do you know, I wouldn't mind betting that you already have another woman in tow—even younger than the last one."

Afterward, he regretted his remark, but his one idea was to wound her:

"How right Father was!"

"About what?"

"When he told me I was a fool to marry your mother's daughter."

Eva stood up, her cigarette between her lips, and looked down on him disdainfully. She seemed taller to him, but that might be due to the clothes she was wearing.

Curtly, she said "Good-by." In a few lithe strides, she'd crossed the terrace to the road where Burns stood waiting. He gave a quick glance at Michel while she said something in his ear.

Michel supposed she was telling him that they had had it out, that all had been said that needed to be said. The Englishman seemed to hesitate; he made some remark to her. But Eva took his arm peremptorily and led him toward the dock.

"Waiter!"

The waiter produced a bill. Michel looked at it and exclaimed:

"Two hundred and fifteen francs! How can that be?"

"The lady and gentleman had lunch here. . . ."

So Michel had to pay for his wife's and Captain Burns's lunch.

When the car reached Saint-Raphaël, at five, the beach was still bright with outfits of every shape and hue. Michel's mood was worse because Baptiste had taken a wrong turn and they had to go by the Upper Corniche, and heights made Michel feel dizzy.

He had a glimpse of his brother's boat, an oddly shaped craft, but seaworthy, it seemed, bobbing on the ripples, resplendent in a coat of scarlet paint.

Mme Donadieu was sitting in the garden with her friends the Krugers, who were still unaware, or discreetly feigned to be unaware, of the fact that Martine had just had a baby.

Martine's window stood open, and her room was bathed in the golden glow of a Riviera afternoon.

To avoid meeting the Krugers, Michel slipped in by the back door, and roamed from room to room, at loose ends. Brooding on what had passed between him and his wife, he found it was her reference to Frédéric that rankled most. What was that nasty thing she'd said in a regretful tone? "Frédéric never wanted it!" Otherwise, she would have . . . But was this the truth?

His shirt was soaked with sweat; he went upstairs to change it, and decided, while he was about it, to change his socks and shoes as well. While he was doing this, his thoughts kept harking back to Frédéric, and other half-forgotten grievances, until he felt an uncontrollable desire to vent his spite on somebody or something. The look of his bedroom sickened him; he realized how ugly and bleak it was. Abruptly, he got up from the bed, went to Martine's door, and knocked.

"Come in."

She was sitting up in bed; her child was asleep in the cradle, and the nurse was ironing baby things. To Martine's disappointment, the doctor had decided that a wet nurse was required. A swarthy young peasant woman with an incipient mustache had been found, and since then there had been no respite from her deep Southern voice.

"Where's Philippe?" asked Michel as he sat down beside the bed.

"He's gone to Monte Carlo. The Grindorges just arrived, for a few days, and they asked him to spend the evening with them. Isn't it lucky he brought his dinner jacket with him?"

This was an unfortunate remark. His grievance against Frédéric was still simmering, and it annoyed Michel to think that Frédéric's son was going to dine at some fancy restaurant with rich Parisians who had sunk a million francs or more in their subsidiary company.

"I must say you *do* look peevish!" Martine exclaimed. She was wearing a curious little bed jacket that gave her the air of a young matron in a musical comedy.

"Do I?"

"You do. What's wrong?"

He shrugged. What *was* wrong? He was in a vile humor; that was all he could have said. Instinctively, he turned the conversation to the object of his rancor.

"Does Philippe see much of his father?"

"I don't think so. He never mentions him to me."

"I wonder . . ."

"What?"

"Oh, nothing." He guessed that the more evasive he appeared,

223

the more questions she would ask. "Anyhow," he added, watching her, "this isn't the time to talk to you about such things."

"What do you mean? What's happened?"

"Nothing's happened. But I've been thinking a good deal lately, and checking up on certain matters. . . ."

"Are you trying to tease me—or what?" She had been looking exceptionally cheerful when he came in; now she was eying her brother apprehensively.

"I've been thinking about Frédéric. And about Father's death. Do you really think he committed suicide?"

"No."

Suicide was indeed the last thing anyone would expect of a man like Oscar Donadieu.

"Exactly!"

"Exactly what? Don't be so tiresome!"

"To my mind, it's equally absurd to suppose there was an accident. Father knew every inch of that area, and, in spite of his age, he was very steady on his feet. One thing's certain: he couldn't have tripped under the influence of drink, because he never touched anything but water at the club."

"Couldn't he have had a stroke?" Martine suggested.

"A stroke that came at the precise moment when he was on the edge of the harbor? That's straining coincidence, isn't it?" A sound was still buzzing in his ears, the noise of a speedboat careering around the bay, with that supercilious young Englishman at the wheel! "I know I really shouldn't talk to you about this—but I'm so cut off from everyone. There are times when I feel I'm the only one of us who gives a thought to our father, who remembers he's a Donadieu. If you want to know what I think, I think Jeannet let us down. He should have checked Frédéric's movements more closely. After all, we have only Frédéric's word for it that he parted company with Father at the corner of Rue Gargoulleau. What Jeannet should have done—"

Martine turned to the nurse.

"Marie, will you finish your ironing in the bathroom?"

"There isn't any wall plug in the bathroom for my iron."

"Please go there anyway."

"Very well, madame."

She turned to Michel.

"Why are you saying all this *now*?"

He was not prepared for the look she gave him, and he lowered his eyes.

"Well?" she asked. "Aren't you going to answer?"

"I don't know. I just happened to be thinking about it."

"What's Eva done to you?"

"What? You . . . you knew about it?"

That made him still more furious. Everyone seemed to have known—except him. And through Frédéric, naturally!

"What's she decided to do?"

"She's going to India."

"Did she say something to you about Frédéric?"

Michel realized that he'd said too much. The question now was how to beat a dignified retreat. He walked to the window and gazed at the beach, the harbor, the esplanade and its trim rows of shade trees.

"She didn't say anything about him. I drew my own conclusions, and I have every right to do so. . . . I forgot for a moment that your husband is his son. I'm very sorry."

He took a step toward the door.

"Michel!"

"Yes. What?"

"Why did you choose today to say all this to me?"

"Didn't you hear me say I was sorry? Don't let's mention it again."

His hand was on the doorknob.

"Michel!"

The door was opening.

"Michel! I wonder if you realize what a really nasty man you are!"

He swung around, wounded to the quick, and shot a furious glance at his sister. Never had she spoken to him that way. He had always looked on her as a mere child, a silly girl who had found nothing better to do than to fling herself into the arms of a cad like Philippe.

As he walked downstairs, he felt lonelier, more cut off from the world than ever before. A drone of women's voices, with occasional ripples of slightly affected laughter, came to him from the garden, where his mother and the Krugers were exchanging Riviera gossip.

On his way through the kitchen to the back door, he caught himself regretting that the servant was a woman of fifty. Presently, still nursing his grievances as he sauntered along the seafront, he noticed that he was passing the Continental. He hardly hesitated a moment, but stepped into the lobby.

"Is Monsieur Freddie in?"

He knew only the young man's Christian name, but that evidently sufficed; the porter promptly ran his eyes over the key rack.

"I think he's out. Are you, by any chance, Monsieur Emile? He said that if you came, you were to be shown up to his room."

So Freddie had remembered, and was playing along! Still, Michel had half a mind to back out of it now that he was standing in the spacious lobby, with its potted palms, pages in blue uniform hovering in the background, elevator boy at his post. Somehow his project seemed out of keeping. . . . But then he heard the porter say:

"Page, take this gentleman to Room 73."

It was too late to back out. He was shown into a rather dark room that smelled of Virginia cigarettes and lavender water.

"Shall I open the shutters, sir?"

"No, thanks." Michel felt in his pocket but failed to find any small change. "I'll see you on my way out."

It was a large, airy room. A stack of pigskin suitcases occupied one corner. There was the gentle drone of an electric fan, and the low bed, with a silk spread, looked so inviting he was tempted to lie down on it and sleep his troubles away. He couldn't have wished for a better place; here, he had a feeling of being worlds away from everything and everyone: from the villa and La Rochelle, from Eva, Frédéric, Philippe, and the Donadieus; out of time and out of space. The furniture was nondescript, comfortable without pretentiousness; the wallpaper and curtains, discreetly subdued. In fact, had it not seemed so silly, Michel would certainly have had a nap.

His eyes fell on a small enameled plaque on the wall, on which, aligned with three buttons, were three tiny figures: a tailcoated headwaiter, a valet with a striped waistcoat, and a coquettish, white-aproned chambermaid. He pressed the third button and heard a faint click; the call light in the hallway over the door of 73 had lighted.

There was no certainty it would be Nina; she had told him she had some hours off every afternoon, when another girl took her place.

He posted himself near the door and soon heard footsteps in the hallway at right angles to the one he was on. At last there was a light tap on the door.

"Come in," he said in a low tone.

She was surprised to find the room almost in darkness, took a few steps forward, then stopped. Meanwhile, Michel had quietly slipped behind her and bolted the door.

"Did you ring, sir?" she asked uncertainly, puzzled at seeing no-body in the room.

When she looked around and discovered Michel, she couldn't decide for a moment whether to laugh or to scream. He had never seen her before in her uniform: a short black skirt, white cap, and apron.

"God! Where did you spring from?"

"Ssh! Not so loud!"

He stood between her and the door. Suddenly he gripped her by the shoulders and forced her toward the bed, panting in her ear:

"Keep quiet! Not a sound, or . . ."

"Let go! You're hurting me."

Strangely, his thoughts were elsewhere—with Eva and her En-glishman, the speedboat, Frédéric. He hardly knew what he was doing, why he was here. Yet another portion of his brain was thinking coherently, or almost so. Thus he was quite aware that the young man from the arsenal, Nina's fiancé, was to arrive the next day. And he wondered if, after what was happening now, he should wait for her as usual at the service door and take her to the cabaret.

He was conscious that Nina, after first struggling—he had needed to exert his strength—was yielding. A look of resignation had settled on her face, and she turned her eyes toward the wall so as not to see him. . . .

Then, standing beside the bed, he looked down at her; she re-mained so still, not even troubling to smooth her dress, that he had a moment of panic.

"What's wrong, Ninouchka? I know I've acted like a brute, but . . . I simply couldn't help it. Do, please, say something."

She hadn't fainted. But she was so revolted that she felt quite sick. At last she rose, slowly, and looked at him with cold disgust.

"Ninouche! Ninouche darling!"

"Shut up!" she snarled, and he was struck by the coarseness of her voice.

"Please don't be angry. If you knew how I've been feeling all afternoon . . ."

"Climbing down, are you?"

She switched on the dressing-table lamp and fixed her hair. Then she went to the bed and smoothed it out.

"I suppose you fixed it up with that gigolo who has this room," she said scornfully. "I'll give him a piece of my mind when I see him next."

"I assure you, Nina . . ."

"Let me tell you this: you're a swine. . . . But I've been really silly. I should've known you'd be up to some dirty trick. I could see from the start you wasn't . . . normal."

Michel stared uncomfortably at the floor.

"Well, I'm leaving," she said after a moment.

"What . . . what are you going to do?"

"Getting cold feet, eh?" Unconsciously, she rubbed her bruised shoulder.

"Listen, Nina! It's just struck me that . . ." Uncertain how to put it, he produced his wallet and began rustling notes in it.

"Don't bother. You ain't got no more than I have."

"What on earth do you mean?"

"I mean that everyone at the Boule Rouge knows you're on your uppers. You've been running a tab for the last month."

"That's why . . ."

"Oh, shut up! I've a good mind to go and tell the police on you. It would serve you damn well right."

With a last vicious glance at him, she walked out. Michel sat down on the bed to give her time to get away, and himself time to steady his nerves. Then, composing his features and adopting a dignified air, he left the room, crossed the lobby under the pages' eyes, and began walking, not toward Villa des Tamaris, but in the opposite direction.

17

One old custom did persist. Whereas on weekdays everybody was up and dressed quite early, no fixed time for rising was observed on Sundays. Most of the family slept late, and when they rose, there was an unusual commotion in the house: doors banging, water running, calling from room to room. And the smell of breakfast hung longer in the air, mingling with steam from baths and whiffs of eau de cologne.

"Hurry up, Mother. It's ten."

"Just a moment."

After glancing into Martine's room, Mme Donadieu, her face lavishly powdered, joined Philippe in the hall. She was out of breath.

"Is the car here?" she asked.

"Yes. It's been waiting with the engine running for five minutes."

The church was only three hundred yards away. But Mme Donadieu's legs had always been capricious: sometimes so swollen that she could just hobble along with the aid of a cane, at other times, quite strong. Her children said that their condition depended on her mood, and what she wanted to do.

The streets brooded in Sunday calm, and they seemed brighter, since there was more space for the sun to play on. The car drew up outside the church; Baptiste got out and opened the door.

The church was very full, and slanting sunbeams, tinged by the stained glass, checkered the aisles. Standing to the right of the altar, the priest was intoning the first prayer, to the accompaniment of discreetly modulated chords from the organ.

"This way, Mother."

As they settled into vacant chairs, the priest moved to the other side of the altar, and everyone stood. Philippe noticed the Kruger family in front of them. They were elaborately dressed, and they, too, exhaled a special Sunday smell.

Chairs scraped on the flagstones, and the sermon began. Philippe's behavior was exemplary: unconstrained, but not irreverent. He stood up, sat down, and knelt at the right moments, crossed himself, and wore throughout a thoughtful, serious expression.

For a while, his eyes, following his mother-in-law's, lingered on Kiki, who had entered the church, accompanied by Edmond, even later than his mother. But it was not his lateness that had struck Mme Donadieu: it was the boy's manner and the look on his face.

The Kruger girls showed all the signs of normal piety. As for Philippe, his bearing of polite indifference was at least suitable. But there, a few rows in front, was Kiki, in the grip of religious ecstasy, induced, no doubt, by the atmosphere of the church, the ritual glamour, the shafts of rosy light falling from the windows, the deep tones of the organ, the incense. . . .

"You see Kiki?" Mme Donadieu whispered.

"Yes."

Both were surprised, almost embarrassed, when at this very moment, though he couldn't possibly have overheard, the boy looked quickly around, blushed when he caught his mother's eye, and resumed his usual, rather grumpy look.

He was still in their minds when the service ended. The blue car was waiting at the church gate, and the people streaming out had to make their way around it.

Bells were ringing, banners waving as an athletic club marched down the street. Perhaps because she had been thinking of Kiki, Mme Donadieu said:

"Have you any idea why Michel went away so suddenly?"

Yesterday, Michel had left for Vittel, saying that his doctor had advised him to take the cure there. Everyone knew that he had something on his mind, and also that it was wiser not to question him.

"I suppose he was more upset than we thought by his meeting with Eva." As a matter of fact, Philippe could have told her the real reason; he had heard about the Nina episode.

They were passing the bandstand on the esplanade, and Mme Donadieu's eyes fell on some empty chairs.

"Let's sit for a while." When they had left the car and sat down, she asked another question:

"What, exactly, have they decided to do? Michel wouldn't tell me anything. He only talked about a misunderstanding, and Eva's health."

"Oh, they've separated for good." He noticed that Mme Donadieu showed no dismay, and little surprise. "Eva's going to India with an English army officer. The children are staying in Switzerland, I think."

Philippe could have sworn a vague smile hovered on his mother-in-law's lips. Flecks of sunlight glowed on her white skirt. A mother-of-pearl lorgnette dangled on her chest, and streaks of powder marked the crannies of her neck.

Both were deep in thought, following their respective interests. The villa was only a hundred yards away, and the garden chairs were much more comfortable than the public ones they were occupying. But it was quite an adventure for Mme Donadieu to be mixing with the crowd on the seafront, and she had no immediate desire to move.

"Michel, I would say, has the worst situation of all of us," she remarked. There was little compassion in her voice; she was merely making an observation, trying to understand something that had always puzzled her. "It's his father's fault really," she continued. "I always told him one shouldn't treat a man over thirty, with a family, as if he were a schoolboy."

Never had she breathed a word of this to her sons or daughters; Philippe was the only person with whom she felt she could be frank— or relatively frank.

"Much good it's done him!" she exclaimed, still thinking of her husband. "Look how things are today! Eva's decamped to India, Michel doesn't know what to do with himself, and Kiki—well, he's such a strange boy it's difficult to know what to make of him. Tell me, Philippe, what do you think of his tutor?"

"I have a feeling that he and Kiki get along somewhat too well together. You would think they were the same age. . . ."

That was as far as he thought he ought to go—the merest hint. With another sigh, Mme Donadieu rose heavily from her chair.

"Well, we'd better be moving. What time are your friends coming?"

"About one, they said."

"I'll have to see about lunch."

On their return to the villa, Philippe went upstairs to his wife.

"Where have you and Maman been all this time?"

"Your mother thought she'd sit for a while on the seafront."

"What did she talk to you about?"

"Oh, nothing in particular. She wanted to know how things stood between Michel and Eva."

A few minutes later she saw him changing his tie and studying his face in the mirror.

"For Madame Grindorge's benefit?" She smiled.

"Don't be silly!" Still, in a way, she was right. Young Mme Grindorge, whose dresses never seemed to fit, had a way of comparing Philippe with her husband when they were together—to the disadvantage of Albert. And unconsciously Grindorge did what was needed to increase his wife's admiration for the younger man:

"You heard what Philippe said?" or "Be nicer to Philippe. Sometimes you're quite short with him."

She had no intention of being "short," but there were times when the way her husband followed a man so much his junior, and accepted his opinions blindly, irritated her.

Since the phonograph venture, in which Philippe had made sixty thousand francs for him without the least risk, and since the Donadieu subsidiary had been established on Philippe's initiative, Grindorge had got into the habit of phoning him several times a day.

"Philippe? I've just been offered some Rand Mines shares. What do you think the chances are of their value increasing?"

Philippe never hesitated—that was where his strength lay—but gave a categorical reply.

"Do you really think so?"

"There's not the slightest doubt."

The Grindorges had come to Monte Carlo just in order to see something of him, and now they were on their way to Villa des Tamaris in their car.

Mme Donadieu had invited the Krugers as well, and was determined to make the lunch a real success. A waiter had been hired, as well as some silver plate, of which there wasn't enough in the villa.

Philippe smiled when he saw the youngest of the Kruger girls, who was greatly smitten with him, cast a sour look at Mme Grindorge. It had taken her only ten minutes to understand. . . .

He was in great form. After lunch, he made his excuses to the Krugers and went to Martine's room with his two friends. The four of them, together again, revived, to some extent, the atmosphere of Paris.

Martine was still confined to her bed, but she was getting back her strength. She proudly exhibited her baby from every angle, and coaxed the Grindorges into declaring that he was the image of his father. Meanwhile, through the open window they could hear the Krugers chattering away—except the youngest girl, who was sulking because of Philippe's absence.

"Will you be staying much longer in Monte Carlo?"

"No. We leave tomorrow. And we'll have to take Philippe back with us; there's a lot of work waiting for him."

Mme Donadieu's voice, in the garden below, was that of a woman in very good humor. This was the life she should always have lived. To think that she'd had to wait until she was nearing sixty—and had Philippe for a son-in-law!

"One day," she was saying, "I'll ask Mrs. Gabell to tea again. She's such a character, I'm sure you'll enjoy it. The tragedy is, I have to leave next week. It's my other children's turn to come here for their vacation, and I'll have to get back into harness."

She and Philippe were yoke fellows. They would run the office together daily while Marthe and her husband were on the Riviera.

There was not the smallest cloud in the sky all day. Mme Donadieu, in one of those moods of rare felicity one wishes would go on forever, refused to hear of her guests leaving.

"Yes, yes, you really must stay to tea. I have some perfectly delicious little cakes, and I want you to try them."

The Grindorges were equally reluctant to go. After tea, Mme Grindorge took her husband aside. After they'd consulted, he went up to Philippe.

"Ask your mother-in-law to come and dine with us at the Casino. . . . Yes, you simply must; it's our last day."

Mme Donadieu accepted, and Philippe, rather shamefaced, went upstairs and told Martine that the four of them were dining out. To his surprise, she showed no resentment.

The sun was setting in a golden haze, and not a breath of wind stirred the trees. Neither Kiki nor Edmond had been seen since the morning service, but no one gave them a thought.

The dinner lasted quite long, and, after it, Grindorge took his guests for a twenty-mile drive along the coast and a final glass of champagne in a new cabaret he'd heard of in Saint-Tropez.

Hanging on André's arm, Nina had been trudging since two o'clock along the dusty, shadeless road that led to Fréjus, where a public fete was taking place. Now and then, when she saw a well-dressed man of Michel's build approaching, she gave a start, and squeezed her companion's arm more tightly.

"I've asked for a transfer to the radio section," he told her, "and if I get it, I'll try to get posted to Saint-Raphaël. That'll be nice, won't it?"

He was puzzled by the change in her; she was much easier to get along with, but also more emotional. When his train had arrived at ten that morning, she was on the platform, and had promptly flung herself into his arms, without a word, weeping profusely.

It was flattering, of course, but he felt foolish, with so many people looking at them.

"Calm down, Nina. Everybody's staring."

Now it occurred to him that she had told him hardly anything about herself.

"What kind of time have you been having these last four months? I suppose Saint-Raphaël's very full now?"

"Oh, not too full."

"Lot of work at the hotel?"

"I have the whole second floor, as usual, but I manage."

"Done much dancing?"

"No. I ain't been to a dance hall twice since you was here last."

That was true. The Boule Rouge didn't count as a dance hall; it was in a different category for them.

"You haven't cheated on me while I've been away?" he said, grinning. He was only teasing; actually, he felt quite confident.

She glanced around nervously as they entered a big room, in which a man in shirtsleeves, standing on a table, was playing a large accordion. Suppose some girl who knew about her was here, and started talking . . . ?

He held her so closely as they danced that their cheeks touched. Suddenly he felt a warm drop fall on his hand. Nina was crying and smiling at the same time.

"Don't look at me like that! I'm not crying, really. It's just being with you again that makes me feel sort of funny."

She caught sight of Jenny, another chambermaid at the Continental, who knew all, or almost all, about her affair with Monsieur Emile. Seeing the anxious look in Nina's eyes, Jenny smiled and made a little reassuring gesture.

The room was very warm. Nina drank lemonade laced with crème de menthe, and soon she was perspiring freely, and her light dress was clinging to her supple body. Her young man began to react.

"How about . . . going somewhere else?" he suggested with a sheepish grin.

"What's the hurry? Let's have another dance first." She kept putting him off. At last he couldn't help noticing.

"I must say you don't seem very interested. . . . I suppose you're in one of your bad moods."

They had danced twenty times before she finally consented to leave. They walked quickly down the street, Nina setting the pace. She was on edge, and she had a moment of panic when they went into a small hotel behind City Hall.

Still, with André it was quite plain sailing. She drew the curtains of the bedroom, turned down the sheet, and made sure the door was securely bolted. Then, as naturally as if she were by herself, she undressed, not forgetting, after taking off her shoes and stockings, to rub her feet, which were aching.

Meanwhile, André smoked a cigarette and continued telling the story he'd started on the way to the hotel.

Then, for the third time that day, she started crying, foolishly, for no reason. André lost patience.

"Damn it all! Ain't you glad to see me back? Why do you keep blubbering, I'd like to know."

"It's nothing really. Don't take no notice."

" 'Nothing'? Do you think it's nice for me, when I get five days' leave, to have you carry on like a regular waterfall?"

Soon he fell asleep, having sat up in the train all night. He was still asleep when night fell. Beside him on the bed, Nina was sitting up, gazing listlessly into the dusk, sometimes casting a quick glance at his face.

The room was pitch-dark when he woke and asked sleepily:

"What's the time?"

"Nearly nine."

"Damn it! You might have waked me. We'll be late for the pictures."

Meanwhile, at Vittel, Michel was vainly trying to stave off disagreeable thoughts. Yet, he consoled himself, what would she gain by giving him away? She hadn't any proof. And, if she didn't really want it, why had she gone with him every evening to the Boule Rouge?

This was the second Sunday on which the Olsens, who had recently bought a car, went out for the day. Marthe drove, with her husband beside her and their small boy, Maurice, behind. This time they ventured farther; they went to Royan, where they had lunch on the terrace of a restaurant overlooking the sea.

"Philippe said you should buy a lighter suit," Marthe reminded her husband. "Yours are much too dark and heavy for the Riviera. What about a light-gray flannel?"

"It would be absurd to order a new suit for just a fortnight."

"But you'll be able to use it again next year."

At the age of thirty-two, Olsen had the reluctance of an old man to spend money, and his thriftiness was of a systematic, not to say scientific, order. He was always well dressed, but he took the utmost care of his clothes, sparing no pains to reduce daily wear and tear. Moreover, he sent for catalogues from all parts of France and compared prices before buying the smallest object for the household or his personal use.

"I'm sure," Marthe said, "that Maman's having the time of her life in Saint-Raphaël. When's Philippe due back?"

"In three days."

"You're quite sure there wasn't any . . . any catch in that agreement?"

Marthe was still suspicious. It was all very well, this windfall that, thanks to Philippe, had swelled the Donadieu coffers at an opportune moment. It enabled each part of the family to spend more freely and enjoy the luxury of a vacation in the South. But Marthe couldn't get rid of a suspicion there must be a "catch" in it.

"Maître Goussard assures me that the agreement's quite in order. I'm satisfied, and I know how to safeguard my interests if I have to. . . . By the way, did I tell you the latest news?"

"No."

"It's about Frédéric. He's in liquidation. And, since he can't raise a sou in La Rochelle—I doubt he can afford a furnished room—it's thought he'll be leaving the city."

"Do you think Philippe will offer to help him?"

"If he does, I'm certain Frédéric will refuse."

"Even if he offers him a job in one of our offices? . . . If he does that, you really must put your foot down. Rightly or wrongly, I've always regarded Dargens as our evil genius. Remember Father's death; Frédéric was the last person seen with him before he died."

But soon the scene around them drew their thoughts away from such a depressing subject. Marthe nudged her husband to point out an enormously fat woman in a red bathing suit. Then her attention was caught by a car like theirs, but with a streamlined body. Maurice started pestering to be allowed to go and paddle. So they settled down contentedly to the mild delights of a small family at the seaside on a fine Sunday afternoon.

Dear Monsieur Dargens: I hope you will forgive me for not writing sooner, after all your kindness to me. I will not try to make excuses. I'm afraid I haven't any. I'll only say I found it difficult to collect my thoughts. That dreadful time in La Rochelle, when you were such a splendid friend in need, still seems so near.

When I got to Paris, I went straight to Mme Jane's hat shop on the Faubourg-St.-Honoré and, thanks to your letter, of course, she was very kind. Too kind, I'm afraid; she engaged me to serve in the shop from the very next morning, and you can imagine what a mess I made of it! Even now, when I see myself in one of the mirrors (this shop is full of mirrors), I realize how dowdy I look, so countrified and gauche.

I am still rather scared of the customers. Luckily, it is now the off-season for hats, and most of the regular customers are away. So Mme Jane has time to show me the ropes, and I think I'm making progress.

I can't say how I feel; I seem to have given up thinking—what with all the noise and bustle, and this great change in my life. Now and then, when I have a moment to myself, I start brooding; but then one of the other girls comes up and makes a joke or scolds me, and I have to laugh. In fact, I can't imagine what you put in that letter to make Mme Jane, and the staff, as well, so nice to me!

I didn't even have to hunt for a place to live. The head saleswoman took me out, and we found a room at once. She has given me all sorts of tips, and is making a black silk dress for me, like the other girls wear.

My address is 28 Boulevard des Batignolles. So if you feel inclined to drop me a line, you know where to send it. I cannot say how grateful I am. I feel like a different person, and if it wasn't that I'm always thinking of poor Father, I could settle down, I'm sure, to quite a happy life.

I thought of writing to him. But he's so obstinate, it would do no good. He wouldn't even read my letter. I am afraid he is terribly unhappy—and all on my account.

Do you think he will be allowed to go back to his job on the railway? How will he manage the house and his meals, now that he's alone? If by any chance you come across him, I do wish you would try to explain things. You would know better than I how to put it.

That is all—except that I want to say again how grateful I am for all your kindness.

Odette

P.S. Please don't show this letter to M. Philippe, or tell him anything, unless he asks about me.

That was a curious Sunday morning for Frédéric Dargens. At nine he was in a shabby waterfront hotel, packing his few belongings in two handsome leather suitcases with his initials stamped on them—last relics of his former affluence.

When a young chambermaid brought his morning coffee, he saw her look of admiration, directed at his silk pajamas and his dressing gown, and smiled wryly.

Downstairs, he said to the proprietor:

"I'm taking the eleven o'clock train. I'll be back in half an hour or so. Will it be all right if I leave my things in my room until then?"

"Yes. But don't be away too long; somebody may want the room."

"Thanks. I'll be as quick as I can."

People were on their way to a Protestant church nearby. Buses were rumbling past, unusually crowded, and a traveling circus had pitched its tent in the center of Place d'Armes.

Frédéric made his way to the outskirts of the city and went down the street on which Baillet lived. Having found the engineer's cottage, not without some difficulty, he stopped at the gate, uncertain what to do, because there was no bell. A woman standing at the door of the next house called to him.

"I think he's at the back, cutting grass for his rabbits. Just open the gate; it's never locked."

He walked around to the back of the cottage, as Odette had done when she came home for the last time. The walls of the yard were lined shoulder-high with hutches, the rabbits in them nibbling green stuff. There was a smell in the air that took Frédéric back to his childhood.

He could see no sign of Baillet. In the center of the back wall was a small, rickety gate, and beyond it lay a stretch of land used by the local garrison. Through the gate, he saw a man, with his back to him, on the far side of this parade ground, cutting grass. He walked quickly across to him.

"Monsieur Baillet?"

The man straightened up and examined Frédéric with mistrust. He was wearing a ragged suit, down-at-heel felt slippers, and a railwayman's cap.

"What do you want with Monsieur Baillet? Who told you I was here?"

He had a small sickle in his hand, and beside him was a basket half full of grass and chicory leaves.

"I'm sorry if I'm disturbing you, but . . ."

"You ain't a reporter, are you?" Baillet, his small eyes screwed up under his bushy brows, was looking more and more suspicious.

"No. I have nothing to do with the press."

"I asked that 'cause I've had two of 'em here already. . . . Oh, you're one of them canvassers for the election." It was Frédéric's clothes that irritated him the most. He'd had enough of the upper class and their ways. "Well, if that's it," he added truculently, "I tell you, it ain't no good trying to talk me around. I'm a Communist, and a Communist I stay."

Frédéric guessed he'd come on a fool's errand. From talk in the cafés, he had learned that the railway company had refused to take Baillet back, but, since he was only a year away from retirement age, had advised him to put in for his pension.

Recently, he had started breeding rabbits, and never left the cottage except on Saturdays, when he went to party meetings in a waterfront café. His comrades may not have taken him seriously, but there was no question he viewed himself as a martyr. He would stalk into the room with the light of combat in his eyes, but he spoke only to voice categorical opinions of the most naïve kind. It was rumored that he was a heavy drinker, and certainly he had the drunkard's habit of making the same remark over and over again, with an inspired air.

"I know what I'm talking about," he would say sternly, "and Baillet ain't one to change his mind once he knows. . . ." Or, "I don't say you ain't men. But there's men and men and, though it's I who says it, to do what I did you got to be a Roman." Evidently, he had heard someone mention the stoic valor of the ancient Romans, and "Roman" was for him synonymous with "hero." Or, "If other folks had the guts to act, like me, there wouldn't be no more exploitation of the workers, no more poverty."

Frédéric was half inclined to leave without saying what he had come to say. Baillet still held his sickle, and his expression was deliberately menacing.

"Please listen, Monsieur Baillet."

"Why should I listen to the likes of you?"

"Couldn't we have a quiet talk, for a minute or two?"

"Talk away!" He feigned not to understand that Frédéric would have preferred moving to the cottage.

"It so happens that I can give you some news of your daughter, and . . ."

The engineer had surely developed a taste for theatrical effects. With a sweeping gesture, he pointed, not to the gate by which Frédéric had come, but to the trees bordering the parade ground, saying:

"That's your way!"

"Let's talk seriously, please. I know you haven't been drinking—it's too early. I have this to tell you. Odette is very unhappy."

"Ain't I told you that's the road, yonder, by them trees. I don't want to hear none of your talk, and that's an end to it. Or do you think that 'cause you wear fancy clothes I got to listen to you?"

Frédéric made a last effort:

"But—suppose Odette were dying?"

"Let her die! It's the best thing she could do."

He turned his back on Frédéric, stooped, and started cutting grass with angry sweeps of his sickle. After a moment, without looking up, he snarled over his shoulder:

"You can tell those fine gentlemen . . . you can tell 'em straight: old Baillet ain't no weathercock; they can't talk him around."

Frédéric glanced back at the cottage. The wall was covered with moss roses. In the next garden, someone was watering a flower bed. Reluctantly, he walked away, crumpling Odette's letter in his pocket. What a damned fool the man was—determined to make the worst of things, at all costs, when a few simple words of explanation might straighten out everything. The truth, of course, was that he had come to enjoy his role of tragic victim, and the more he drank, the more intractable he would become.

It took Frédéric longer than he expected to get back to the city by the way Baillet had indicated, and he had to hurry to catch his train. For the first time in his life he himself had to carry, the full length of Quai Vallin, the two big suitcases, which slapped his calves at every step. There were taxis waiting outside the station, and some of the drivers grinned ironically when they saw him; two, however, raised their caps with a slightly sheepish air.

He swallowed hard before saying: "Third, single, Paris."

Previously, he had always taken the night train, reserving the one and only sleeper on it, and giving a large tip to the attendant.

A porter came up and offered to help him with his luggage.

"No, thanks. I can manage."

Since this was the first time he was traveling third class, he walked along the corridor looking for a place and was surprised to find the train so crowded. At last he discovered a few inches of seat unoccupied, in a compartment full of soldiers.

"Is that seat free?"

"Can't you see it is?"

He hoisted his suitcases over their heads into the rack, which consisted of three strips of wood. After sitting for a moment, he went out into the corridor and pressed his face to the window just as the train was passing a big sign, on which was painted, in red letters, LA ROCHELLE.

When he went back to his seat, the young fellow beside him started peeling an orange.

III

PARIS

18

She made him think of one of those matrons with sagging breasts, common sights on every fashionable beach, who, with placid shamelessness, wear bathing suits so absurdly large and loose that at the least movement they disclose portions of their anatomy better kept concealed. Like them, Paulette Grindorge had the outward aspect of a respectable married woman, and, like them, she flaunted her nakedness so unself-consciously that it took one's breath away.

Philippe had nearly finished dressing and was knotting his tie in front of the dressing table when she emerged from the bathroom without a stitch on, and made her usual exclamation:

"What! You're dressed already? I'm afraid I always make you wait."

She didn't seem to realize that, after a certain moment, the necessary thing was to escape as soon as possible from the depressing atmosphere of this hotel bedroom, rented for the afternoon. Her instincts led her to do just the opposite. With the meticulousness of a good housewife, she spread a towel on the seat of a red plush armchair before sitting down and beginning to pull on a gray silk stocking.

"I'm sorry to be so slow. Still, it's so nice having a little time to talk all by ourselves, isn't it?"

There was a hiss of rain on the street outside, the lights of Rue Cambon glimmered across the curtains, and a steady drone of traffic came from nearby boulevards. It was one of those cold, clammy evenings Paris has in late autumn, when even the lights seem steeped in moisture, sidewalks are black with jogging umbrellas, and taxis swish in never-ending lines over the slippery asphalt.

"That's an awfully pretty tie. I don't know how you manage it, Philippe, but you always look so much more chic than other men."

Philippe did not turn, but he could see her in the mirror, looking rather ungainly, one leg cocked up, with a stocking half on. She had changed hardly at all in the last five years: her face still had its sallow shapelessness, her figure its crude profusion; her hair was the same lackluster brown. Her legs curved slightly inward and, when she hurried, her knees kissed.

At last she moved again. After fastening the stocking, she began hunting for the other in a heap of clothes on a chair.

"You know, Philippe, if you're really in a hurry, you needn't wait."

"That's all right."

"Do you have people coming for dinner this evening?"

"I don't think so. Unless Martine's invited someone."

"You're quite sure she . . . she doesn't suspect anything?"

If only the woman had the sense to spare him this tiresome quarter of an hour! But that was too much to hope for. He suspected she deliberately dawdled. His eyes hardened as he watched her in the mirror making comical grimaces as she twisted to fasten her brassiere.

He lit a cigarette and, for want of anything better to do, strolled over to the window and peered out through the curtains. Suddenly he exclaimed:

"God damn it!"

It was so unexpected, and so unlike him, that Paulette jumped up and ran to him, half naked as she was.

"What's the matter? Is it . . . ?"

For months, she'd felt sure this would happen someday—and now it *had* happened! On the far side of the street was a small green car with a white top: Martine's car!

"Can you see your wife?"

"No."

"Has she been there long?"

"How can I tell?"

She pressed against him, smelling of face powder and bath salts.

There was no shop nearby, nor any other reason Philippe could imagine for Martine's being on this street. Looking to the right, he saw the brilliantly lighted window of an Alsatian restaurant. It was just possible that she was buying something there. From above, there was no way to see if anyone was in the car.

"What shall we do?"

"Get dressed first," he said crossly. It was an effort, just then, to conceal his distaste.

"Angry with me, Philippe?"

"Don't be silly. Why should I be? It's not your fault."

"What are you going to tell her?"

"Ask me another! But for God's sake get your clothes on."

She looked grotesque with her dress half on, tugging at it, wriggling like an eel.

"Is there a back way out?"

He made an irritated gesture. His eyes were still on the little car, beyond which people were hurrying along the sidewalk.

"You can say you had a business appointment. After all, it's just an ordinary hotel."

She might think so, but most Parisians knew better. This hotel was notorious for catering to amorous occasions.

She was smearing her pouting lips in front of the mirror. At last she put the lipstick in her bag and went back to Philippe's side.

"Are you quite sure it's her car?"

He was. The body had been specially made for Martine, and there was no other car like it in Paris. As a matter of fact, he had given it to her for the fourth anniversary of their wedding day.

Paulette had a glimpse of Philippe's face, and its look of concentrated fury made her gasp. He swung around and started across the room.

"She'll stay until we come out; that's certain. I suspect she's been trailing us for some time."

"Do you think she'll . . . she'll make a scene?"

"A scene? No; that's not her way. But it's rotten, all the same. Especially because it will be much more difficult for us to meet after this."

Paulette had a pleased smile.

"Are you happy about our meeting?"

"Don't be silly. Of course I am."

"Philippe darling, there's no need to worry. We're sure to find some way of . . ."

"If only you were free!"

"What would you do?"

"Marry you, of course."

"But you have a wife . . . and a son."

He shrugged, as if implying that these were details. But he was stealthily watching her, and he saw that his words had moved her deeply. There were tears in her eyes.

"Albert would never hear of a divorce," she said sadly.

"I know that."

That wasn't what he wanted.

"Well then? I don't . . ."

"That's enough. . . . We can't stay in this room forever. I'll leave first. You can watch what happens."

She helped him into his blue overcoat, brought his gray felt hat from the mantel, and held her face toward him for the usual kiss.

"When?" That question, too, had become a habit.

"How can I say?" He sighed and gave a slight lift of his arm toward the curtained window, the street where the car persisted in remaining.

They went together to the stairs, and Paulette leaned over the banister to watch him going down. Then she ran back to the window. She could see only the far half of the street. Philippe entered her field of vision, walking straight toward the car.

Just as he reached it, the car moved off. For a moment, Philippe seemed at a loss. Then he glanced up at the hotel window with a shrug, and stretched out his arm to hail a passing taxi.

Were Philippe's ears burning? And Martine's? They might have been, for they were being talked about three hundred miles away, in Mme Brun's living room, where an unfamiliar scent hung in the air.

The Paris drizzle was here replaced by a downpour, and throughout La Rochelle the boom of a heavy sea could be heard.

Françoise, Mme Brun's daughter, had arrived unexpectedly, swathed in expensive furs and redolent of perfume. Though it was a year since her last visit, she'd already told her mother she would be leaving the next day.

"Paul's expecting me in London. I'm going via Dieppe and will have to make an early start."

She gave the old lady a long look.

"It's extraordinary, really. You haven't changed a bit."

After that, she peered at Charlotte, who was sitting in a dark corner and hadn't said a word.

"What's the trouble, Charlotte? Not feeling any better?"

"No. Worse!"

"It's in . . . the same place as before?"

"Yes," Charlotte said, adding in a harsh tone: "In the uterus, if you must know."

The unfairness of it! she was thinking. Other women can have a host of lovers and get away with it. And I, with my two poor little love affairs, have to be singled out!

After half an hour in the company of her mother and her mother's prematurely aged companion, Françoise felt as if she were being slowly suffocated. Taking advantage of a moment when Charlotte was out of the room, she asked Mme Brun:

"How do you two manage with the housework?"

How did they manage? Well, because Mme Brun disliked seeing new faces around her, the caretaker's wife did the heavy work. And, things being as they were, it was Mme Brun who waited on Charlotte, oftener than not! That was how they managed.

But Charlotte never showed a spark of gratitude; instead, she was always whining:

"I know what you'd like best: for me to die. I'm just a burden for you, and I know it! If you were to put poison in my food someday, I wouldn't be surprised."

Much against her wishes, Françoise had agreed to stay with her mother overnight. It was the least she could do, considering how rare her visits were. She felt thoroughly ill at ease in this huge sad house. And, as Philippe was doing at almost the same time in the hotel bedroom, she walked to a window and drew aside a curtain. Looking at the house next door, she asked:

"How are the Donadieus getting along?"

"Getting fewer." Her mother smiled. She affected laconic answers, which she took for witticisms. She had lost none of her archness with the years, and wore a band of watered silk to hide the wrinkles of her neck and the dresses of an Old World coquette.

"Only Marthe and her husband," she explained after a moment, "are here now. The Queen Mother, as Charlotte calls her, lived for a while in the lodge at the entrance to the drive, but I rather think her daughter disapproved of this. Anyhow, she's moved to Paris."

"So Martine told me."

"Oh? So you've seen her there?"

"We have the same dressmaker. And we sometimes meet at parties. She's developed into quite a beauty, and she's always exquisitely dressed." She leaned forward to look at the house, where lights were showing only on the ground floor. "Doesn't Marthe find it rather boring?"

"Oh, no. She's quite a social leader nowadays, or thinks she is. Whenever a lecturer comes to La Rochelle, she gives a reception in his honor. Last week she had a marshal of France to dinner."

"What's Michel doing?"

"He's on the Riviera, but I don't know where. Since his wife left him, he hardly ever comes to La Rochelle."

"Any news of Eva?"

"No."

From the dark corner came a shrill, embittered voice:

"What earthly interest can they have for you, those people and their doings?"

Charlotte resented the idea of a third party being let into *their* secrets, the tittle-tattle with which she and her employer whiled away their days.

"What does Martine have to say? Do you see her often?"

"Only now and then. I think maybe things aren't too smooth between her and Philippe. I don't know anything definite, but I gathered it from friends who sometimes have dinner at their house."

Charlotte, who seemed to think her disease gave her every right, cut in rudely:

"Can't you two stop talking? Or at least change the subject?"

Philippe had begun by telling the taxi driver to take him to Avenue des Champs-Elysées. He'd had a quick glimpse of his wife's face through the window of the car. Why she should have left like that completely baffled him; though, at the time, he'd thought she was smiling mischievously, like someone who's successfully played a practical joke. But perhaps that was only an illusion, due to the glass and the lights of passing cars.

The avenue looked like a river that evening, or a canal, with taxis plying continuously in both directions, held up, as at a lock gate, at each crossing. The driver looked around to be told where to stop.

"Drop me at Fouquet's, please."

He went there daily at about this hour. Tonight his car was waiting for him outside. Félix, his chauffeur, hurried toward him and deferentially asked for orders.

"Stay here. I'll be back presently."

The doorman held a big red umbrella over his head. About to enter, Philippe stopped, went back to his car, and asked Félix:

"Did you see my wife before you left? Did she ask you anything?"

"No, sir. I didn't see anyone."

That made it more perplexing. Whenever he met Paulette at the hotel on Rue Cambon, he always arranged for his car to be waiting outside Fouquet's. It was a sort of alibi.

Either Martine had followed him from the start, or somebody who knew had told her.

Fouquet's was crowded, as usual, and there was a babel of talk in many tongues. After a waiter had helped him off with his coat and taken it, with his hat, to the checkroom, Philippe instinctively glanced at his reflection in a mirror and ran his hand over his hair.

Paulette's right, he thought. It's a little unusual to wear this lemon-yellow tie with a double-breasted suit. But somehow I can carry it off; it doesn't look too outré. His hands were white and expertly manicured, and his small mustache emphasized the whiteness of his teeth.

On his way to the bar, he greeted two or three acquaintances with an absent-minded air, as though he hardly recognized them. This was not owing to his present frame of mind; it was one of his mannerisms.

The bartender greeted him with a flash of his shaker.

"Good evening, Monsieur Philippe."

"Here's Philippe!" There were six or seven people at the bar, and, though they never met elsewhere, they called each other by their first names. The usual jests were exchanged.

"Well, this *is* a surprise! I thought you must be in jail."

"Why?"

"Oh, I heard they'd rounded up another broker. That's the fourth this week."

"How about the film producers?" Philippe retorted. "They've pulled in a fifth—not counting the two who got across the border in the nick of time."

Dice rattled for another round. Philippe dabbed his forehead with his handkerchief. His thoughts were still on Martine and the way she had driven off without a word.

Saying to the man beside him, "Back in a moment," he hurried downstairs. The telephone operator and checkroom and lavatory attendants all knew him.

"Get me Turbigo 3721."

While waiting, he lit a cigarette and examined his face again in a mirror, making fretful little noises, like a busy man resenting every wasted moment.

"Your number, Monsieur Dargens."

"Hello! Is that you, Mother? I wonder if you'd eat dinner with us tonight. . . . No. At home. There's no need to dress. I don't think there'll be anybody else. Good! I'll send Félix with the car to get you. Glad you can come."

He stepped out of the booth, and stared at the floor, thinking quickly.

"Call my apartment." He had no need to give the number.

"Who's this? . . . Oh, it's you, Rose. Has your mistress come back? . . . Yes? . . . No, don't disturb her. Just tell her that Madame Donadieu will be dining with us. . . . Yes. I'll be home in an hour or so."

Had he acted wisely? There was no telling. However, her mother's presence would give him a breathing space; he could postpone the irksome task of "explaining."

When he returned to the bar, Albert Grindorge was there; he, too, came nearly every evening. The two men greeted each other like the old friends they were.

"Everything all right, Philippe?"

"Yes, thanks." Leaning on the bar, Philippe skimmed the evening paper in silence. So absorbed was he that he forgot to send the car for Mme Donadieu. A quarter of an hour later, he remembered and sent a page to Félix with a message.

"I have to be off," Albert announced. "I promised to meet Paulette at half past seven. What are you and Martine doing tonight?"

"We'll stay in, I think. My mother-in-law's coming to dinner."

"Meet us after the theater."

"Well, I can't promise."

There was no need to name the meeting place. The two young couples went almost everywhere together. They even went to the same places for vacation, and often took long car trips together on weekends.

"You don't look well, old friend," Albert remarked.

"Nonsense. I'm quite all right."

"Business?"

"No. I just have a slight headache this evening. I don't know why."

"See you later, then?"

"Perhaps."

"Do come. Paulette will be so pleased."

Philippe couldn't help murmuring under his breath: "You fool!"

But an amiable fool, almost pathetic in his devotion to his friend Philippe, who had opened to him new horizons, jolted him from the rut into which he'd been settling.

People were starting dinner and, one after the other, the drinkers left the bar. Soon, Philippe found himself alone. Now and then he cast a nervous glance at the clock, but not until it said eight-thirty did he toss away the paper, pay for his drinks, and beckon to the page waiting with his coat and hat.

"Is your car here, sir?"

"No. Get a taxi."

He gave the driver his address: 28 Avenue Henri-Martin.

It was a huge building with modern apartments. A wrought-iron door, backed with a mirror, led into a spacious, pillared lobby.

Philippe entered the elevator and rang at a door on the third floor. After his valet had helped him off with his coat, he drew a deep breath, like a man about to take a plunge, and walked resolutely to the living room.

"Good evening, Mother! It was nice of you to come." He kissed her on the forehead, as usual, then turned to his wife, who was sitting in an armchair.

"Evening, Martine dear," he murmured, in his usual vaguely affectionate tone.

She accepted his kiss tranquilly and continued talking to her mother. Mme Donadieu was in the best of spirits, as always when she had an opportunity to breathe the atmosphere of luxury pervading this area. Tonight, she merely regretted that there were no guests and that they hadn't dressed for dinner.

She had not changed greatly. Only one of her weaknesses had grown: a passion for jewelry of all kinds. Unable to afford the real thing, she bedecked herself with imitations.

"So you think it's the same story?"

Philippe, who had no idea what they were talking about, helped himself to half a glass of port.

"From what she says in her letter, I gather he has the same strange moods. In her place, I'd be very careful. Remember our mistake in giving him that tutor."

He concluded they were talking about Kiki, comparing him with Marthe's son, who, as Mme Donadieu had remarked, seemed to take after him in being moody and hostile toward his parents. But Philippe was too preoccupied with his own troubles to pay much attention. The voices of the two women were no more than a vague burden to his thoughts.

"Dinner is served, madame."

Philippe heaved a sigh of relief. The first phase was over. His mother-in-law took the seat on his left, Martine sat facing him. Their small son, Claude, always had his meals in the nursery.

"You like trout in Chablis, don't you, Mother?"

"Very much! Trout's always been my favorite fish. The trouble is it's so terribly expensive now, even in the Saint-Antoine market, where

I do my shopping. And everything there is only half the price you have to pay in this part of Paris."

Martine's face betrayed no emotion of any kind. Though usually she changed for dinner, she was still in the tailored suit she'd worn in the afternoon. She carried out her duties as hostess with perfect ease, giving almost imperceptible signs to the white-gloved butler.

Philippe gave her a tentative look and pursed his lips in a humorously childish pout. This usually worked when they'd had an argument, and he wanted to make peace. But she merely raised her eyebrows a little, as if wondering what he meant.

The conversation turned to a play Mme Donadieu had seen. She had become a great theatergoer, and Philippe frequently supplied her with tickets. She did complain about the number of small expenses connected with going: the program, the checkroom charge, the tip expected by the usher.

"When you add the taxi fare, it comes to twenty francs, sometimes more."

The butler heard all this without surprise; he was used to old Mme Donadieu. Philippe ate without knowing what he was doing and wiped his lips too often. From time to time, he looked at Martine and sighed.

"Lucky fellow!" his friends said. "His wife's one of the prettiest women in Paris."

That was true. Even Mme Donadieu was impressed by Martine's grace, especially when she thought of Marthe, who was getting fat, and Michel, with his flabby cheeks and big pouches under his eyes. Martine's appearance had steadily improved, and now there was something dazzling about her beauty.

Added to this, she had poise, an unfailing self-possession that warned off male admirers and made other women ill at ease. Some accused her of "putting on airs"; others, of being "an iceberg."

"Serve the coffee in the living room, please."

She rose first, and was followed by her mother. When Philippe joined them, smoking a cigarette, she paid no attention to him.

"I suppose you young people want to go out." Mme Donadieu smiled. "Don't let me keep you."

"No, Maman. We have no plans tonight."

"If you have, you mustn't mind about me. . . . You'll let me have the car to go home in, won't you, Philippe?"

"How about a liqueur, Maman," Martine suggested.

Mme Donadieu nodded cheerfully. Now that she was living by herself, she had developed a fondness for such small self-indulgences as sweet liqueurs, bonbons, and frequent visits to the cinema, sometimes seeing two shows in one afternoon.

"Is the business doing well, Philippe?"

"Excellently."

"Then you're one of the lucky ones. I hear nothing but grumbles about the depression. Yet the worse things get, the more money you seem to make. Poor Frédéric was telling me only yesterday . . ."

Conscious that she had made a slip, she coughed and reached toward the sugar bowl. Philippe sprang to his feet.

"How many lumps?"

"Two, please."

Though apparently calm, Philippe felt an unusual sense of insecurity. He kept giving his wife imploring glances, as if to say: "Let's make up. Don't harden your heart against me. I can explain everything. I didn't mean to hurt you."

It was he, however, who pressed Mme Donadieu to stay—so much did he dread being alone with Martine.

Finally, she stood up.

"Well, my dears, I really must be off. For once, you haven't any guests, so you can enjoy a nice quiet evening by yourselves."

Martine merely smiled, and Philippe didn't dare insist any longer.

After the front door had closed and the butler had removed the coffee tray, Martine casually picked up a book.

"Please listen to what I have to say," Philippe began.

Looking up, she stared at him steadily. And he forgot what he'd planned to say. A wave of anger surged over him, anger at himself, the world at large, and his wife.

"Do you intend to go on sulking all evening?" he asked harshly.

"Sorry . . . I didn't know I was sulking."

"No cheap irony, please. You know quite well we have to have a talk, you and I."

"Was it I who asked Maman to dinner this evening?"

"Oh, so that's what you think now? I mustn't ask your mother to come when *I* feel like it?"

She pretended to be absorbed in her book. He jumped up, snatched it from her hand, and flung it across the room.

"I insist that you listen to me."

Docilely, she waited.

"I wonder if you realize how ridiculously you're behaving? It's all very well to adopt that superior air, but . . . I suppose you know that everybody's complaining about the business slump and cutting down their expenses. Well, I'm making all the money I want, and there's never been a question of cutting down on expenses as far as you're concerned. That's a fact, isn't it? I let you have everything you want, don't I?"

She kept quite still, and her aloofness enraged him still more.

"To do that I have to work twenty hours a day. And I can assure you that some of those hours are hellish. And yet . . . you're jealous, vulgarly jealous, like any stupid little bourgeoise, and, instead of helping, you try to make things harder."

At last she spoke.

"Are you referring to our friend Madame Grindorge?"

"I'm referring to your jealousy in general, and especially to . . ."
He fumbled for words.

"To what happened this afternoon, you mean, don't you? Please notice that you were the first to mention it. I haven't said a word."

"Maybe not. But your . . . your whole attitude this evening was just the same as . . ."

"Now listen to me, Philippe." She stood, as though to stress the seriousness of what she had to say. "It's no use shouting . . . or destroying the furnishings." He had grabbed a Sèvres statuette and looked about to dash it to the floor. "I won't ask you how long you've been going to that hotel on Rue Cambon with Paulette. I won't speak about all those nights the four of us spent together at cabarets, dances, and the rest of it."

"You'd need some nerve!"

"Really?"

"Do you imagine it's for the pleasure of their company that I cultivate the Grindorges? Must I say it all over again—what I've told you dozens of times? It's thanks to their money that we could make a start, and if I'm able to go on now, it's because I have behind me the capital that Albert—"

"There's no need to shout. The servants will hear every word."

"It's your fault if . . ."

"No. Please let me speak, Philippe." Her tone was mild, conciliatory. "I'm not going to scold you. I want to say something, and after that I'll leave you in peace. Do you remember telling me one evening that you'd successfully carried out a big coup, and how pleased you were with yourself? There was nothing, you said, you couldn't do, once you set your mind to it." He must have said it in some boastful moment, and it bothered him to know she'd stored it in her memory. "And then you laughed and said you could at last confess how you'd forced your way into the Donadieu home. Into the Donadieu home, mind you—not my bedroom."

He dropped his eyes, uneasy. What a stupid fool he'd been to give himself away like that, in a moment of senseless pride!

"You told me about that poor woman, Charlotte, who used to let you in by the garden door, and then you had to make love to her on the way back. . . . That wasn't all. Do you remember saying—"

"Stop!"

"I'm almost finished. I'll repeat, word for word, the last thing you said. It was this: 'One should stop at nothing when one sees the way to success. Charlotte served as a stepping-stone, and a very useful one she was.' "

Philippe, still holding the little statuette, turned away from her.

"I have only one thing more to tell you, Philippe. *I refuse to serve as a stepping-stone.* Is that quite clear? . . . No, don't go away. Answer me, please."

He could not get a word out. There was something so uncanny in her springing this on him today, of all days, that he felt a twinge of fear. With an effort, he pulled himself together. It must be pure co-incidence, no more than that. Though Martine had a curious knack of reading the minds of others—his, especially, he had often noticed—there was nothing supernatural about her insight. She could not possibly know what he'd been saying to Paulette as she nestled against him in the hotel bedroom:

"If only you were free!"

Or her reply—each word of that short colloquy had stuck in his mind.

"Albert would never hear of a divorce." And, "But you have a wife . . . and a son. . . ."

The gesture he had made came back to him so vividly—and the unspoken thought that lay behind it—that again he gave Martine a nervous glance, half afraid that she had read his mind. Abruptly, he walked out, and shut himself in his bedroom.

"I refuse to serve as a stepping-stone."

He could hear her giving orders to the butler and the cook, and remembered that a member of the government was coming to lunch with them next day.

"After the hors d'oeuvres . . ." she was saying.

He flung the window open. The leafless branches of the trees along the avenue were slowly dripping in the calm air. Some patches of the sidewalk were bone-dry, he noticed; others glistened with moisture. Footsteps receded, stopped; a door closed.

19

In the big house in La Rochelle, life went on to the ordered rhythm that had been set, once and for all, in Oscar Donadieu's lifetime. The sounds, the lighting, even the smell of the place were much the same as always.

In Paris, Philippe had created, not only a Dargens atmosphere, but also a Dargens style. Thus, on opening his eyes the next morning, when his valet drew back the curtains on a drab, rain-dim sky, the first thing his gaze fell on was the glossy Russia leather that covered the walls of his room. It had been one of his innovations, using leather instead of wallpaper.

Much of his early pleasure had disappeared, but he still felt pleased with his originality every time he saw the walls. The curtains, too, were leather, jade green, as was his bedspread. The dressing gown handed to him was a yellow that just missed being garish.

It was seven o'clock. Only in early rising did the Dargens order conform with Donadieu tradition. However late he got to bed, even if he was not home until daybreak, Philippe invariably rose at seven. And from the moment his eyes opened, his mind began to move.

This morning, as he put on his slippers and glanced at the bare branches and cheerless sky, he frowned and sighed heavily. Like a swarm of pestering insects, his anxieties of the previous night had come back in full force.

"The blue suit, sir?"

Absentmindedly, he said:

"No. The dark gray."

He wondered if it wouldn't have been better to have stayed and had things out with Martine last night. In his black-marble bathroom, he washed, brushed his teeth, and, still frowning, went into his dressing room, which was also a miniature gymnasium.

"Morning, Pedretti."

He had no need to see the man. He knew he was standing there, waiting, the boxing gloves ready. He almost said:

"I don't feel like sparring this morning. You can go."

But he did not say it. Exercise might do him good, take his mind off his troubles. He held out his wrists to Pedretti, to have the gloves adjusted. But his thoughts were still on Martine, and he kept glancing toward the wall next to her room.

"That's enough for today, Pedretti. Tomorrow, as usual."

He dressed with his usual brisk precision, and at eight-fifteen was ready to leave. After a moment's hesitation, he started toward Martine's room.

"Is your mistress up yet, Rose?"

"No, sir. She told me last night she wasn't to be waked on any account." The girl seemed ready to bar his access to the room.

With a slight shrug, he went on to the nursery. The Alsatian nurse was rubbing his five-year-old son with a huge soapy sponge.

After a glance, he closed the door again. There was no time to waste. As he went down the front steps, Félix raised his cap politely and held the door of the car open. Without asking where to go, he started down Avenue Henri-Martin.

The "Dargens touch" was apparent also in the large building on the Champs-Elysées, where, though his offices occupied only one floor, Philippe had a private elevator and his own doorman, in a green uniform, waiting on the ground floor. A monogram, R.M.C., prefixed and followed by a star, was much in evidence: on the wrought-iron gate of the elevator, on the doorman's coat, and woven into the office curtains.

Philippe's style of dressing made him look younger than his years, and also somewhat like a gigolo, but he carried it off well. As he walked into his spacious office, he looked like a man who has made good in life and is used to being obeyed.

The layout of his offices copied American business premises he had seen in films. A roomy reception area, to which the public had access, extended the full length of the floor. Separated from this by a counter with a grille, like those in banks, was a row of offices, each with a brass plate bearing an employee's name and function. Beyond these offices was a row of frosted-glass doors inscribed ASSISTANT MANAGER, MANAGER, ACCOUNTANT, and so forth.

The time clock was for everyone, including Philippe and Albert. As the employees took off their coats, they greeted the head of the firm.

"Good morning, Monsieur Philippe."

He had made it known that he liked being addressed that way, rather than as Monsieur Dargens.

The walls in his office, too, were covered with leather, embossed at intervals with the firm's monogram and the stars. To the left of his desk was another door, which still bore the letters P.E.M., for the now defunct business Philippe had launched with Albert soon after his elopement with Martine.

The mail was brought, ten minutes after his arrival, to Philippe for sorting; he made a point of doing this himself. There were envelopes bearing postmarks from every part of France, addressed to the Raw Materials Corporation or just R.M.C., containing checks, money orders, and bills, among other items.

Albert arrived, a few minutes late, and, after knocking, stepped into the office.

"Feeling better? You didn't look too well last night. . . . Good. See you later."

Albert was not even the assistant manager. His office door bore the title STATISTICS, and he spent his days immured in it, with his clerk, a rather pretty girl. Though greatly smitten, he dared not make advances; Michel Donadieu's mishap had left a deep impression on him.

By eight-thirty, work was in full swing. A lighted board began to blink with the changing prices of commodities in various world markets. Caron entered, closed the door carefully behind him, and sat down facing Philippe.

Pale, his eyes dulled by insomnia, his unkempt mustache straggling over his upper lip, he looked out of place in the luxurious office. Yet Philippe had made this man, who had started as a clerk in Accounting, his second in command. He was the only member of the firm who knew its true position. Philippe gave him a questioning look.

"I'll have the forty thousand by lunchtime."

"Good. That will see us through."

"Only until the next due day. In my opinion, we'd do well to wind up R.M.C. before things get too hot."

They spoke in whispers. With Caron, Philippe had no need to bluff or keep up appearances. In the bleak morning light, the signs of strain on his face were cruelly apparent.

"Well, that gives us a couple of months, doesn't it?"

"Maybe . . . But what will we do then?"

"You'll see." Hadn't he always risen to the occasion in a crisis? And weren't all his operations part of a set plan?

The phonograph venture had served its turn. By enabling Albert to make some easy money, it had established, once and for all, his confidence in Philippe.

With the subsidiary company he'd floated in La Rochelle, the major part of the Donadieu business had come under Philippe's control. A year later, he'd bought out Michel's interest for cash. So he now held a majority of the shares in the family concern. But these ventures were small-time. There was no big money in them, although, from an investment angle, they paid reasonably well.

Only one of his ventures had failed, a cooperative known as Home Fisheries. The capital came from hundred-franc shares. Each share entitled its holder to a specified quantity of fish, delivered weekly to his door at the wholesale price. Somewhere in the office were dusty files relating to this company, and, though three years had passed since its demise, now and then some provincial would call to find out the market value of his shares.

The R.M.C. operated on a larger scale altogether. It had a staff of fifty to sell, to the public, futures in rubber, copper, sugar, wool, and similar commodities. Albert Grindorge was on the board of directors and had been allotted a task after his own heart: the collation of statistics. He had antlike industry and a methodical mind, and he spent long hours tabulating figures in market reports and financial reviews from every quarter of the globe. His results were not of any value to the company, but the work kept him out of mischief and under Philippe's supervision, until he stepped into his father's fortune.

This fortune was somewhere between a hundred and two hundred million francs. Yet, in getting around Paris, old Grindorge never used anything but the Métro.

"Hello! Ask my wife to come to the telephone, please. . . . Martine? Philippe."

He spoke in a low voice, cupping the phone with his hand, his eyes fixed on the door of his office.

"I've been thinking about that lunch we have scheduled for today. The Grindorges are coming, too; remember? I was wondering . . ." He fumbled for words, gripping the phone with unnecessary strength. "Did you hear what I said?"

"Yes . . . What about it?" Her voice had no trace of anger. She was merely waiting to hear what he had to say.

"Well, I was wondering if . . . if, under the circumstances, I ought to put them off. Or perhaps . . ."

"Why should we put them off?"

"I thought . . . Oh, all right, we'll let it stand. Sure you don't mind?"

"Why should I?"

"Good. That's settled, then. . . . Sorry I bothered you. I'll see you soon."

The important thing was to keep his head, and Philippe was sure he could. He'd been in tight corners often enough, and always got out. To touch everyday life again, he visited the outer offices, where, as Caron put it, "things were humming." Ten or so typewriters were clicking merrily, office boys were hurrying messages from one department to another, and beyond the grille a number of customers were waiting their turn. Several of the girls raised their eyes from their typewriters, to gaze ecstatically at their handsome young boss, so like a film hero.

Philippe dropped in on Albert.

"Everything going well?"

"Fine . . . Do you know, I've just discovered that in the period from 1900 to 1905 the export of Australian wool was . . ."

"Sorry, I can't stay now. Tell me later."

He still felt unsettled, and this made him furious with himself. Back in his office, he picked up the telephone on his right, which bypassed the office switchboard.

"Is that you, Paulette?"

She gave a little cry, then asked him to hold on while she shut the door. He could picture her, half dressed, in her untidy bedroom, all aflutter now that the call she'd been waiting for all morning had come.

"Well? What did she say?" she asked quickly.

"There's no need to get flustered. Nothing terrible happened. Martine took it quite sensibly."

"Does she know it was I . . . ?"

"No, she doesn't."

"Are you quite sure? She's very clever, you know. She may be pretending. If you knew how awful I feel about it! I didn't sleep a wink last night."

"I'm sorry, but I have a lot to do. I can't talk now. Anyhow, I'll see you at lunch. Just be natural, and, you'll see, everything will go smoothly."

"Oh, I can't face it! I won't come."

"You've got to. I insist. Au revoir, dear."

"But—"

He hung up; then stared at the telephone as if wondering who else he could call.

"I refuse to serve as a stepping-stone." The words kept ringing in his ears. It was the worst blow to his pride he'd ever experienced. Even when going through the liquidation of Home Fisheries, he had felt less embarrassed, less humiliated.

And it was Martine who had dealt this blow—Martine, whom he had shaped little by little to his liking, who was, in a sense, his creation. Never during all the years of their married life had he thought of her as a young woman with a personality and a will of her own, who might stand up to him with a decided "No!"

Her No was not even a Donadieu No. That could be circumvented. The other members of the family had all given in. Michel, to start with. He no longer dared go back to La Rochelle, now that old Baillet, during his Saturday drinking bouts, had taken to declaring to all and sundry that he'd get even with the bastard who had ruined his daughter; if he ever set eyes on him, he'd shoot on sight!

It had been easy for Philippe to persuade his brother-in-law that, with his weak heart, absolute rest was necessary. The result was that Michel had sold his interest in the family business and now led an idle life on the Riviera.

All Marthe and her husband had wanted was the big house on Rue Réaumur, their place in the business hierarchy of La Rochelle, and to sit daily in the gloomy sanctum of old Oscar Donadieu, dispensing orders. To all this they were welcome, as far as Philippe was concerned; they could run the fisheries and shipping businesses as they thought fit.

As for Mme Donadieu, it was really Marthe who slowly but surely edged her out. And it was Philippe who had given the older woman a warm welcome, encouraged her to visit, and sent her theater tickets.

Kiki and the odd young tutor had completely vanished. Police inquiries all over France had discovered nothing.

But now it was Martine who, with no show of anger—an angry outburst might have been easier to cope with than her air of quiet resolution—was the one to stand her ground, to say: "Thus far—and no farther!"

A telephone shrilled—a business call. Philippe referred the man to Caron; he knew he wasn't up to useful work this morning. November gloom brooded on the Champs-Elysées. Philippe's dark-blue, discreetly sumptuous limousine, with only the tiniest of monograms glinting on the doors, was waiting at the curb.

"If only you were free!"

Philippe had never tolerated anyone's putting a spoke in his wheel; even as a child he had flared up when his plans were crossed.

Suddenly he picked up his hat and coat, stopped again at Albert's office, and said:

"I'm going out. See you in an hour."

Without waiting for a reply, he crossed the reception area with the air of a man used to stares from envious or curious eyes, and hurried down to his car.

"To the Marboeuf Club."

The club was quite near his office, and he sometimes went there in the morning for a dip in the swimming pool. This time his visit had another object.

The lounge was empty, as was the wide stairway. Without troubling to knock, he entered the secretary's office, sat down on the arm of a chair, and said, with a slight sigh:

"Good morning."

"Morning," Frédéric replied, looking up over his spectacles from the pile of vouchers he was checking. "What's the trouble?"

"Do I look as if I was in trouble?"

"Yes. Tell me about it."

"Oh, it's nothing, really." Philippe had been strongly against his father's taking this job. He had offered him a position on the board of directors of R.M.C., but Frédéric had refused.

Frédéric's hair was now white, some of the briskness had left his movements, and his gaze was more serene, but he carried his age remarkably well.

"How's Odette?" Philippe asked.

"Quite well."

Knowing that Philippe would soon come out with the reason for his visit, Frédéric bent once more over his work. There was a long silence. Philippe lit a cigarette and held his case out to his father.

"Have you forgotten I don't smoke?"

He had had some trouble with his heart; nothing very serious, but it had been a warning.

"I'd like you to have a talk with Martine."

"Oh? Have you had a fight?"

"Well, something rather tiresome happened yesterday." Philippe's tone betrayed his embarrassment. "She saw me leaving a hotel on Rue Cambon. You can guess what sort of hotel. She knows I was with Paulette."

"Yes? How did she take it?"

"That's what baffles me. She didn't make a scene at all. In fact, if I hadn't brought the subject up, she might not have said anything. . . . I do wish you'd talk to her."

"What do you want me to say?"

"Anything you want to. You might explain that I don't really like Paulette. But if it weren't for the Grindorges' money, we'd still be in that gloomy house in La Rochelle. . . . One of these days, the old man will die, and the Grindorges will step into a big fortune, well over a hundred million francs."

Frédéric, who had taken off his spectacles, looked at his son's face as calmly as Martine had, and his voice was as calm as hers when he asked:

"Yes? And what then?" When Philippe looked uncomfortable, and made no reply, Frédéric added dryly: "Do you think Grindorge will give you a free hand with his money just because you're sleeping with his wife?"

"Don't be absurd!"

"Well then, I simply don't . . ."

"Neither do I," retorted Philippe. "But that doesn't matter. My instinct has served me pretty well so far—you can't deny that. I don't have to think through every detail. . . . Anyhow, Paulette can twist her husband around her little finger. And I need him. In fact, I need him more than . . . than anyone else."

"Are you referring to Martine?"

"I'm referring to anyone who is fool enough to stand in my way. Of course, if you prefer to take her side against your son's . . ." He was blundering, and knew it; and he was once more furious with himself, for letting his tongue run away with him, for voicing thoughts he should have kept to himself. He added bitterly: "You've always sided with the Donadieus against me."

"If that's true"—there was a hint of sadness behind the tone of irony—"I haven't brought them much luck."

"What do you mean by that?"

"Never mind. . . . Philippe, you'd better go. I have a lot of work to attend to."

"You won't see Martine?"

"I'll call her one of these days."

"Au revoir."

"That's right. Au revoir."

It would look better if he entered hastily, like a man who's been detained to the last moment by urgent business. His overcoat dangling on his arm, he plunged into the living room and held out his hand to the minister, a very ordinary man in his forties.

"So sorry to be late."

In passing, he dabbed his wife's forehead with his lips, and a moment later was bending over Paulette's hand.

"Really I'm inexcusable. I didn't see you at first."

He gave Albert a friendly wave.

A brief silence followed, during which his guests tried to remember what they'd been talking about when he came in.

"Let's go in to lunch," Martine said quickly.

Naturally, Paulette had to be on Philippe's right, and the first thing she did was to drop her fork. Her hands were trembling, and she hardly dared look at Martine. Yet, try as she might to prevent it, her eyes kept turning to the face of her hostess.

Philippe, watching her, said:

"How do you like your new apartment?" His offhandedness was slightly forced.

The new apartment, like the Grindorges' car, the hunting lodge they rented near Orléans, and their house in Trouville, had been chosen by Philippe. The habit of taking his advice on such matters had continued after those early days, when they were as unsophisticated as the callowest provincial, and he had opened the world to them. Before meeting Philippe, Albert, like his father, had always used the Métro in Paris, and his clothes, if not ready-made, always looked it. Paulette got her dresses from obscure dressmakers who professed to copy the models of the important fashion houses. For their vacations, they usually went to some family resort, such as Royan, and took one floor of a villa.

Philippe had changed all that. He had introduced them to cabarets where one has supper luxuriously in the small hours, to the glamour of first nights and private showings. Now, Albert had the same tailor he had, a man who came over from London once a month and met customers at the Ritz.

Martine, facing him, was perfectly composed. The guest of honor, who was minister of education, was talking to her about the shortage of playing fields, compulsory Latin, the drawbacks of the examination system, and other such topics.

Philippe kept trying to catch her eye, but, when he did manage it, he could tell how aloof from him she still was, and, like last night, without a trace of hostility.

She spoke to Paulette once or twice, amiably but in the faintly condescending tone she always used with her.

"By the way, what's your son's age exactly now?"

"Just turned six." Paulette's voice trembled, and she gave Martine a grateful look, as if she'd done her a favor to address her.

Albert was as boring as usual. Statistics had also opened up a new world, in which, for him, but for him only, everything was delightful, even thrilling. There was excitement in juggling huge figures and making surprising discoveries: the amount of sugar consumed per capita in different countries, for instance; or the exact zones of commercial influence the various nations controlled. His conversations almost always began with:

"Do you know how many . . . ?"

How many tons of coal or yards of cotton cloth were consumed in a given country; how many working hours were required to produce . . .

Today at lunch, everything, state education included, was no more than a background against which Martine's calm, serious face shone, as if a spotlight were directed on it, her lips moving to utter tactful commonplaces, her gaze coldly unresponsive to Philippe's pleading looks.

Only his wife knew what they meant, this way his eyes sought hers incessantly, the nervous twitching of his fingers, the slight pout when she looked toward him. It was as if Philippe were saying to her across the table, in so many words:

"Let's make peace, dear. Surely it's obvious that you have nothing to fear from a brainless little frump like Paulette, who's scared to death of you. That Albert's a tiresome oaf. And that precious minister you're playing up to is nothing but a windbag, blathering like a politician or complaining like an old maid. In this room, only you and I matter; the rest simply don't count."

He had always felt that Martine and he were alike, and of a race apart. That brief scene last night had been a revelation. He had tried to mold her in his own image, and now, for the first time, he knew she was no pale replica, but his equal. He could no longer run things alone; he had his wife to reckon with.

Meanwhile, that fool Paulette could find nothing better to do than press her knee against his. It was, perhaps, to reassure herself, or to convey to him that she was his, body and soul. . . . The others were still making conversation.

"So you think that afternoons should be devoted to games at every school?"

"I wonder. You know Professor Carel's view: that games retard a boy's mental development."

Paulette's knee was getting more insistent; she had drunk two glasses of wine, and that always made her sentimental. Really, Philippe thought, it was almost pathetic that, though she must have seen herself thousands of times in her mirror, she could seriously believe he was in love with her, and ready to discard for her sake the woman who sat facing him, who had grace, clean-cut beauty, superb poise. . . .

Paulette was also trying to get him to talk.

"I'm sure you have your own ideas on the subject. Do let's hear them."

"I've never given it a moment's thought."

"Personally . . ." began Grindorge, after carefully wiping his mouth with his napkin, which was a sure sign that he proposed to speak at length.

His opinion was, naturally, based on figures, such as the percentages of mental deficiency and suicide in U.S. universities, the decline of TB in elementary schools since . . .

Once again a rush of emotion, genuine emotion, came over Philippe, and he tried with all his might to flash an unspoken message to Martine across the table. "Surely you realize now that we two are people apart and should stick together, whatever happens. Instead of being annoyed, you should sympathize with me for having to waste two afternoons a week with this absurd—"

Just then Paulette upset the salt, and Philippe, who was superstitious, turned on her quite rudely:

"Why can't you be more careful!"

She looked as though she would burst into tears. He pulled himself together.

"Sorry! My nerves are rather bad today. . . . And I do hate quarrels. When one upsets the salt, it means . . ."

"I know. But it was I who upset it. So it's Albert and I who will quarrel."

Even more exasperating was the fact that this boring lunch was merely the means to a wholly banal end. The minister had been invited solely because, sometime in the near future, he might introduce Philippe to the minister of finance, from whom Philippe hoped to glean some advance information about impending changes in the import duty on certain raw materials.

Did the minister of education suspect this, Philippe wondered. If not, it did little credit to his intelligence. Or maybe he loved eating lunch out and accepted every invitation on principle. If he'd guessed the object of this one, it would be odd, since no one had breathed a word on the subject throughout the meal.

Martine rose and walked into the living room. Paulette, like a schoolgirl in the throes of first love, lingered to squeeze Philippe's arm and whisper passionately:

"I love you!"

He muttered something as he looked down at her face.

Her expression startled him. She had always been delicate, and her health had gotten worse recently. Her cheeks had a strange, unhealthy pallor, and became mottled with red blotches under the stress of emotion. But it was the look in her eyes that surprised him: a look of mystical exaltation he hadn't seen before.

She said in a low, clear voice:

"You'll see!"

There was no time to ask what she meant. A moment later they had joined the rest around a low, gateleg table.

Coffee cup in hand, Albert continued expounding his views to the minister, while Martine, carrying another cup, walked over to Paulette.

"Coffee, dear?"

Philippe felt almost sorry for Albert and vaguely annoyed with Martine. And he felt, faintly, very faintly, a touch of fear—for himself. He had always been sure he would have the master hand in any situation, however dangerous. Indeed, the more critical things became, the surer he felt that he would rise to the occasion, dominate their course, and keep his head whatever happened.

Now, as his gaze shifted from Paulette's eyes to Martine's, he was conscious of an unknown factor, of impending developments in which he might not have the upper hand. Who would be the gainer, who the loser, he had no idea.

"I refuse to serve as a stepping-stone." That crude word "stepping-stone"—what a fool he'd been to use it!—kept running through his head.

And that damn-fool Paulette had to blurt out—with the maudlin earnestness women of her kind put into the promises they make their lovers—her cryptic "You'll see!" See what? When? Did she even know what she meant?

He heard the great man asking:

"Would you permit me to use your telephone? I must call my secretary."

While the butler guided him to a small adjoining room, where he could telephone unheard, Albert took the opportunity to declare:

"A charming fellow, isn't he? Very sound in his views."

Martine sank back in her chair and drew her hand slowly across her forehead. Philippe moved restlessly around the room. Paulette broke the silence.

"We must have a housewarming—for the new apartment. What evening will suit you?"

"Oh, any evening you like," said Martine politely.

"Tonight?"

Her husband demurred.

"No. That wouldn't give us time to make preparations."

"How about tomorrow?"

"We're going to an opening night," Philippe said.

"Then let's make it Sunday." Since Martine had not cold-shouldered her, she was getting bolder.

When the minister returned, she said to him, with a smile:

"Do come, too! It would give us so much pleasure."

"Come to what?"

"To . . ."

Philippe had had enough. Muttering an excuse, he left the room.

20

"But I told you to go. I quite understand."

He hurried after her, with a show of contrition.

"It's a damn nuisance. I don't want to go at all, but you know how important it is for me. . . ."

"Yes, Philippe, I know. And it's high time for you to start."

". . . and I promised Albert to pick him up on the way."

"Yes, so you told me."

"What are you going to do today?"

"I have no plans."

"Not fed up with me?"

"No. . . . If you waste any more time, there won't be any point in going."

Like a schoolboy, he ran off to his room to dress. In less than a quarter of an hour, he managed to get into his ornate hunting outfit, which made him look more than ever like a film star.

I mustn't seem too pleased, he thought. For three days, he hadn't once laughed in Martine's presence, to make her understand that he was fully aware of the seriousness of what had happened. They had studiously refrained from speaking about it. Philippe had risked only a vague allusion:

"Then everything's all right now?"

"Quite all right."

"You won't think about it again?"

"About what?"

At all costs, he wanted to avoid a real explanation, which might put him in a bad light. So he made sure his wife and he were rarely alone together.

"I must give Claude a kiss before I go."

He drew on his warm gloves. It was still raining heavily and, glancing at the window, he made a slight grimace, still playing the part of a man who resents the necessity of going out.

"Let's hope I can fix up that business with Weil. It's exceedingly important."

His valet carried his gun to the car, which at last started off down the slippery avenue.

It was a cold morning, and the windows of all the apartments were shut. When making plans for a housewarming, Paulette had overlooked one thing: the hunting season was in full swing.

When the car stopped at the apartment building where the Grindorges lived, Philippe told his chauffeur to blow the horn three times. Albert had only to put on his hat and kiss his wife.

"If you feel bored, go chat with Martine, or ask her to come here."

"Perhaps I will. . . . Off you go!"

The windows of the car were misted, and both men were smoking. On either side, the vast bare cornfields of La Beauce stretched to the gray horizon. It was a fairly long trip to the château on the Loire owned by the millionaire Weil, known as Flour Weil, to distinguish him from Weil the film magnate, who was said to be heading for bankruptcy court.

Martine lacked the energy to dress and go to Mass. Until noon, she busied herself with small domestic duties: checking the linen, pointing out to her maid a tear in one of her dresses and explaining how to mend it, watching her son play, giving orders to the cook. But she did it all so listlessly that afterward she could not have said how she had spent her time.

The valet asked Rose, her maid:

"Know if she's going out this afternoon?"

"I don't think so."

The man sighed. For all her seeming apathy, Martine was quite capable of devoting the afternoon to a general inspection of closets and wardrobes, or checking the accounts of the various members of her staff.

"I don't want any lunch," she announced. "A glass of milk will do."

In other parts of Paris, there would be people coming and going, but whenever Martine glanced from her window, her eyes fell on an empty street. Even the old general had stayed indoors. Martine did not know him, but she saw him every morning, leaving at nine-thirty, punctual as clockwork, and getting on the horse his orderly had brought to the door. She picked up a novel but couldn't settle down to it; she allowed Claude to come into the living room to play, but soon he got on her nerves, and she rang for the nursemaid.

What she felt was enormous lethargy, as if she were floating in a vacuum, without a foothold anywhere.

At loose ends, she wandered from room to room. The truth was, she realized in a moment of bleak lucidity, that she had identified herself too completely with Philippe. Yet, after all, that was natural enough; she had only come alive when he had taken her in hand; before that, she'd been a nonentity.

And, strangely, something of the sort was true of Philippe, too. In those early days, his personality had, like hers, been rough. Life together had gradually shaped them both. Never had she thought of keeping back any fragment of herself, or of excluding him from any of her interests or activities. But, out of the blue . . . !

Philippe had noticed nothing, but she had had exactly the sensation that comes in certain dreams when suddenly you start slipping into a fathomless abyss.

"Go for your hunting," she had told him that morning.

He had been hovering around her with a hangdog air, waiting for the permission he dared not request. It had been a shock to discover something she had never suspected: that there was a streak of cowardice in his nature. And she also knew that if she insisted on his staying, he'd use every possible expedient to keep from having a tête-à-tête with her.

Perhaps it was better this way. Still, she'd have liked . . . No. What was the use of brooding? Philippe was what he was.

Her servants found their apprehensions justified when, ruthlessly forgetting that it was Sunday afternoon and they were dying to go to see a film, she opened the first closet that caught her eye and summoned her maid. Next, it was the cook's turn; after hers, the butler's.

"Is that you, Frédéric? . . . Are you busy? . . . No? Can I come around for an hour or so?"

Mme Donadieu was also at loose ends. The view from her windows, over Place des Vosges—its railings blacker than usual in the steady drizzle, and the fountain playing as if there weren't enough water coming down already—was no less dismal than the aspect on Avenue Henri-Martin.

After lunch, she spent a good hour dressing. Halfway across the square, she stopped, and went back to pour milk into her cat's saucer.

A visit with Frédéric, she had found, was the best solution on Sunday afternoons like this. The only trouble was that he lived so far away, out near Porte Champerret, in one of the new buildings, honeycombed with tiny apartments, that had sprung up on the western edge of Paris.

She decided against the Métro, too depressing on a day like this, and boarded a bus. There was at least the interest of streets and shops, lights and traffic, that way.

Across from Frédéric's was a bakery, and she knew what kind of cake to buy. Then she had to take the elevator, which always made her nervous, because once it had stopped between two floors when she was alone.

"Good afternoon, Frédéric. How are you, Odette?"

At first, she had found Odette's presence here slightly embarrassing. But the girl had shown so much tact, and her manners were so gentle, that this embarrassment had quickly disappeared.

Their brief encounter in La Rochelle had stirred Frédéric's compassion, and he had learned since that Odette had a nice disposition. He had met her again in Paris when he looked up his friend Jane at the hat shop where Odette worked. She had been in Paris only a fortnight, but the change in her was remarkable. She seemed to have acquired Parisian chic, or, rather, her carriage and demeanor, which previously impressed him most, showed hidden gracefulness.

"I hope you'll come to dinner with me one of these days." He had to be vague because he was so short of money that it was all he could do to pay for his own meals.

That was how it had started, much as such things happen to young people, and actually Frédéric was in the same position as a young man scouring Paris for a job. He had to take great care of his shirts and shoes, and often his dinner consisted of café au lait and a few rolls.

Then a day came . . . Really, at his age, it was preposterous! Tears came to his eyes and he had to blow his nose when he remembered it. A day came when this amazing young woman, to all appearances so commonplace and unperceptive, began to guess how things stood with him and asked him now and then to dinner. One evening, she had broached the subject, shyly at first, then in more pressing terms:

"Please, Frédéric, don't refuse. It would make me so happy. And in a few months, when you're in a position . . ."

He was being offered money, like a gigolo! But he was deeply moved—and that evening was the beginning.

A week later, he got the job as secretary at the Marboeuf Club. They started going out together in the evening, but there was never any talk of love.

People alone in Paris, like these two, very soon get sick of living in a hotel or a furnished room. After a few weeks, Odette started hunting for a place of her own. When he had time to spare, Frédéric went with her.

He was with her when she inspected the apartment near Porte Champerret. It cost four thousand francs a year, plus the usual extra charge for heat.

"It's far too big for one person," Odette decided, with regret. "I hate to let it go. The view is so nice, and everything's so clean and new."

Then and there they decided to share it. They settled in, and a month went by before anything took place between them. But it was bound to happen, and one night, quite naturally, indeed almost casually, she became his mistress.

When Mme Donadieu came to live in Paris, Frédéric sometimes went to see her, as he used to do in La Rochelle.

"I'd love to visit you, too, but I'm so afraid that . . ."

"There's nothing to be afraid of. Come. You'll find it will go quite smoothly."

It went so smoothly that whenever Mme Donadieu was lonely on Sunday, she dropped in on Frédéric and Odette, bringing the usual cake. If anything disconcerted her, it was the apartment. Her own was on the third floor of a very old building; it had thick walls, huge windows, and in it Mme Donadieu could enjoy a more or less familiar setting.

But here everything was cramped; it was like being in a box. Frédéric, who was tall, could touch the ceiling with his hand. The furniture was made to scale; too thickly varnished, too new and glossy, it might have come from the toy department of one of the big stores.

"It's so easy to keep clean," Odette pointed out.

And proudly she opened what looked like a closet and disclosed a chute, down which trash of all kinds was precipitated to a bin on the street level.

"Clever, isn't it?"

Though that Sunday it was raining just as hard at Porte Champerret as elsewhere in Paris, and the spectacle of streaming buses had been far from cheerful, Mme Donadieu was in a happy mood. Indeed, as she often told her friends, she was never bored—least of all when she had someone to talk to.

"Do you remember, Frédéric?"

The older she grew, the further she harked back for reminiscences; she was now full of the period when she wore girlishly short shirts and a pigtail down her back.

Odette was brewing coffee, which they all preferred to tea. There was a cobwebbed bottle of Armagnac on the table, and Frédéric made no secret of the fact that it came from the Marboeuf Club.

"I can't help wondering what they find to do there all day, the two of them."

She was referring to Marthe and Olsen, her husband, still interned, as she regarded it, in the old La Rochelle house.

"You can't imagine what I endured every winter. The place was a regular icebox. Of course, poor Oscar had central heating put in, but that was years ago, and the furnaces in those days weren't what they are now." She seldom mentioned her dead husband, but this evening something prompted her to add: "It's odd, but I can't help feeling he knew the time had come for him to go. . . ."

Looking at Frédéric, she saw that he understood her and seemed to agree.

"Yes," she went on, "and it's not the first time I've had that idea. I often wonder if he hadn't lost heart. No, that's not it. I can't find the right word, I'm afraid. But just think of what has happened since he died! You know, Frédéric, how proud he used to be of the House of Donadieu, and everything connected with it. And now there's no one except a son-in-law. And it was another son-in-law who saved the business when things were going wrong.

"I was always telling him he was getting more and more disagreeable every year, becoming a regular old bear! One day, I really lost my temper and called him a selfish beast because he wouldn't allow any freedom to any of us, but expected us all to toe the line. Now, I wonder . . ."

She paused. Her thoughts were unclear, and she frowned.

"Yes, I wonder if it wasn't always on his mind that there was no one to succeed him—no one like him, I mean. I'm sure he loathed

Kiki. . . . Poor Kiki! What would his father say if he knew . . . ?"

Half closing her eyes, Mme Donadieu sank back in her chair. She didn't like to have such thoughts, but there were moments, especially when she was with Frédéric, when they forced themselves on her.

Wasn't the whole family to blame, in some way, for what had happened to poor Kiki? He was born too late, when his parents no longer had the patience needed to handle a small, rather difficult boy. As for his brother and sisters, they had their own interests, and left him to himself. Kiki had never had a fair chance. The greatest mistake, however, had been to give him that tutor, Edmond, about whose character no serious inquiry had been made, even though for a domestic servant one insisted on references.

Marthe had been the first to sound a note of warning, pointing out that the two boys were not part of the family's life; they were too wrapped up in each other. They had no friends their own age, read none of the books boys usually read, and they carried physical culture to such an excess that it wasn't healthy; it seemed more like an obsession. Marthe had finally declared:

"The best thing would be to send Kiki to a good boarding school. That would knock the nonsense out of him."

They had taken her advice, and sent him to a Jesuit school in Brussels.

Two months later, they learned that Kiki had run away. And Edmond had disappeared, too.

"What do you think, Frédéric? Has he come back to France?"

"Most unlikely, I would say."

"Poor boy! In two months, he'll be twenty-one. Philippe reminded me of it the other day, because of the new arrangements we'll have to make—with the estate, I mean. . . . But let's not think about that. Turn on the radio, Frédéric. Try to get something pleasant."

He was twiddling the knobs when the telephone rang, though because of loud music they nearly missed hearing it. It was five o'clock; streetlights were on, and rain was still falling.

Mme Donadieu, who felt quite at home, answered, and the voice at the other end sounded confused.

"Is this Monsieur Dargens's apartment? . . . Oh, it's you, Maman. I didn't recognize your voice. Do I hear music?"

"It's Martine," Mme Donadieu told the others.

"Is Frédéric in?" Martine went on. "Ask him if he'd mind my coming over."

When Mme Donadieu had hung up, they looked at each other with some surprise. Martine saw Frédéric fairly often, but almost always at her apartment or in a restaurant. They all felt there was something behind this call, something less trivial than a mere wish for company.

"I suppose Philippe's gone shooting, and she doesn't know what to do with herself." Mme Donadieu preferred to brush aside disagreeable thoughts.

Of them all, it was she who had the happiest temperament; so she was the least susceptible to the depressing atmosphere of this wet Sunday afternoon.

"Perhaps I'd better wait till she comes," Odette said, "before cutting the cake."

Instinctively, she began moving around the room, making sure everything was in order—as though Martine was a guest different from others.

"Is this all right here?" She had placed the small alabaster lamp on a low table near the sofa. Raindrops were flashing down the windowpanes, which glimmered blue against the falling night.

"What do you think about Philippe's business?" Mme Donadieu asked Frédéric. "Is it really doing as well as he says? When I think of all the money they must spend, living the way they do . . ."

"There she is!" Odette had seen the small green car drawing up outside.

Frédéric went to the elevator to meet Martine and was surprised to see the plain black dress under her raincoat.

It made her look like a young schoolgirl—a schoolgirl in mourning. Her mother was quite startled, and asked impulsively:

"What's wrong?"

"Nothing. What made you think there was?"

She stood outside the little pool of light cast by the alabaster lamp, and they could not see her face. But, by some trick of the light, though she seemed only a darker shadow against shadows, her outline was sharply defined.

"Let me help you with your coat, Madame Dargens." Martine was one of her customers at Jane's, and Odette always sounded obsequious when addressing her.

Something in the atmosphere of the dim room, a curious oppression, made Martine feel as if she were suffocating. To dispel the feeling, she said briskly:

"Well, Maman?"

"Yes, my dear? What is it?"

Martine could bear it no longer.

"Why are you all staring at me? . . . I suppose it's that funny little lamp that makes you look so strange. Turn on the big light, please."

But when Frédéric did, she blinked and put her hand over her eyes.

"No. It's too strong. It was nicer before."

"What have you been doing all day?" her mother asked.

"Oh, Philippe went off to hunt. So I've been putting in a spell of domestic drudgery. An hour ago, I'd had enough, so I thought I'd drop in for a chat with Frédéric and Odette."

None of them was deceived by her pretense of cheerfulness. And it didn't help when, pointing to the cake, she cried:

"Oh, how nice! That's a mocha cake, isn't it? The one cake I like. Did you guess I was coming? . . . Why did you turn off the radio?"

"For your telephone call."

"What were you talking about when I came in?"

"I don't remember. What were we talking about, Frédéric? . . . About you and Philippe very likely . . . I daresay Marthe's by herself, too, in dull old La Rochelle. Jean's sure to be at Esnandes today. Your father was the only one who never cared for hunting. . . . *Where* did you get that dress?"

She seemed quite annoyed with her daughter for looking so plain.

"I unearthed it when I was going through my closet. It must be at least four years old. . . . Yes, I remember now; I got this dress soon after Claude was born. What's wrong with it?"

"It's not your style. A little depressing, to my mind."

"Then it suits the weather." Martine laughed.

She kept moving around; she poured the coffee, asked for milk, and even started toward the kitchen to get it.

"No, really you mustn't!" Odette protested. She seemed quite shocked at the thought of Martine's helping in her duties as hostess.

"And how's life been treating you, Frédéric?" Martine asked, for the sake of saying something.

"Oh, once a man's turned the corner, as I have . . ."

"What corner?"

"You'll understand someday—many, many years ahead."

"Don't pretend to be so venerable. You don't look a day more than forty-five."

Somehow, though they all were doing their best to keep the conversation alive, everything they said fell flat. There was silence again, broken only by the clink of forks. Then Martine asked:

"Isn't it rather annoying having streetcars and buses passing all day?"

"We're hardly ever here in the daytime," Odette pointed out with a smile. "There aren't so many in the evening, thank goodness!"

Martine looked at her almost enviously. For most of the day, she and Frédéric were at their jobs, with no time to think about themselves or their personal troubles. When they came home, they had only an hour or two to go before sleep brought oblivion.

"By the way," said Mme Donadieu, "if Philippe brings back some partridges, do remember to send me one. Not a big one, though; I like them young and tender. My teeth, you know . . ."

She was about to laugh, but Martine sprang from her chair, so abruptly it almost upset, and walked quickly to the window, where she stood quite still, pressing her face to the glass.

"What's the matter, darling?" her mother asked in alarm.

The others rose in clumsy haste.

"Martine, what's wrong?" They could hear her gasping, trying to catch her breath. "Are you feeling ill? Shall I get you something?"

Martine shook her head, and made a little gesture of impatience. Why couldn't they leave her alone? That was all she wanted. But they would crowd around her!

"Odette, bring some vinegar," cried Mme Donadieu.

At last Martine managed to speak.

"No! Leave me alone!" Her voice was shrill with exasperation.

"Martine! Do try to calm yourself!"

The attack was passing. Martine's body relaxed, her shoulders sagged, and she gazed dully at the others.

"Please let me alone for just a minute."

What had come over her? It was a sudden, frantic impulse to burst into tears, to fling herself down on a bed the way Kiki used to, to grit her teeth and score the sheets with her fingernails, to cry and whimper—somehow to give vent to her suppressed feelings.

With a weak attempt at a smile, she came back to the table.

"I'm awfully sorry. It's over now."

"Have some water. I'm afraid you're too nervous again. But it's only a passing phase, I believe."

Martine guessed what was in her mother's mind, and knew she

was mistaken. Frédéric, she felt sure, had never for a moment thought she was going to have another child. His face was turned away, but she could see he was worried. When she saw a hard look settle in his eyes, she knew he was thinking of Philippe.

"I feel so ashamed of myself," she said. "I've spoiled your evening." Her one desire now was to get away.

All over Paris, caged indoors, people were grumbling, fidgeting, getting on one another's nerves.

In the Grindorges' apartment, too, that morning a woman, irritated by her husband's show of reluctance when, she knew quite well, he was itching to be off, had kept repeating:

"Yes, yes. Go off to your hunting. Don't bother about me."

"If I hadn't promised Philippe . . ."

"There's no need to make excuses. Of course you must go."

And, to complete the resemblance, Paulette, too, had resolved to devote this wet Sunday to household chores. In her case, of course, there was more reason. The Grindorges had only just moved; nothing was in its final place, so there was plenty to be done.

She began by sending the children, with their nursemaid, to her father-in-law's house, and telling the cook to go to the cinema.

She wanted to be alone. Yet, when she had the place to herself, she seemed unable to settle down, and drifted from room to room, sinking wearily now and then to a chair or a bed.

At these moments she imagined the scene at Flour Weil's estate: Philippe and Albert trudging across muddy fields, with the barking of dogs and the cries of beaters echoing around them. At the château, their hostess would be busy supervising preparations for a midday dinner to which thirty or forty would sit down. Fifteen or twenty cars would be parked in the courtyard, and soon one of the keepers would be sorting out the collective bag.

Paulette hadn't set eyes on Philippe for three days—except for a glimpse from her third-floor window when he stepped out of his car to help Albert stow his guns in the back.

And he had telephoned only once.

"Paulette? Look, we'll have to go slow for a while. Martine's on the warpath. She even came to the office this morning. I keep running into her everywhere, so it wouldn't be safe. . . ."

"But, Philippe . . ." She gave a little sob.

"I'm afraid it can't be helped, dear. I don't see much hope for the present. . . . Unless, someday, I've had enough and . . ."

"Don't say that! You frighten me. Philippe, promise me not to . . . to do anything rash."

There was a click. He had hung up.

All the lights were on in the apartment and most of the doors were open. Everywhere, Paulette saw her reflected self in a mirror; she patted her hair or drew her dressing gown together; though it was now five in the afternoon, she had not yet dressed.

She picked up a big doll sprawled on the sofa, carried it to the nursery door, and tossed it into the room. A dozen times, she was on the brink of tears, yet her eyes remained dry. She could not shake off the feeling of oppression that weighed on her.

It was as wearing as a sleepless night, and she was conscious of being in a curious physical state, neither well nor ill. Still, her nerves seemed to be under control, because she managed to lie quite still on her bed for an hour, gazing at the ceiling. Then she started roaming again. The place was so new to her that only after pushing repeatedly at one of the doors, and thinking it must be locked, did she remember that it opened the other way, toward her.

A dozen times she stopped at the telephone, only to turn away with a despondent gesture. She could think of no one to call, and, really, she had nothing to say. To make things worse, almost every room had a telephone. It had been Philippe's idea, and Albert had adopted it, as he did with all Philippe's ideas. So, wherever she went, the sleek black coil of a phone met her eye.

It was six when she visited the kitchen and pantry, to make sure the servants were still out. She locked the service door, as she had the front door. Every time she heard the elevator going up or down, she gave a start.

Finally, she called her father-in-law, who answered the telephone himself.

"Are the children all right? . . . No. There's no hurry at all. I'm very busy trying to make some sort of order here. . . . Yes, certainly they can eat with you. . . . Thanks. Good night, Father."

The children were at the other end of Paris, where old Grindorge was still living, a hundred yards from the factory he had built thirty years before. Its output of machine tools had made it the second or third largest in France. And Albert was in the country, on the other side of Orléans.

With brisk, precise gestures—as if all her desultory movements had been leading up to this—Paulette opened a bookcase, the one in the smoking room, which contained only bulky reference books, bound in red or green leather. She took down a volume of the encyclopedia, the one marked "S–Tr," and began reading, still jumping each time she heard the elevator.

Strychnine. A highly poisonous vegetable alkaloid, $C_{21}H_{22}N_2O_2$ . . . Nearly insoluble in water . . . affects all parts of the nervous system . . . Symptoms usually appear within twenty minutes of ingestion, starting with stiffness at the back of the neck and twitching of the muscles . . . violent tetanic convulsions. . . . Death follows rapidly, consciousness being retained throughout.

She closed the book abruptly and replaced it on its shelf. Then, as if coming to a decision, she took down another, from the same group.

Laudanum. A simple alcoholic tincture of opium. . . . The patient who has swallowed a lethal dose usually passes at once into the narcotic state. . . . Breathing becomes progressively slower and shallower, until finally it ceases altogether.

She could have sworn the elevator had stopped at their floor, on which theirs was the only apartment. Yet there was no ring. She went to the hall and pressed her ear to the door, but could hear nothing.

Still convinced that someone was lurking outside, she hurried to the bedroom, took Albert's revolver from a drawer, and went back to the front door. After flinging it open, she switched on the landing light.

No one. Her imagination had tricked her. She bolted the door again and put the revolver back in the drawer with trembling hands. She was shaken by the thought that she might easily have fired it without thinking.

She ate nothing. She had told the servants she was dining out. At nine, there was a ring at the door, but at the same moment she heard her children's voices.

Why did they stare at her so? Was there something strange in her appearance? After kissing them, she ran to the living room and studied her face in a mirror. All she noticed was that a strand of hair was falling down her cheek and her eyes had a peculiar fixity.

Her temples were throbbing; she was in for a bad headache.

When Albert got home, at one in the morning, he was somewhat surprised to find a volume of the encyclopedia lying open on the smoking-room table. Giving no further thought to it, he took off his hunting boots, put his guns back in the rack, and smoked a final cigarette.

On tiptoe, though light was shining under the door, he entered the bedroom he shared with his wife because his father had been profoundly shocked when he spoke of having separate bedrooms.

The bed had not been turned down. Paulette, still in her dressing gown, was lying across it, one slipper dangling from her bare foot. Her face was drawn, her breathing labored, and she seemed to be in the throes of a bad dream.

21

"Monsieur Michel Donadieu wishes to know if he can see you, madame."

"Where is he?"

"In the hall."

At another time Martine might have smiled at the thought of her brother waiting, with dignity, and gloves in hand.

"Show him into the living room, please."

It was the Wednesday following that memorably rainy Sunday, on which, the newspapers had declared, the rainfall had exceeded the record amount for any day in the last twenty years. There was a bite in the air, though winter had not yet definitely set in. As she walked into the room, Martine glanced at the clock; it was ten minutes past eleven.

"Good morning, Michel."

As usual, she inclined her forehead for him to kiss—a family tradition. Then she curled up in a corner of the sofa, drawing her dressing gown over her legs.

"Keeping well?" she asked. It was difficult to tell. Not only his limbs, but his features, too, had become almost shapeless, both buried in layers of fat.

"No," he replied dolefully. "I've been anything but well for the last month or so."

Martine was only vaguely sorry for him. Actually, he rather disgusted her, and she had a shrewd idea of the object of this visit: once again he wanted money. She could see him wondering how to steer the conversation into a favorable channel.

"Have you come from Antibes?" That was the last address he had given. He had moved several times, and for the usual reason: he had "got into trouble" with a girl.

"No. I'm staying in Cannes. The hotel's ridiculously cheap, but they provide for one quite well, considering. . . . How's your husband?"

Just then the telephone rang. With a languid gesture, Martine reached for it.

"Yes? Who is it? . . . Oh, good morning, Paulette. How are you?"

Unobservant though he normally was, Michel was startled by the change that came over his sister. She had stiffened, and her eyes, narrowed to pinpoints, were fixed on the carpet in a concentrated stare.

On the other end Paulette answered, somewhat shakily:

"Quite well, thanks. It's ages since we last saw each other . . ."

"Ages?"

"Well, not since lunch last week. But I've just been given four seats for the opening night of that new American film everybody's talking about. It's going to be a big evening. People are paying fabulous prices for standing room, I hear. . . . Are you there?"

"Yes. When is it?"

"Tonight. Will you come?"

"I can't be sure whether Philippe has made another engagement. Call him and ask."

"I'd rather not."

"Why?"

"Oh, I don't much care for calling men, especially in their offices. . . . He *is* in his office, isn't he?" Then, on the spur of the moment, she had a bold idea. "I've just remembered that I have to go to the Champs-Elysées this morning, and I'll drop in on Albert. . . . By the way, it's a full-dress show. Tails, glad rags, and all the rest of it. Au revoir."

Michel, who was watching his sister, asked in a casual tone:

"Who was that?"

"Someone asking us to a film this evening."

"As I was saying . . . But what on earth's come over you, Martine?"

"Nothing's come over me."

"You look awfully pale. . . . Shall I leave you now, and come back later?"

"No, of course not. Tell me what you have to say."

"It's not so very urgent. But I've had some heavy bills to meet lately, and I'm a little short. Do you think you could persuade Philippe to give me an advance on the next half-year's allowance? Not a lot— say, twenty thousand francs."

That "next half-year" was, as Martine knew, a euphemism. Philippe had already come to her brother's rescue several times, and the advance, if any, would come from—at the earliest—the second period of the following year.

"And I swear this is the last time I let a girl get me into her clutches," Michel blustered. "I'm through with women."

Usually Martine was patient with her brother, but today—why, she had no idea—he truly nauseated her.

"You'd better tackle Philippe yourself."

"Why? Aren't you getting on together?"

"That's not it. It would be better if this request didn't always come from me."

Though Martine was giving her attention to the conversation, other thoughts were hovering in her mind: the sound of Paulette's voice on the telephone; all sorts of trivial happenings in the last few days. Was Philippe sincere when, at meals, he used a cheerful tone and seemed to assume that all was forgiven, or forgotten? He had never again referred to that fateful afternoon, and he refrained from speaking of Paulette, or even of going out with the Grindorges—which was a great change. . . . Michel's voice broke through her musings.

"He's not having trouble with his business, is he?"

"Not that I know of."

For the first time since he had come, Michel dropped the sycophantic, almost humble tone he had been using. There was a hint of bitterness in his voice when he said:

"In that case, I don't see why he should make a fuss about advancing me a paltry twenty thousand. Any bank would do it right away. If I ask him, it's precisely because he might not care to have it known that his brother-in-law . . ."

"Why not go and tell him that at the office?"

"I suppose you think I haven't the nerve to do it? . . . But really he has no right to put on airs. If he's a rich man now, it's thanks to us. And that's putting it in the kindest way. If one wanted to be nasty . . ."

"Michel! I suggest that you go now."

"Of course you *would* take his side."

"I'm not taking his side. Only, I don't like to hear you talking nonsense."

"You call it nonsense? I defy you to deny that Philippe has, to all intents and purposes, turned us out of our own home."

She eyed him with distaste. There were sallow half-moons under his eyes, gray hairs in his mustache, but, in spite of the weather, he was as neat as a tailor's dummy, and there wasn't a particle of dust or mud on his shoes—which he still cleaned himself.

"Ask Maman, or Marthe, Olsen, anyone you like, what they think."

Michel was now pacing the room, whose air of luxury seemed to add weight to his assertions.

"Shall I tell you once and for all how I feel about it, Michel? If I do, don't forget you asked for it. . . . No. We'd better drop the subject. All you have to do is to see Philippe in his office. I'll be surprised if he refuses what you ask."

"No. Tell me what you think. I'd rather know."

"Have it your own way! My opinion is that, if Philippe hadn't stepped in, the Donadieu business would be in worse shape than it is. In fact, it would have passed out of the family's hands altogether. Papa had sized you up, and he never let you take the least initiative. I don't want to hurt your feelings and I won't go into details. As for Olsen, he has just brains enough to make a good chief clerk, nothing more. And Maman—well, she was full of good intentions, but after a few months of her regime she'd managed to get one of the best-organized businesses in France into the most hopeless tangle. So, for heaven's sake, don't start telling me that Philippe—"

"Naturally you stick up for your husband." Michel began hunting for his hat, which he had handed to the valet on entering.

"I'm not sticking up for anyone or anything, but I loathe the sort of nonsense you indulge in. I wouldn't be at all surprised if the real cause of Papa's death was that he simply despaired of the whole lot of us. . . . Well? Have you anything else to say to me?"

"Er—no. I don't think so."

"Then, au revoir. I must go see what Claude is up to."

All she had just said she meant—but she knew there was more to it than that. Indeed, the way she had put it garbled her real thoughts. But Michel had brought it on himself; he should have chosen a better moment.

In her bedroom, she picked up the telephone and called the R.M.C.

"Monsieur Dargens, please . . . Is that you, Philippe? I'm sorry to disturb you at work. . . . Is Paulette there, by any chance? I want to speak to her."

"Hello? Yes, it's me!" There was a nervous tremor in Paulette's voice.

"I forgot to ask you what color you'll be in tonight—so our dresses don't clash."

She could swear Philippe was listening in, on the extension, and that Paulette had turned to him with a questioning look. He was probably whispering to her what dress to wear.

"Pale blue? Thanks. Remember me to Albert, won't you?"

She remained sitting by the telephone, frowning—as she often sat for hours when Philippe was away.

". . . and Jesus laid his hands on them." For some time this fragment of the Gospel had been running through her head. Suddenly she knew the reason. If only someone were beside her now, to lay his hand on her forehead, a cool, firm, healing hand! Everyone took her for a levelheaded young woman—some even accused her of being hard-boiled—yet, under the surface, she felt things so deeply that there were moments when she could have cried with pain.

Five minutes passed. Then she called Philippe again.

"I thought I'd better let you know: Michel is coming to see you. . . . Yes, for the usual thing. Do as you please about it. . . . Is Paulette still there?"

He answered "No," but could she believe him? And, even if it were true, there had been plenty of time for them to arrange another meeting.

It wasn't only that fragment of the Gospel that she had come to understand. She saw in a new light the visits Frédéric used to pay in the old days to the two women in her parents' house: first to Mme Donadieu, who confided to him all her small vexations; then to Eva, in that exotic boudoir with the black curtains, where, squatting on cushions on the floor, they smoked endless cigarettes. . . .

But she was different; she wanted neither men nor women friends. She wanted only Philippe!

They met in the American bar in the neighborhood; it was their usual rendezvous when they were having a night out together. Paulette was in pale blue, the one color she should avoid, since it emphasized her awkward figure and the grayness of her skin.

She usually patronized the same shops Martine did, so, as it so happened, both were wearing almost identical ermine capes.

They had only a hundred yards to go from the bar to the theater, and they decided to walk. Albert stepped to Martine's side, and Philippe, after a brief hesitation that did not escape his wife, offered his arm to Paulette.

"Don't you think she's looking rather run-down?" Albert murmured in a tone of husbandly concern. "I've been quite worried these last few days. You have so much influence on her, I wish you'd try to buck her up."

For this gala night, an awning had been put up out to the sidewalk, and they entered the brilliantly lighted lobby between resplendent members of the Republican Guard standing at attention. What happened next was embarrassing and took all four by surprise. There was a crowd, including the usual gate-crashers watching for their chance, and the ushers checking the invitations were alert.

Albert handed the two cards to a young man in a dinner jacket, who promptly announced:

"Two seats in box 5. Two in the orchestra. This way."

Noticing that Albert seemed flustered, Philippe intervened.

"I'm Philippe Dargens, of R.M.C.," he said in a peremptory tone. "There has been some mistake. We wish to sit together."

"Can't be managed," said the young man, who was already inspecting another card.

"Excuse me. I must insist. . . . You heard my name?"

"Afraid I don't know you. You'd better see the manager."

For the first time in several days, Martine actually smiled. Then, when she saw how pale Philippe had turned at this rebuff, she felt some compassion.

He turned on his heel and hurried to the box office, where he had a colloquy with a man in full evening dress, evidently someone in charge.

Paulette naïvely remarked:

"What earthly difference can it make if we aren't together while the film is on?"

She was probably counting on being with Philippe, while her husband sat beside Martine.

They waited for ten minutes, during which a dignified man, probably the manager, appeared from a side door and could be seen talking earnestly with Philippe. Nothing could be done, it seemed; every seat was taken, and, if they delayed, they might lose the seats allotted them—so Philippe announced, in a voice rough with indignation.

On their way to the wide marble staircase, Martine, with a quick, possessive gesture, took her husband's arm and said:

"We'll sit in the orchestra, Philippe. I like being near the screen, as you know. The Grindorges can have the seats in the box."

It was too late for discussion. The auditorium had darkened and an usherette was beckoning them forward with her flashlight.

Another attendant had pounced on the Grindorges and was guiding them to the staircase leading to the boxes. The film had started, and some of the audience protested when Philippe seemed to linger.

"Sit down!"

Martine was trembling at her audacity. She could see Philippe's face in the brightness from the screen; its look was ominous.

"Angry with me?" she whispered in his ear.

"No."

"What's wrong then?"

"Nothing . . . Don't talk, please."

Though there was no physical contact between them, she knew he was sitting bolt upright, every muscle tense, gazing ahead with unseeing eyes, indifferent to the black-and-white figures forming and fading on the screen. And she could picture Paulette, too, in the box, snapping at her husband and twisting her handkerchief between her fingers.

When the intermission came, but before the lights had come on, Philippe got up and, taking no notice of his wife or of the protests of the people in their row, walked to one of the exits.

Martine had not been prepared for this. After a moment's indecision, she followed him. But by then everybody was standing, and the aisles were so full that she felt something like panic, the dismay of a child lost in a crowd.

Looking up at the boxes, she saw that the Grindorges, too, had left their seats, so she looked for them in the lobby. The theater was one of the largest in Paris and, this being a gala night, it was packed with people. Hardly knowing what she was doing, Martine, murmuring "Excuse me!," pushed her way through, but didn't see Philippe or the Grindorges.

She thought of sending for the car and going home, but she couldn't bring herself to leave, and continued looking for the others. She felt a woman's hand on her arm.

"Hello! Where were you?"

Paulette and Albert seemed surprised to see her by herself. Without thinking, she asked:

"Have you seen Philippe?"

"No. We're looking for him. We thought he was with you. Any idea where he's gone?"

The intermission was nearly over when at last they discovered Philippe in one of the bars, staring gloomily at the glass in his hand, which was trembling slightly.

"So this is where you were! We've been hunting for you," said Albert breezily. He guessed that Philippe and Martine had had some disagreement.

"Yes, this is where I was."

After a glance at the whisky-and-soda he was holding, Martine said deliberately:

"I think I'll have a drink too. Bartender, another whisky, please."

It was really obvious by now, to the Grindorges, that under the surface a struggle was in progress. Martine did not like whisky, and Philippe, who had been having trouble with his digestion, was on a diet that limited him to claret; all alcohol, whisky especially, had been ruled out.

"What will you have?" he asked in a surly voice, turning to Paulette.

"Nothing, thanks. We'd better be getting back to our seats. It's time, Albert, isn't it?"

They left, and the bar rapidly emptied. Philippe ordered another whisky-and-soda.

"How many does that make?" Martine asked.

"Three."

Quite coolly she said to the bartender:

"Two whiskies for me, please." And added, aside, to Philippe:

"That'll make us even, won't it?"

She heard him draw a deep, sibilant breath, and saw his grip tighten on the brass railing until his knuckles showed white.

"Do you propose to stay here for the rest of the show?" she asked.

"Yes."

"In that case, I'm staying, too."

He was holding himself in, but the effort was great. Twice his eyes settled on his wife, and she could see hatred in them. To all appearances, she was perfectly at ease, though it was all she could do to remain on her feet.

Under her breath she whispered a last appeal:

"Philippe!"

"Yes?"

"Don't you think we could go home now?"

"No."

"All right. Then we'll stay."

She could not get through the three whiskies. Ordering them had been mere bravado. After the first sips, she felt quite sick.

The doors had been closed; a faint sound of music came through from the auditorium, then a ripple of applause when the producer's name was flashed on the screen.

"You're very unkind, Philippe."

That set him off, despite the presence of the bartender, who, however, was tactful enough to retreat to the far end of the bar.

"Unkind! I like that! You insult me in public—and not me only, but also our friends—and then you tell me I'm unkind."

"I only did it because I wanted to be with you."

"Well, you had no right to do it. For one thing, they're our hosts tonight."

"Oh, come on, Philippe! Don't exaggerate."

He gripped her arm roughly and almost shouted in her face:

"I've had enough! Do you hear? Enough! You've been making my life unbearable these last days, and it's got to stop."

"What have I done?"

"Damn it! You know quite well. Do you think I don't know what lies behind your air of . . . of disdainful calm? . . . And you're only acting like this because I was silly enough to spend an afternoon with a woman in a hotel bedroom!"

"No, Philippe, that's not true."

"Well, what else have you got against me? . . . You should have more sense. She doesn't attract me in the least. She's a complete dud—you know that as well as I do. But I happen to need her husband, and when she flung herself at me, I didn't dare turn her down."

"You're hurting me, Philippe."

He released her arm. There was a red circle above her wrist.

"I suppose it's easy enough to work yourself up into a state of idiotic jealousy when you have nothing to do all day, but—"

"Not so loud, please!" a voice said from the door to the auditorium. An usher was standing there watching them.

But Philippe was beyond caring. Now that he'd shown his anger, he was determined to vent all his grievances. There was a vicious edge to his voice, but, in curious contrast, an almost pleading look in his eyes.

"I'm aiming high, Martine, and I mean to get there, no matter what it costs. I work like a slave—twenty hours a day. And it's a hell of a struggle, I assure you, to keep going. If I let down for a minute, everything would collapse like a house of cards. Because I give you everything you ask for, and I never tell you about my worries, you probably think it's all smooth sailing. . . ."

Had Martine been unable to see his face, she might have let herself be moved, but she could watch him, and, for all his accent of sincerity, perhaps made more effective by the drinks, she felt sure he was acting.

"Please don't say any more, Philippe. . . . Shall we go home now?"

"No."

"What do you propose to do?"

"The Grindorges have asked us to supper. I'm waiting for them."

"What if I don't want to come?"

"That's your problem. You can go home if you want to."

"Oh, Philippe!"

"No! It's no use whimpering 'Oh, Philippe!' I know what's in your mind. You're afraid I'm going to make a scene. You keep looking at that damn fool at the door who said, 'Not so loud, please!' "

He was conscious, however, that he was calmer, so he drank another whisky while he tried to think of a reason for another outburst.

"Let's take this opportunity to talk business, for a change. You don't approve of that subject, do you? It's much too sordid for your ladyship. Money is vulgar—to make, anyhow; not to spend. . . . Well, get this into your head: I'm in a jam. Somehow or other I've got to get eight hundred thousand francs before the fifteenth of this month. And if I haven't raised a million and a half within two months, R.M.C. will have to be liquidated. . . . Does that mean anything to you? . . . You *would* choose a time like this for scenes of jealousy, for trailing me wherever I go like a detective and pumping my chauffeur about my movements. . . . It's no use shaking your head; I know all about it."

"Philippe!"

He gave a short laugh.

"This morning, for instance—really you overdid it. You called me twice within five minutes—in the office—just because Paulette happened to be there. . . . Yesterday afternoon you called with a crazy story of wanting a key, and you knew quite well I didn't have it. How do you expect me to do any work? I have to keep my head clear and—"

"I'm going." She turned toward the door.

He grabbed her wrist again, more roughly than before.

"No, you don't! And it's no use looking around like that. I'm not afraid of making a scene. I don't care how many people see us—the more the merrier."

He gave her a venomous look. She lowered her head; tears were rolling down her cheeks.

"Please, Philippe, do try to calm down. Don't drink any more."

"Why not? I'm not drunk."

To humor him, she, too, had to act a part, to plead, to pretend to agree with what he said.

"No, you're not drunk. But . . . you're upset tonight. Let's go back to our seats, or go home, whichever you prefer."

"No."

"I promise not to reproach you with anything."

"That's not it."

"What do you mean?"

"I mean, I'd rather you did. Ever since . . . since last Thursday, you haven't had a word to say. You go around looking very calm and dignified—much too much the grand lady to condescend to anything so vulgar as a quarrel. That wouldn't matter so much, except that you've been spying on me, watching everything I do, even the expression on my face! Yesterday you called Fouquet's, and you had absolutely nothing to tell me. It's come to the point where I can't take a step without wondering how it will be interpreted. . . ."

"And, as a result, you don't dare have any more meetings with Paulette," she added sadly.

"Damn it all! Haven't you understood? Must I start all over again from the beginning? I told you the position I'm in—about R.M.C., I mean."

Cold sweat was breaking out on her forehead; her cheeks were deathly pale. To steady herself, she leaned against the bar. But Philippe had no compassion.

"That's an old trick! When I say something you don't like, you pretend you're going to faint."

She felt a spasm of nausea, and heard herself exclaim in a voice she hardly recognized:

"How I loathe you!"

But it wasn't true. It was the exact opposite of the truth. She hungered for him with every fiber. And she stayed there, under the bartender's pitying gaze, courting the risk of an even more painful outbreak—to prevent his having a few moments alone with that miserable woman! That's what I'm reduced to! she thought sadly.

Philippe was indulging in an orgy of self-pity, and he, too, felt like weeping. How unfair that a woman's senseless jealousy should stand between him and the realization of his ambitions!

"For six years," he said in a plaintive tone, "I've fought my way, inch by inch, to where I am now. But the point I've reached is only a beginning; the real struggle lies ahead. And now your ladyship thinks fit to get on your high horse because I . . . No, damn it all, you can't seriously imagine I get any pleasure out of sleeping with a creature like that! You've only got to look at her. That's why it's so ridiculous to be jealous. There's nothing to be jealous of." He was talking more to himself than to Martine, bewailing the injustice of his lot, his wife's incomprehension. Yet all the time he was lying, or, rather, garbling the truth.

It was true that, as he said, he never spared himself and he did sacrifice everything to his ambition; but he failed to add—what Martine knew only too well—that he was quite prepared to sacrifice her, too, when the time came—if, indeed, he had not done so already.

A tumult of clapping and bravos poured in; all the padded doors had opened simultaneously.

"Philippe, I'm awfully tired, and I'm not feeling well. Let's go home."

"Go home if you want to."

"For the last time, I beg you: please, let's go. If you have any pity . . ."

"And for the last time I tell you to go home if you want to."

Hastily, he drained the whisky in his glass and started looking for the Grindorges with a casual air, though he seemed a little unsure of his movements. Martine tried to keep him in sight among the crowd.

"Where were you? We've been hunting for you everywhere."

"Oh, Martine was feeling tired." Philippe had quickly recovered his aplomb.

"I'm sorry to hear that, Martine. Do you want to go home?"

"No."

Her "No" sounded like a threat.

"Would you get our coats, Albert?"

They had supper at Maxim's. As usual on such occasions, Philippe got up several times in the course of the meal to shake hands with people he knew. Watching him, Martine could see that he was nervous, but the signs were too slight to be noticed by others.

She felt as if all the vitality had been drained out of her. Her head ached, and waves of nausea kept surging up. In fact, when the meal was over, she had to hurry to the ladies' room, where she was sick. She would have given a lot for a breath of fresh air, but she'd resolved to see it through. As she was freshening her makeup in front of the mirror, she felt sure Philippe had taken this opportunity to ask Paulette to dance with him.

Her intuition was correct. When she opened the door, Paulette, to whom Philippe was talking in a low voice, squeezed his arm and whispered:

"Be careful. Your wife's back."

Martine could not hear this, but she'd seen Paulette's glance, and guessed what she'd said. Slowly, she crossed the dance floor to their table. Albert was smoking.

"Don't you think she's looking better?" he said to Martine. "These last few weeks she's been off color—I suppose you've noticed it, too—and moody sometimes and overexcited at others. I've been quite worried. I hope it doesn't mean another baby's on the way."

"Yes, indeed let's hope not." Martine's voice was so strange that Albert gave her a puzzled, rather anxious look.

The dance ended, Philippe slumped heavily into his chair and, though they were Albert's guests, beckoned to the headwaiter.

"The check, please."

"But . . ."

"Sorry, Albert, I really must go home. I've been feeling under par all evening, and that dance . . ."

It was not the dance that had upset him. It was what Paulette had whispered, with an almost crazy look in her eyes, when they were at the far end of the dance floor:

"You remember what you said to me?"

When he pretended not to, she became explicit.

"Are you quite sure you'd marry me if . . . ?"

At that moment he had been strangely shaken, and he couldn't remember now if he had said anything or merely nodded.

22

"Come in, Frédéric. I hope you're not angry with me for taking you away from work?"

"Not in the least. I never have much to do until five."

"Have a cigar."

It was Saturday. A time was to come when they would try to recall each date, and fix events in the right order. But there was little likelihood that anyone, with the possible exception of Frédéric, would be able to do that.

It was the Saturday following that memorably rainy Sunday when Mme Donadieu met Martine at Frédéric's apartment, and after the gala night at the cinema and the supper at Maxim's. There would be no difficulty in getting the week right, anyhow, because every newspaper had photographs of floods in Paris suburbs, of firemen in boats rescuing people from half-submerged houses, of a village in the Rhone district threatened by a landslide—not to mention the usual picture of the Zouave statue beside Pont de l'Alma, the Parisians' gauge for measuring the height of the Seine.

The incessant rain had affected everybody's nerves. It had lasted too long, and everyone was sick of living in perpetual moisture.

"Why don't you have a cigar?"

"I'm not smoking. Doctor's orders."

"Oh, once in a while won't harm you. And I'll open a bottle of some excellent Bordeaux I got recently."

Actually, Mme Donadieu was eager to launch into her subject. But she could not bring herself to break with this time-honored custom. In La Rochelle, the Donadieus had few callers, but when one came, even if he was a mere salesman, cigars and wine or liqueur were invariably produced. There were, however, several varieties of cigar, graded to the status of the visitor.

"Perhaps I shouldn't have called you. But all morning I've been dreadfully worried. . . . First, please tell me if you've seen Martine or Philippe lately."

"Not since Sunday." To please his hostess, Frédéric had lit a cigar.

The room had an unusual formality, thanks to its tall windows and the antique furniture Mme Donadieu had brought from La Rochelle.

"I can't imagine what's going on," she continued, "but I feel sure there's something wrong. I rarely let a day go by without calling Martine and having a chat with her. I find it does me good; and I like to keep in touch. After that, I can think about what she said, and try to picture what she's doing. . . . Well, yesterday morning I called her three times, when I know she's always in, and her maid told me she was out. I felt so uneasy that I called Philippe, at his office, though I know he hates being disturbed there. He told me he was sure Martine was in; he'd been talking to her on the telephone a few minutes before."

Frédéric found his attention straying from what Mme Donadieu was telling him, to her appearance. She was seated in a way that put her face beside an enlarged photograph of Kiki, taken a month before he disappeared. As often in enlargements of snapshots, the profile was indistinct; the whole face, in fact, had a curious evanescence. It struck Frédéric that Mme Donadieu's face, in this uncertain light, had something of the same wraithlike quality. He was calculating her age, when a mention of his son brought him back to what she was saying.

"I quite understand that Martine has her own interests and anxieties, and may not always feel like chattering with her old mother. But yesterday morning Philippe's voice sounded so strange that I decided to risk going to Avenue Henri-Martin—in that pouring rain too!"

"Did you see her?"

"The butler said he'd see if she was in. I'm positive I heard Martine's voice, but he told me she was out.

"This morning I called her again. No luck. When I telephoned Philippe, all he said was that he didn't understand, that when Martine was out of sorts she often behaved oddly. I can't help feeling there may be something seriously wrong. What do you think, Frédéric?"

It was a difficult question to answer. Frédéric was aware that all was not well between his son and Martine. Philippe had told him about the incident at the hotel on Rue Cambon, and about Martine's jealousy. He, too, felt alarmed.

"Oh, I suppose they've had a fight." He felt he had to comfort his old friend as best he could.

"Don't answer if you'd rather not, but there's something else I'd like to ask, and I hope you won't mind telling me what you think. Do you consider Philippe's business sound?"

"That depends on what you mean by 'sound.' There's no knowing, really. Sometimes a well-established, conservative firm comes a financial cropper, while a speculative business like Philippe's forges steadily ahead."

"Don't you worry sometimes? Please remember that I have nothing against Philippe or his methods. I accept him as he is."

Though it was only three in the afternoon, the light was failing.

"Oh, well," Mme Donadieu said, with a sigh, "at my age it's no use worrying. . . ." She turned and gazed at Kiki's picture. "If only I could see my boy—just once again!" Her eyes grew moist. "Isn't it extraordinary that we've never been able to find out anything about him? Philippe must have spent a small fortune trying to trace him, and I'll always be grateful to him for that, whatever else he may do."

"It's seldom that young fellows who disappear like that are traced," Frédéric observed.

"Why?"

"Because there are too many of them. There's little the police can do, really, especially when they've gone abroad."

"But why doesn't Kiki write? . . . That's another thing in Philippe's favor. When Kiki vanished, he insisted on my taking his share, in full. That was kind, wasn't it?"

Ingenuously, the old lady mixed money matters with questions of the heart—as had all the Donadieus.

"I'm wondering," she continued, "what sort of arrangement will be made next month—for the final settlement of the estate, I mean. Michel dropped in yesterday, and he assured me that a declaration by the court that Kiki is untraceable will be enough."

The room was full of dusk. The two wineglasses stood empty on a low Empire table. When a clock struck four, Frédéric rose. Mme Donadieu had wept a little, and was nervously squeezing her handkerchief. As she saw Frédéric out, she switched the light on in the hall.

"Do please let me know at once if . . . if you hear anything. Remember me to Odette."

Unexpectedly, she found herself smiling as she went back to her chair. The mention of Odette's name had recalled a remark Michel had made:

"Is that girl still living with Frédéric?"

His mother had noticed an undertone of rancor, and guessed he hoped to hear they had parted. He was hardly less jealous of Frédéric than of Philippe; both father and son, to his thinking, had trespassed on his preserve.

Next morning, when Mme Donadieu called her daughter, the butler promptly replied:

"They're both out for the day, madame—hunting." And for once he was telling her the truth.

This Sunday was almost as wet as its predecessor, and the two cars, the Grindorges' and Philippe's, were traveling, one behind the other, through heavy rain. Albert was driving his car; he had never dared to have a chauffeur, because of his father, who strongly disapproved of a man's not driving his own car if capable of doing so. Paulette, beside him, looked more run down than ever. When he tried to start a conversation, she promptly shut him up, saying she wanted to sleep.

"Yes, do have a short nap; it may do you some good. I'd like you to be all right when we're with Pomeret."

The minister of education, with whom they'd had lunch at the Dargenses', had consented to join the party, after being assured there would be only the five of them, and everything would be quite informal. Despite his appearance, he was a shy man who had started his career as a teacher. As much as possible, he avoided social functions.

He sat beside Martine in the back of the other car. Philippe, who sat facing them, had dark rings around his eyes, like a man who has been sleeping badly. Nevertheless, he did his best to keep the conversation going.

"Look! We're just coming to the end of it. You remember that farmhouse I showed you fifteen minutes ago. Well, all the cornfields we've been passing since then belong to Grandmaison. I'd guess he owns about a third of La Beauce corn land. Have you met him?"

"No," the minister confessed. As a matter of fact, it amazed him to learn that a third of La Beauce, the "granary of France," was in the hands of a single man.

"I'd say he and his family are the 'safest' millionaires in the country right now. All their money's in land."

Martine, watching Philippe's face, repressed a smile, less of irony than of sympathetic understanding. She had been struck by the way he'd said, "All their money's in land."

How mistaken people were who regarded him as a born gambler, a man who enjoyed walking a financial tightrope! There had been a glint of envy in his eyes when he uttered those words. She had seen that look before, when they were traveling.

At one of the hotels in which they stayed, he had drawn her attention to a rather oddly shaped whisky bottle, placed in a prominent position behind the bar.

"Just think, Martine! We could drop into bars in China, Australia, South America, or even northern Alaska, and we'd see a bottle like that. It makes you think, doesn't it?"

Martine had smiled. It didn't make *her* think, and she disliked whisky.

"Don't you see what I mean? Think of the number of bottles of this brand that are consumed every day. Think of the thousands and thousands of cases of it being shipped all the time to every corner of the world. And—just think—it all belongs to one man! One man in England raking in the profits, thousands of pounds a day coming in from everywhere. That's what I call a big business, something to be proud of."

The road was in bad repair, and they were constantly thrown from side to side. Soon after they passed Pithiviers, the chauffeur drew back the glass panel to ask where to turn. Philippe couldn't remember, and they had to wait for the Grindorges to catch up.

Albert took over the lead. They had started before sunrise, because the men had been unable to leave Paris the previous day. Now the sun was up; men with guns on their shoulders could be seen trudging through stubble fields and along the grassy edges of the road. As they drove through villages, they met groups of people coming from early Mass.

"It's interesting, isn't it? Weil, 'Flour' Weil, as everyone calls him, has control, direct or indirect, over all the corn that's milled in France. Not a grain escapes him."

Martine marveled at his composure. How could he appear so calm, talk so easily on trivial subjects, after the emotional crisis he had been through so short a time before? She was quite incapable, especially after getting up at five in the morning, of making small talk.

It was a relief when, after going through a hamlet lost in the forest, they turned right into a spacious drive leading to a rather dreary-looking château. It was even less imposing than Esnandes, which at last the family had brought themselves to sell, because it was not worth its keep.

Albert, who had bought this château the previous year, could not refrain from pointing out to the minister the traces of a coat of arms over the doorway. Under it was a worn date, ANNO MDC . . . The final figures were eroded. But among the crumbling scrollwork, Albert professed to distinguish three inverted fleurs-de-lis, and announced that he was going to have some research done.

Strangely, four of the five of them would have been quite unable to explain why they were here. The weather was atrocious, and, hemmed in by the huge trees of the forest of Orléans, the place was darker and damper than the house at Esnandes. All the game in the five or six acres of fields belonging to the estate had already been shot. So the men had to make their way into the woods, where every step brought down a shower of icy drops.

The gamekeeper was surly, the dogs seemed half asleep, and, though all the rabbits were put up near the minister, he invariably missed them.

This expedition had been organized on a few hours' notice. On Saturday morning, there had been no question of it. Albert proposed to devote Sunday to reading a book on statistics he had been keeping in reserve for such a day. Since Friday evening, Philippe had been in such a vile humor that his staff worked in fear and trembling. Martine was sulking—that, anyway, was how Philippe described her persistent seclusion in her bedroom or in the nursery. She had always been an affectionate mother, but not to the point of staying with her small son all day. She'd suddenly decided to undertake the job of teaching him to read.

What, then, had induced the four of them to get up in the dark and endure a sixty-mile journey in the rain, with the sole object of floundering ankle-deep in mud and lunching uncomfortably in a dreary château?

As soon as they got there, Paulette said to Martine, with affected cheerfulness:

"Make yourself at home, dear. You can have the run of the whole place—we haven't any secrets! I must ask you to excuse me while I see about lunch."

Martine did not even wonder how to spend her morning. On entering the living room, she'd noticed a sofa, upholstered in pale pink, and had dropped down on it like a log. She lay there on her back, looking idly at the branch of a cedar tree that hung across a window. Various sounds came to her; some of them she identified, but without real interest.

There was, for instance, the crackle of burning pinecones; the air in the room was heavy with their aromatic smell. A woman in the kitchen grumbled because no truffles had been brought to serve with the fowl. Now and then, Martine heard the thud of a gunshot, the bark of a dog.

She gave herself up to daydreaming, following whatever thoughts and pictures floated into her mind. That bottle of whisky, for example . . . What Philippe really wanted to be was the maker of that whisky, or the owner of a third of La Beauce, or at least of a business as substantial as the Donadieus' had been in her father's time, but on a far larger scale.

There was more in common between the outlook of those two, her father and Philippe, than she had imagined. Only, where Philippe used the term "dynasty," Oscar Donadieu had spoken of "the family," in much the same respectful tone as a statesman uses when mentioning "the nation."

Another shot. Martine seemed to see a rabbit rolling over, pawing the air in its death agony.

Then a picture floated into consciousness of the poster for a popular toothpaste, which Philippe had pointed to one day.

"Do you know how much they spend in advertising every year, with one agency alone? Ten million francs!"

This recalled another remark of his, referring to a well-known laxative:

"Eight million of those pills are taken every day."

But he'd also said, regretfully, that to bring businesses like these to dominance takes three generations, or start-up capital of many millions.

"It was through Charlotte you forced your way into the Donadieu home. . . ."

She heard his voice beyond the crackling of the pinecones, which were shooting volleys of red sparks across the hearth. Twice Paulette looked in.

"Bored, all by yourself?"

No, she wasn't bored. She wanted to think. She had done little else for the last three days, but there seemed no limit to her capacity for thought.

"It was through Charlotte . . ."

Suddenly she had a morbid craving to evoke cruel, sordid pictures: Philippe and Charlotte, in the wet darkness of Mme Brun's garden, locked in a crude embrace. But quickly this passed, and, yielding to a gentler mood, she recalled Philippe in his moments of affection, when his voice lost its harshness and his eyes glowed softly as he drew her lips to his.

He was only thirty, and yet he had already created, almost out of nothing, a setting for his life that anyone might envy: the apartment on Avenue Henri-Martin, his luxurious office on the Champs Elysées. And if Michel could now lead idle days on the Riviera, running after chambermaids to his heart's content; if Mme Donadieu was now living in a comfortable apartment in Paris—these, too, were Philippe's work. All this, as he had reminded her on that unforgettable night when he had dropped the mask of self-control and spoken his mind—all this he had achieved single-handed. After all . . .

For a while she reproached herself for judging him so harshly, and an almost tender smile hovered on her lips. But it soon faded, and her eyes grew hard.

Why should she be added to the list of his victims? In a flash of cruel insight, she'd realized that the people she'd been recalling were not mere puppets, whom Philippe had manipulated to serve his ends; they were living victims, sacrificed to his star. All of them—Charlotte, Michel, Albert . . .

She refused to be another Charlotte. Definitely, with all her will-power, she refused!

ANOTHER VICTIM OF MOLEBANE

A lamentable case of poisoning is reported from the Chenerailles district. M. Eugène Terret, a gardener employed at the Château d'Orgnac, after preparing a paste for the destruction of moles with the well-known poison Molebane, neglected to wash his hands before picking and eating a tomato. Half an hour later, feeling severe griping pains, he hurried to the doctor, who administered an antidote. It was too late, however, and, like Mme Fauveau, the Parisian fireman's wife, whose death was reported in these columns last week, he rapidly succumbed, in excruciating agony.

This paragraph had appeared in Saturday morning's paper, before there had been any talk of going hunting on the following day. At eleven, the newspaper lying on her dressing table, Paulette had called her husband.

"That you, Albert? Look, I've just remembered there are some winter pears at Chenevières that we ought to pick before the frost gets them."

He mumbled something, and his wife continued:

"I suggest we go there tomorrow, and combine it with a little hunting. . . . Are you listening?"

"Yes."

"You remember Monsieur Pomeret, the education minister? . . . You rather liked him, didn't you? Ask him to join us. And of course the Dargenses should come. Do try to arrange it."

"All right. I'll see what can be done."

"Yes, do. It will be such a nice change. I've been so terribly bored lately."

Albert had promptly gone to Philippe's office.

"My wife's anxious to go to Chenevières tomorrow, and she wants you and Martine and Pomeret to come along. I'm not particularly happy with the idea, but she's been so low recently that I don't want to disappoint her."

Philippe's face darkened; he was silent for a moment.

"You'd better call Pomeret," he said at last, "and see how he feels about it."

"Couldn't *you* call him?"

"I'm too busy."

At home, he said to Martine:

"I think we'll be going to Chenevières tomorrow, for some hunting."

"I won't go."

There was challenge in the eyes of both, not for the first time.

Philippe repeated:

"We're going to Chenevières tomorrow. If you want to know why, I'll tell you. Pomeret's coming."

"In that case—all right!"

It was better to give in; otherwise Philippe would lose his temper again, as he had at the film gala, and accuse her of making difficulties, of wrecking his career for a mere caprice.

"And you might try to be a little more amiable."

"To whom?"

"To everyone. Your mother's even called me, twice, to tell me you always pretend you're out when she calls."

"I didn't feel like talking."

307

He clenched his fists. Ten times in the last two days they had been on the brink of a violent argument. Martine conjured up a smile.

"Don't worry, Philippe. I'll make myself as amiable as you could wish."

So now they were at Chenevières. Neither had the least inkling that they owed this ill-timed, indeed pointless, hunting party to a casual article in the paper.

Pomeret was full of excuses for his bad marksmanship. Philippe had shot two rabbits and a pheasant. Albert, who had brought down nothing yet, tried to cover his embarrassment with feeble jokes.

The gamekeeper had evidently had other plans for his Sunday; he was barely polite, and made a point of taking them on paths on which they constantly had to wriggle under barbed-wire fences.

Meanwhile, Paulette was behaving so oddly that Naomi, the game-keeper's wife, who acted as cook on these occasions, followed her with her eyes, now and then murmuring plaintively:

"I'd much rather you let me do the work by myself, madame."

Paulette pretended not to hear; she seemed determined to lend a hand, and even began to pluck a chicken, making a complete mess of it. She also seemed determined to keep up a conversation.

"Are you still quite happy here, Naomi? I'm afraid you must have had a dreadful week, what with all this rain."

"I'd have been happier if we could have had this Sunday off, seeing as my husband's brother's come all the way from Orléans to see us today. He's in the cottage now, and real bored he must be, left by himself like that."

"Ask him to come over here. He can have his lunch with you in the kitchen."

"Maybe he wouldn't want to. He's a truck driver, and doesn't like being told what to do. Now, madame, you'd better leave me to myself; I get along with my work better when there's nobody around."

Paulette complied, but ten minutes later she was back. She acted like someone who dreads being left alone.

"Tell me, Naomi. Are there many rats here?"

"Rats? Not that many, I don't think."

"But there are some, aren't there?"

"Oh, there's sure to be some in a big house like this. But we needn't take no notice."

Paulette poured herself a glass of water. Her hands were trembling so much that it slipped through her fingers and broke on the floor.

She gazed at the broken glass with dismay that seemed out of all proportion to its cause. "It's plain glass," Naomi observed. "That means good luck."

With an effort, Paulette pulled herself together.

"What about dessert, Naomi? Do you have something ready?"

"You know I haven't had no time. If you wanted dessert, why didn't you bring it with you? But no, you never thought of that. You didn't even think of bringing some chocolates for my little girl, like you said you would next time you came."

"Next Sunday I'll bring some. I promise you I won't forget again."

She went out, then hurried back again, and had more rambling talk with Naomi. Her cheeks had a cadaverous pallor, and each time there was a shot outside she jumped.

"The woman's crazy," Naomi muttered to herself.

In her aimless roaming, Paulette frequently stopped at a certain spot, hesitated, then turned and walked quickly away.

It was at the end of a hallway paved with blue-gray flagstones. A rarely used door opened on the yard, and through it you could cross directly to the washhouse without passing through the kitchen or scullery. Since the washing was now done in the yard, under a faucet, the washhouse had been converted into a storeroom, where objects of all kinds—game bags, cartridge belts, white coats for the beaters, fox traps—were kept.

There was an immense fireplace, with a long mantelpiece above it. It was here that, two weeks earlier, when planning a general cleaning of the ground-floor rooms, Paulette had noticed some dusty bottles, left by the previous owners of the château. Among them was a small brown jar labeled, she was almost certain, MOLEBANE.

She could not decide if she should go to the washhouse through the kitchen or the door at the end of the hallway. Her mind was curiously lucid, yet somehow her thoughts seemed out of her control, though they followed each other with logical precision. As she moved restlessly from room to room, the lines in the newspaper and the label on the jar stood out before her, like captions on a screen. It was as if the jar had become something she must procure for its own sake; she had forgotten why she needed it.

The frantic days she had been living through in Paris, when she'd toss for hours on her bed, or pass into a sort of waking dream in which all kinds of fantastic schemes raced through her mind, were ended. That scheme, for instance, of filing halfway through an axle of her husband's car or tampering with the lugs on one of the wheels. Absurd, on the face of it. Were she to go to the garage and start tinkering with the car, somebody would be sure to ask what she was up to. And, in any case, Albert always drove so slowly, he would come to no great harm.

Then she had thought of going to some small pharmacy in the suburbs and asking for a bottle of laudanum. But that, too, was impractical. The pharmacist wouldn't let her have it, most likely, and, if he did, he might remember her face. She had to think of something else. . . .

Her brain had raced on like a machine out of control; there had been no stopping it. She had not only worked out each successive scheme down to its smallest detail, but also thought out the consequences: what she would have to say to her friends, and to the police who questioned her; the funeral arrangements, even the mourning clothes she would need to buy. Yet, amazingly, in the fever of those vision-haunted hours, she had managed, outwardly, to appear quite calm.

During these periods of intense thought, which lasted sometimes only a few minutes, and sometimes went on for hours, she was in a sort of trance. When she came out of it, she felt as vacant and exhausted as a drug addict after an orgy. When Albert came home she hardly knew if he was the Albert of her dream or the living Albert, her husband, in flesh and blood.

"You should take things easy for a while," he counseled. "Why don't you see the doctor?"

She had shaken her head.

"Well, if you won't rest, try to do something outside, instead of moping around the apartment. Ask Martine to go with you."

For the sake of peace, she had said, "All right."

Now the bottle of Molebane was only a few yards away, on the other side of that wall. She went back to the kitchen. Naomi heaved a prodigious sigh, as if she were trying to empty her enormous breasts, and scowled.

"Have the winter pears, the ones on the espaliers, been picked?"

"Dunno. Maybe my husband's picked them."

"Give me a basket, please."

"Can't you see it's raining cats and dogs?"

"I'll wear a raincoat."

"You'd better put on boots, too," advised Naomi, handing her the basket with a sulky look.

Paulette stopped in the living room on her way out.

"Sure you don't mind my deserting you? I'm going out to pick some pears. Do you want to come?"

"Thanks," Martine said, "but I'd rather stay here."

Paulette blushed; she'd almost made a slip—said "tomatoes" instead of "pears." Because of the paragraph in the paper, of course. That wretched man had eaten a tomato. This time it would be pears.

"I'll have some port sent in."

"Don't bother. It's so nice and warm here. I'm quite comfortable. But you might tell your maid to put some more logs on the fire."

Paulette herself put the logs on, in order not to return to the kitchen.

"Are you quite sure there's nothing you'd like, dear?"

Paulette was conscious that no one wanted her, neither Martine nor Naomi, but she didn't care.

"Well, I'll go and pick those pears for lunch," she repeated deliberately.

The espaliers flanked the kitchen-garden wall. As she approached, she heard dogs barking less than five hundred yards away. The last shots of the day were fired quite near the wall, where a hare had taken cover in a tangle of grass and nettles. Pomeret had the first shot, but Philippe fired a second later and bowled the hare over while Albert was just taking aim.

23

"Donad!" said Mrs. Goudie severely, and, as if incapable of further speech, or preferring to keep it for weightier occasions, shot a pointed glance, first at the paper the young man was reading as he lounged against the sideboard, then at his vacant chair at the dining table.

The young man, so tall that people turned to stare at him in the street, blushed and stammered an apology. Pushing the paper into his pocket, he hurried, with awkwardness due as much to shyness as to his lanky limbs, toward the empty chair. On his right sat Davidson, a war veteran, and on his left Mrs. Hirst, the fastest typist in Big Hole City, and also the swarthiest; the black down on her upper lip was thicker than the incipient mustache on Donad's.

Once at the table, none of the eight men and three women said a word. They were here to eat, not to babble. The hired girl brought in a soup tureen, and each in turn passed his or her soup plate to Mrs. Goudie, who plied her ladle with the skill that comes of constant practice.

The soup was promptly followed by Indian corn pudding, and this was the time to keep watch, covertly of course, on one's neighbor's plate. The tall, shy young man did this with the utmost discretion, but he could not help casting an envious glance at Davidson, who had got the largest helping. To console himself, he reflected that there might be some left over, in which case Mrs. Goudie might say, as she often did:

"Donad shall have it. He's the biggest, and he's a growing boy. What's more, he works the hardest."

The trouble was that today, because his paper had arrived, he had been slow in taking his place, and was probably in Mrs. Goudie's black book.

Not until the last mouthful of pudding had been eaten, and they were rolling up their napkins and slipping them into rings, did anyone dare speak. There was a sudden bustle as they all rose at once, some going upstairs to their bedrooms, while others moved into the parlor, where there was a piano and a phonograph.

By common consent, Mrs. Goudie's boardinghouse was the best establishment of its kind in Big Hole City. For one thing, it was a brick house, whereas nearly all the others were wooden. Also, since there was room for only eleven lodgers, one had to wait until someone left; and then, not to rent a room, but to submit an application for one, with due form and ceremony. Mrs. Goudie, a model of rectitude, insisted on references.

Roughhousing was unknown under her roof. No drinking of strong liquor was allowed, and smoking was tolerated only in the parlor; Mrs. Goudie disapproved of tobacco smoke in the bedrooms no less than in the dining room.

"Let's have a page," young Donad said to a shorter, more sparely built young man sitting beside him on the sofa. They settled down to reading the Paris newspaper that had come in that morning's mail.

The atmosphere of the boardinghouse was as restful as that of a convent or a museum. The dark, impersonal furniture of the parlor contributed to the lethargy of the after-dinner hour, inducing a gentle coma.

Edmond ventured, as he read, to smoke a cigarette, but Donad— as he now called himself to sound more American—had as much aversion to tobacco as to strong drink and light women.

Outside, it was blowing up for a gale, perhaps a hurricane. Now and then, the young man raised his head, listened to the gusts, and heaved a sigh.

"Did you manage all right at the fourth pylon?" Edmond asked as he turned to a new page of the paper.

"Yes. I stuck it out till the whistle blew."

Big Hole City was not a town, strictly speaking, but a mushroom growth of shacks and warehouses that had sprung up, almost over-night. It lay at the foot of a huge dam being erected to divert a river, and later to supply power for the biggest hydroelectric plant in the world.

For three years, an army of American, Italian, German, and other workmen, foremen, engineers, and office employees had been living here, all their activities and interests centered on the slowly rising wall. It was estimated that another three years' work lay ahead.

Edmond was employed in a drafting office. Donad could have done similar work, but he had wanted manual labor, the harder the better. Often, at the close of the day, though he had an appetite like his brother Michel's, he was so exhausted that he went straight to bed.

His worst problem, after the dam had reached a certain height, was to conquer a tendency to dizziness. Only to Edmond had he spoken of this weakness, and none of his fellow workers had noticed the greenish pallor of his cheeks as he edged his way along a plank a hundred feet above the ground or straddled the hook of a crane swinging him high in the air.

"Read this," Edmond said.

If, instead of khaki shirt and shorts, Donad had been wearing some loose-fitting brown garment, he would have made a splendid model for a monk in a stained-glass window, because of his great stature and the look of mystic exaltation on his gaunt face. Everyone thought he was as strong as an ox, and took care not to upset him. In reality, though he had his father's build, his body had the softness of Michel's and his mother's.

"What do you want me to read?"

"Look at the bottom of the 'Personal' column."

Without the least sign of interest, he read:

Re Oscar Donadieu, Shipowner, La Rochelle, deceased. Maître Goussard, attorney-at-law, La Rochelle, requests M. Oscar Donadieu, Jr., now age 21, to communicate with him at once.

"That's right! I *have* come of age," murmured Donad, as though this fact had just struck him for the first time.

"What will you do about it?"

"Nothing, of course. What did you expect me to do?"

Wasn't he perfectly happy in Big Hole City, where he had settled into a groove that fitted him perfectly? Like all the others, he was roused from sleep by the blast of a whistle, and soon hurried downstairs to join his fellow workers at Mrs. Goudie's breakfast table. Like the others, he wore a khaki shirt and shorts, waterproof boots and oilskins, and on his way to the site swung his shoulders to the same rhythm as the rest, and made the same gestures when he clocked in.

Then came the grim but glorious struggle to control his nerves while he was being hoisted to the dizzy summit. And how wonderful, almost ecstatic, was his joy when another blast of the whistle signaled release, the end of his ordeal.

"Don't you ever feel like going back?" Edmond asked.

"Certainly not. Do you?"

"No, of course not," Edmond answered, a shade too quickly. "But it's different for me. You're a rich man. In two or three years, the dam will be finished, and . . ."

"There'll be other dams to build, won't there?"

In a sense, his life was dedicated to the building of the dam, and no other interest could compete with it. He was not the only one who felt like this. That huge, imposing structure slowly rising from the valley dominated the thoughts and activities of the entire army of workers serving its ascent. Few of them bothered to learn the latest news from New York or Chicago. If they sometimes grumbled about the weather, this was not due to the hardships it imposed on them in the open, but because autumn rains might cause a landslide, or early frost play havoc with unset concrete.

For Donad's leisure hours, there was the comfortable warmth of Mrs. Goudie's parlor, and three times a week a "social" organized by the local minister.

This evening, such a gathering was taking place, and at five minutes to eight Edmond and Donad put on their caps and set out for the meetinghouse. On their way, they passed a tavern. Someone was playing a concertina, and women were sitting at the bar. Donad gave them a brief glance, shook his head sadly, but made no comment.

Standing on the threshold of the barnlike room where the socials took place, the Reverend Cornelius Hopkins shook hands with each new arrival, calling him by his Christian name and adding some words of personal greeting. He had an intimate knowledge of the lives of his flock; even their differences with foremen or the management.

"Good evening, Donad. Have you put up a good fight?"

Since the young man was impervious to moral temptations, his meaning was clear: had he mastered his dread of heights?

"Yes. I held out till the whistle blew."

"God will reward you, my boy. To fight weakness is as salutary for the soul as for the body."

The lighting was poor, and the dark timbered walls made the room gloomier still. Gymnastic apparatus occupied one end, for use on Sundays and summer evenings. The weather had turned cold, and the early arrivals had annexed the seats nearest the big stove in the middle of the room.

Looking around, Donad noticed Edmond having a whispered conversation with the minister, but thought nothing of it.

"What's the program this evening?" he asked the man beside him.
"Have no idea."

Some evenings, the minister gave a short talk on a Bible subject; on others, he sat down at the harmonium, and they learned new hymns and part-songs. If the attendance was small, they merely talked among themselves, supposedly on edifying subjects, which somehow always turned to progress on the dam.

Edmond, without saying anything, sat down next to Donad just as the minister was ringing a small bell and seating himself behind the reading desk on which the Bible lay. To his horror, Donad noticed that he had the French newspaper in his hand. He blushed, gave Edmond a reproachful look, and stirred uneasily, with half a mind to leave.

"Dear friends . . ."

The wind was rising; now and again it would bring the sound of the concertina, which everyone tried to ignore.

"Dear friends, I had intended to speak to you tonight on the sermon in the wilderness, but . . ."

He opened the newspaper, and abruptly, amazingly, the Donadieu family entered the life of Big Hole City.

". . . I cannot pass over in silence the conduct of our dear brother Donad, one of our best workers in the Lord's vineyard. I have just read in a newspaper from his country . . ."

One after the other, everyone turned to stare at the young man, who was blushing like a girl. After reading the notice in halting French and translating it, the minister expatiated on the sacrifice brother Donad wished to make—of a fortune of many thousands of dollars—in order to continue leading a simple, ascetic life and keep himself unspotted in this world.

Then he opened his Bible at the passage telling how Esau bartered his birthright for a mess of pottage. Donad, who had been too flustered to follow the preacher's words, began to pay serious attention.

"When evil triumphs in high places, as it does today, have we the right to set our personal peace of mind above the task that God may have allotted us? Have we the right, I say, in times of worldwide turmoil, when the devil is putting forth his utmost efforts, to stand aside from the fight with folded arms?"

Donad, aside from watching Edmond from the corner of an eye, felt certain he had come to an understanding with the preacher. Suddenly, deep depression settled over him. The tenor of his life was threatened; with all his heart, he rebelled against the thought of being torn away from Big Hole City, from these gatherings at the meeting-house, from those silent meals at Mrs. Goudie's, where he watched with anxious eyes the sharing of the pudding. He had almost stopped listening to what was being said, but he could see the preacher's face glimmering moonlike above the feeble lamp, whereas his flock remained in heavy shadow, like figures in a Rembrandt print.

There were moments when he could hardly believe it was he who was being preached at; others when he envied the men around him, who hadn't had the misfortune of being mentioned in a newspaper and thus being put in a situation that could be cleared up only through Biblical precedent.

"Our brother must take humble thought as to his duty. If he should go to France, our prayers will follow him. They will have power, I do not doubt, to bring him back to us, rich with new capacity for good, and better armed to fight the good fight against the powers of evil, which have never been more active than today."

When everyone rose, Donad felt uneasy, as though he were already removed from his fellow workers.

The minister had come up and was handing the French paper to him. "At Sunday service tomorrow, we shall all pray for you to be guided aright in this crisis of your life."

In the street, Donad said nothing to Edmond, who walked beside him with his head hanging. When they passed the tavern, where dancing had now begun, Donad looked away.

He had forgotten it was Saturday. He would have been greatly surprised to learn that Frédéric and his mother had spent a full hour talking about him, in an old-fashioned Paris apartment. In a dim way, he realized how strange it was that a man like the Reverend Cornelius Hopkins, Australian by birth but now an American citizen, should, though several thousand miles from them, be showing so much interest in the Donadieu family's affairs.

The Sunday that the workers on the big dam joined in prayer for the guidance of Donad was the same Sunday on which, at Chene-vières, once lunch was over, the two couples fell to wondering how to kill time until they started back to Paris.

When Donad fell asleep, he was pouting like a sulky child, and his fists were clenched in his passionate resolve not to give up his work on the dam, whatever pressure was put on him. He had much the same feeling toward his work as a recluse has for his monastery, or another type of man for the army—for an organization in which one can escape from oneself, can merge one's personality in communal life.

"Shall we play bridge?"

Unfortunately, Pomeret had never learned to play that game, or any other. Nor did he see any necessity for a game; he was faintly puzzled by his hosts' evident desire for diversion.

He had been shown around the château, and had duly appreciated the old atmosphere of the rooms, their dark wainscoting, enormously thick walls, and windows opening on forest, now lashed by wind and rain.

The smell of burning pine logs tickled his nostrils agreeably; the sight of the flames dancing in the huge fireplace pleased his eye. He would have been quite content to sit for hours in his comfortable armchair, nursing a glass of old brandy between his palms and smoking a Havana cigar, putting in an occasional leisurely remark on any subject that came up.

He was not in the least put out at having missed all his birds and hares, and during lunch had given humorous descriptions of similar misadventures at other hunting parties.

"I don't suppose you will believe me when I say I do it almost— mind you, only *almost*—on purpose. But really . . ."

Now that they no longer had the stimulus of sitting around a table, each was thrown back on himself. There was something lugubrious about the silences that fell, more and more frequently, on their conversation.

Martine, who was again lying on the sofa, kept looking at Philippe, then Albert, as if she were weighing them against each other. And, indeed, the contrast was striking: Albert's mild appearance and lamblike manners against Philippe's lithe grace and ruthlessness. Philippe was the jungle beast who had laid the foundations of his success by making love to a whore like Charlotte in a decrepit summerhouse.

His eyes were fixed on the leaping flames, and it was impossible to guess his thoughts. Albert seemed restless; after a long silence, he said to his wife:

"Would you get the bicarbonate, dear? I'm having trouble with my stomach."

She hurried out of the room. Soon there was a shrill sound of voices arguing in the kitchen.

Philippe stretched and turned toward Martine.

"What shall we do? I'm afraid it's too wet for a walk in the forest."

"Need we really do anything?" Pomeret said, and smiled.

"The best thing," Martine remarked, "would be to get back to Paris while there's some daylight left. There's nothing to prevent our having dinner together in a restaurant. I know it's not very nice on a Sunday. Still, it's better than nothing."

They took a quarter of an hour to decide. Then there was a general move to the hall for hats and coats. When Martine and Paulette happened to be side by side, Paulette asked:

"How shall we arrange ourselves in the cars?"

"Arrange ourselves?" Martine sounded surprised. Surely it was obvious they would go back as they had come, with Pomeret in their larger car and the Grindorges in their small one.

"Oh, it doesn't really matter. Only, I was thinking . . ."

What was she thinking? Her nerves were in such a state that she could hardly button her coat.

"Where shall we meet?"

Philippe decided for them.

"At my place."

"Look," Pomeret put in, "I won't inflict my company on you any longer. If you'll drop me at Porte d'Orléans, I'll take a taxi from there."

"No, no. You really must stay with us. We would be *so* disappointed."

Actually he hadn't the slightest wish to stay with them, but, out of politeness, he dared not insist.

Paulette continued behaving strangely. Now she appealed to Philippe.

"Couldn't we all go back in your car?"

Philippe looked puzzled, and Albert protested energetically:

"Don't be absurd, Paulette! I'd have to come back again to get my car, or do without it all week."

"Oh, for all the use you make of it . . ."

Martine was watching her and, though she had no inkling of what was to come, noting every detail; Paulette's remark, for instance, when the two cars were about to start:

"You go in front. You drive faster than we do. And we'll all meet at your place."

In the lead car, conversation turned naturally to the Grindorges. To keep Paulette out of it as much as possible, Philippe enlarged on Albert's passion for statistics. The subject was harmless enough, and from statistics the talk veered to economics, and to the activities of the R.M.C.

Rain was coming down in torrents when they drove through Pithiviers, and then Arpajon. As they were approaching Longjumeau they had a flat tire—the first time with this car. They stayed inside while the chauffeur got the toolbox from the back and set his tools out on the roadside in the rain.

They had a spare, and the job should not have taken more than ten minutes. Instead, they were held up for half an hour, because the jack wouldn't work, and Félix had to borrow another from a café five hundred yards away.

Suddenly Martine said:

"That's curious! The Grindorges haven't caught up yet."

This was surprising, because they had not been driving at all fast.

"I wonder what's happened?" Pomeret remarked.

Philippe thought it best to take it lightly.

"Oh, they probably discovered they'd forgotten something and had to go back for it."

"Or," the minister suggested, "they, too, may have had a flat tire."

He looked at Philippe as he spoke and noticed that the rings around his host's eyes seemed darker than usual. Though he had no idea of the relationship between the two young couples, he had a vague suspicion that something was wrong. This was one of the reasons why, when they were entering Paris, he again insisted on taking a taxi home, on the pretext that he had just remembered an official function he had to attend that evening.

When he got out, Philippe moved over beside his wife; he disliked traveling backward in the car. Then he stretched his legs, sighed, and ran his hand over his forehead.

"What a day!"

"Still, you had her near you."

He frowned and muttered irritably:

"Don't talk nonsense!"

Martine, he felt, should have had more sense than to increase the strain on him by a display of petty jealousy. Yes, she, too, was a fool, with a one-track mind, for all her seeming intelligence!

She should have realized that love had nothing to do with it; that the one thing on his mind was how to stop Paulette from doing something foolish. But Martine, like all jealous women, kept brooding on his physical relations with her "rival," those dreary, futile sessions in hotel bedrooms rented for the afternoon.

One thing in particular had added to his anxiety this evening: the odd way Paulette had shaken hands with him through the window of the car. She had dug her nails into his flesh so deeply that his thumb was bleeding, and he had to keep his handkerchief around it.

What on earth could they be up to in the car behind? And why had Paulette proposed that they leave it in Chenevières, and then suggested that they arrange themselves differently for the drive back? He cast a sour glance at Martine. Really, it was her fault; for the last week she had made it impossible for him to have a quiet talk with Paulette. It was not for lack of trying that he'd failed. But she'd kept track of his movements, called the office repeatedly, or called Paulette, to make sure where each of them was at any given moment.

At last the car stopped; they had reached home. Martine went straight to the nursery, and found it empty. Her heart missed a beat. Then she saw a note lying on the table.

Madame, Your mother called to ask me to bring Master Claude to her apartment for the afternoon. I did not like to say no. I hope I did the right thing. I will take great care of him. . . .

"What is it?" asked Philippe, who had followed her.

"Claude is at Maman's, with the nurse."

"You know I don't like his going there."

He had no particular reason for this, except, perhaps, that he wanted to keep his son under his influence as long as possible.

"Call and tell the nurse to bring him back," he said.

To his surprise, she did so at once. Receiver in hand, she turned to him.

"Maman wants to know if she can bring him back herself."

He hesitated. Then it struck him that this would mean another person in the house if . . . if anything happened.

"Certainly. Tell her to come."

"Yes, Maman, it's quite all right. And you must stay to dinner."

It was six o'clock, and the servants were coming back from their afternoon off. Philippe, going to his room to change, lingered for some time in front of his mirror, gazing hard into his own eyes. There was a trace of playacting in his pose, and he was congratulating himself on his imperturbability.

"Luck's dead against me for the moment," he murmured, quickly adding: "But I'm keeping my head. And I'll keep it, whatever happens."

Otherwise, heaven alone knew what might follow. "If only you were free!" Yes, when he said that, he'd meant it; half meant it, anyhow. But there were . . . reservations. Were Paulette to become free now, it would serve no purpose; old Grindorge was still alive. In a year or so, when Albert had inherited his father's fortune—yes, *then* it would be different.

What an imbecile the woman was! She actually believed he loved her for herself, enjoyed her clumsy caresses, her maudlin sentimentality! And, in her infatuation, she was quite capable of pushing her folly to extremes.

He took a bottle of iodine from a shelf, and was dabbing it on the wound her nail had made on his thumb, when the bell rang.

It was not the Grindorges, but his son, escorted by Mme Donadieu and the nurse. Claude promptly went to his father, like a well-mannered child, and held out his forehead for a kiss. His cheeks were cool and moist from the fresh air.

Mme Donadieu kissed her daughter with more than her usual warmth, and gave her a long look.

"I'm so pleased . . ."

Pleased to see her again and, still more, to find her looking so composed.

"I've been rather out of sorts these last few days," Martine said, to excuse herself.

"Well, you seem all right now. That's the main thing. But you know what I'm like. I've only got you two . . ."

"Didn't Michel see you?"

"Yes, and he told me your husband had been quite nice to him. Still . . ."

Again she left her thought unspoken. Michel was her son, of course, just as Marthe, whom she went to see twice a year in La Rochelle, was her daughter. Yet somehow when they were together they never found anything to say to each other. In fact, the atmosphere at their rare meetings was much like that at Chenevières that afternoon.

"Anyhow, he's the only one in the family who's like that," added Mme Donadieu as she took off her hat.

She did not go into details; that would have been both painful and superfluous. They all kept to the vaguest terms when talking about

322

Michel. Everyone knew what was meant: he was gradually sinking deeper into a morass of corruption, and the end was bound to be disastrous.

"Perhaps his wife's behavior affected him more than we suspected at the time."

A lame excuse. He had begun before that: first with a nursemaid, then with Odette.

Philippe, his forehead pressed to the window, was watching for the Grindorge car. The trees along the avenue were dripping; at the corner, where the Bois de Boulogne began, a policeman, on duty, shivered under his blue cape.

"Some tea, Maman?"

"No, thanks. We've already had tea. But I'd love a glass of port."

Martine rang for the butler and gave the order. Then she went and stood at Philippe's side. Both seemed to have the same thought in mind, for she asked:

"No sign of them yet?"

"Are you expecting people for dinner?" asked Mme Donadieu from her armchair.

"Only the Grindorges. But perhaps they won't come."

Philippe gave a start and looked hard at his wife. Then he was furious with himself for yielding to this nervous reflex, which he felt sure she'd noticed.

She added, by way of explanation:

"It's such dreadful weather. And Albert was complaining of pains in his stomach."

Philippe could bear it no longer and walked out of the room.

Martine called after him:

"Do you want some port?"

"I'll be back in a minute," he said, from the hall.

He locked himself in his bedroom, and stood again in front of the mirror. After a sharp glance at his face, he went to the telephone on his bedside table and called the Grindorges' apartment.

"Hello?" He kept his voice low; his gaze shifted from his reflection to the door, and back again.

"Yes? Who's that? . . . Oh, it's you, Florence. This is Monsieur Dargens. Are Monsieur and Madame Grindorge back?"

"Oh, were they to come back this afternoon?"

"I don't know."

"Because the cook hasn't made dinner."

"Well, as I said, I don't know what their plans were. I called on the off-chance."

Even if they'd been doing only twenty miles an hour, they should have been back by now. And if the car had broken down, Albert would surely have telephoned, since, for all he knew, Pomeret might be waiting for them at a restaurant.

Philippe sat down on the edge of his bed, letting the receiver fall back with a weary gesture. He had a sense of imminent danger, such as he'd never felt in his life before. For the last half-hour drops of sweat had been oozing from his forehead.

There were footsteps in the hall. Someone tried to open his door.

"Are you there, Philippe?"

Suddenly he saw red. Turning the key, he flung the door open. His wife was standing there.

"Yes, I'm here. What the hell do you want *now*?"

He knew his behavior was absurd, that what had prompted her to come wasn't curiosity, but her woman's instinct, a desire, perhaps, to help him. But it was too late; he had let his nerves take charge and, before he could stop it, he said, crudely:

"So I can't be left in peace—even when I go to the toilet!"

It was noon in Big Hole City, and Donad was taking his place at Mrs. Goudie's table, embarrassed by the knowledge that the eyes of all the boarders, who now regarded him as the most eccentric of millionaires, were fixed on him. His embarrassment reached its climax when the good lady served him first, and gave him an enormous helping—without the least sign of protest from the others.

24

Could things have turned out differently if the old gentleman in the lobby below had not been so impatient?

Mme Donadieu had dined with her daughter and son-in-law, and it was Philippe, as much as Martine, who had pressed her into staying late. As a special treat, Claude had been allowed to have his dinner with the grown-ups.

Then, out of the blue, as she was seeing her mother to the elevator, Martine broke down. Her eyes were blurred with tears as she said, "Au revoir, Maman," in a choking voice. Instead of bestowing the usual kiss on Mme Donadieu's forehead, she flung herself into her mother's arms, pressing herself to the old woman's ample breast.

"What's the matter, darling? Tell your old mother about it."

But Martine pointed to the open door of the elevator and, instead of speaking, gulped down a sob.

"Is it Philippe?" Mme Donadieu's voice was almost drowned by the shrilling of the bell. The old gentleman on the ground floor was summoning the elevator.

"Martine, don't frighten me! Tell me what it is."

Again there was a loud peal of the bell.

"No. Don't worry. It's nothing." With an effort, Martine got these words out.

She almost pushed her mother into the waiting elevator and stood watching her go down, dwindling to a head and shoulders, then a head only, then a hat. Looking up, Mme Donadieu saw her daughter's form receding in the opposite order, until finally nothing was visible but the hem of a skirt.

Martine lingered there to steady herself, and she saw the impatient old gentleman carried up to the apartment above, and even noticed that he had a brown wart on his nose.

On returning to the apartment, she went first to her room, to comb her hair and dab some powder on her cheeks. Philippe had stayed in the living room. Presently she joined him there, and hovered uncertainly, pretending to be looking for something. Suddenly, she stopped in front of him.

"Philippe!"

He was holding a magazine, but she could see he was not reading, and guessed he was as upset as she was if not more.

"Philippe! Are you listening?"

"Yes. What is it?"

"The Grindorges aren't back yet." She watched his face, which was relatively calm.

"How do you know?"

"I just called."

"Why did you do that?"

"Oh, no special reason. The maid answered. . . . Philippe!"

"Yes? What do you want *now*?"

"Look at me, please."

She had mastered her emotion, and her voice was steady, her gaze calm and searching. He was seated, and Martine, who was standing, seemed to dominate the situation, not only by her height, but also by the firmness of her attitude and tone.

"Listen to me, Philippe. And please don't try to put me off with lies. What I'm asking now I ask for the sake of all that's dearest to us—our love, our little boy. . . . Have you nothing to tell me, Philippe?"

There was dark compulsion in her eyes, which never shifted from her husband's, as if determined to wrest the truth from him. And her voice had an unusual deep fervor.

"There's still time," she continued. "I won't try to work on your feelings; I won't remind you of those nights in my bedroom in La Rochelle, or our first weeks in Paris. But I beg you, Philippe . . . Look! I'm going on my knees to you! . . . I beseech you to answer. . . . Have you nothing to tell me?"

She had sunk to her knees, and was holding her clasped hands toward him, incapable of saying another word.

Philippe tried to look away, but her eyes held his, and he knew that as long as he stayed in the chair there was no escape. With an effort, he rose, turned his back on his wife, and began to move toward the door, muttering uncomfortably:

"What should I have to tell you? Really, you must be going crazy!"

Martine was still on her knees when he walked out. Not until he was entering his bedroom did he hear her getting up. Thinking she was going to run after him, to make a last desperate appeal, he quickly turned the key.

She heard the sound, stopped a few yards from his door, then slowly went to her own room.

Philippe undressed with his usual neat precision, though hardly conscious of what he was doing. He measured sixty drops of his sleeping medicine into a tumbler. Sitting up in bed, he opened a newspaper and waited for the drug to take effect. He was no more aware of the printed words before him than he had been in the living room. But his brain was active, and the pictures in his mind had a strange lucidity, like the light sometimes seen in theaters, which is so sharply focused it brings out unexpected details. As though disembodied, he saw himself lying in bed, in a luxurious room smelling faintly of leather, with the pale glow from a bedside lamp playing on the pillow. He saw his face, a glimmering oval under a mass of brown hair brushed smoothly back from his temples. And a voice, his own, kept echoing in his ears: "I won't! I won't give in!"

He was only thirty, and was convinced that great achievements lay within his reach. Only thirty, with half a life before him. Abruptly, on this thought, he fell into a deep, dreamless sleep.

Martine stayed awake until four or five in the morning. Twice in the course of the night she walked barefoot to her husband's door.

It was broad daylight when she woke, with a start. The wind had risen, and a shutter was banging in the apartment above. She sat up, haunted by a dim, unformulated fear, before her mind began to function clearly. Then she rang for her maid.

"Good morning, Rose. What's the time? . . . Has Monsieur Dargens left?"

"Yes, madame. At the usual time. It's after nine."

She hurried to Philippe's room. A dressing gown was thrown on the bed, boxing gloves lay on a stool, the water in the bath was still tepid, and blue with soap. So Philippe had had his usual sparring match with Pedretti! In a way, this reassured her, but at the back of her mind was a feeling that there had been something not quite right in this.

"Tell him my husband's always in his office by eight-thirty."

"The gentleman insists on seeing you, madame."

The butler handed her a card on a tray, and it seemed to her that

327

there was something unusual in his attitude. But perhaps that was only a trick of her nerves.

Try as she might to persuade herself that this morning was like any other, even the light in the apartment seemed different, and the butler, waiting, tray in hand, looked like a figure of impending doom. She glanced at the card:

ANDRÉ LUCAS
DIVISIONAL SUPERINTENDENT
POLICE JUDICIAIRE

"Where is he?"

"In the hall, madame."

"Show him into the living room."

She was still in her dressing gown, but that didn't seem to matter. Just then it struck her that she hadn't given her son his good-morning kiss, so she went first to his room. Claude was pleased.

On entering the living room, she quite unconsciously assumed her most stately manner, and the superintendent was apologetic.

"I am exceedingly sorry to trouble you, madame. I asked to see Monsieur Dargens, but was told that he had left already."

"My husband always gets to his office by eight-thirty."

"So your butler told me. I'll go and see him presently. Before that, may I ask you one or two questions?"

"Won't you sit down?"

She, too, sat down, and her long, pale, slightly iridescent silk dressing gown made her look slimmer and taller than normal.

"I understand that you were part of a hunting party yesterday in the neighborhood of Orléans."

Martine could take no credit for her reaction; she was not so much composed, as stunned. The words came at her like so many missiles, which she strained to catch, even to intercept before they reached her ears.

The superintendent misread her calmness, and observed:

"I see you don't know what's happened. You haven't read this morning's paper?"

The newspapers were lying near her, on a silver tray.

"Monsieur Albert Grindorge died yesterday afternoon, at a hospital in Arpajon."

Had she guessed this before? It didn't take her by surprise, and

328

she waited quietly to hear what would come next. She could have sworn she knew that, too. . . .

"He died under tragic circumstances. Death was due to poisoning. The local police gave us a full report this morning, and . . ."

"Would you excuse me for a moment?" Martine stood up quickly.

"Certainly."

Like a sleepwalker, she moved into her bedroom, grabbed the first coat she saw, her mink, and slipped it over her dressing gown.

Then she ran to the door and down the stairs, hailed a passing taxi, and gave the address of Philippe's office.

It had happened just outside the market at Arpajon. Albert had been fidgeting and, after looking vainly for a restaurant, had stopped the car outside a rather unprepossessing little café.

"I must get out for a moment," he said to his wife. "Shall I bring a drink to warm you up?"

She shook her head, and he hurried inside.

"The lavatory?" he asked, before ordering a drink.

"At the back of the yard, on your right. Just beyond the chicken run. It's dark, I'm afraid."

The place was neither town nor country. What the landlord called a yard was more like a kitchen garden, with a few forlorn cabbage stumps surviving among piles of empty bottles, casks, and crates. Chickens ran as Albert groped his way along the muddy path.

The landlord's wife, who had been listening, remarked:

"He's found it."

Leaning against the zinc counter, her husband resumed his conversation with a cart driver.

"I told him right off. It ain't fair that just because we're in the trade we got to pay through the nose all the time, when other folks get off scot-free. 'I voted for you last election,' I says, 'but this time . . .' "

There were three tables, some chairs, a small billiard table in a corner.

"Listen, Eugène!"

"Eh?"

"Sounds like someone groaning, don't it?"

All three listened. The landlord frowned.

"That's odd."

"Perhaps he's sick."

It was a rare event for owners of private cars to stop here.

"Hadn't you better go and see?"

"Oh, let's wait a while. May be nothing." He was about to resume his conversation when his wife tapped him on the shoulder.

"Don't you hear? He's calling for help."

Actually, the sound that came from the yard was more like a foghorn than a human cry.

"Well? Why don't you go?"

"Hey," said the landlord to the driver, "*you* come, too. It'd be better if there was two of us."

"Here, take this." His wife handed him a small flashlight.

The battery was almost completely run down. In the yard, the groaning could be heard distinctly. There was no doubt the man was in great pain. Beyond the chicken run was the small, tumbledown shed with a roughly made seat and squares of newspaper on a rusty hook.

The man was lying on the floor, writhing convulsively.

"What's wrong? Got the bellyache?"

The woman, who had lingered in the background, suggested they carry him inside.

"Mind where you put him," she added. "He's filthy from rolling in that muck."

It was the cart driver who raised Albert by the shoulders and dragged him inside, through the kitchen.

"Where shall I put him?"

"On the bench."

The man rolled off the bench at once, so they hoisted him onto the billiard table, after spreading newspapers on it.

Paulette, whom the woman had gone out to call, came in. She looked frightened out of her wits.

"Feeling ill, Albert? Shall I send for a doctor?"

As the landlord's wife was to tell the police next day, Paulette seemed to be "not quite all there."

She turned and asked shakily:

"Is there a doctor near here?"

The woman ran out to get him, while the landlord, aided by the driver, tried to force some fiery raw brandy between Albert's tight-set lips.

"Let me have some, too," said Paulette, who had sat down on a rush-bottomed chair. She jumped each time her husband groaned.

The brandy was so strong that she coughed most of hers up. There was the sound of hurried steps, and the woman came in, followed by a young doctor, who hovered around his patient for some time with an embarrassed air. At last he made up his mind.

"He must go to the hospital at once. . . . How did it start?"

"I don't know. He was driving. He seemed all right. Then he stopped the car."

"The minute he came in," added the landlord, "he asked the way to the w.c."

Albert had died in the hospital at about the same time Mme Donadieu, accompanied by her grandson, entered her daughter's apartment.

Paulette had been told to stay in the hospital waiting room; it had white tile walls, some wooden benches, and an electric heater. Every five minutes a nurse came to give her the latest news or to ask a question.

"Can you tell us what he ate today?"

Paulette answered promptly, giving every detail she could remember.

". . . and, after the cheese, he had a pear, one of the winter pears from our orchard."

The car had been left beside the market. A policeman, after talking to the owner of the café, came to the hospital. After a brief conversation with the doctor in charge, he called headquarters.

In the bare, harshly lighted waiting room, where nothing cast a shadow except herself, Paulette remained seated, her hands clasped on her knees, staring vacantly.

"I am afraid, madame, that a postmortem examination will be necessary. I don't know what arrangements you propose to make. Are there any relatives to notify?"

"Yes. There's his father." Somehow she got the words out, adding old Grindorge's address and telephone number.

"We can arrange for you to stay here for the night. You look as if you needed some sleep."

Yes, she needed sleep, and she didn't want to go to the apartment. The doctor, who was watching her covertly, exchanged a glance with the nurse, as if to say: "Strange bird, isn't she?" When she'd been told that Albert had died, she refused to go see him.

She was given a small bedroom with a hospital bed. An hour later, when a nurse came to ask if she wanted anything, she was sleeping soundly.

The taxi driver, who could see her in his mirror, was puzzled by his new fare. For one thing, he'd noticed that under her fur coat she was wearing a silk dressing gown. And she was leaning forward, as if by so doing she could make the taxi go faster.

Martine had only one idea—to get there in time. Without stopping to pay the driver, she ran in the building and asked the elevator boy, as he opened the door:

"Has my husband gone out?"

"I don't think so. I haven't seen him, anyhow."

Still running, she crossed the reception area while the clerks stared at her across the counter. When she passed the door with Albert's name on it, she was shocked: for the first time she fully realized that he was dead, that they would never see him again.

"Philippe!" she cried.

Thank heaven, he was still here! She looked at him, then put her hand on his shoulder. "You must come at once. There's a policeman at our apartment."

He took it so quietly that she felt herself grow calmer.

"Well, what if there is? Really, Martine, you shouldn't get into such a state over—"

"You don't know?"

"That Albert's dead? I know. What about it?"

She stared at him. Surely he couldn't be so unconcerned! Almost angrily she repeated:

"Come!"

"If the police have anything to ask me, they can come here. I'm not going to them."

But when she said "Come!" once more, her tone was so compelling that he rang for Caron.

"I must go out. I'll be back in an hour."

"I regret having made you wait, Superintendent, but I wanted my husband to be present."

She was so cold that she kept her fur coat on. Philippe sat down facing the policeman, crossed his legs, and lit a cigarette.

"You'd better leave us, Martine. You're too upset." And he told a lie; a deliberate, disgusting lie. Turning to the superintendent, he said, quite coolly: "You must excuse my wife; she is in an interesting condition, and I can see the news you brought has upset her seriously."

"It's I," Lucas replied politely, "who should apologize, for disturbing you like this. . . . There are complications in this case, it happens: the parties concerned all live in Paris, but the death took place at Arpajon, and the crime, if there was a crime, must have been committed in the Orléans district. So far, I have read only the report of the local police. Since you and Madame Dargens spent yesterday with the Grindorges . . ."

"Monsieur Pomeret, the minister of education, was there too."

"I know. I have an appointment with him at eleven." The superintendent glanced at his watch. "The five of you left Paris together, I believe. Would you give me an account of all that happened in the course of the day?"

Philippe did so, at considerable length, smoking one cigarette after another. Martine, who, despite her husband's advice, had stayed in the room, did not see him betray the least uneasiness, even when the superintendent asked:

"You were very friendly with the Grindorges, I gather. Can you tell me if you ever noticed anything in their attitude toward each other . . . ?"

"I know nothing of their private lives."

"You never saw any signs that they . . . they didn't hit it off?"

"Certainly not. That's so, isn't it, Martine?"

She nodded.

"I must apologize for my next question. Monsieur Grindorge, Senior, whom I visited this morning before coming here, alleges that ever since his son and daughter-in-law became intimate with you, he has noticed a great change in his son's behavior."

"I quite agree. The Grindorges started going out much more, leading a happier life, if I may say so."

"Thank you . . . I presume that you have no intention of leaving Paris during the next few days?"

"No. I have no such intention," Philippe replied in a toneless voice.

"Because, if you have occasion to leave, I must ask you to let the Police Judiciaire know."

He murmured excuses and bowed to Martine. Soon they heard him going down in the elevator.

It seemed then as if the big apartment had suddenly become bigger, but completely empty—a hollow shell containing two people, Martine and Philippe. Martine was shivering slightly in her fur coat. Philippe, after shaking ash from his cigarette, irritably stubbed it out in the ashtray.

Once the elevator door had clanged below, and the butler had left the room, there was dead silence. Slowly, Philippe raised his head and looked at Martine. Now at last it came to him that the time for lies was over. He understood why she had come to his office to summon him and forced him to return with her to the apartment.

He was struck by the change in her appearance. Her features had grown hard—whether from despair or implacable resolve, he couldn't tell. All she said was:

"Well? What do you propose to do?"

There was something so scornful and so imperious in her tone that Philippe quailed. He began to pace restlessly up and down the room. When he wanted to light another cigarette, his fingers were trembling so violently that he could not make the lighter work.

"You heard my question, Philippe?"

"I don't know what you mean," he muttered, looking away.

"Philippe!"

"Yes?"

"Look at me. Don't be a coward as well. I asked: What do you propose to do?"

"And I ask you: What's the point of an idiotic remark like that?"

Then an amazing thing happened. She walked up to him, impressive in her long, heavy fur coat; when he started to turn his head away again, she slapped his face. The gesture was impulsive, and no sooner had she made it than she cried in an anguished tone:

"Philippe!"

He nearly returned the blow. For a moment it seemed that both would lose self-control completely, and there would be a real brawl. He steadied himself, however, and began to walk toward the door.

Martine moved in front of him and barred the way.

"No. You will not leave. Don't you understand—even now?"

"I understand that you're really going crazy."

"Don't be disgusting! If anyone's going crazy, you know quite well it isn't I, but that poor woman. . . . Now I'll repeat my question—for the last time: What do you propose to do?"

"There's not a scrap of evidence that Paulette . . ."

"Do you mean to say you didn't notice the way that policeman looked at you when he repeated what Albert's father told him?"

"I haven't committed any crime. They can't do anything to me."

"That's not the point. The policeman's not here now. . . . I want to know your plans."

There was a cocktail cabinet in the corner, and he began to pour himself a drink. Martine snatched the glass from him and flung it on the floor.

"Are you really such a coward?"

"Not so loud! The servants . . ."

"What do they matter—considering the point that things have come to? Confess, Philippe. You were thinking of leaving, weren't you?"

There, she was mistaken. The idea had crossed his mind last night, but, on thinking it over in his office this morning, he had convinced himself that nothing could possibly be charged against him. It was not a criminal offense to have a married woman as a mistress, or even to express a wish that she were free.

"Let me tell you," Martine went on, "I'll never, never agree to that."

He gave a short laugh.

"Very flattering! I suppose this is what they call 'love'!"

"I don't know if it's love or hatred"—her voice lost its firmness for a moment—"but I do know that you and I have built a life together. I know, too, that you're quite capable of starting another, somewhere else. And that's something I absolutely refuse to let you do."

"Please, talk more quietly."

"I don't care who hears me."

"Our son . . ."

"*Your* son, Philippe; that's what you've always called him. . . . Now, at last, you must tell me, frankly, what you're going to do."

Neither of them could know that at this moment Paulette Grindorge was seated in a small office on Quai des Orfèvres, confronting a superintendent of the C.I.D. who for two hours had been going back, like Martine, to the same question.

"Why did you poison your husband?"

And always the same answer:

"I didn't poison him."

A policeman who had been sent to Chenevières on his motorcycle to question Naomi had just come back with a statement, part of which the superintendent read to Paulette.

" 'During that Sunday morning did your mistress appear to be in her usual state of mind?'

" 'No.'

" 'What did you notice about her that seemed different?'

" 'Everything! It was like a madhouse all morning. Madame kept walking around like a lost soul, and popping into the kitchen every few minutes. Sometimes she went out into the yard, in all that teeming rain, and came back looking like death warmed over, as they say. . . .'

" 'Did you hear her quarreling with her husband that morning?'

" 'She didn't have a chance. He was out hunting in the forest with the other gentlemen.'

" 'Do you know if she had a lover?'

" 'That's no business of mine, and I ain't saying anything.'

" 'You are bound by law to tell me all you know. This is a police inquiry. You will be examined again, under oath. Might as well answer my question now.'

" 'I can't answer it. I don't know.'

" 'Well, have you noticed anything in Madame Grindorge's behavior that—'

" 'I once saw her slip a note into Monsieur Philippe's hand.'

" 'Was that all?'

" 'Another day I caught them kissing on the landing.'

" 'What rooms did Madame Grindorge enter Sunday morning?'

" 'I don't know. But I couldn't help wondering what she was up to in the washhouse.' "

The policeman had added a note:

"I have made an inventory of the objects in this washhouse, which is now used as a storeroom. I found a bottle of Molebane. The cork was moist, though the liquid reached only halfway up the bottle. I took possession of it and hand it in with this report."

The Seine was in flood, and from the windows of the office on the quai, a turbid mass of dark-brown water could be seen plunging under the arches of the bridge. The superintendent asked:

"Do you recognize this bottle of Molebane? I must warn you, before you reply, that fingerprints have been found on it."

The question had a result that took the superintendent by surprise. Paulette jerked her head up, with a grimace that had a faint resemblance to a smile, and calmly said:

336

"You can kill me if you like. I don't mind dying." There was a radiance in her eyes, as if, beyond the gray walls of the office, she glimpsed celestial visions.

Martine had kept her eyes fixed on her husband's face. Now she sighed:

"My poor Philippe!"

Poor, indeed, this man in whom she had once believed, and who was again slinking into his bedroom. Stepping quickly forward, she jointed him on the threshold, entered, and turned the key on the inside.

"Don't you realize that after all the things you've done I couldn't dream of letting you go? Remember Charlotte. Remember all the Donadieus, whom you . . . No, I won't reproach you; I'm quite as much to blame myself. In fact, that's why . . ."

"Look," he broke in roughly, "will you tell me plainly what you're getting at?"

But it sounded hollow. His one idea was to escape. Had there been any way, he would have taken it.

"It's no use, Philippe. You've got to face what's coming. Soon, this evening or tomorrow, they'll be here, questioning you, putting you through the whole thing. . . ."

"I haven't done anything!"

"Perhaps not. But the fact remains that we're at the end of our rope."

"I'm only thirty," he pointed out with a touch of defiance.

"And I'm only twenty-two, Philippe. Albert was thirty-five. Paulette has two small children and . . ."

"That's enough! Anyhow, is it *my* fault?"

"Try to be a man, and hear what I have to say. Claude will be all right. Maman will look after him."

His eyes widened.

"What are you saying?"

"I said Maman will look after Claude. One must know when one is beaten. . . . Look at me, Philippe, I beg you."

He'd never seen that look in Martine's eyes, a look of infinite, devoted love. It amazed him. He'd half expected to see hatred.

"Philippe! It's time for us to go. . . ."

He misunderstood, and almost smiled. Then he saw that she was holding out to him the revolver she'd taken from his drawer.

"I won't repeat . . . all you've done to me. That's over with. But I spent a good part of the night thinking about it. And I wasn't quite sure yet—though I had a sort of hunch. . . . This morning, when I didn't find you here, I really thought you'd gone for good."

The idea crossed Philippe's mind of seizing the revolver and flinging it through the window.

Martine seemed to guess his thought. All the color left her cheeks, and she cried beseechingly:

"No, Philippe. Please, *please* don't do that. Don't spoil . . ."

He lunged forward, tried to grip her wrist and twist it. She fired two shots in quick succession; watched him swaying, swaying, his hand pressed to his chest. She bent toward him as he fell, her arms outstretched.

"Philippe! My Philippe!" Her voice broke on a sob.

Could he still see her? Could he see her eyes aglow with love as she crouched over him, hear the last fond words she murmured, feel a tear fall on his cheek? Pressing the revolver to her breast, she pulled the trigger.

"My Philippe!"

The servants were trying to break through the door. Martine's maid had run to the telephone and was frantically calling the police.

Death was slow in coming to Martine as she lay stretched on her husband's body. She reached out for the revolver, put its muzzle in her mouth, and fired again.

"Phil . . . !"

25

Donad had just time enough in Paris to buy a ready-made black suit. As might have been expected, it was too small; an inch or so of cuff protruded from each sleeve and an equal length of sock below each trouser leg.

The people in La Rochelle found him changed out of recognition. He was pointed at in the street, and those who spoke to him were struck by his voice.

"Why, he's picked up an American accent!"

That was true. During the last six years, even with Edmond, he hadn't spoken a word of French. Now, in this small city, its inhabitants so diverse in temperament and outlook, he felt wholly out of place, and his old shyness returned when he had to talk to any of them.

Impressed by his height and apparent strength, they could hardly believe he was Michel's brother.

By the strict letter of ecclesiastical law, one, at least, of the Dargens couple should have been refused Catholic rites. But, after having inquiries made in Paris, the local clergy came to the conclusion that there was no knowing which of the two had committed suicide. The bishop ruled that, under the circumstances, it was more charitable to give both the benefit of the doubt and grant them Christian burial.

For the first time in many years the house on Rue Réaumur was full from top to bottom. The large living room had been converted into a mortuary chapel; the portraits of Oscar Donadieu and his wife were shrouded in black crepe.

Mme Donadieu stayed in the lodge at the end of the drive, where she had lived for some months before Philippe and Martine left for Paris.

Michel had the second floor to himself; the rooms had been left exactly as they were when he lived there with Eva. His son had come from Grenoble, where he was in school during the summer; he spent his winters at a higher altitude.

"Why not stay in our house?" Mme Donadieu had suggested to Frédéric.

But he preferred to go to the Hôtel de France, from which, on the morning of the funeral, he had a ten-minute talk with Odette, over the telephone, to reassure her. The previous evening, old Baillet had gone on one of his drinking bouts and was in a dangerous mood. Hearing this, Frédéric had gone to the superintendent of police and had a long talk with him.

"I suggest," he said finally, "that you find some pretext for keeping him locked up tomorrow, if only for three hours."

A pretext was duly found, though rather lame. It was that Baillet had been seen trespassing on military property, the parade ground where he cut grass for his rabbits. He had had several drinks by the time a policeman came to arrest him, and put up a stout resistance.

In jail, he started yelling so loudly that his invective against the government, the police, and the Donadieus could be heard halfway down Rue du Palais.

All the notables of La Rochelle attended the funeral: among them, Camboulives—whose two daughters had been married the previous week—the Varins, the Mortiers, Limaille the lawyer, and Maître Goussard. The crews of the Donadieu fishing fleet, and all those who could be spared from the colliers and freighters, the office staff and warehouse workers, and the local agents for Donadieu Briquets, turned out in force, some of them carrying wreaths they'd pooled their money to buy.

Even the Krugers, of Mulhouse, took notice, though they had been out of touch with Mme Donadieu for several years. They sent her a forty-word telegram of condolence.

Six years had passed since the Donadieus were last seen together. The general verdict was that Mme Donadieu looked much livelier and healthier than in the past, whereas Michel had become a sorry, not to say repulsive, sight.

People were so used to seeing the Olsens that they hardly noticed them. It was Kiki who was the focus of interest.

"Are you sure it's he?"

All sorts of fantastic rumors had been going around.

"Just imagine! He's become a naturalized American, so they say."

Others went further and, probably because they'd heard tales of

340

the young man's mystical proclivities, asserted that he had "gone Mormon!"

"He has a job in a gold mine over there. You wouldn't think it to look at him. Did you ever see such a suit! But he has more money than all the other Donadieus put together."

Edmond, afraid of a cold reception, had stayed in Paris; Donad was to call him the moment the ceremony ended.

There had been fears of a disturbance at the funeral, not only because of old Baillet's threats—though no one now took him very seriously—but also because of the dockworkers' strike that had started three days ago, about which Olsen was taking a firm line, as representative of the Donadieu interests.

Everyone had read in the morning paper the latest news of the "Dargens Tragedy."

> After a lengthy examination by two eminent specialists, Mme Grindorge has been declared of unsound mind, and transferred to an asylum.

Hidden under a mass of flowers, the coffins lay side by side on the same catafalque, in the central aisle. Of the women seated on the left, in the pale glow of candles and the bleak autumnal light falling from the high windows, it was Marthe who had shed the most tears. Mme Donadieu held herself very erect and gazed fixedly at the altar and the officiating priest.

On the right of the aisle, Kiki stood with folded arms, and even at the elevation, out of forgetfulness perhaps, did not kneel. He, like his mother, gazed straight ahead; but whereas her eyes were dark with grief and indignation, his had the serenity of one who has found his path in life. His heart and soul were overseas, in Big Hole City. This was a mere passing affair, signifying nothing. He had resolved to leave on the first train the next day.

Olsen, who had been watching him with a puzzled look, whispered in his ear:

"Do you propose to stay some time in France?"

And Michel, while, to the burden of deep organ notes, boys' voices sang the Dies Irae, was hoping that Philippe had forgotten to enter in his accounts that fifteen thousand francs' advance made to him the previous week. He had asked for twenty thousand, but Philippe always gave him less.

The service proceeded, the congregation kneeling, standing, or crossing itself according to the rubric. Now and then, the silvery chimes of a small bell sounded through the dim, incense-laden air.

"*Libera nos, Domine . . .*"

Mme Donadieu had been asked if she wished the rite of kissing the pax and an offertory included in the service. She couldn't decide at first.

"Is it done usually?"

"Six times out of ten."

So the mourners walked in single file to the altar steps, kissed the tablet, and dropped their alms in the plate held by an acolyte.

"*Pater noster . . .*"

Twice the priest walked slowly around the catafalque on which Martine and Philippe lay in their coffins. The first time, he censed it; on the second round he sprinkled holy water.

"*Et ne nos inducas in tentationem . . .*"

Deep voices, sustained by organ notes, sounded from the choir loft.

"*Sed libera nos a malo.*"

"*A porta inferni . . .*"

"*Erue, Domine, animas eorum . . .*"

"*Amen.*"

There came a sudden hush—even the organ was silent—while, bearing a cross, an acolyte stepped quickly forward and took his stand before the catafalque. Carefully, the undertaker's men extracted the two coffins, which looked unexpectedly narrow, from the black-and-silver pyramid.

From the organ loft three soft notes sounded, giving the pitch to the priest. He began intoning again, this time in minor key, while the congregation shuffled out, their shoes rasping on the dusty flagstones. A master of ceremonies in a cocked hat mustered them as they came out, and a long line of cars formed beside the wall.

"*Erue me . . .*"

The priest went on intoning in the front car, seated between two boys in surplices. In the second car were Mme Donadieu, Olsen, Marthe, and Michel. Kiki was in the third, with his nephew, the two lawyers, and two men who were strangers to him.

People stopped to stare at the long black procession as it crawled through the streets, then along the harbor, passing the Donadieu offices on Quai Vallin, which were closed for the day. Almost a thousand people on foot, including delegates with banners, followed the ten cars heading the cortège.

"Do you intend to go back to America, Monsieur Oscar?" asked Goussard.

Kiki hesitated before replying; he was so used to being called Donad that it flustered him to be addressed as Monsieur Oscar. Also, all this pomp accompanying a burial, once so familiar, now struck him as completely futile, indeed unseemly.

"Yes," he said at last, "I'm leaving on the *Ile-de-France*, the day after tomorrow."

"Well, you're quite fit and strong now . . ." the lawyer pointed out.

Goussard was like the others: none of them understood that this was precisely why he must go. His hard-won strength had no scope here.

At the end of Quai Vallin was the canal, and they passed the exact spot where, one night years ago, thirty feet from the drawbridge, old Oscar Donadieu had met his end.

Some people commented on this, but the family kept away from the subject. Olsen was saying:

"If the rest of you had taken my advice . . ."

Mme Brun had managed to squeeze into a car, but Charlotte went on foot, in spite of her incurable disease. Referring to it, she had said to her employer the previous evening:

"I'm sure it's his fault. He was so rough!"

She seemed to have, however, a morbid satisfaction in her "growth," bearing it with the same stoical complacence shown by the small acolyte who carried the large topheavy cross at the head of the procession.

The two coffins, so similar that the undertaker's men failed to distinguish one from the other, entered the cemetery, where a double grave waited. Michel had firmly refused to let them be placed in the Donadieu family vault.